The stirring story of the life a
Alexander Kent's bestselling n

ALEXANDER KENT

Honour This Day

arrow books

This edition published by Arrow Books in 2006

5 7 9 10 8 6

First published in the United Kingdom in 1987 by William Heinemann
First published by Arrow Books in 2000

Arrow Books
The Random House Group Limited
20 Vauxhall Bridge Road, London SW1V 2SA

www.rbooks.co.uk

Addresses for companies within The Random House Group Limited
can be found at:
www.randomhouse.co.uk/offices.htm

The Random House Group Limited Reg. No. 954009

A CIP catalogue record for this book
is available from the British Library

ISBN 9780099497721

The Random House Group Limited supports The Forest Stewardship
Council (FSC), the leading international forest certification organisation.
All our titles that are printed on Greenpeace approved FSC certified paper
carry the FSC logo. Our paper procurement policy can be found at:
www.rbooks.co.uk/environment

Printed and bound in Great Britain by
Cox & Wyman Ltd, Reading, Berkshire

For Kim, with so much love

Mourn, England, mourn and complain
For the brave Lord Nelson's men
Who died upon that day
All on the main. . . .

Broadsheet ballad, 1805

Contents

Antigua

1804

1

Memories

English Harbour, in fact the whole island of Antigua, seemed to crouch motionless as if pinned down by the noon sun. The air was humid and oppressively hot, so that the many vessels scattered at anchor were blurred in heavy haze, like reflections in a steamy looking-glass.

This October in 1804 was only days old, the middle of the hurricane season, and one of the worst on record. Several ships had been lost at sea, or driven ashore when they had been caught in some dangerous channel.

English Harbour was the important, some said vital, headquarters for the fleet which served the Caribbean and to the full extent of the Leeward and Windward Islands. Here was a fine anchorage, a dockyard where even the most serious damage and refitting could be carried out. But peace or war, the sea and the weather were constant enemies, and whereas almost every foreign flag was assumed to be hostile, the dangers of these waters were never taken for granted.

English Harbour was some twelve miles from the capital, St John's, and so the social life in and around the dockyard was limited. On a flagged terrace of one of the better houses flanking the hillside behind the harbour, a group of people, mostly officials and their ladies, stood wilting in the unmoving air watching the approach of a man-of-war. It seemed to have taken an eternity for the newcomer to gain substance and shape through the shimmering haze, but now she stood, bows-on to the land, her sails all but flat against her stays and yards.

Ships of war were too commonplace for mention. After years of conflict with France and her allies, such sights were part of these people's daily lives.

This one was a ship-of-the-line, a two-decker, her rounded black and buff hull making a sharp contrast with the milky water and the sky which seemed without colour in the unwavering heat. The sun stood directly above Monk's Hill and was encircled with silver; somewhere out at sea there would be another storm very soon. This ship was different in one respect from other comings and goings. News had been brought by a guardboat that she was from England. To those watching her painstaking approach, just the name of England created so many images. Like a letter from home, a description from some passing sailor. Uncertain weather, shortages, and a daily fear of a French invasion across the Channel. As varied as the land itself, from lush countryside to city squalor. There was hardly a man or woman watching the two-decker who would not have traded Antigua for a mere glimpse of England.

One woman stood apart from the others, her body quite still, except for her hand, which used a fan with economical care to revive the heavy air.

She had tired long ago of the desultory conversation of the people she had come to know and recognise out of necessity. Some of their voices were already slurred with overheated wine, and they had not even sat down to eat as yet.

She turned to conceal her discomfort as she plucked the ivory gown away from her skin. And all the while she watched the ship. *From England.*

The vessel could have been quite motionless but for a tiny feather of white foam beneath her thrusting, gilded figurehead. Two longboats were leading her inshore, one on either bow; she could not see if they were attached to their mother ship by line or not. They too were barely moving, and only the graceful rise and fall of their oars, pale like wings, gave a hint of effort and purpose.

The woman knew a great deal about ships; she had travelled many hundreds of leagues by sea, and had an eye for their

4

complex detail. A voice from the past seemed to linger in her mind, which had described a ship as man's most beautiful creation. She could hear him add, *and as demanding as any woman*.

Someone behind her remarked, 'Another round of official visits, I suppose?' No one answered. It was too hot even for speculation. Feet clattered on stone steps and she heard the same voice say, 'Let me know when you get any more news.'

The servant scurried away while his master opened a scrawled message from somebody in the dockyard.

'She's the *Hyperion*, seventy-four. Captain Haven.'

The woman watched the ship but her mind was drawn to the name. Why should it startle her in some way?

Another voice murmured, 'Good God, Aubrey, I thought she was a hulk. Plymouth, wasn't it?'

Glasses clinked, but the woman did not move. Captain Haven? The name meant nothing.

She saw the guardboat pulling wearily towards the tall two-decker. She loved to watch incoming ships, to see the activity on deck, the outwardly confused preparations until a great anchor splashed down. These sailors would be watching the island, many for the first time. A far cry from the ports and villages of England.

The voice commented, 'Yes, she was. But with this war spreading every day, and our people in Whitehall as unprepared as ever, I suspect that even the wrecks along our coastline will be drummed into service.'

A thicker tone said, 'I remember her now. Fought and took a damned great three-decker single-handed. No wonder the poor old girl was laid up after that, eh, what?'

She watched, hardly daring to blink as the two-decker's shape lengthened, her sails being brailed up while she swung so slowly into whatever breeze she could discover.

'She's no private ship, Aubrey.' Interest had moved the man to the balustrade. 'God, she wears an admiral's flag.'

'*Vice*-Admiral,' corrected his host. 'Very interesting. She's apparently under the flag of Sir Richard Bolitho, Vice-Admiral of the Red.'

The anchor threw up a column of spray as it fell from the

5

cathead. The woman flattened one hand on the balustrade until the heat of the stone steadied her.

Her husband must have seen her move.

'What is it? Do you know him? A true hero, if half what I've read can be believed.'

She gripped the fan more tightly and pressed it to her breast. *So that was how it would be.* He was here in Antigua. After all this time, after all he had endured.

No wonder she had remembered the ship's name. He had often spoken so affectionately of his old *Hyperion*. One of the first ships he had ever commanded as a captain.

She was surprised at her sudden emotion, more so at her ability to conceal it.

'I met him. Years ago.'

'Another glass of wine, gentlemen?'

She relaxed, muscle by muscle, aware of the dampness of her gown, of her body within it.

Even as she thought about it she cursed herself for her stupidity. It could not be like that again. *Never.*

She turned her back on the ship and smiled at the others. But even the smile was a lie.

Richard Bolitho stood uncertainly in the centre of the great stern cabin, his head cocked to the sudden thud of bare feet across the poop. All the familiar sounds crowded into the cabin, the muffled chorus of commands, the responding squeal of blocks as the yards were braced round. And yet there was hardly any movement. Like a phantom ship. Only the tall, shimmering bars of gold sunlight which moved along one side of the cabin gave any real hint that *Hyperion* was swinging slowly into the off-shore wind.

He watched as the land edged in a green panorama across the first half of the stern windows. *Antigua.* Even the name was like a stab in the heart, a reawakening of so many memories, so many faces and voices.

It was here in English Harbour where, as a newly appointed commander, he had been given his very first command, the small, lithe sloop-of-war, *Sparrow.* A different kind of vessel, but then the war with the rebellious Americans had been different also. How long ago it all seemed. Ships and faces, pain and elation.

He thought of the passage here from England. You could not ask for a faster one – thirty days, with the old *Hyperion* responding like a thoroughbred. They had stayed in company with a convoy of merchantmen, several of which had been packed with soldiers, reinforcements or replacements for the chain of English garrisons throughout the Caribbean. More likely the latter, he thought grimly. Soldiers were known to die like flies out here from one fever or another without ever hearing the crack of a French musket.

Bolitho walked slowly to the stern windows, shading his eyes against the misty glare. He was again aware of his own resentment, his reluctance at being here, knowing the situation would require all the diplomacy and pomp he was not in the mood to offer. It had already begun with the regular crash of salutes, gun for gun with the nearest shore battery, above which the Union Flag did not even ripple in the humid air.

He saw the guardboat riding above her own reflection, her oars stilled as the officer in charge waited for the two-decker to anchor.

Without being up there on the poop or quarterdeck Bolitho could visualise it all, the men at braces and halliards, others strung out along the great yards ready to fist and furl the sails neatly into place, so that from the land it would look as if every stitch of canvas had vanished to the touch of a single hand.

Land. To a sailor it was always a dream. A new adventure.

Bolitho glanced at the dress coat which hung across a chairback, ready for the call to commence his act. When he had been given command of *Sparrow* all those years ago he would never have believed it possible. Death by accident or in the cannon's mouth, disgrace, or the lack of opportunity to distinguish yourself or gain an admiral's favour, made any promotion a hard climb.

Now the coat was a reality, bearing its twin gold epaulettes with their paired silver stars. And yet . . . He reached up to brush the loose lock of hair from above his right eye. Like the scar running deep into his hairline where a cutlass had nearly ended his life, nothing changed, not even uncertainty.

He had believed that he might be able to grow into it, even though the step from command to flag rank was the greatest stride of all. Sir Richard Bolitho, Knight of the Bath, Vice-Admiral of the Red, and next to Nelson the youngest on the List. He gave a brief smile. The King had not even remembered his name when he had knighted him. Bolitho had also managed to accept that he was no longer involved with the day-to-day running of a ship, *any* ship which flew his flag. As a lieutenant he had often glanced aft at the captain's remote figure, and had felt awe, if not always respect. Then as a captain himself he had so often lain awake, fretting, as he listened to the wind and shipboard noises, restraining himself from dashing on deck when he thought the officer of the watch was not aware of the dangers around him. It was hard to delegate; but at least the ship had been his. To the ship's company of any man-of-war their captain was next only to God, and some said uncharitably that that was only due to seniority.

As a flag officer you had to stay aloof and direct the affairs of all your captains and commanders, place whatever forces you controlled where they would serve to the best effect. The power was greater, but so too was the responsibility. Few flag officers had ever allowed themselves to forget that Admiral Byng had been shot for cowardice by a firing party on the deck of his own flagship.

Perhaps he would have settled down to both his rank and unfamiliar title but for his personal life. He shied away from the thought and moved his fingers to his left eye. He massaged the lid and then stared hard at the drifting green bank of land. Sharp and clear again. But it would not last. The surgeon in London had warned him. He needed rest, more treatment, regular care. It would have meant remaining ashore – worse than that, an appointment at the Admiralty.

So why had he asked, almost demanded, another appointment with the fleet? Anywhere, or so it had sounded at the time to the Lords of Admiralty.

Three of his superiors there had told him that he had more than earned a London appointment even before his last great victory.

8

Yet when he had persisted, Bolitho had had the feeling they were equally glad he had declined their offers.

Fate – it must be that. He turned and looked deep into the great cabin. The low, white deckhead, the pale green leather of the chairs, the screen doors which led to the sleeping quarters or to the teeming world of the ship beyond, where a sentry guarded his privacy around the clock.

Hyperion – it had to be an act of Fate.

He could recall the last time he had seen her, after he had worked her into Plymouth. The staring crowds who had thronged the waterfront and Hoe to watch the victor returning home. So many killed, so many more crippled for life after their triumph over Lequiller's squadron in Biscay, and the capture of his great hundred-gun flagship *Tornade* which Bolitho was later to command as another admiral's flag captain.

But it was this ship which he always remembered. *Hyperion*, seventy-four. He had walked beside the dock in Plymouth on that awful day when he had said his last farewell; or so he had believed. Battered and ripped open by shot, her rigging and sails flayed to pieces, her splintered decks darkly stained with the blood of those who had fought. They said she would never stand in the line of battle again. There had been many moments while they had struggled back to port in foul weather when he had thought she would sink like some of her adversaries. As he had stood looking at her in the dock he had almost wished that she had found peace on the seabed. With the war growing and spreading, *Hyperion* had been made into a stores hulk. Mastless, her once-busy gundecks packed with casks and crates, she had become just a part of the dockyard.

She was the first ship-of-the-line Bolitho had ever commanded. Then, as now, he remained a frigate-man at heart, and the idea of being captain of a two-decker had appalled him. But then, too, he had been desperate, although for different reasons. Plagued by the fever which had nearly killed him in the Great South Sea, he was employed ashore at the Nore, recruiting, as the French Revolution swept across the continent like a forest fire. He could recall joining this ship at Gibraltar as if it was yesterday. She had been old and tired and yet she had taken him to her, as if in some way they needed each other.

Bolitho heard the trill of calls, the great splash as the anchor plummeted down into the waters he knew so well.

His flag captain would come to see him very soon now for orders. Try as he might, Bolitho could not see Captain Edmund Haven as an inspiring leader or his personal adviser.

A colourless, impersonal sort of man, and yet even as he considered Haven he knew he was being unfair. Bolitho had joined the ship just days before they had weighed for the passage to the Indies. And in the thirty which had followed, Bolitho had stayed almost completely isolated in his own quarters, so that even Allday, his coxswain, was showing signs of concern.

It was probably something Haven had said on their first tour of the ship, the day before they had put to sea.

Haven had obviously thought it odd, eccentric perhaps, that his admiral should wish to see anything beyond his cabin or the poop, let alone show interest in the gundecks and orlop.

Bolitho's glance rested on the sword rack beside the screen. His own old sword, and the fine presentation one. How *could* Haven have understood? It was not his fault. Bolitho had taken his apparent dissatisfaction with his command like a personal insult. He had snapped, 'This ship may be old, Captain Haven, but she has out-sailed many far younger! The Chesapeake, the Saintes, Toulon and Biscay – her battle honours read like a history of the navy itself!' It was unfair, but Haven should have known better.

Every yard of that tour had been a rebirth of memory. Only the faces and voices did not fit. But the ship was the same. New masts, and most of her armament replaced by heavier artillery than when she had faced the broadsides of Lequiller's *Tornade*, gleaming paint and neatly tarred seams; nothing could disguise his *Hyperion*. He stared round the cabin, seeing it as before. *And she was thirty-two years old*. When she had been built at Deptford she had had the pick of Kentish oak. Those days of shipbuilding were gone forever, and now most forests had been stripped of their best timber to feed the needs of the fleet.

It was ironic that the great *Tornade* had been a new ship, yet she had been paid off as a prison-hulk some four years back. He felt his left eye again and cursed wretchedly as the mist seemed to drift across it. He thought of Haven and the others who served this old ship day and night. Did they know or guess that the man whose flag flew from the foremast truck was partially blind in his left eye? Bolitho clenched his fists as he relived that moment, falling to the deck, blinded by sand from the bucket an enemy ball had blasted apart.

He waited for his composure to return. No, Haven did not seem to notice anything beyond his duties.

Bolitho touched one of the chairs and pictured the length and breadth of his flagship. So much of him was in her. His brother had died on the upper deck, had fallen to save his only son Adam, although the boy had been unaware that he was still alive, at the time. And dear Inch who had risen to become *Hyperion*'s first lieutenant. He could see him now, with his anxious, horse-faced grin. Now he too was dead, with so many of their 'happy few'.

And Cheney had also walked these decks – he pushed the chair aside and crossed angrily to the open stern windows.

'You called, Sir Richard?'

It was Ozzard, his mole-like servant. It would be no ship at all without him.

Bolitho turned. He must have spoken her name aloud. How many times; and how long would he suffer like this?

He said, 'I – I am sorry, Ozzard.' He did not go on.

Ozzard folded his paw-like hands under his apron and looked at the glittering anchorage.

'Old times, Sir Richard.'

'Aye.' Bolitho sighed. 'We had better be about it, eh?'

Ozzard held up the heavy coat with its shining epaulettes. Beyond the screen door Bolitho heard the trill of more calls and the squeak of tackles as boats were swayed out for lowering alongside.

Landfall. Once it had been such a magic word.

Ozzard busied himself with the coat but did not bring either sword from the rack. He and Allday were great friends even though most people would see them as chalk and cheese. And Allday would not allow anyone but himself to clip on the sword. Like the old ship, Bolitho thought, Allday was of the best English oak, and when he was gone none would take his place.

11

He imagined that Ozzard was dismayed that he had chosen the two-decker when he could have had the pick of any first-rate he wanted. At the Admiralty they had gently suggested that although *Hyperion* was ready for sea again, after a three-year overhaul and refit she might never recover from that last savage battle.

Curiously it had been Nelson, the hero whom Bolitho had never met, who had settled the matter. Someone at the Admiralty must have written to the little admiral to tell him of Bolitho's request. Nelson had sent his own views in a despatch to Their Lordships with typical brevity.

Give Bolitho any ship he wants. He is a sailor, not a landsman.

It would amuse Our Nel, Bolitho thought. *Hyperion* had been set aside as a hulk until her recommissioning just a few months ago, and she was thirty-two years old.

Nelson had hoisted his own flag in *Victory*, a first-rate, but he had found her himself rotting as a prison hulk. He had known in his strange fashion that he had to have her as his flagship. As far as he could recall, Bolitho knew that *Victory* was eight years older than *Hyperion*.

Somehow it seemed right that the two old ships should live again, having been discarded without much thought after all they had done.

The outer screen door opened and Daniel Yovell, Bolitho's secretary, stood watching him glumly.

Bolitho relented yet again. It had been easy for none of them because of his moods, his uncertainties. Even Yovell, plump, round-shouldered and so painstaking with his work, had been careful to keep his distance for the past thirty days at sea.

'The Captain will be here shortly, Sir Richard.'

Bolitho slipped his arms into the coat and shrugged himself into the most comfortable position without making his spine prickle with sweat.

'Where is my flag lieutenant?' Bolitho smiled suddenly. Having an official aide had also been hard to accept at the beginning. Now, after two previous flag lieutenants, he found it simple to face.

'Waiting for the barge. After that,' the fat shoulders rose

cheerfully, 'you will meet the local dignitaries.' He had taken Bolitho's smile as a return to better things. Yovell's simple Devonian mind required everything to remain safely the same.

Bolitho allowed Ozzard to stand on tip-toe to adjust his neck-cloth. For years he had always hung upon the word of admiralty or the senior officer present wherever it happened to be. It was still difficult to believe that this time there was no superior brain to question or satisfy. He *was* the senior officer. Of course in the end the unwritten naval rule would prevail. If right, others would take the credit. If wrong, he might well carry the blame.

Bolitho glanced at himself in the mirror and grimaced. His hair was still black, apart from some distasteful silver ones in the rebellious lock of hair covering the old scar. The lines at the corners of his mouth were deeper, and his reflection reminded him of the picture of his older brother, Hugh, which hung in Falmouth. Like so many of those Bolitho portraits in the great grey stone house. He controlled his sudden despair. Now, apart from his loyal steward Ferguson and the servants, it was empty.

I am here. It is what I wanted. He glanced around the cabin again. *Hyperion. We nearly died together.*

Yovell turned aside, his apple-red face wary. 'The Captain, Sir Richard.'

Haven entered, his hat beneath one arm.

'The ship is secured, sir.'

Bolitho nodded. He had told Haven not to address him by his title unless ceremony dictated otherwise. The division between them was already great enough.

'I shall come up.' A shadow moved through the door and Bolitho noticed just the briefest touch of annoyance on Haven's face. That was an improvement from total self-composure, he thought.

Allday walked past the flag captain. 'The barge is alongside, Sir Richard.' He moved to the sword rack and eyed the two weapons thoughtfully. 'The proper one today?'

Bolitho smiled. Allday had problems of his own, but he would keep them to himself until he was ready. Coxswain? A true friend was a better description. It certainly made Haven frown that one so lowly could come and go as he pleased.

Allday stooped to clip the old Bolitho sword to the belt. The leather scabbard had been rebuilt several times, but the tarnished hilt remained the same, and the keen, outmoded blade was as sharp as ever.

Bolitho patted the sword against his hip. 'Another good friend.' Their eyes met. It was almost physical, Bolitho thought. All the influence his rank invited was nothing compared with their close bond.

Haven was of medium build, almost stocky, with curling ginger hair. In his early thirties, he had the look of a sound lawyer or city merchant, and his expression today was quietly expectant, giving nothing away. Bolitho had visited his cabin on one occasion and had remarked on a small portrait, of a beautiful girl with streaming hair, surrounded by flowers.

'My wife,' Haven had replied. His tone had suggested that he would say no more even to his admiral. A strange creature, Bolitho thought; but the ship was smartly run, although with so many new hands and an overload of landsmen, it had appeared as if the first lieutenant could take much of the credit for it.

Bolitho strode through the door, past the rigid Royal Marine sentry and into the glaring sunlight. It was strange to see the wheel lashed in the midships position and abandoned. Every day at sea Bolitho had taken his solitary walks on the windward side of the quarterdeck or poop, had studied the small convoy and one attendant frigate, while his feet had taken him up and down the worn planks, skirting gun tackles and ringbolts without any conscious thought.

Eyes watched him pass, quickly averted if he glanced towards them. It was something he accepted. He knew he would never grow to like it.

Now the ship lay at rest; lines were being flaked down, petty officers moved watchfully between the bare-backed seamen to make sure the ship, no longer an ordinary man-of-war but an admiral's flagship, was as smart as could be expected anywhere.

Bolitho looked aloft at the black criss-cross of shrouds and rigging, the tightly furled sails, and shortened figures busily working high above the decks to make certain all was secure there too.

14

Some of the lieutenants moved away as he walked to the quarterdeck to look down at the lines of eighteen-pounders which had replaced the original batteries of twelve-pounders.

Faces floated through the busy figures. Like ghosts. Noises intruded above the shouted orders and the clatter of tackles. Decks torn by shot as if ripped by giant claws. Men falling and dying, reaching for aid when there was none. His nephew Adam, then fourteen years old, white-faced and yet wildly determined as the embattled ships had ground together for the last embrace from which there was no escape for either of them.

Haven said, 'The guardboat is alongside, sir.'

Bolitho gestured past him. 'You have not rigged winds'ls, Captain.'

Why could he not bring himself to call Haven by his first name? *What is happening to me?*

Haven shrugged. 'They are unsightly from the shore, sir.'

Bolitho looked at him. 'They give some air to the people on the gundecks. Have them rigged.'

He tried to contain his annoyance, at himself, and with Haven for not thinking of the furnace heat on an overcrowded gundeck. *Hyperion* was one hundred and eighty feet long on her gundeck, and carried a total company of some six hundred officers, seamen and marines. In this heat it would feel like twice that number.

He saw Haven snapping his orders to his first lieutenant, the latter glancing towards him as if to see for himself the reason for the rigging of windsails.

The first lieutenant was another odd bird, Bolitho had decided. He was over thirty, old for his rank, and had been commander of a brig. The appointment had not been continued when the vessel had been paid off, and he had been returned to his old rank. He was tall, and unlike his captain, a man of outward excitement and enthusiasm. Tall and darkly handsome, his gipsy good looks reminded Bolitho of a face in the past, but he could not recall whose. He had a ready grin, and was obviously popular with his subordinates, the sort of officer the midshipmen would love to emulate.

Bolitho looked forward, below the finely curved beakhead where he could see the broad shoulders of the figurehead. It was what he had always remembered most when he had left the ship at Plymouth. *Hyperion* had been so broken and damaged it had been hard to see her as she had once been. The figurehead had told another story.

Under the gilt paint it may have been scarred too, but the piercing blue eyes which stared straight ahead from beneath the crown of a rising sun were as arrogant as ever. One outthrust, muscled arm pointed the same trident towards the next horizon. Even seen from aft, Bolitho gained strength from the old familiarity. *Hyperion*, one of the Titans, had overthrown the indignity of being denigrated to a hulk.

Allday watched him narrowly. He had seen the gaze, and guessed what it meant. Bolitho was all aback. Allday was still not sure if he agreed with him or not. But he loved Bolitho like no other being and would die for him without question.

He said, 'Barge is ready, Sir Richard.' He wanted to add that it was not much of a crew. *Yet.*

Bolitho walked slowly to the entry port and glanced down at the boat alongside. Jenour, his new flag lieutenant, was already aboard; so was Yovell, a case of documents clasped across his fat knees. One of the midshipmen stood like a ramrod in the sternsheets. Bolitho checked himself from scanning the youthful features. It was all past. He knew nobody in this ship.

He looked round suddenly and saw the fifers moistening their pipes on their lips, the Royal Marines gripping their pipeclayed musket slings, ready to usher him over the side.

Haven and his first lieutenant, all the other anonymous faces, the blues and whites of the officers, the scarlet of the marines, the tanned bodies of the watching seamen.

He wanted to say to them, 'I am your flag officer, but *Hyperion* is still *my* ship!'

He heard Allday climb down to the barge and knew, no matter how he pretended otherwise, he would be watching, ready to reach out and catch him if his eye clouded over and he lost his step. Bolitho raised his hat, and instantly the fifes and drums snapped into a lively crescendo, and the Royal Marine guard presented arms as their major's sword flashed in salute.

Calls trilled and Bolitho lowered himself down the steep tumble-home and into the barge.

His last glance at Haven surprised him. The captain's eye were cold, hostile. It was worth remembering.

The guardboat sidled away and waited to lead the barg through the anchored shipping and harbour craft.

Bolitho shaded his eyes and stared at the land.

It was another challenge. But at that moment it felt like run ning away.

2

A Sailor's Tale

John Allday squinted his eyes beneath the tilted brim of his hat and watched the inshore current carry the guardboat momentarily off course. He eased his tiller carefully and the freshly painted green barge followed the other boat without even a break in the stroke. Allday's reputation as the vice-admiral's personal coxswain had preceded him.

He stared along the barge crew, his eyes revealing nothing. The boat had been transferred from their last ship *Argonaute*, the Frog prize, but Bolitho had said that he would leave it to his coxswain to recruit a new crew from *Hyperion*. That was strange, he had thought. Any of the old crew would have volunteered to shift to *Hyperion*, for like as not they would have been sent back to sea anyway without much of a chance to visit their loved ones. He dropped his gaze to the figures who sat in the sternsheets. Yovell who had been promoted from clerk to secretary, with the new flag lieutenant beside him. The young officer seemed pleasant enough, but was not from a seagoing family. Most who seized the chance of the overworked appointment saw it as a sure way for their own promotion. Early days yet, Allday decided. In a ship where even the rats were strangers, it was better not to make hasty decisions.

His eyes settled on Bolitho's squared shoulders and he tried to control the apprehension which had been his companion since their return to Falmouth. It ought to have been a proud homecoming despite the pain and the ravages of battle. Even the

18

damage to Bolitho's left eye had seemed less terrible when set against what they had faced and overcome together. It had been about a year ago. Aboard the little cutter *Supreme*. Allday could recall each day, the painful recovery, the very power of the man he served and loved as he had fought to win his extra battle, to hide his despair and hold the confidence of the men he led. Bolitho never failed to surprise him although they had stayed together for over twenty years. It did not seem possible that there were any surprises left.

They had walked from the harbour at Falmouth and paused at the church which had become so much a part of the Bolitho family. Generations of them were remembered there, births and marriages, victories at sea and violent death also.

Allday had stayed near the big doors of the silent church on that summer's day and had listened with sadness and astonishment as Bolitho spoke her name. *Cheney*. Just her name; and yet it had told him so much. Allday still believed that when they reached the old grey stone house below Pendennis Castle it would all return to normal. The lovely Lady Belinda who in looks at least was so like the dead Cheney, would somehow make it right, would comfort Bolitho when she realised the extent of his hurt. Maybe heal the agony in his mind which he never mentioned, but which Allday recognised. *Suppose the other eye was somehow wounded in battle?* The fear of so many sailors and soldiers. Helpless. Unwanted. Ferguson, the estate's steward who had lost an arm at the Saintes what seemed like a million years back, his rosy-cheeked wife Grace the housekeeper, and all the other servants had been waiting to greet them. Laughter, cheers, and a lot of tears too. But Belinda and the child Elizabeth had not been there. Ferguson said that she had sent a letter to explain her absence. God knew it was common enough for a returning sailor to find his family ignorant of his whereabouts, but it could not have come at a worse moment or hit Bolitho so hard.

Even his young nephew Adam, who now held his own command of the brig *Firefly*, was not able to console him. He had been ordered back to take on supplies and fresh water.

Hyperion was real enough, though. Allday glared at the stroke

19

oarsman as his blade feathered badly and threw spray over the gunwale. Bloody bargemen. They'd learn a thing or two if he had to teach every hand separately.

The old *Hyperion* was no stranger, but the people were. Was that what Bolitho wanted? Or what he needed? Allday still did not know.

If Keen had been flag captain – Allday's mouth softened. Or poor Inch even, things would seem less strange.

Captain Haven was a cold fish; even his own coxswain, a nuggety Welshman named Evans, had confided over a *wet* that his lord and master was without humour, and could not be reached.

Allday glanced again at Bolitho's shoulders. How unlike their own relationship. One ship after the other, different seas, but usually the same enemy. And always Bolitho had treated him as a friend, *one of the family* as he had once put it. It had been casually said, yet Allday had treasured the remark like a pot of gold.

It was funny if you thought about it. Some of his old messmates might even have jibed him had they not been too respectful of his fists. For Allday, like the one-armed Ferguson, had been pressed into the King's service and put aboard Bolitho's ship, the frigate *Phalarope* – hardly an ingredient for friendship. Allday had stayed with Bolitho ever since the Saintes when his old coxswain had been cut down.

Allday had been a sailor all his life, apart from a short period ashore when he had been a shepherd, of all things. He knew little of his birth and upbringing or even the exact whereabouts of his home. Now, as he grew older, it occasionally troubled him.

He studied Bolitho's hair, the queue tied at the nape of his neck which hung beneath his best gold-laced hat. It was jet-black, and in his appearance he remained youthful; he had sometimes been mistaken for young Adam's brother. Allday, as far as he knew, was the same age, forty-seven, but whereas he had filled out, and his thick brown hair had become streaked with grey, Bolitho never appeared to alter.

At peace he could be withdrawn and grave. But Allday knew most of his sides. A tiger in battle; a man moved almost to tears and despair when he had seen the havoc and agony after a sea-fight.

The guardboat was turning again to pass beneath the tapering jib-boom of a handsome schooner. Allday eased over the tiller and held his breath as fire probed the wound in his chest. That too rarely left his mind. The Spanish blade which had come from nowhere. Bolitho standing to protect him, then throwing down his sword to surrender and so spare his life.

The wound troubled him, and he often found it hard to straighten his shoulders without the pain lancing through him as a cruel reminder.

Bolitho had sometimes suggested that he should remain ashore, if only for a time. He no longer offered him a chance of complete freedom from the navy he had served so well; he knew it would injure Allday like a worse wound.

The barge pointed her stem towards the nearest jetty and Allday saw Bolitho's fingers fasten around the scabbard of the old sword between his knees. So many battles. So often they had marvelled that they had been spared once again when so many others had fallen.

'*Bows!*' He watched critically as the bowman withdrew his oar and rose with a boathook held ready to snatch for the jetty-chains. They looked smart enough, Allday conceded, in their tarred hats and fresh checkered shirts. But it needed more than paint to make a ship sail.

Allday himself was an imposing figure, although he was rarely aware of it unless he caught the eye of some girl or other, which was more often than he might admit. In his fine blue coat with the special gilt buttons Bolitho had presented to him, and his nankeen breeches, he looked every inch the Heart of Oak so popular in theatre and pleasure-garden performances.

The guardboat moved aside, the officer in charge rising to doff his hat while his oarsmen tossed their looms in salute.

With a start Allday realised that Bolitho had turned to look up at him, his hand momentarily above one eye as if to shield it from the glare. He said nothing, but there was a message in the glance, as if he had shouted it aloud. Like a plea; a recognition which excluded all others for those few seconds.

Allday was a simple man, but he remembered the look long after Bolitho had left the barge. It both worried and moved him.

As if he had shared something precious.

He saw some of the bargemen staring at him and roared, 'I've seen smarter Jacks thrown out of a brothel, but by God you'll do better next time, an' that's no error!'

Jenour stepped ashore and smiled as the solitary midshipman blushed with embarrassment at the coxswain's sudden outburst. The flag lieutenant had been with Bolitho just over a month, but already he was beginning to recognise the strange charisma of the man he served, his hero since he had been like that tongue-tied midshipman. Bolitho's voice scattered his thoughts.

'Come along, Mr Jenour. The barge can wait; the affairs of war will not.'

Jenour hid a grin. 'Aye, Sir Richard.' He thought of his parents in Hampshire, how they had shaken their heads when he had told them he intended to be Bolitho's aide *one day*.

Bolitho had seen the grin and felt the return of his sense of loss. He knew how the young lieutenant felt, how he had once been himself. In the navy's private world you found and hung on to friends with all your might. When they fell you lost something with them. Survival did not spare you the pain of their passing; it never could.

He stopped abruptly on the jetty stairs and thought of *Hyperion*'s first lieutenant. Those gipsy good looks – *of course*. It had been Keverne he had recalled to mind. They were so alike. Charles Keverne, once his first lieutenant in *Euryalus*, who had been killed at Copenhagen as captain of his own ship.

'Are you all right, Sir Richard?'

'*Damn you, yes!*' Bolitho swung round instantly and touched Jenour's cuff. 'Forgive me. Rank offers many privileges. Being foul-mannered is not one of them.'

He walked up the stairs while Jenour stared after him.

Yovell sighed as he sweated up the steep stone steps. The poor lieutenant had a lot to learn. It was to be hoped he had the time.

The long room seemed remarkably cool after the heat beyond the shaded windows.

Bolitho sat in a straight-backed chair and sipped a glass of hock, and marvelled that anything could stay so cold. Lieutenant

Jenour and Yovell sat at a separate table, which was littered with files and folios of signals and reports. It was strange to consider that it had been in a more austere part of this same building that Bolitho had waited and fretted for the news of his first command.

The hock was good and very clear. He realised that his glass was already being refilled by a Negro servant and knew he had to be careful. Bolitho enjoyed a glass of wine but had found it easy to avoid the common pitfall in the navy of over-imbibing. That could so often lead to disgrace at the court martial table.

It was too easy to see himself in those first black days at Falmouth, where he had returned there expecting – expecting what? How could he plead dismay and bitterness when truthfully his heart had remained in the church with Cheney?

How still the house had been as he had moved restlessly through the deepening shadows, the candles he held aloft in one hand playing on those stern-faced portraits he had known since he was Elizabeth's age.

He had awakened with his forehead resting on a table amidst puddles of spilled wine, his mouth like a birdcage, his mind disgusted. He had stared at the empty bottles, but could not even remember dragging them from the cellar. The household must have known, and when Ferguson had come to him he had seen that he was fully dressed from the previous day and must have been prowling and searching for a way to help. Bolitho had had to force the truth out of Allday, for he could not recall ordering him out of the house, to leave him alone with his misery. He suspected he had said far worse; he had later heard that Allday had also drunk the night away in the tavern where the inn-keeper's daughter had always waited for him, and hoped.

He glanced up and realised that the other officer was speaking to him.

Commodore Aubrey Glassport, Commissioner of the Dockyard in Antigua, and until *Hyperion*'s anchor had dropped, the senior naval officer here, was explaining the whereabouts and dispersal of the local patrols.

'With a vast sea area, Sir Richard, we are hard put to chase and detain blockade-runners or other suspect vessels. The French and their Spanish allies, on the other hand –'

Bolitho pulled a chart towards him. The same old story. Not enough frigates, too many ships-of-the-line ordered elsewhere to reinforce the fleets in the Channel and Mediterranean.

For over an hour he had examined the various reports, the results which had to be set against the days and weeks of patrolling the countless islands and inlets. Occasionally a more daring captain would risk life and limb to break into an enemy anchorage and either cut out a prize or carry out a swift bombardment. It made good reading. It did little to cripple a superior enemy. His mouth hardened. Superior in numbers only.

Glassport took his silence for acceptance and rambled on. He was a round, comfortable man, with sparse hair, and a moon-face which told more of good living than fighting the elements or the French.

He was to have been retired long since, Bolitho had heard, but he had a good rapport with the dockyard so had been kept here. Judging by his cellar he obviously carried his good relations to the victualling masters as well.

Glassport was saying, 'I am fully aware of your past achievements, Sir Richard, and how *honoured* I am to have you visit my command. I believe that when you were first here, America too was active against us, with many privateers as well as the French fleet.'

'The fact we are no longer at war with America does not necessarily remove the threat of involvement, nor the increasing danger of their supplies and ships to the enemy.' He put down the chart. 'In the next few weeks I want each patrol to be contacted. Do you have a courier-brig here at present?' He watched the man's sudden uncertainty and astonishment. The upending of his quiet, comfortable existence. 'I shall need to see each captain personally. Can you arrange it?'

'Well, er, ahem – yes, Sir Richard.'

'Good.' He picked up the glass and studied the sunlight reflected in its stem. If he moved it very slightly to the left – he waited, sensing Yovell's eyes watching, Jenour's curiosity.

He added, 'I was told that His Majesty's Inspector General is still in the Indies?'

Glassport muttered wretchedly, 'My flag lieutenant will know exactly what –'

Bolitho tensed as the glass's shape blurred over. Like a filmy curtain. It had come more quickly, or was it preying on his mind so much that he was imagining the deterioration?

He exclaimed, 'A simple enough question, I'd have thought. Is he, or is he not?'

Bolitho looked down at the hand in his lap and thought it should be shaking. Remorse, anger; it was neither. Like the moment on the jetty when he had turned on Jenour.

He said more calmly, 'He has been out here for several months, I believe?' He looked up, despairing that his eye might mist over once more.

Glassport replied, 'Viscount Somervell is staying here in Antigua.' He added defensively, 'I trust he is satisfied with his findings.'

Bolitho said nothing. The Inspector General might have been just one more burden to the top-hamper of war. It seemed absurd that someone with such a high-sounding appointment should be employed on a tour of inspection in the West Indies, when England, standing alone against France and the fleets of Spain, was daily expecting an invasion.

Bolitho's instructions from the Admiralty made it clear that he was to meet with the Viscount Somervell without delay, if it meant moving immediately to another island, even to Jamaica.

But he was here. That was something.

Bolitho was feeling weary. He had met most of the dockyard officers and officials, had inspected two topsail cutters which were being completed for naval service, and had toured the local batteries, with Jenour and Glassport finding it hard to keep up with his pace.

He smiled wryly. He was paying for it now.

Glassport watched him sip the hock before saying, 'There is a small reception for you this evening, Sir Richard.' He seemed to falter as the grey eyes lifted to him again. 'It hardly measures up to the occasion, but it was arranged only after your, er, flagship was reported.'

Bolitho noted the hesitation. Just one more who doubted his choice of ship.

Glassport must have feared a possible refusal and scampered on, 'Viscount Somervell will be *expecting* you.'

'I see.' He glanced at Jenour. 'Inform the Captain.' As the lieutenant made to excuse himself from the room Bolitho said, '*Send* a message with my cox'n. I need you with *me*.'

Jenour stared, then nodded. He was learning a lot today.

Bolitho waited for Yovell to bring the next pile of papers to the table. A far cry from command, the day-to-day running of a ship and her affairs. Every ship was like a small town, a family even. He wondered how Adam was faring with his new command. All he could find as an answer to his thought was envy. Adam was exactly like he had been. More reckless perhaps, but with the same doubtful attitude to his seniors.

Glassport watched him as he leafed through the papers while Yovell stooped politely above his right shoulder.

So this was the man behind the legend. Another Nelson, some said. Though God alone knew Nelson was not very popular in high places. He was the right man to command a fleet. Necessary, but afterwards? He studied Bolitho's lowered head, the loose lock above his eye. A grave, sensitive face, he thought, hard to picture in the battles he had read about. He knew Bolitho had been badly wounded several times, that he had almost died of a fever, although he did not know much about it.

A Knight of the Bath, from a fine old seafaring family, looked on as a hero by the people of England. All the things which Glassport would like to be and to have.

So why had he come to Antigua? There was little or no prospect of a fleet action, and provided they could get reinforcements for the various flotillas, and a replacement for – He wilted as Bolitho touched on that very point, as if he had looked up quickly to see right into his mind with those steady, compelling grey eyes.

'The Dons took the frigate *Consort* from us?' It sounded like an accusation.

'Two months back, Sir Richard. She drove aground under fire. One of my schooners was able to take off most of her company before the enemy stood against her. The schooner did well, I thought that –'

'The *Consort*'s captain?'

'At St. John's, Sir Richard. He is awaiting the convenience of a court martial.'

'Is he indeed.' Bolitho stood up and turned as Jenour re-entered the room. 'We are going to St. John's.'

Jenour swallowed hard. 'If there is a carriage, Sir Richard –' He looked at Glassport as if for guidance.

Bolitho picked up his sword. 'Two horses, my lad.' He tried to hide his sudden excitement. Or was it merely trailing a coat to draw him from his other anxiety? 'You are from Hampshire, *right*?'

Jenour nodded. 'Yes. That is –'

'It's settled then. Two horses immediately.'

Glassport stared from one to the other. 'But the reception, Sir Richard?' He sounded horrified.

'This will give me an appetite.' Bolitho smiled. 'I shall return.' He thought of Allday's patience, Ozzard and the others. '*Directly*.'

Bolitho peered closely at his reflection in an ornate wall mirror, then thrust the loose lock of hair from his forehead. In the mirror he could see Allday and Ozzard watching him anxiously, and his new flag lieutenant Stephen Jenour massaging his hip after their ride to St. John's and back to English Harbour.

It had been hot, dusty but unexpectedly exhilarating, and had almost been worthwhile just to see the expressions of passers-by as they had galloped along in the hazy sunshine.

It was dark now, dusk came early to the islands, and Bolitho had to study himself very carefully while his ear recorded the sound of violins, the muffled murmur of voices from the grand room where the reception was being held.

Ozzard had brought fresh stockings from the ship, while All-day had collected the fine presentation sword to replace the old blade Bolitho had been wearing.

Bolitho sighed. Most of the candles were protected by tall hurricane glasses so the light was not too strong. It might hide his crumpled shirt, and the stain left by the saddle on his breeches. There had been no time to return to *Hyperion*. *Damn Glassport and his reception*. Bolitho would much rather have stayed in his cabin and sifted through all which the frigate captain had told him.

Captain Matthew Price was young to hold command of so fine a vessel. The *Consort* of thirty-six guns had been working through some shoals when she had been fired on by a coastal battery. She had been that close inshore when she had unfortunately run aground. It was much as Glassport had described. A schooner had taken off many of *Consort*'s people, but had been forced to run, her task incomplete, as Spanish men-of-war had arrived on the scene.

Captain Price was so junior that he had not even been posted, and if a court martial ruled against him, which was more than likely, he would lose everything. At best he might return to the rank of lieutenant. The worst did not bear thinking about.

As Price sat in a small government-owned house to await the calling of the court martial he had plenty to ponder about. Not least that it might have been better had he been taken prisoner, or killed in battle. For his ship had been refloated and was now a part of His Most Catholic Majesty's fleet at La Guaira on the Spanish Main. Frigates were worth their tonnage in gold, and the navy was always in desperate need of them. When Bolitho had been in the Mediterranean there were only six frigates available between Gibraltar and the Levant. The president of Price's court martial would not be able to exclude that fact from his considerations.

Once, in desperation, the young captain had asked Bolitho what he thought of the possible outcome.

Bolitho had told him to expect his sword to point towards him at the table. To hazard his ship was one thing. To lose it to a hated enemy was another entirely.

There had been no sense in promising Price he could do something to divert the court's findings. Price had taken a great risk to discover the Spanish intentions. Laid beside what Bolitho already knew, his information could be invaluable. But it would not help the *Consort*'s captain now.

Bolitho said, 'I suppose it is time.' He looked at a tall clock and added, 'Are our officers present yet?'

Jenour nodded, then winced as the ache throbbed through his

thighs and buttocks. Bolitho was a superb horseman, but then so was he, or so he had believed. Bolitho's little joke about people from Hampshire being excellent riders had acted as a spur, but at no time had Jenour been able to keep pace with him.

He said, 'The first lieutenant arrived with the others while you were changing, Sir Richard.'

Bolitho looked down at the immaculate stockings and remembered when he had been a lowly lieutenant with only one fine pair for such occasions as this. The rest had been darned so many times it had been a wonder they had held together.

It gave him time to think about Captain Haven's request to remain aboard ship. He had explained that a storm might spring up without warning and prevent his return from the shore in time to take the necessary precautions. The air was heavy and humid, and the sunset had been like blood.

Hyperion's sailing master, Isaac Penhaligon, a fellow Cornishman by birth at least, had insisted that a storm was very unlikely. It was as if Haven preferred to keep to himself, even though someone at the reception might take his absence as a snub.

If only Keen was still his flag captain. He had but to ask, and Keen would have come with him. Loyalty, friendship, love, it was something of each.

But Bolitho had pressed Keen to remain in England, at least until he had settled the problems of his lovely Zenoria. More than anything else Keen wanted to marry his dark-eyed girl with the flowing chestnut hair. They loved and were so obviously *in* love that Bolitho could not bring himself to separate them so soon after they had found each other.

Or was he comparing their love with his own house?

He stopped his thoughts right there. *It was not the time.* Maybe it never could be now.

Perhaps Haven did not like him? He might even be afraid of him. That was something Bolitho had often found hard to believe in his own days as a captain. When he had first stepped aboard a new command he had tried to hide his nervousness and apprehension. It had been much later when he had understood that a ship's company was far more likely to be worried about him and what *he* might do.

Jenour asked politely, 'Shall we go, Sir Richard?'

Bolitho wanted to touch his left eye but stared instead at the nearest hurricane glass and the tendril of black smoke which rose straight up to the ceiling. It was clear and bright. No shadows, no mist to taunt him and take him off-guard.

Bolitho glanced at Allday. He would have to speak to him soon about his son. Allday had said nothing about him since the young sailor had left *Argonaute* on their return to England. *If I had had a son perhaps I would have wanted too much. Might have expected him to care about all the same things.*

A pair of handsome doors were pulled open by footmen who had hitherto been invisible in the shadows.

The music and babble of voices swept into the room like surf on a reef, and Bolitho found himself tensing his muscles as if to withstand a musket ball.

As he walked down the pillared corridor he pondered on the minds and the labour which had created this building on such a small island. A place which through circumstances of war had many times become a vital hinge for England's naval strategy.

He heard Jenour's heels tapping on the floor, and half-smiled as he recalled the lieutenant's eagerness to ride neck-and-neck with him. More like two country squires than King's officers.

He saw the overlapping colours of ladies' gowns, bare shoulders, curious stares as he drew closer to the mass of people. They had had little notice of his coming, Commodore Glassport had said, but he guessed that any official visitor or a ship from England was a welcome event.

He noticed some of *Hyperion*'s wardroom, their blues and whites making a clean contrast with the red and scarlet of the military and Royal Marines. Once again he had to restrain himself from searching for familiar faces, hearing voices, as if he still expected a handshake or a nod of recognition.

There were some steps between two squat pillars, and he saw Glassport peering along the carpet towards him. Relieved no doubt that he had actually arrived after his ride. One figure stood in the centre, debonair and elegant, and dressed from throat to ankle in white. Bolitho knew very little of the man he had come to meet. The Right Honourable the Viscount Somervell, his Majesty's

Inspector General in the Caribbean, seemed to have little which equipped him for the appointment. A regular face at Court and at the right receptions, a reckless gambler some said, and a swordsman of renown. The last was well-founded, and it was known that the King had intervened on his behalf after he had killed a man in a duel. To Bolitho it was familiar and painful territory. It hardly qualified him for being here.

A footman with a long stave tapped the floor and called, 'Sir Richard Bolitho, Vice-Admiral of the Red!'

The sudden stillness was almost physical. Bolitho felt their eyes following him as he walked along the carpet. Small cameos stood out. The musicians with their fiddles and bows motionless in mid-air, a young sea-officer nudging his companion and then freezing as Bolitho's glance passed over him. A bold stare from a lady with such a low-cut gown that she need not have covered herself at all, and another from a young girl who smiled shyly then hid her face behind a fan.

Viscount Somervell did not move forward to greet him but stood as before, one hand resting negligently on his hip, the other dangling at his side. His mouth was set in a small smile which could have been either amusement or boredom. His features were of a younger man, but he had the indolent eyes of someone who had seen everything.

'Welcome to —' Somervell turned sharply, his elegant pose destroyed as he glared into a trolley of candelabra which was being wheeled into the room behind him.

The sudden glare of additional light at eye-level caught Bolitho off-balance just as he raised his foot to the first of the steps. A lady dressed in black who had been standing motionless beside the Viscount reached out to steady his arm, while through the mass of candles he saw staring faces, surprise, curiosity, caught like onlookers in a painter's canvas.

'I beg your pardon, Ma'am!' Bolitho regained his balance and tried not to shade his eye as the mist swirled across it. It was like drowning, falling through deeper and deeper water.

He said, 'I am all right —' then stared at the lady's gown. It was not black, but of an exquisite green shot-silk which shone, and seemed to change colour in its folds and curves as the light that

31

had blinded him revealed her for the first time. The gown was cut wide and low from her shoulders, and the hair he remembered so clearly as being long and as dark as his own, was piled in plaits above her ears.

The faces, the returning murmur of speculative chatter faded away. He had known her then as Catherine Pareja. *Kate*.

He was staring, his momentary blindness forgotten as he saw her eyes, her sudden anxiety giving way to an enforced calm. She had known he was to be here. His was the only surprise.

Somervell's voice seemed to come from a great distance. He was calm again, his composure recovered.

'Of course, I had forgotten. You have met before.'

Bolitho took her proffered hand and lowered his face to it. Even her perfume was the same.

He heard her reply, 'Some while ago.'

When Bolitho looked up she seemed strangely remote and self-assured. Indifferent even.

She added, 'One could never forget a hero.'

She held out her arm for her husband and turned towards the watching faces.

Bolitho felt an ache in his heart. She was wearing the long gold filigree earrings he had bought her in that other unreal world, in London.

Footmen advanced with trays of glittering glasses, and the small orchestra came to life once again.

Across the wine and past the flushed, posturing faces their eyes met and excluded everyone.

Glassport was saying something to him but he barely heard. After all that had happened, it was still there between them. It must be quenched before it destroyed them both.

3

King's Ransom

Bolitho leaned back in his chair as a white-gloved hand whisked away the half-emptied plate and quickly replaced it with another. He could not remember how many courses he had been offered nor how many times the various goblets and fine glasses had been refilled.

The air was full of noise, the mingled voices of those present, at a guess some forty officers, officials and their ladies with the small contingent from *Hyperion*'s wardroom divided amongst them. The long room and its extended table was brightly lit by candles, beyond which the shadows seemed to sway in a dance of their own as the many footmen and servants bustled back and forth to maintain a steady supply of food and wine.

They must have garnered servants from several houses, Bolitho thought, and he could gather from the occasional savage undertones of the senior footman that there had been several disasters between kitchen and table.

He was seated at Catherine's right hand, and as the conversation and laughter swirled around them he was very aware of her, although she gave little hint of her own feelings at his presence. At the far end of the table Bolitho saw her husband, Viscount Somervell, sipping his wine and listening with apparent boredom to Commodore Glassport's resonant and thickening tones. Occasionally Somervell appeared to glance along the table's length, excluding everyone but his wife or Bolitho. Interest, awareness? It was impossible to determine.

As the doors swung open from time to time to a procession of sweating servants Bolitho saw the candles shiver in the smoky air. Otherwise there was little hint of movement, and he pictured Haven, safe in his cabin, or brooding over his possible role in the future. He might show more animation when he learned what was expected of him and his command.

She turned suddenly and spoke directly to him. 'You are very quiet, Sir Richard.'

He met her gaze and felt his defence falter. She was just as striking, more beautiful even than he had remembered. The sun had given her neck and shoulders a fine blush, and he could see the gentle pulse of her heart where the silk gown folded around it.

One hand lay as if abandoned beside her glass, a folded fan close by. He wanted to touch it, to reassure himself or to reveal his own stupidity.

What am I? So full of conceit, so shallow that I could imagine her drawn to me again after so long?

He said instead, 'It must be seven years.'

Her face remained impassive. To anyone watching she might have been asking about England or the weather.

'Seven years and one month to be exact.'

Bolitho turned as the Viscount laughed at something Glassport had said.

'And then you married *him*.' It came out like a bitter accusation and he saw her fingers move as if they were listening independently.

'Was it so important?'

She retorted, 'You delude yourself, Richard.' Even the use of his name was like the awakening of an old wound. 'It was not so.' She held his gaze as he turned again. Defiance, pain, it was all there in her dark eyes. 'I need security. Just as you need to be loved.'

Bolitho hardly dared to breathe as the conversation died momentarily around him. He thought the first lieutenant was watching them, that an army colonel had paused with his goblet half-raised as if to catch the words. Even in imagination it felt like a conspiracy.

'Love?'

34

She nodded slowly, her eyes not leaving his. 'You need it, as the desert craves for rain.'

Bolitho wanted to look away but she seemed to mesmerise him.

She continued in the same unemotional tone, 'I wanted you then, and ended almost hating you. *Almost.* I have watched your life and career, two very different things, over the past seven years. I would have taken anything you offered me; you were the only man I would have loved without asking for security in marriage.' She touched the fan lightly. 'Instead you took another, one you imagined was a substitute –' She saw the shot strike home. '*I knew it.*'

Bolitho replied, 'I thought of you often.'

She smiled but it made her look sad. 'Really?'

He turned his head further so that he could see her clearly. He knew others might watch him for he appeared to face her directly, but his left eye was troubled by the flickering glare and the swooping shadows beyond.

She said, 'The last battle. We heard of it a month back.'

'You knew I was coming here?'

She shook her head. 'No. He tells me little of his government affairs.' She looked quickly along the table and Bolitho saw her smile as if in recognition. He was astonished that the small familiarity with her husband should hurt him so much.

She returned her gaze to his. 'Your injuries, are they –?' She saw him start. 'I helped you once, do you not remember?'

Bolitho dropped his eyes. He had imagined that she had heard or detected his difficulty in seeing her properly. It all flashed through his mind like a wild dream. His wound, the return of the fever which had once almost killed him. Her pale nakedness as she had dropped her gown and folded herself against his gasping, shivering body, while she had spoken unheard words and clasped him to her breasts to repulse the fever's torment.

'I shall *never* forget.'

She watched him in silence for some moments, her eyes moving over his lowered head and the dangling lock of hair, his grave sunburned features and the lashes which now hid his eyes, glad that he could not see the pain and the yearning in her stare.

Nearby, Major Sebright Adams of *Hyperion*'s Royal Marines was expounding on his experiences at Copenhagen and the bloody aftermath of the battle. Parris, the first lieutenant, was propped on one elbow, apparently listening, but leaning across the young wife of a dockyard official, his arm resting against her shoulder which she made no attempt to remove. Like the other officers, they were momentarily free of responsibility and the need to keep up any pretence and the posture of duty.

Bolitho was more aware than ever of a sudden isolation, the need to tell her his thoughts, his fears; and was revolted at the same time by his weakness.

He said, 'It was a hard fight. We lost many fine men.'

'And *you*, Richard? What more did you have to lose that you had not already abandoned?'

He exclaimed fiercely, 'Let it be, Catherine. It is over.' He raised his eyes and stared at her intently. 'It must be so!'

A side door opened and more footmen bustled around, but this time without new dishes. It would soon be time for the ladies to withdraw and the men to relieve themselves before settling down to port and brandy. He thought of Allday. He would be out there in the barge with his crew waiting for him. Any petty officer would have been sufficient, but he knew Allday. He would allow no other to wait for him. He would have been in his element tonight, he thought. Bolitho had never known any man able to drink his coxswain under the table, unlike some of the guests.

Somervell's voice cut along the littered cloth although he seemed to have no problem in making it carry.

'I hear that you saw Captain Price today, Sir Richard?'

Bolitho could almost feel the woman at his side holding her breath, as if she sensed the casual remark as a trap. Was guilt that obvious?

Glassport rumbled, 'Not captain for long, I'll wager!' Several of the guests chuckled.

A black footman entered the room and after the smallest glance at Somervell padded to Bolitho's chair, an envelope balanced carefully on a silver salver.

Bolitho took it and prayed that his eye would not torture him now.

Glassport was going on again. 'My only frigate, by God! I'm dashed hard put to know –'

He broke off as Somervell interrupted rudely, 'What is it, Sir Richard? Are we to share it?'

Bolitho folded the paper and glanced at the black footman. He was in time to see a strange sympathy on the man's face, as if he knew.

'You may be spared the spectacle of a brave officer's dishonour, Commodore Glassport.' His voice was hard and although it was directed at one man it gripped the whole table.

'Captain Price is dead.' There was a chorus of gasps. 'He hanged himself.' He could not resist adding, 'Are you satisfied?'

Somervell pushed himself back from the table. 'I think this may be a suitable moment for the ladies to retire.' He rose effortlessly to his feet, as if it was a duty rather than a courtesy.

Bolitho faced her and saw the concern stark in her eyes as if she wanted to tell him out loud.

Instead she said, 'We will meet.' She waited for him to raise his head from a brief bow. 'Soon.' Then with a hiss of silk she merged with the shadows.

Bolitho sat down and watched unseeingly as another hand placed a fresh glass by his place.

It was not their fault, not even the mindless Glassport's.

What could I have done? Nothing could interfere with the mission he intended to undertake.

It might have happened to any one of them. He thought of young Adam instead of the wretched Price sitting alone and picturing the grim faces of the court, the sword turned against him on the table.

It was curious that the message about Price's death had been sent directly from St. John's to *Hyperion*, his flagship. Haven must have read and considered it before sending it ashore, probably in the charge of some midshipman who in turn would hand it to a footman. It would not have hurt him to bring it in person, he thought.

He realised with a start that the others were on their feet, glasses raised to him in a toast.

Glassport said gruffly, 'To our flag officer, Sir Richard Bolitho, and may he bring us fresh victories!' Even the huge amount of wine he had consumed could not hide the humiliation in his voice.

Bolitho stood up and bowed, but not before he had seen that the white-clad figure at the opposite end had not touched his glass. Bolitho felt his blood stir, like the moment when the topsails of an enemy revealed their intentions, or that moment in early dawn when he had faced another in a duel.

Then he thought of her eyes and her last word. *Soon.*

He picked up his own glass. *So be it then.*

The six days which followed *Hyperion*'s arrival at English Harbour were, for Bolitho at least, packed with activity.

Every morning, within an hour of the guardboat's delivery of messages or signals from the shore Bolitho climbed into his barge and with a puzzled flag lieutenant at his elbow threw himself into the affairs of the ships and sailors at his disposal. On the face of it, it was not a very impressive force. Even allowing for three small vessels still in their patrol areas, the flotilla, for it was no more than that, seemed singularly unsuited for the task in hand. Bolitho knew that their lordships' loosely-worded instructions, which were locked in his strongbox, carried all the risk and responsibility of direct orders given to a senior captain, or a lowly one like Price.

The main Antigua squadron, consisting of six ships-of-the-line, were reported as being scattered far to the north-west in the Bahama Islands, probably probing enemy intentions or making a show of force to deter would-be blockade runners from the Americas. The admiral was known to Bolitho, Sir Peter Folliot, a quiet, dignified officer who was said to be sorely tried by ill-health. Not the best ingredients for aggressive action against the French or their Spanish ally.

On the sixth morning, as Bolitho was being carried across the barely ruffled water towards the last of his command, he considered the results of his inspection and studies. Apart from *Obdurate*, an elderly seventy-four, which was still undergoing storm repairs in the dockyard, he had a total of five brigs, one sloop-of-war, and *Thor*, a bomb-vessel, which he had left until last. He could have summoned each commander to the flagship; it would have been what they were expecting of any flag officer, let alone one of Bolitho's reputation. They were soon to learn that he liked to discover things for himself, to get the feel of the men he would lead, if not inspire.

He considered Somervell, and his failure to visit *Hyperion* as he had promised after the reception. Was he making him wait deliberately, to put him in his place, or was he indifferent to the final plan, which they would need to discuss before Bolitho could take decisive action?

He watched the rise and fall of the oars, the way the bargemen averted their eyes whenever he glanced at them, Allday's black shadow across the scrubbed thwarts, passing vessels and those at anchor. Antigua might be a British possession, one so heavily defended that a need for more ships was unnecessary, but there were plenty of traders and coastal sailing-masters, who, if not actual spies, would be ready and willing to part with information to the enemy if only for their own free passage.

Bolitho shaded his eyes and looked towards the nearest hillside, to a battery of heavy guns marked only by a rough parapet and a lifeless flag above it. Defence was all very well, but you won wars by attacking. He saw dust along the coast road, people on the move, and thought again of Catherine. She had been rarely out of his thoughts, and he knew in his heart he had worked himself so hard to hold his personal feelings at bay where they could not interfere.

Perhaps she had told Somervell everything which had happened between them. Or maybe he had forced it out of her? He dismissed the latter immediately. Catherine was too strong to be used like that. He recalled her previous husband, a man twice her age, but one of surprising courage when he had tried to help Bolitho's men defend a merchant ship from corsairs. Catherine had hated him then. Their feelings for each other had grown from that animosity. Like steel in the livid heat of a forge. He was still not sure what had happened to them, where it might otherwise have led.

Such a short climax in London after their meeting outside the Admiralty, when Bolitho had just been appointed commodore of his own squadron.

Seven years and one month. Catherine had forgotten nothing. It was unnerving, and at the same time exciting, to realise how she had managed to follow his career, and his life; two separate things as she had put it.

Allday whispered, 'They've manned the side, Sir Richard.'

Bolitho tilted his hat and stared towards the bomb-vessel. His Britannic Majesty's Ship *Thor*.

Small when compared with a frigate or line-of-battleship, but at the same time heavy-looking and powerful. Designed for bombarding shore installations and the like. *Thor*'s main armament consisted of two massive thirteen-inch mortars. The vessel had to be powerfully built to withstand the downward recoil of the mortars, which were fired almost vertically. With ten heavy carronades and some smaller six-pounders, *Thor* would be a slow sailer. But unlike many of her earlier consorts which had been ketch-rigged, *Thor* mounted three masts and a more balanced ship-rig, which might offer some improvement in perverse winds.

A shadow passed over Bolitho's thoughts. Francis Inch had been given command of a bomb-vessel after he had left *Hyperion*.

He looked up and saw Allday watching him. It was uncanny.

Allday said quietly, 'The old *Hekla*, Sir Richard – remember her?'

Bolitho nodded, not seeing Lieutenant Jenour's mystified stare. It was hard to accept that Inch was dead. Like so many now.

'*Attention on deck!*'

Calls trilled and Bolitho seized a ladder with both hands to haul himself through the low entry port.

The vessels he had already visited in harbour had seemed startled by his arrival on board. Their commanders were young; all but one had been lieutenants just months ago.

There was no such nervousness about *Thor*'s captain, Bolitho thought as he doffed his hat to the small quarterdeck.

Commander Ludovic Imrie was tall and narrow-shouldered, so that his solitary gold epaulette looked as if it might fall off at any moment. He stood over six feet, and when you considered

Thor's headroom, four feet six inches in some sections, it must have seemed like being caged.

'I bid you welcome, Sir Richard.' Imrie's voice was surprisingly deep, with a Scottish burr which reminded Bolitho of his mother. Bolitho was introduced to two lieutenants and a few junior warrant officers. A small company. He had already noted their names, and sensed their reserve giving way to interest or curiosity.

Imrie dismissed the side-party and after a brief hesitation ushered Bolitho below to his small stern-cabin. As they stooped beneath the massive deck beams, Bolitho recalled his first command, a sloop-of-war; how her first lieutenant had apologised for the lack of space for the new commander. Bolitho had been almost beside himself with glee. After a lieutenant's tiny berth in a ship-of-the-line it had seemed like a palace.

Thor's was even smaller. They sat opposite one another while a wizened messman brought a bottle and some glasses. A far cry from Somervell's table, Bolitho thought.

Imrie spoke easily about his command, which he had held for two years. He was obviously very proud of *Thor*, and Bolitho sensed an immediate resentment when he suggested that bombs, for the most part, had achieved little so far in the various theatres of war.

'Given a chance, sir –' He grinned and shrugged his narrow shoulders. 'I beg your pardon, Sir Richard, I should have known.'

Bolitho sipped the wine; it was remarkably cool. 'Known what?'

Imrie said, 'I'd heard you tested your captains with a question or two –'

Bolitho smiled. 'It worked this time.' He remembered some of the others he had met in Antigua. He had felt something akin to hostility, if not actual dislike. Because of Price, perhaps? After all, they had known him, had worked in company with his frigate. They might think that he had killed himself deliberately because Bolitho had refused to intervene. Bolitho could think of several occasions when he had felt much the same.

Imrie stared through the skylight at the empty sky.

'If I could lie near a good target, sir, I'd put down such a barrage, the enemy'd think Hell had dropped amongst them. The Dons have never faced –' He faltered and added apologetically, 'I mean, that is, if we were against the Spaniards at any time –'

Bolitho eyed him steadily. Imrie had worked it out all by himself. Why else would his vice-admiral bother to call on him? Price's exploits and disaster on the Spanish Main linked with *Thor*'s obvious advantages in the shallows where *Consort* had run aground had formed their own picture in his mind.

Bolitho said, 'That is well thought, Commander Imrie. I will trust you to keep your suppositions to yourself.' It was odd that none of the others, not even Haven, had once questioned their motives for being here.

Bolitho rubbed his left eyelid and then withdrew his hand quickly. 'I have studied the reports, and have re-read the notes my aide took down when I spoke to Captain Price.'

Imrie had a long face with a craggy jaw and looked as if he could be a formidable opponent in any circumstances. But his features softened as he listened to Bolitho. Perhaps because he had referred to the dead man by his full rank. It offered some small dignity, a far cry from the lonely grave below the East Battery.

Bolitho said, 'The approaches are too well protected for what I must keep in mind. Any well-sited artillery can destroy a slow-moving vessel with ease, and with heated shot the effect would be disastrous.'

Imrie rubbed his chin, his eyes far away. As Bolitho had noticed, they were unmatched, one dark and the other pale blue.

He said, 'If we are both thinking of the same patch of coast, Sir Richard, and of course we can't be *sure* of that –'

Jenour watched, fascinated. These two officers, each a veteran in his own field, yet able to discuss something he still could not grasp, and chuckle over it like two conspiring schoolboys. It was unbelievable.

Bolitho nodded. 'But *if* –'

'Even *Thor* might have to lay-off too far to use the mortars, Sir Richard.' He scanned his face as if expecting an argument or disappointment. 'We don't draw much less than *Consort* did.'

A boat thudded alongside and Bolitho heard Allday barking at someone for interrupting their conference.

Then his face appeared in the skylight. He said, 'Beggin' your pardon, Sir Richard. Message from *Hyperion*. The Inspector General is come aboard.'

Bolitho concealed a tremor of excitement. Somervell had given in to curiosity at last. Or was he imagining that also? That there was already some kind of contest between them?

Bolitho stood up and winced as his head struck one of the beams.

Imrie exclaimed, 'God damn it, Sir Richard, I should have warned you!'

Bolitho reached for his hat. 'It acted as a reminder. It was less painful than the memory.'

On deck, the side-party had assembled and Bolitho saw *Hyperion*'s jolly-boat already pulling back to the ship. Allday clambered fuming down to the waiting barge. He had sent that pink-faced midshipman off with a flea in his ear. Young puppy. He glared at the bargemen. 'Stand by in the boat, damn you!'

Bolitho made a decision. 'Tell your senior to take over, Imrie. I wish you to accompany me directly.'

Imrie's jaw dropped open. 'But, Sir Richard –'

Bolitho saw his first lieutenant watching them. 'He is just aching to take command, albeit for a day – it is every first lieutenant's dream!' He was amazed at his own good humour. It was like a dam holding all the worries here and at home back and out of view.

He stooped over as if to examine one of the snout-nosed twenty-four pounder carronades. It gave him time to massage his eye again, to drive off the mist which the sharp sunlight had thrown at him as if to crack his confidence.

Imrie whispered to Jenour, 'What a man, eh? I think I'd follow him to hell *and* back!'

Jenour watched Bolitho's shoulders. 'Aye, sir.' It was only a guess, but he saw more than anyone of Bolitho apart from Allday and the cabin staff. It was strange that they never mentioned it. But Jenour's uncle was a physician in Southampton. He had spoken of something like this. Jenour had seen Bolitho caught off balance, like the moment when the Viscount's beautiful wife had reached out to aid him, and other times at sea before that.

But nothing was ever said about it. He had to be mistaken.

All the way across the anchorage Bolitho pondered over his mission. If he had frigates, even one at his disposal, he could plan around the one, formidable obstacle.

La Guaira, the Spanish port on the Main and gateway to the capital Caracas, was impregnable. That was only because nobody had ever attempted it before. He could feel Imrie's curiosity and was glad he had visited the *Thor* before discussing the venture with Haven and the others.

Imrie would be confident but not reckless. Price had believed he could do it, although for different reasons. Had he succeeded, it was unlikely that even a tiny fishing dory could slip through the Dons' defences afterwards.

Allday muttered, 'We have to put round t'other side, Sir Richard.' He sounded irritated, and Bolitho knew that he was still brooding over his newly-discovered and as quickly lost son.

Jenour stood up and swayed in the barge. 'The water-lighters are alongside, Sir Richard. Shall I signal them to stand away for you?'

Bolitho tugged his coat. 'Sit down, you impatient young upstart.' He knew the young lieutenant was smiling at his rebuke. 'We need fresh water, and *Hyperion* does have two sides to her!'

They pulled around the bows and past the out-thrust trident. Bolitho glanced up at the figurehead's fierce stare. Many a man must have seen that lancing through the gunsmoke and felt a last fear before he was cut down in battle.

He found Haven agitated and probably worried that Bolitho would berate him.

'I am sorry about the lighters, sir! I was not expecting you!'

Bolitho crossed the deck and looked down. Again, it was to test his eye, to prepare it for the cool shadows between decks.

'No matter.' He knew Haven was watching Imrie with suspicion and said, 'Commander Imrie is my guest.' He rested his hands on the sun-baked woodwork and regarded the nearest lighter. They were huge, flat-bottomed craft, their open hulls lined with great casks of water. One line of casks had already been hoisted up and lowered inboard on tackles; and Bolitho saw Parris, the first lieutenant, one foot resting negligently on a hatch coaming, watching Sheargold the beaky-faced purser check each cask before it was sent below. He was about to turn away and then said, 'The lighter is still on even keel, yet all the casks are on the outboard side.'

Haven observed him warily, as if he thought Bolitho had been too long in the sun.

'They are so constructed, sir. Nothing will tilt them.'

Bolitho straightened his back and looked at Imrie.

'*There you have it*, Imrie. A platform for your mortars!' He ignored their combined astonishment.

'*Now*, I must meet the Inspector General!'

In the bars of bright forenoon sunlight, The Right Honourable the Viscount Somervell lounged against a leather-backed chair and listened without interruption. He was dressed in very pale green with brocade and stitching which would put any prince to shame. Close-to and in the brilliant glare Somervell looked younger, mid-thirties, her age or perhaps less.

Bolitho tried not to think beyond the outline of his plan, but Catherine seemed to linger in the great cabin like a shadow, as if she too was making comparisons.

Bolitho walked to the stern windows and looked out at some passing fishing boats. The anchorage was still flat and calm, but the mist was drifting seawards, and the pendant above an anchored brig was lifting occasionally to a lifeless breeze.

He said, 'Captain Price –' He paused, expecting Somervell to interrupt, or to voice some scathing comment. He did not. '– made a practice of patrolling that section of the Main where he was eventually forced to abandon *Consort*. He took careful note of everything he saw, and searched or destroyed some twenty enemy vessels in the process. Given time –'

This was Somervell's cue. 'It ran out for him.' He leaned forward in his chair, his pale eyes unblinking despite the harsh glare. 'And you have actually *discussed* some of this secret matter with, er, a Commander Imrie?' He spoke the man's name indifferently, as a landowner might speak of a lowly farm labourer. 'That is surely an extra risk?'

Bolitho replied, 'Imrie is an intelligent officer, shrewd too.

When I spoke to my other commanders earlier I had the impression that they were convinced I intended to try and cut out the *Consort*, or *Intrépido* as she has been renamed.'

Somervell pressed his fingertips together. 'You *have* done your work well, Sir Richard!'

Bolitho continued, 'Imrie would guess immediately that I had something else in mind. He knew that his *Thor* is too heavy and slow for a cutting-out expedition.'

'I am relieved to know that you have told him no more at present.'

Bolitho lowered his eyes to the chart, unnerved that Somervell could get under his skin so easily.

'Every year, Spanish treasure convoys set sail from the Main with each ship carrying a King's ransom. Between them, the church and the army have raped the continent, and now the King of Spain needs gold all the more. His French masters are making certain of their share.'

Somervell stood up and walked casually to the chart. Everything he did looked bored and unhurried, but his reputation as a swordsman made a lie of that.

He said, 'When I first came out here at His Majesty's *direction* –' He dabbed his mouth with a silk handkerchief and Bolitho thought it was to hide a small smile, 'I considered that the capture of such treasure might be just another dream. I know that Nelson has had some luck, but that was at sea where the chance of finding such booty is even more difficult.'

He traced the lines with one finger. 'La Guaira is well defended. It is where they will have taken the *Consort*.'

'With respect, my lord, I doubt that. La Guaira is the gateway to the capital, Caracas, but it is not suitable to refit a man-of-war, and it seems likely she will have been damaged after driving ashore.' Before Somervell could disagree he touched the coast away from La Guaira. 'Here, my lord, Puerto Cabello, seventy miles to the west'rd. It would be a far more likely destination.'

'Hmm.' Somervell leaned over the chart and Bolitho noticed a livid scar below his ear. A close call, he thought grimly.

Somervell continued, 'It is rather near to your intended operation. I am really not convinced.' He stood up and walked around

46

the cabin as if pacing out a rectangle. 'Price saw vessels at anchor, and I have had reports that treasure-ships are using La Guaira. The place is well defended, with at least three fortresses, and as *Consort* discovered to her cost, some other batteries, probably horse-artillery, for good measure.' He shook his head. 'I don't like it. If we still had the frigate it might, and I only say *might*, be different. Should you attack, and the Dons repulse you, we shall toss away every chance of surprise. The King of Spain would lose a fleet, rather than surrender his gold. I am *not* convinced.'

Bolitho watched him and felt strangely calm. In his mind the hazy plan had become suddenly real, like a shoreline hardening through a dawn mist. War at sea was always a risk. It took more than skill and plain courage; it took what his friend Thomas Herrick would describe as the work of Lady Luck. Friend? Was he still that after what had happened?

'I am prepared to take that chance, my lord.'

'Well, maybe I am not!' Somervell swung round, his eyes cold. 'There is more than glory at stake here!'

'I never doubted it, my lord.'

They faced one another, each testing the other's intentions.

Somervell said suddenly, 'When I first came to this damned place I imagined that some well-tried and gallant captain would be sent to seek out and capture one of the *galleons*.' He almost spat out the word. 'I was informed that a squadron would eventually come and seal off the escape routes which these Spanish *ladies* take on their passage to the Canaries and their home ports.' He held out one hand as if about to bow. 'Instead, *you* are sent, like a vanguard, to give the matter weight, to carry it through *no matter what*. So if we fail, the enemy victory will seem all the greater – what do you say about that?'

Bolitho shrugged. 'I think it can be done.' It came to him like a cry in the night. Somervell needed it to succeed more than anyone. Because of disfavour at court or because he was in some sort of trouble which a share of the prize money would readily take care of?

He said flatly, 'There is no time left, my lord. If we wait until reinforcements arrive from England, and I must stress that I am only expecting three more liners, the whole world will be after us. A victory may help our finances, but I can assure you that it will more than damage the Franco–Spanish alliance.'

Somervell sat down and carefully arranged his coat to give his thoughts time to settle.

He said irritably, 'The secret will out anyway.'

Bolitho watched him pout his lips and tried not to imagine them touching her neck, her breast.

Then Somervell smiled; it made him appear momentarily vulnerable. 'Then I agree. It shall be done as you describe. I am empowered to get you any assistance you need.' The smile vanished. 'But I cannot help you if –'

Bolitho nodded, satisfied. 'Yes, my lord, that word *if* can mean so much to a sea-officer.'

He heard someone hailing a boat, the clatter of oars nearby and guessed that Somervell had planned his departure, like his visit, to the minute.

Bolitho said, 'I shall tell Captain Haven at once.'

Somervell was only half-listening but he said, 'As little as possible. When two men share a secret, it is no longer a secret.' He looked at the screen door as Ozzard entered carrying his hat with elaborate care.

Somervell said quietly, 'I am glad we met. Though for the life of me I cannot imagine why you insisted on taking this mission.' He eyed him quizzically. 'A death-wish perhaps? You must surely have no need for more glory.' Then he turned on his heel and strode from the cabin.

At the entry port he glanced indifferently at the rigid marines and waiting side-party, then at Imrie's lanky shape by a poop ladder.

'I would imagine that the Lady Belinda is displeased about your zest for duty so soon after your recent victory?' He smiled wryly, then walked to the entry port without another glance.

Bolitho watched the smart launch being pulled away from *Hyperion*'s shadow and pondered what they had discussed; more, what they had left unsaid.

The reference to Belinda, for instance. What had Somervell expected to incite? Or was it merely something he could not restrain when neither of them had once mentioned Catherine?

Bolitho looked at the nearest anchored brig, the *Upholder*. Very like Adam's command, he thought.

Haven moved nearer and touched his hat. 'Any orders, Sir Richard?'

Bolitho pulled out his watch and snapped open the guard. Exactly noon, yet it felt like no time since he had left to visit *Thor*.

'Thank you, Captain Haven.' Their eyes met, and Bolitho could feel the other man's reserve, a wariness which was almost physical. 'I shall require all our captains on board at the close of the afternoon watch. Bring them aft to my quarters.'

Haven swallowed. 'The rest of our vessels are still at sea, sir.'

Bolitho glanced round, but the guard was dismissed, and only a few idlers and the master's mate of the watch were nearby.

He said, 'I intend to up-anchor within the week, as soon as there is wind enough to fill our canvas. We shall sail southwest to the Main and stand off La Guaira.'

Haven had ruddy, sunburned cheeks which matched his hair, but they seemed to pale. 'That's six hundred miles, sir! In this ship, without support, I'm not certain –'

Bolitho lowered his face and said, 'Have you no stomach for it, man? Or are you seeking an early retirement?' He hated himself, knowing that Haven could not hit back.

He added simply, 'I need you, and so does this ship. It has to be enough.' He turned away, despairing at what he saw in Haven's eyes.

He noticed Imrie and called, 'Come with me, I wish to pick your brains.'

Bolitho winced as a shaft of sunlight lanced down through the mizzen shrouds. For just those few seconds his eye was completely blind, and it was all he could do not to cry out.

A death-wish, Somervell had said. Bolitho groped into the poop's shadows and felt the bitterness coursing through him. Too many had died because of him, and even his friends were damaged by his touch.

Imrie ducked his head beneath the poop and walked beside him into the gloom between decks.

'I have been thinking, Sir Richard, and I've a few ideas –'

He had not seen the dismay on his admiral's face, nor could he guess how his simple remarks were like a lifeline for him.

Bolitho said, 'Then we shall quench our thirst while I listen.'

Haven watched them leave the quarterdeck and called for the signals midshipman. He told the boy the nature and time of the signal for the other captains to repair on board, then turned as the first lieutenant hurried towards him.

Before the lieutenant could speak Haven rasped, 'Do I have to perform your duties too, damn you?' He strode away adding, 'By God, if you cannot do better, I'll see you cast ashore for good!'

Parris stared after him, only his tightly bunched fists giving a hint of his anger and resentment.

'*And God damn you too!*' He saw the midshipman staring owlishly at him and wondered if he had spoken aloud. He grinned wearily. 'It's a fine life, Mr Mirrielees, provided you hold your tongue!'

At eight bells that afternoon, the signal was run up to the yard. It was begun.

4

Storm Warning

Bolitho stood in the centre of the deserted boatshed and allowed his eyes to grow accustomed to its shapes and shadows. It was a great, ramshackle building, lit by just a few guttering lanterns which swayed on long chains to reduce the risk of fire, and which gave the impression that the place was moving like a ship.

It was evening outside, but unlike the previous ones the darkness was alive with sounds, the creak and slap of palm fronds, the uneasy ripple of wavelets beneath the crude slipway upon which the water-lighter had been prepared for its passage south. The boatshed had been a hive of activity, with shipwrights and sailors working against time to rig extra bilge pumps and fit iron crutches along the bulwarks so that it could be manhandled by long sweeps when required.

Bolitho felt the loose sand in his shoes from his walk along the foreshore while he went over his plans for the hundredth time. Jenour had kept him close company, but had respected his need to be alone, at least with his thoughts.

Bolitho listened to the lap of water, the gentle moan of wind through the weather-worn roof. They had prayed for wind; now it might rise and turn against them. If the lighter was swamped before it could reach the rendezvous he must decide what to do. He would either have to send *Thor* inshore unsupported, or call off the attack. He thought of Somervell's eyes, of the doubt he had seen there. No, he would not back down from the attack; it was pointless to consider alternatives.

He glanced around at the black, inert shadows. Skeletons of old boats, frames of others yet to be completed. The smells of paint, tar and cordage. It was strange that it never failed to excite him even after all the years at sea.

Bolitho could recall the sheds at Falmouth, where he and his brother, Hugh, and sometimes his sisters had explored all the secret places, and had imagined themselves to be pirates and princesses in distress. He felt a stab in his heart as he pictured his child, Elizabeth. How she had plucked at his epaulettes and buttons when he had first seen her, had picked her up so awkwardly.

Instead of drawing him and Belinda closer, the child had done the opposite. One of their disputes had been over Belinda's announcement that she wanted her daughter to have a governess and a proper nurse to care for her. That, and the proposed move to London, had sparked it off.

She had exclaimed on one occasion, 'Because you were raised in Falmouth with other village children, you cannot expect me to refuse Elizabeth the chance to better herself, to take proper advantage of your achievements.'

It had been a difficult birth, while Bolitho had been away at sea. The doctor had warned Belinda against having another child, and a coldness had formed between them which Bolitho found hard to accept and understand.

She had said sharply on another occasion, 'I told you from the beginning, I am not Cheney. Had we not looked so much alike I fear you would have turned elsewhere!'

Bolitho had wanted to break down the barrier, take her to him and pour out his anguish. To tell her more of the damage to his eye, admit what it might mean.

Instead he had met her in London, and there had been an unreal, bitter hostility which both of them would regret.

Bolitho touched his buttons and thought of Elizabeth again. She was just sixteen months old. He stared around with sudden desperation. Would she never play in boatsheds like this one? Romp on the sand and come home filthy to be scolded and loved? He sighed, and Jenour responded immediately. '*Thor* should be well on her way, Sir Richard.'

Bolitho nodded. The bomb-vessel had sailed the previous night. God alone knew if spies had already gleaned news of her proposed employment. Bolitho had made certain that rumours had been circulated that *Thor* was taking the lighter in tow to St Christopher's, and even Glassport had put aside his resentment to provide some deck cargo with the senior officer's name and destination plainly marked.

Anyway, it was too late now. Perhaps it had been so when he had insisted on sailing in advance of his new squadron, to deal with the King's need for gold in his own way. *Death-wish*. It stuck in his mind like a barb.

He said, 'Imrie will doubtless be glad to be at sea.'

Jenour watched his upright figure and saw that he had removed his hat and loosened his neckcloth as if to draw every benefit from this last walk ashore.

Bolitho did not notice the glance, but was thinking of his other commanders. Haven had been right about one thing. The remaining three vessels of his small force had not yet returned to English Harbour. Either Glassport's schooner had been unable to find them, or they had separately decided to drag out their time. He thought of their faces when they had gathered in the great cabin. Thynne, of the third-rate *Obdurate* which was still completing repairs to storm-damage, was the only post-captain amongst them. Bolitho's main impression had been one of youth, the other that of polite wariness. They had all known the dead Price, and perhaps they saw in Bolitho's strategy something stolen, by which their admiral intended to profit.

He had remarked as much to Jenour, not because his young flag-lieutenant had either the experience or the wisdom to comment, but because he needed to share it with someone he could trust.

Typically, Jenour had insisted, 'They all know your record, Sir Richard. That is enough for any man!'

Bolitho glanced at him now. A pleasant, eager young man who reminded him of no one. Maybe that was the reason for his choice. That and his unnerving knowledge of his past exploits, ships and battles.

The three brigs, *Upholder*, *Tetrarch* and *Vesta*, would weigh tomorrow and sail with their flagship. It was to be hoped they did not run down on some enemy frigates before they reached the Main. The brigs mounted only forty-two pop-guns between them. If only the one sloop-of-war had received his recall signal. The *Phaedra* at least looked like a small frigate, and in proper hands could double as one. Or was he again thinking of his first command, and the luck he had enjoyed with her?

Bolitho walked slowly to the end of the slipway where it dipped into the uneasy catspaws. The water looked like ebony, with only occasional shadows and reflections from riding-lights, or as in *Hyperion*'s case, the checkered lines of open gunports. He felt the warm breeze stir his coat-tails and tried to picture his chart, the uncertainties which marked each of the six hundred miles as surely as any beacons.

Bolitho tried not to become irritated when he thought of Haven. He was no coward, but had shown himself to be beset by other, deeper anxieties. Whatever he really believed about being given command of a veteran like *Hyperion*, Bolitho knew differently. Old she might be, but she was a far better sailer than most. He smiled sadly, recalling her as she had been when he had first taken command as a young captain. She had been in commission so long without entering harbour for a refit that she was unbearably slow. Even with her copper-sheathing, the weed on her bottom had been yards long, so that under full sail she could only manage half the speed of her companions.

It was unusual for any captain to antagonise his admiral, whether he hated him or not. The climb to promotion was hard enough without flinging down more obstacles. Haven refused every offer of personal contact, and when, on the passage from England, tradition had insisted on his presence at table while Bolitho had entertained some of the junior officers, he had kept to himself. Alone amongst so many. He thought of the picture of Haven's pretty wife. Was she the cause of his moods? Bolitho grimaced in the darkness. *That* he would understand well enough.

A shadowy fishing-boat slipped past the nearest anchored brig. She could be carrying a message to the enemy. If the Dons found out what they intended, the admiral in Havana would have a whole squadron at sea within hours of receiving the news.

It was time to return to the jetty where his barge would be waiting, but he felt a reluctance to leave. It was peaceful here, an escape from danger and the call of duty.

The fishing-boat had vanished, unaware of the thoughts it had roused.

Bolitho stared at *Hyperion*'s glowing lines of open ports. As if she was still hanging on to the angry sunset, or was burning from within. He thought of the six hundred souls packed into her rounded hull and once again felt the pain of his responsibility, which wrongly directed could destroy them all.

They did not ask for much, and even the simplest comforts were too often denied them. He could picture these faceless men now, the Royal Marines in their *barracks*, as they termed their section of the deck, polishing and cleaning their equipment. At other mess tables between the guns where sailors lived out their watches below, some seamen would be working on delicate scrimshaw, or making tiny models of bone and shell. Seamen with hands so roughened by cordage and tar, yet they could still produce such fine results. The midshipmen, of which *Hyperion* carried eight, would be performing their studies for promotion to the godly rank of lieutenant, sometimes working by the smallest light, a glim set in an old shell.

The officers had not yet emerged except for brief contact on deck, or at dinner in his cabin. Given time they would show what they could or could not do. Bolitho swung his hat at some buzzing insect in the darkness. *Given leadership*. It all came down to that. He heard Jenour's shoes scrape on the rough ground as he turned towards the top of the boatshed.

Then he heard the carriage wheels, the stamp of a restless horse, and a man calling out to calm it.

Jenour whispered hoarsely, ' 'Tis a lady, Sir Richard.'

Bolitho turned, only his heart giving away his feelings. Not once did he question who it might be at this hour. Perhaps he had inwardly been expecting her, hoping she might find him. And yet he knew otherwise. He felt off-guard, as if he had been stripped naked.

They met below the propped-up bow of an old boat and Bolitho saw that she was covered from head to toe in a long cloak; its cowl hung loosely over her hair. Beyond her he could see a carriage on the road, a man at the horse's head, two small lamps casting an orange glow across the harness.

Jenour made to leave but she waved his apology aside and said, 'It is well. I have my maid with me.'

Bolitho stepped closer but she did not move towards him. She was completely hidden by the cloak, with just the oval of her face and a gold chain at her throat to break the darkness.

She said, 'You are leaving very soon.' It was a statement. 'I came to wish you luck with whatever –' Her voice trailed away. Bolitho held out his hand, but she said quickly, 'No. It is unfair.' She spoke without emotion, so that her voice seemed full of it. 'You met my husband?'

'Yes.' Bolitho tried to see her eyes but they too were in deep shadow. 'But I want to speak about you, to hear what *you* have been doing.'

She lifted her chin. 'Since you left me?' She half turned away. 'My husband spoke to me of your private meeting. You impressed him. He does not admire others very often. The fact you knew of the frigate's new name . . .'

Bolitho persisted, 'I need to talk, Kate.' He saw her shiver.

She said quietly, 'I once asked you to call me that.'

'I know. I do not forget.' He shrugged and knew he was floundering, losing a battle he could not fight.

'Nor I. I read everything I could, as if I expected that with time I could lose what I had felt. Hatred was not enough. . . .' She broke off. 'I was hurt – I bled because of you.'

'I did not know.'

She did not hear him. 'Did you imagine that your life meant so little to me that I could watch years of it pass and *not* be hurt? Years I could never share . . . did you think I loved you so little?'

'I thought you turned aside, Kate.'

'Perhaps I did. There was nothing offered. More than anything I wanted you to succeed, to be recognised for what you are. Would you have had people sneer when I passed as they do at Nelson's whore? How would you have ridden *that* storm, tell me?'

Bolitho heard Jenour's shoes as he moved away, but no longer cared.

'Please give me the chance to explain –'

She shook her head. 'You married another and have a child, I believe.'

Bolitho dropped his hands to his sides. 'And what of you? You married him.'

'*Him?*' She showed one hand through the cloak but withdrew it again. 'Lacey needed me. I was able to help him. As I told you, I wanted security.'

They watched each other in silence and then she said, 'Take care in whatever madness you are involved. I shall probably not see you again.'

Bolitho said, 'I shall sail tomorrow. But then he doubtless told you that too.'

For the first time her voice rose in passion and anger.

'Don't you use that tone with me! I came tonight because of the love I believed in. Not out of grief or pity. If you think –'

He reached out and gripped her arm through the cloak.

'Do not leave in anger, Kate.' He expected her to tear her arm away and hurry back to the coach. But something in his tone seemed to hold her.

He persisted, 'When I think of never seeing you again I feel guilty, because I know I could not bear it.'

She said in a whisper, 'It was your choice.'

'Not entirely.'

'Would you tell your wife you had seen me? I understand she is quite a beauty. Could you do that?'

She stepped back slightly. 'Your silence is my answer.'

Bolitho said bitterly, 'It is not like that.'

She glanced round towards the carriage and Bolitho saw the cowl fall from her head, caught the gleam of the lamps on her earrings. The ones he had given her.

She said, 'Please leave.' When he made to hold her again she backed away. 'Tomorrow I shall see the ships stand away from the land.' She put her hand to her face. 'I will feel nothing, Richard, because my heart, such as it is, will sail with you. *Now go!*'

Then she turned and ran from the shed, her cloak swirling about her until she reached the carriage.

Jenour said huskily, 'I am indeed sorry, Sir Richard –'

Bolitho turned on him. 'It's *time* you grew up, Mr Jenour!'

Jenour hurried after him, his mind still in a whirl from what he had seen and unwillingly shared.

Bolitho paused by the jetty and looked back. The carriage lamps were still motionless, and he knew she was watching him even in the darkness.

He heard the barge moving towards the jetty and was suddenly thankful. The sea had claimed him back.

At noon on the third day at sea Bolitho went on deck and walked along the weather side. It was like the other days, as if nothing, not even the men on watch, had changed.

He shaded his eyes to glance up at the masthead pendant. The wind was steady, as before, across the starboard quarter, creating a long regular swell which stretched unbroken in either direction. He heard the helmsman call, 'Steady as she goes, sir! Sou' west by west!' Bolitho knew it was more for his benefit than the officer-of-the-watch.

He looked at the long swell, the easy way *Hyperion* raised her quarter and allowed it to break against her flank. A few men were working high above the deck, their bodies tanned or peeling according to their time at sea. It never stopped. Splicing and reeving new lines, tarring-down and refilling the boats with water on their tier to keep the seams from opening in the relentless glare.

Bolitho felt the officer-of-the-watch glancing at him and tried to remember what he could about him. In a fight, one man could win or lose it. He paced slowly past the packed hammock nettings. Vernon Quayle was *Hyperion*'s fourth lieutenant, and unless he was checked or possibly killed he would be a tyrant if he ever reached post-rank. He was twenty-two, of a naval family, with sulky good looks and a quick temper. There had been three men flogged in his division since leaving England. Haven should have a word with the first lieutenant. Maybe he had, although the captain and his senior never appeared to speak except on matters of routine and discipline.

Bolitho tried not to think of *Hyperion* as she had once been. If any man-of-war could be said to be a happy ship in days like these, then so she had been then.

He walked forward to the quarterdeck rail and looked along the upper deck, the market-place of any warship.

The sailmaker and his mates were rolling up repaired lengths of canvas, and putting away their palms and needles. There was a sickly smell of cooking from the galley funnel, though how they could eat boiled pork in this heat was hard to fathom.

Bolitho could taste Ozzard's strong coffee on his tongue, but the thought of eating made him swallow hard. He had barely eaten since leaving English Harbour. Anxiety, strain, or was it still the guilt of seeing Catherine again?

Lieutenant Quayle touched his hat. '*Upholder* is on station, Sir Richard. The masthead makes a report every half-hour.' It sounded as if he was about to add, 'or I'll know the reason!'

Upholder was hull-down on the horizon and would be the first to signal that she had sighted *Thor* at the rendezvous. *Or not.* Bolitho had placed the brig in the van because of her young commander, William Trotter, a thoughtful Devonian who had impressed him during their first few meetings. It needed brains as well as good lookouts when so much depended on that first sighting.

Tetrarch was somewhere up to windward, ready to dash down if needed, and the third brig, *Vesta*, was far astern, her main role to ensure they were not being followed by some inquisitive stranger. So far they had seen nothing. It was as if the sea had emptied, that some dreadful warning had cleared it like an arena.

Tomorrow they would be near enough to land for the masthead to recognise it.

Bolitho had spoken to *Hyperion*'s sailing master, Isaac Penhaligon. Haven was fortunate to have such an experienced master, he thought. *So am I.* Penhaligon was a Cornishman also, but in name only. He had been packed off to sea as a cabin-boy at the tender age of seven years, and had walked ashore very little since. He was now about sixty, with a deeply-lined face the colour of leather, and eyes so bright they seemed to belong to a younger person trapped within. He had served in a packet-ship, in East Indiamen, and eventually had, as he had put it, donned the King's coat as a master's mate. His skill and knowledge of the oceans and their moods would be hard to rival, Bolitho thought. An additional piece of luck was that he once sailed in these same waters, had fought off buccaneers and slavers, had done so much that nothing seemed to daunt him. Bolitho had watched him checking the noon sights, his eyes on the assembled midshipmen whose navigation and maritime knowledge lay in his hands, ready to make a rough comment if things went wrong. He was never sarcastic with the *young gentlemen*, but he was very severe, and they were obviously in awe of him.

Penhaligon had compared his charts and notes with Price's own observations and had commented sparingly, 'Knew his navigation, that one.' It was praise indeed.

A petty officer approached the lieutenant and knuckled his forehead. Bolitho was thankful to be left alone as Quayle hurried away. He had seen the petty officer's expression. Not just respect for an officer. It was more like fear.

He stroked the worn rail, hot from the sunlight. He thought of that last meeting in the boatshed, Catherine's voice and fervour. He had to see her again, if only to explain. *Explain what?* It could do nothing but harm to her. To both of them.

She had seemed unreachable, eager to tell him the hurt he had done her, and yet. . . .

He remembered vividly their first meeting, and when she had cursed him for the death of her husband. Her *second* husband. There had also been the one she rarely mentioned, a reckless soldier-of-fortune who had died in Spain in some drunken brawl. Who had she been then, and where had she come from? It was hard to see her, so captivating and striking as she was now, set against the squalor she had once touched on in a moment of intimacy.

And what of Somervell? Was he as cold and indifferent as he appeared? Or was he merely contemptuous; amused perhaps while he watched the reawakening of old memories, which he might use or ignore as he chose?

Would he ever know, or would he spend the rest of his life remembering how it had once been for so short a time, knowing that she was watching from a distance, waiting to learn what he was doing, or if he had fallen in battle?

Quayle had gone to the helm and was snapping something at

the midshipman-of-the-watch. Like the others, he was properly dressed, although he must be sweating fire in this heat.

Had Keen been his flag captain he would have – Bolitho called, 'Send for my servant!'

Quayle came alive. 'At *once*, Sir Richard!'

Ozzard emerged from the shadows of the poop and stood blinking in the glare, more mole-like than ever. Small, loyal and ever ready to serve Bolitho whenever he could. He had even read to him when he had been partially blinded, and before, when he had been smashed down by a musket. Meek and timid, but underneath there was another kind of man. He was well-educated and had once been a lawyer's clerk; he had run away to sea to avoid prosecution, and some said the hangman's halter.

Bolitho said, 'Take my coat, if you please.' Ozzard did not even blink as the vice-admiral tossed his coat over his arm and then handed him his hat.

Others were staring, but by tomorrow even Haven might tell his officers to walk the decks in their shirts and not suffer in silence. If it took a uniform to make an officer, there was no hope for any of them.

Ozzard gave a small smile, then scurried thankfully into the shadows again.

He had watched most faces of Bolitho, his moods of excitement and despair. There had been too many of the latter, he thought.

Past the marine sentry and into the great cabin. The world he shared with Bolitho, where rank was of little importance. He held up the coat and examined it for traces of tar or strands of spun yarn. Then he saw his own reflection in the mirror and held the coat against his own small frame. The coat hung almost to his ankles and he gave a shy smile.

He gripped the coat tightly as he saw himself that terrible day when the lawyer had sent him home early.

He had discovered his young wife, naked in the arms of a man he had known and respected for years.

They had tried to bluff it out and all the while he had been *dying* as he had stared at them.

Later, when he had left the small house on the Thames at

Wapping Wall, he had seen the shopkeeper's name opposite. *Tom Ozzard*, Scrivener. He had decided then and there it was to be his new identity.

Never once had he looked back to the room where he had stopped their lies with an axe, had hacked and slashed until there was nothing recognisable in human form.

On Tower Hill he had found the recruiting party; they were never far away, always in the hopes of a volunteer, or some drunkard who would take a coin and then find himself in a man-of-war until he was paid off or killed.

The lieutenant in charge had regarded him with doubt and then amusement. Prime seamen, strong young men, were what the King needed.

Ozzard carefully folded the coat. It was different now. They would take a cripple on two crutches if they got the chance.

Tom Ozzard, servant to a vice-admiral, afraid, no, terrified of battle when the ship quaked and reeled around him, a man with no past, no future.

One day, deep in his heart, Ozzard knew he would go back to that little house at Wapping Wall. Then, only then, he would give in to what he had done.

From the masthead lookout, curled up in the cross-trees, to Allday, sprawled in his hammock while he slept off the aftermath of several *wets*, from Ozzard to the man in the great cabin whom he served, most thoughts were on tomorrow.

Hyperion in all her years, and over the countless leagues she had sailed, had seen many come and go.

Beyond the figurehead's trident lay the horizon. Beyond that, only destiny could identify.

5

Leadership

Bolitho walked up the wet planking to the weather side of the quarterdeck and steadied himself by gripping the hammock nettings. It was still dark, with only spectres of spray leaping over the hull to break the sea's blackness.

Darker shadow moved across the quarterdeck to merge with a small group by the rail, where Haven and two of his lieutenants received their reports and passed out new orders.

Voices murmured from the gundeck, and Bolitho could picture the hands at work around the invisible eighteen-pounders, while on the deck below the heavier battery of thirty-two pounders, although equally busy, remained silent. Down there, beneath the massive deckhead beams, the gun crews were used to managing their charges in constant gloom.

The hands had been piped to an even earlier breakfast, probably an unnecessary precaution because when dawn found them they would still be out of sight of land – except, with any luck, by the masthead lookouts. In the past hour *Hyperion* had altered course, and was heading due west, her yards close-hauled with their reduced canvas of forecourse and topsails. It explained the uneasy, turbulent motion, but Bolitho had noticed the difference in the weather as soon as his feet had touched the damp rug by his cot.

The wind was steady but had risen; not much, but after the seemingly constant calm or glassy swell, it seemed violent by comparison.

Everyone nearby knew he was on deck and had discreetly crossed to the lee side to give him room to walk if he chose. He looked up at the rigging and saw the braced topsails for the first time. They were flapping noisily, showing their displeasure at being so tightly reined.

He had been awake for most of the night, but when the hands were called, and the work of preparing the ship for whatever lay ahead begun, he had felt a strange eagerness to sleep.

Allday had padded into the cabin, and while Ozzard had magicked up his strong coffee, the big coxswain had shaved him by the light of a spiralling lantern.

Allday had still not unburdened himself about his son. Bolitho could remember his elation when he had discovered he had a son of twenty, one he had known nothing about, who had decided to join him when his mother, an old love of Allday's, had died.

Then aboard the cutter *Supreme* after Bolitho had been cut down and almost completely blinded, Allday had nursed an anger and a despair that his son, also named John, was a coward, and had run below at the very moment when Bolitho had needed him most.

Now he knew differently. Afraid of the fire of battle perhaps, but no coward. It took a brave heart to disguise fear when the enemy's iron raked the decks.

But his son had asked to leave the ship when they had docked. For Allday's sake and for everyone's peace of mind Bolitho had spoken to the officer in charge of the coastguard near Falmouth, and asked him to find a place for him. His son, John Bankart as he was named after his mother, had been a good seaman, and could reef, splice and steer with the most experienced Jack. He had been performing the duties of second-coxswain in the prize *Argonaute* to help Allday, who was too proud to admit that his terrible wound was making things hard for him. Also, Allday had been able to keep an eye on him, until the day when Bolitho had been wounded whilst aboard the little cutter.

Bolitho disliked asking favours of anyone, especially because of his rank, and now he was unsure that he had done the right thing. Allday brooded about it, and when not required on duty spent too much time alone, or sitting with a tot in his hand in Ozzard's pantry.

We are both in need. Like dog and master. Each fearful that the other would die first.

A youthful voice exclaimed, 'Sunrise, sir!'

Haven muttered something, then crossed to the weather side. He touched his hat in the darkness.

'The boats are ready for lowering, Sir Richard.' He seemed more formal than ever. 'But if *Upholder* is on station we should get plenty of warning if we need to clear for action.'

'I agree.' Bolitho wondered what lay behind the formality. Was he hoping to see *Upholder*'s signal flying to announce she had *Thor* in sight? Or was he expecting the sea to be empty, the effort and the preparation a waste of time?

He said, 'I never tire of this moment.' Together they watched the first glimpse of sunlight as it rimmed the horizon like a fine gold wire. With *Hyperion* on her present tack the sun would rise almost directly astern, to paint each sail by turn then reach out far ahead, as if to show them the way to the land.

Haven commented, 'I just hope the Dons don't know we're so near.'

Bolitho hid a smile. Haven would make Job seem like an optimist.

Another figure crossed the deck and waited for Haven to see him. It was the first lieutenant.

Haven moved a few paces away. 'Well? What now?' His voice was hushed, but the hostility was obvious.

Parris said calmly, 'The two men for punishment, sir. May I tell the master-at-arms to stand over their sentence until –'

'*You shall not*, Mr Parris. Discipline is discipline, and I'll not have men escape their just deserts because we may or may not be engaging an enemy.'

Parris stood his ground. 'It was nothing that serious, sir.'

Haven nodded, satisfied. 'One of them is from your part-of-ship, am I right? Laker? Insolent to a petty officer.'

Parris's eyes seemed to glow from within as the first weak sunlight made patterns on the planking.

'They both lost their tempers, sir. The petty officer called him a whore's bastard.' He seemed to relax, knowing the battle was already lost. 'Me, sir, I'd have torn out his bloody tongue!'

Haven hissed, 'I shall speak with *you* later! Those men will be seized up and flogged at six bells!'

Parris touched his hat and walked away.

Bolitho heard the captain say, '*Bloody hound!*'

It was no part of his to interfere. Bolitho looked at the sunrise, but it was spoiled by what he had heard.

He would have to speak to Haven about it later when they were alone. He glanced up at the mizzen topmast as a shaft of light played across the shrouds and running rigging. If he waited until action was joined it might be too late.

The words seemed to echo around his mind. *If I should fall . . .* Every ship was only as strong as her captain. If there was something wrong . . . He looked round, Haven brushed from his thoughts, as the masthead yelled, 'Sail in sight to the sou'-west!'

Bolitho clenched his hands into fists. It must be *Upholder*, right on station. He had been right in his choice for the van.

He said, 'Prepare to come about, Captain Haven.'

Haven nodded. 'Pipe the hands to the braces, Mr Quayle.'

Another face fitted into the pattern; Bolitho's companion of the forenoon watch the day before. The sort of officer who would have no compassion when it came to a flogging.

Bolitho added, 'Do you have a good man aloft today?'

Haven stared at him, his face still masked in shadow. 'I – I believe so, sir.'

'Send up an experienced hand. A master's mate for my money.'

'Aye, sir.' Haven sounded tense. Angry with himself for not thinking of the obvious. He could scarcely blame Parris for that.

Bolitho glanced around as the shadows nearby took on shape and personality. Two young midshipmen, both in their first ship, the officer-of-the-watch, and below the break in the poop he saw the tall, powerful figure of Penhaligon the master. If he was satisfied with their progress you would never know, Bolitho thought.

'Deck there! *Upholder* in sight!'

Bolitho guessed the voice was that of Rimer, master's mate of the watch. He was a small, bronzed man with features so creased that he looked like some seafarer from a bygone age. The other vessel was little more than a blur in the faint daylight, but Rimer's experience and keen eye told him all he needed to know.

Bolitho said, 'Mr Jenour, get aloft with a glass.' He turned aside as the young lieutenant hurried to the shrouds. 'I trust you climb as fast as you ride?'

He saw the flash of teeth as Jenour grinned back at him. Then he was gone, his arms and legs working with all the ease of a nimble maintopman.

Haven crossed the deck and looked up at Jenour's white breeches. 'It will be light enough soon, sir.'

Bolitho nodded. 'Then we shall know.'

He bunched his fists together under his coat-tails as Jenour's voice pealed down.

'Signal from *Upholder*, sir! *Thor in company!*'

Bolitho tried not to show excitement or surprise. Imrie had done it.

'*Acknowledge!*' He had to cup his hands to shout above the slap of canvas and rigging. There was no further signal from *Upholder*. It meant nothing had gone wrong so far, and that the ungainly lighter was still safely in tow.

He said, 'When the others are in sight, Captain Haven, signal them to proceed while we are all of one mind. There is no time for another conference. Even now there is a chance we might be discovered before we are all in position.'

He walked to the nettings again. There was no point in showing doubt or uncertainty to Haven. He looked aloft as more and more of the rigging and spars took shape in the sunlight. It was strange that he had never mastered his dislike of heights. As a midshipman he had faced each dash aloft to help shorten or make more sail as a separate challenge. At night in particular, with the yards heeling over towards the bursting spray and the deck little more than a blur far beneath his feet, he had felt an enduring terror.

He saw some Royal Marines on the mizzen-top, their scarlet coats very bright while they leaned over the barricade to watch for the brig *Upholder*. Bolitho would have dearly liked to climb up past them without caring, as Jenour had done. He touched his left eyelid, then blinked at the reflected sunlight. Deceptively clear, but the worry was always there.

He looked along the upper deck, the gun crews standing down to go about their normal tasks as the first tension disappeared with the night.

So many miles. Too many memories. During the night when he had lain awake in his cot listening to the sluice and creak of the sea around the rudder he had recalled another time when *Hyperion* had sailed this far, while he had been her captain. They had slipped past the Isles of Pascua in the darkness and Bolitho could remember exactly that dawn attack on the French ships anchored there. And it was nine years ago. The same ship. But was he still the same man?

He glanced up at the mizzen top and was suddenly angry with himself.

'Hand me that glass, if you please.' He took it from a startled midshipman and walked purposefully to the weather shrouds. He could feel Haven watching him, saw Parris trying not to stare from the larboard gangway where he was in discussion with Sam Lintott, the boatswain. Probably telling him when to rig the gratings so that punishment could be carried out as ordered.

Then he saw Allday squinting up from the maindeck, his jaw still working on a piece of biscuit while he, too, stared with astonishment. Bolitho swung himself up and around the shrouds and felt the ratlines quiver with each step while the big signals telescope bounced against his hip like a quiver of arrows.

It was easier than he would have believed, but as he clambered into the top he decided it was far enough.

The marines stood back, nudging and grinning to each other. Bolitho was able to recall the name of the corporal, a fierce-looking man who had been a Norfolk poacher before he signed on with the Corps. Not before time, Major Adams had hinted darkly.

'Where is she, Corporal Rogate?'

The marine pointed. 'Yonder, sir! Larboard bow!'

Bolitho steadied the long telescope and watched as the brig's narrow poop and braced yards leapt into view. Figures moved about *Upholder*'s quarterdeck, steeply angled as the ship heeled over to show her bright copper to the early sunshine.

Bolitho waited for *Hyperion* to sway upright and for the

mizzen topmast to restrain its shivering, and beyond *Upholder* he saw a tan-coloured pyramid of sails. *Thor* was ready and waiting.

He lowered the glass as if to bring his thoughts into equal focus. Had he decided from the very beginning that he would lead the attack? If it failed, he would be taken prisoner, or. . . . He gave a grim smile. The *or* did not bear thinking about.

Corporal Rogate saw the secret smile and wondered how he would describe it to the others during the next watch below. How the admiral had spoken to him, just like another Royal. *One of us.*

Bolitho knew that if he sent another officer and the plan misfired, the blame would be laid at his door anyway.

They had to trust him. In his heart Bolitho knew that the next months were crucial for England, and for the fleet in particular. Leadership and trust went hand in hand. To most of his command he was a stranger and their trust had to be earned.

He considered his argument with sudden contempt. *Death-wish.* Was that a part of it too?

He concentrated on the brig's sturdy shape as she ducked and rose across steep waves. In his mind's eye he could already see the land as it would appear when they drew nearer. The anchorage at La Guaira consisted mainly of an open roadstead across the front of the town. It was known to be heavily defended by several fortresses, some of which were quite newly constructed because of the comings and goings of treasure-ships. Although La Guaira was just six miles or so from the capital, Caracas, the latter could only be reached by a twisting, mountainous road some four times that distance.

As soon as *Hyperion* and her consorts were sighted the Spanish authorities would send word to the capital with all the haste they could manage. Because of the time it would take on that precarious road, La Guaira might just as well be an island, he thought. All the intelligence they had been able to gather from traders and blockade-runners alike pointed to the captured frigate *Consort* being at Puerto Cabello, eighty miles further westward along the coast of the Main.

But suppose the enemy did not fall for the ruse, would not

believe that the British men-of-war were intending to cut out the new addition to their fleet?

So much depended on Price's maps and observations, and above all, luck.

He looked down at the deck far below and bit his lip. He knew he would never have sent a subordinate to carry out such a mission even nine years back when he had commanded the old *Hyperion*. He glanced at the marines. 'There's work for all of you soon, my lads.'

He swung himself down on to the futtock shrouds, more conscious of their faces split into huge grins than of the wind which flapped around his coat as if to fling him to the deck. *It was so easy*. A word, a smile, and they would die for you. It made him feel bitter and humble at the same time.

By the time he had reached the quarterdeck his mind had cleared. 'Very well. In one hour we shall alter course to the sou' west.' He saw the others nod. 'Have *Upholder* and *Tetrarch* tack closer to the land. I don't want the Dons to get near enough to see our strength.' He saw Penhaligon the sailing master give a wry smile and added, 'Or our lack of it. *Thor* will hold to windward of us in company with *Vesta*. Let me know when it is light enough to make signals.' He turned towards the poop and then paused. 'Captain Haven, a moment if you please.'

In the great cabin the strengthening sunlight made strange patterns on the caked salt which had spattered the stern windows. Most of the ship had been cleared for action before dawn. Bolitho's quarters were like a reminder of better times, until these screens were taken down, and the cabin furniture with all traces of his occupation here were taken to the security of the hold. He glanced at the black-barrelled nine-pounders which faced their closed ports on either side of the cabin. Then these two beauties would have the place to themselves.

Haven waited for Ozzard to close the screen door and withdraw, then stood with his feet apart, his hat balanced in both hands.

Bolitho looked at the sea beyond the smeared glass. 'I intend to shift to *Thor* at dusk. You will take *Hyperion* with *Vesta* and *Tetrarch* in company. By first light tomorrow you should be in sight of Puerto Cabello and the enemy will be convinced that you intend to attack. They will not know your full strength – we have been lucky in reaching this far undetected.' He turned in time to see the captain gripping his hat so fiercely that it buckled in his fingers. He had expected an outburst or perhaps the outline of an alternative strategy. Haven said nothing, but stared at him as if he had misheard.

Bolitho continued quietly, 'There is no other way. If we are to capture or destroy a treasure-ship it must be done at anchor. We have too few ships for an extended search if she slips past us.'

Haven swallowed hard. 'But to go *yourself*, sir? In my experience I have never known such a thing.'

'With God's help and a little luck, Captain Haven, I should be in position in the shallows to the west of La Guaira at the very moment you are making your mock attack.' He faced him steadily. 'Do not risk your ships. If a large enemy force arrives you will discontinue the action and stand away. The wind is still steady at north-by-west. Mr Penhaligon believes it may back directly which would be in our favour.'

Haven looked around the cabin as if to seek an escape.

'He may be wrong, sir.'

Bolitho shrugged. 'I would not *dare* to disagree with him.'

But his attempt to lighten the tension was lost as Haven blurted out, 'If I am forced to withdraw, who will believe –'

Bolitho looked away to hide his disappointment. 'I will have new orders written for you. No blame will be laid at your door.'

Haven said, 'I was not suggesting it merely for my own benefit, sir!'

Bolitho sat down on the bench seat and tried not to think of all those other times when he had sat here. Hopes, plans, anxieties.

He said, 'I shall want thirty seamen from your company. I would prefer an officer whom they know to command them.'

Haven said instantly, 'May I suggest my first lieutenant, sir?'

Their eyes met. *I thought you might.* He nodded. 'Agreed.'

Calls trilled from the quarterdeck and Haven glanced at the door.

Bolitho said abruptly, 'I have not yet finished.' He tried to remain calm but Haven's behaviour was unnerving. 'If the enemy does throw a force against you there is no way that you can cover my withdrawal from La Guaira.'

Haven lifted his chin slightly. 'If you say so, Sir Richard.'

'I do. In which case you will assume command of the flotilla.'

'And may I ask what you would do, sir?'

Bolitho stood up. 'What I came to do.' He sensed that Allday was waiting close by the door. Another argument, when he told him he was not coming over to *Thor* with him.

'Before you leave, Captain Haven.' He tried not to blink as the mist filtered persistently across his left eye. 'Do not have those men flogged. I cannot interfere, because everyone aboard would know that I had taken sides, as you already knew when you crossed swords with your senior in my presence.' He thought he saw Haven pale slightly. 'These people have little enough, God knows, and to see their messmates flogged before being ordered into battle can do nothing but harm. Loyalty is all-important, but remember that while you are under my flag, loyalty goes both ways.'

Haven backed away. 'I hope I know my duty, Sir Richard.'

'So do I.' He watched the door close, then exclaimed, '*God damn him!*'

But it was Jenour who entered, wiping tar from his fingers with a piece of rag.

He watched as if to gauge Bolitho's mood, and said, 'A fine view from up there. I have come to report that your signals have been made and acknowledged.' He glanced up as feet thudded overhead and voices echoed from the maindeck. 'We are about to change tack, Sir Richard.'

Bolitho barely heard. 'What is the matter with that man, eh?'

Jenour remarked, 'You have told him what you intend.'

Bolitho nodded. 'I'd have thought any captain would have jumped at the chance to cast his admiral adrift. I know I did.' He stared round the cabin, searching for ghosts. 'Instead, he thinks of nothing but –' He checked himself. It was unthinkable to discuss the flag captain with Jenour. Was he so isolated that he could find no other solace?

Jenour said simply, 'I am not so impertinent as to say what I think, Sir Richard.' He looked up and added, 'But I would stand by whatever you ordered *me* to do.'

Bolitho relaxed and clapped him on the shoulder. 'They say that faith can move a mountain, Stephen!'

Jenour stared. Bolitho had called him by name. It was probably a mistake.

Bolitho said, 'We will transfer to *Thor* before dusk. It must be smartly done, Stephen, for we have a long way to travel.'

It was not a mistake. Jenour seemed to glow. He stammered, 'Your coxswain is waiting outside, Sir Richard.' He watched as Bolitho strode across the cabin, then chilled as he cannoned into a chair which Haven must have moved.

'Are you all right, Sir Richard?' He fell back as Bolitho turned towards him. But this time there was no anger in his sensitive features. Bolitho said quietly, 'My eye troubles me a little. It is nothing. Now send in my cox'n.'

Allday walked past the lieutenant and said, 'I have to speak my piece, Sir Richard. When you goes across to that bomb,' he almost spat out the word, 'I'll be beside you. Like always, an' I don't give a bugger, beggin' your pardon, Sir Richard.'

Bolitho retorted, 'You've been drinking, Allday.'

'A bit, sir. Just a few wets afore we leave the ship.' He put his head on one side like a shaggy dog. 'We *will*, won't we, sir?'

It came out surprisingly easily. 'Yes, old friend. Together. One more time.'

Allday regarded him gravely, sensing his despair. 'Wot is it, sir?'

'I nearly told that youngster, Jenour. Nearly came right out with it.' He was talking to himself aloud. 'That I'm terrified of going blind.'

Allday licked his lips. 'Young Mr Jenour looks on you as a bit of a hero, sir.'

'Not like you, eh?' But neither of them smiled.

Allday had not seen him like this for a long while, not since. . . .

He cursed himself, took the blame for not being here when he was needed. It made him angry when he compared Haven with Captain Keen, or Herrick. He looked around the cabin where they had shared and lost so much together. Bolitho had nobody to share it with, to lessen the load. On the messdecks the Jacks thought the admiral wanted for nothing. By Jesus, that was just what he had. Nothing.

Allday said, 'I know it's not my place to say it, but –'

Bolitho shook his head. 'When did that ever stop you?'

Allday persisted, 'I don't know how to put it in officers' language like.' He took a deep breath. 'Cap'n Haven's wife is havin' a baby, probably dropped it by now, I shouldn't wonder.'

Bolitho stared at him. 'What of it, man?'

Allday tried not to release a deep breath of relief as he saw the impatience in Bolitho's grey eyes.

'He thinks that someone else may be the father, so to speak.'

Bolitho exclaimed, 'Well, even supposing –' He looked away, surprised, when he ought not to have been, at Allday's knowledge. 'I see.' It was not the first time. A ship in dock, a bored wife and a likely suitor. But it had taken Allday to put his finger on it.

Bolitho eyed him sadly. How could he leave him behind? What a pair. One so cruelly wounded by a Spanish sword thrust, the other slowly going blind.

He said, 'I shall write some letters.'

They looked at each other without speaking. Cornwall in late October. Grey sky, and rich hues of fallen leaves. Chipping-hammers in the fields where farmers took time to repair their walls and fences. The elderly militia drilling in the square outside the cathedral where Bolitho had been married.

Allday moved away towards Ozzard's pantry. He would ask the little man to write a letter for him to the innkeeper's daughter in Falmouth, though God alone knew if she would ever get it.

He thought of Lady Belinda and the time they had found her in the overturned coach. And of the one named Catherine who might still harbour feelings for Bolitho. A fine-looking woman, he thought, but a lot of trouble. He grinned. A sailor's woman, no matter what airs and graces she hoisted at her yards. And if she was right for Bolitho, that was all that mattered.

Alone at his table Bolitho drew the paper towards him and watched the sunlight touch the pen like fire.

In his mind he could see the words as he had written them before. '*My dearest Belinda.*'

At noon he went on deck for his walk, and when Ozzard entered the cabin to tidy things he saw the paper with the pen nearby. Neither had been used.

6

'In War There Are No Neutrals —'

The transfer from *Hyperion* to the bomb-vessel *Thor* was carried out just before sunset, without mishap. Men and weapons with extra powder and shot were ferried across, the boats leaping and then almost disappearing between the crests of a deep swell.

Bolitho watched from the quarterdeck while *Hyperion* lay hove-to, her canvas booming in protest, and once again marvelled at the sunset's primitive beauty. The long undulating swell, like the boats and their labouring crews, seemed to glow like rough bronze, while even the faces around him looked unreal; like strangers.

With two of *Hyperion*'s boats and thirty of her men safely transferred, Bolitho made the final crossing in a jolly boat.

He had barely been received aboard *Thor* before he saw *Hyperion*'s yards swinging round, her shadowed outline shortening as she turned away to follow the two brigs into the last of the sunset.

If Commander Ludovic Imrie was bothered by having his flag officer coming aboard his modest command, he did not show it. He displayed more surprise when Bolitho announced that he did not intend to wear his epaulettes, and suggested that Imrie, as *Thor*'s commander, should follow his example.

He had remarked calmly, 'Your people know you well enough. I trust that they will know me too when this affair is finished!'

Bolitho was able to forget *Hyperion* and the others as they headed further and further away towards Puerto Cabello. He could feel the tension mount around him as *Thor* made more sail and steered, close-hauled, towards the invisible shoreline.

Hour followed hour, with hushed voices calling from the chains where two leadsmen took regular soundings, so that their reports could be checked carefully against the chart and the notes Bolitho had made after his meeting with Captain Price.

The noise was loud, but deceptive. Astern on its tow-line, the clumsy lighter was pumped constantly in a battle which Imrie had admitted had begun within hours of leaving harbour. Any rise in the sea brought instant danger from flooding, and now, with both *Thor*'s heavy mortars and their crews on board, the lighter's loss would spell disaster.

Bolitho prowled restlessly around the vessel's quarterdeck and pictured the land in his mind, as he had seen it that late afternoon. He had made himself climb aloft just once more, this time to the maintop, and through a rising haze had seen the tell-tale landmarks of La Guaira. The vast blue-grey range of the Caracas Mountains, and further to the west the impressive saddle-shaped peaks of the Silla de Caracas.

Penhaligon could be rightfully proud of his navigation, he thought. Allday barely left his side after they had come aboard, and Bolitho could hear his uneven breathing, his fingers drumming against the hilt of a heavy cutlass.

It made Bolitho touch the unfamiliar shape of the hanger at his belt. The prospect of action right inside the enemy's territory occupied everyone's mind, but Bolitho doubted if Allday had missed his decision to leave the old family sword behind in *Hyperion*. He had almost lost it once before. Allday would be remembering that too, thinking Bolitho had left it with Ozzard only because he believed he might not return.

Adam would wear the sword one day. It would never fall into enemy hands again.

Later, in Imrie's small cabin, they peered at the chart behind shuttered stern windows. *Thor* was cleared for action, but her chance would come only if the first part succeeded. Bolitho traced the twisting shallows with the dividers, as Price must have done before his ship had driven ashore. He felt the others crowding around and against him. Imrie and his senior master's mate,

Lieutenant Parris, and *Thor*'s second lieutenant, who would cover the attack.

Bolitho wondered momentarily if Parris was thinking about the floggings, which had been cancelled at Haven's order. Or of the fact that Haven had insisted that the two culprits should be included in the raiding party. All the bad eggs in one basket maybe, he thought.

He pulled out his watch and laid it beneath a low-slung lantern.

'*Thor* will anchor within the half-hour. All boats will cast off immediately, the jolly boat leading. Soundings must be taken, but not unnecessarily. Stealth is vital. We must be in position by dawn.' He glanced at their grim expressions. 'Questions?'

Dalmaine, *Thor*'s second lieutenant, raised his hand.

'What if the Don has moved, sir?'

It was amazing how easy they found it to speak up, Bolitho thought. Without the intimidating vice-admiral's epaulettes, and in their own ship, they had already spoken of their ideas, their anxieties as well. It was like being in a frigate or a sloop-of-war, all over again.

'Then we will be unlucky.' Bolitho smiled and saw Jenour's eyes watching the brass dividers as he tapped the chart. 'But there have been no reports of any large ships on the move.'

The lieutenant persisted, 'And the battery, sir. Suppose we cannot take it by surprise?'

It was Imrie who answered. 'I would suggest, Mr Dalmaine, that all your pride in your mortars will have been misplaced!'

The others laughed. It was the first healthy sign.

Bolitho said, 'We destroy the battery, then *Thor* can follow through the sandbars. Her carronades will more than take care of any guardboats.' He stood up carefully to avoid the low beams. 'And then we shall attack.'

Parris said, 'And if we are repulsed, Sir Richard?'

Their eyes met across the small table. Bolitho studied his gipsy good looks, the reckless candour in his voice. A West Country man, probably from Dorset. Allday's blunt words seemed to intrude, and he thought of the small portrait in Haven's cabin.

He said, 'The treasure-ship must be sunk, fired if possible. It may not prevent salvage, but the delay will be considerable for the Don's coffers!'

'I see, sir.' Parris rubbed his chin. 'The wind's backed. It could help us.' He spoke without emotion, not as a lieutenant who might well be dead, or screaming under a Spanish surgeon's knife by morning, but as a man used to command.

He was considering alternatives. *Suppose, if, perhaps.*

Bolitho watched him. 'So shall we be about it, gentlemen?' They met his gaze. Did they know, he wondered? Would they still trust his judgment? He smiled in spite of his thoughts. Haven certainly trusted nobody!

Imrie said cheerfully, 'Och, Sir Richard, we'll a' be rich men by noon!'

They left the cabin, stooping and groping like cripples. Bolitho waited until Imrie alone remained.

'It must be said. If I fall, you must withdraw if you think fit.'

Imrie studied him thoughtfully. 'If *you* fall, Sir Richard, it will be because I've failed you.' He glanced around the cramped cabin. 'We'll make you proud, you'll see, sir!'

Bolitho walked out into the darkness and stared at the stars until his mind was steady again.

Why did you never get used to it? The simple loyalty. Their honesty with one another, which was unknown or ignored by so many people at home.

Thor dropped anchor, and as she swung to her cable in a lively current, the boats were manhandled alongside or hoisted outboard with such speed that Bolitho guessed that her commander had been drilling and preparing for this moment since he had weighed at English Harbour.

He settled himself in the sternsheets of the jolly boat, which even in the darkness seemed heavy, low in the water with her weight of men and weapons. He had discarded his coat and hat and could have been another lieutenant like Parris.

Allday and Jenour were crowded against him, and while Allday watched the oarsmen with a critical eye, the flag lieutenant said excitedly, 'They'll never believe this!'

By they, he meant his parents, Bolitho guessed.

It seemed to sum up his whole command, he decided. Captains

or seamen, there were more sons than fathers.

He heard the grind of long sweeps as the lighter was cast adrift from *Thor*'s quarter, spray bursting over the blades until two more boats flung over their tow-lines.

It was a crazy plan, but one which might just work. Bolitho plucked his shirt away from his body. Sweat or spray, he could not be sure. He concentrated on the time, the whispered soundings, the steady rise and fall of oars. He did not even dare to peer astern to ensure that the others were following.

The boats were at the mercy of the currents and tides around the invisible sandbars. One minute gurgling beneath the keel, and the next with all the oars thrashing and heaving to prevent the hull from being swung in the wrong direction.

He pictured Parris with the main body of men, and Dalmaine in the lighter with his mortars, the hands baling to keep the craft afloat. So close inshore he would not dare to use the pumps now.

There was a startled gasp from the bows, and the coxswain called hoarsely, '*Oars!* Easy, lads!'

With the blades stilled and dripping above either beam, the jolly boat pirouetted around in the channel like an untidy sea-creature. A man scrambled aft and stared at Bolitho for several seconds.

He gasped, 'Vessel anchored dead ahead, sir!' He faltered, as if suddenly aware that he was addressing his admiral. 'Small 'un, sir. Schooner mebbee!'

Jenour groaned softly. 'What damned luck! We'd never –'

Bolitho swung round. 'Shutter the lantern astern!' He prayed that Parris would see it in time. An alarm now would catch them in the open. It was too far to pull back, impossible to slip past the anchored ship without being challenged.

He heard himself say, 'Very well, Cox'n. Give way all. Very steady now.' He recalled Keen's calm voice when he had spoken with his gun crews before a battle. Like a rider quieting a troubled mount.

He said, 'It's up to us. No turning back.' He made each word sink in but it was like speaking into darkness or an empty boat. 'Steer a little to larboard, Cox'n.' He heard a rasp of steel, and a petty officer saying in a fierce whisper, 'No, don't load! The first man to loose off a ball will feel my dirk in 'is belly!'

And suddenly there she was. Tall, spiralling masts and furled sails, a shaded anchor light which threw thin gold lines up her shrouds. Bolitho stared at it as the boat glided towards her bows and outstretched jib-boom.

Was it to be here, like this?

He heard the oars being hauled inboard with elaborate care, the sudden scramble in the bows where the keen-eyed seaman had first sighted this unexpected stranger.

Allday muttered restlessly, 'Come on, you buggers, let's be 'avin' you!'

Bolitho stood up and saw the jib-boom swooping above him as the current carried them into the hull like a piece of driftwood. Jenour was crouching beside him, his hanger already drawn, his head thrown back as if expecting a shot.

'Grapnel!'

It thudded over the bulwark even as the boat surged alongside.

'*At 'em, lads!*' The fury of the man's whisper was like a trumpet call. Bolitho felt himself knocked and carried up the side, seizing lines, scrabbling for handholds, until with something like madness they flung themselves on to the vessel's deck.

A figure ran from beneath the foremast, his yell of alarm cut short as a seaman brought him down with a cudgel; two other shapes seemed to rise up under their feet and in those split seconds Bolitho realised that the anchor watch had been asleep on deck.

Around him he could sense the wildness of his men, the claws of tension giving way to a brittle hatred of anything that spoke or moved.

Voices echoed below deck, and Bolitho shouted, 'Easy, lads! Hold fast!' He listened to one voice in particular rising above the rest and knew it was speaking a language he did not recognise.

Jenour gasped, 'Swedish, sir!'

Bolitho watched the boarding party prodding at the schooner's crew, as singly or in small groups they clambered through two hatches to gape at their change of circumstances.

Bolitho heard the stealthy movement of oars nearby and guessed that Parris with one of his boats was close alongside. He had probably been expecting a sudden challenge, the raking murder of swivels.

81

Bolitho snapped, 'Ask Mr Parris if he has one of his Swedish hands on board!' Like most men-of-war *Hyperion* had the usual smattering of foreign seamen in her company. Some were pressed, others volunteers. There were even a few French sailors who had signed on with their old enemy rather than face the grim prospects of a prison hulk on the Medway.

A figure strode forward until Allday growled, 'Far enough, *Mounseer*, or whatever you are!'

The man stared at him, then spat, 'No need to send for an interpreter. I speak English – probably better than you!'

Bolitho sheathed his hanger to give himself time to think. The schooner was unexpected. She was also a problem. Britain was not at war with Sweden, although under pressure from Russia it had been close enough. An incident now, and. . . .

Bolitho said curtly, 'I am a King's officer. And you?'

'*I* am the master, Rolf Aasling. And I can assure you that you will live to regret this – this act of piracy!'

Parris slung his leg over the bulwark and looked around. He was not even out of breath.

He said calmly, 'She's the schooner *Spica*, Sir Richard.'

The man named Aasling stared. '*Sir* Richard?'

Parris eyed him through the darkness. 'Yes. So mind your manners.'

Bolitho said, 'I regret this inconvenience – Captain. But you are anchored in enemy waters. I had no choice.'

The man leaned forward until his coat was touching Allday's unwavering cutlass.

'I am about my peaceful occasions! You have no right –'

Bolitho interrupted him. 'I have every right.' He had nothing of the kind, but the minutes were dashing past. They must get the mortars into position. The attack had to begin as soon as it was light enough to move into the anchorage.

At any second a picket ashore might notice something was wrong aboard the little schooner. She might be hailed by a guardboat, and even if Parris's men overwhelmed it, the alarm would be raised. The helpless lighter, *Thor* too if she tried to interfere, would be blown out of the water.

Bolitho dropped his voice and turned to Parris. 'Take some

men and look below.' His eyes were growing used to the schooner's deck and taut rigging. She mounted several guns, and there were swivels where they had rushed aboard, more aft by the tiller. They had been lucky. She did not have the cut of a privateer, and the Swedes usually kept clear of involvement with the fleets of France and England. A trader then? But well armed for such a small vessel.

The master exclaimed, 'Will you leave my ship, sir, and order your men to release mine!'

'What are you doing here?'

The sudden question took him off balance. 'I am trading. It is all legal. I will no longer tolerate –'

Parris came back and stood beside Jenour as he said quietly, 'Apart from general cargo, Sir Richard, she is loaded with Spanish silver. For the Frogs, if I'm any judge.'

Bolitho clasped his hands behind him. It made sense. How close they had been to failure. Might still be.

He said, 'You lied to me. Your vessel is already loaded for passage.' He saw the man's shadow fall back a pace. 'You are waiting to sail with the Spanish treasure convoy. *Right?*'

The man hesitated, then mumbled, 'This is a neutral ship. You have no authority –'

Bolitho waved his hand towards his men. 'For the moment, Captain, I have just that! Now answer me!'

Spica's master shrugged. 'There are many pirates in these waters.' He raised his chin angrily. 'Enemy warships too!'

'So you intended to stay in company with the Spanish vessels until you were on the high seas?' He waited, feeling the man's earlier bombast giving way to fear. 'It would be better if you told me now.'

'The day after tomorrow.' He blurted it out. 'The Spanish ships will leave when –'

Bolitho hid his sudden excitement. *More than one ship*. The escort might well come from Havana, or already be in Puerto Cabello. Haven could run right into them if he lost his head. He felt Parris watching him. What would *he* have done?

Bolitho said, 'You will prepare to up-anchor, Captain.' He ignored the man's immediate protest and said to Parris, 'Pass the word to Mr Dalmaine, then bring your boats alongside and take them in tow.'

The Swedish master shouted, 'I will not do it! I want no part in this madness!' A note of triumph moved into his tone. 'The Spanish guns will fire on us if I attempt to enter without orders!'

'You *do* have a recognition signal?'

Aaseling stared at his feet. 'Yes.'

'Then use it, if you please.'

He turned away as Jenour whispered anxiously, 'Sweden may see this as an act of war, Sir Richard.'

Bolitho peered at the black mass of land. 'Neutrality can be a one-sided affair, Stephen. By the time Stockholm is told of it, I hope the deed will be done and forgotten!' He added harshly, 'In war there are no neutrals! I've had a bellyful of this man's sort, so put a good hand to guard him.' He raised his voice so that the master might hear. 'One treacherous sign and I'll have him run up to the yard where he can watch the results of his folly from the end of a halter!'

He heard more seamen clambering aboard with their weapons. What did they care about neutrality and those who hid behind it so long as they could profit from it? To their simple reasoning, either you were a friend, or you were just as much a foe as Allday's *mounseers*.

'Space out your men, Mr Parris. If we are driven off at the first attempt –'

Parris showed his teeth in the darkness. 'After this, Sir Richard, I think I'd believe anything.'

Bolitho massaged his eye. 'You may have to.'

Parris strode away and could be heard calling out each man by name. Bolitho noticed the familiar way they responded. No wonder the schooner's small company were so cowed. The British sailors bustled about on the unfamiliar deck as if they had been doing it all their lives.

Bolitho remembered what his father had once told him, with that same grave pride he had always displayed when it came to his seamen.

'Put them on the deck of any ship in pitch darkness and they will be tripping aloft in minutes, so well do they ply their trade!'

What would he make of this, he wondered?

'Capstan's manned, sir!'

That was a midshipman named Hazlewood, who was aged thirteen, and on his first commission in *Hyperion*.

Bolitho heard Parris telling him sharply to stay within call. 'I don't want any damned heroes today, Mr Hazlewood!'

Like Adam had once been.

'Heave away, lads!'

Some wag called from the darkness, 'Our Dick'll get us Spanish gold for some grog, eh?' He was quickly silenced by an irate petty officer.

Bolitho stood beside the vessel's master and tried to contain the sympathy he really felt for the man.

After this night his life would be changed. One thing was certain; he would never command any vessel again.

'Anchor's aweigh, sir!'

'Braces, lads!' Bare feet skidded on damp planking as the schooner curtsied round, freed from the seabed, her mainsail filling above their crouched figures to make the stays hum and shiver to the strain.

Bolitho clung to a backstay and made himself remain patiently silent until the schooner had gathered way, and with the boats veering astern, pointed her bowsprit to the east.

Parris seemed to be everywhere. If the attack was successful, he might end up as the senior survivor. Bolitho was surprised that he could consider the possibility of dying without dispute.

Parris crossed the deck to join him. 'Permission to load, Sir Richard? I thought it best to double-shot the six-pounders, and it all takes time.'

Bolitho nodded. It was a sensible precaution. 'Yes, do it. And, Mr Parris, impress on your people to watch the crew. In all conscience, I could not batten them below in their own hull in case the batteries fire on us before we can fight free, but I'd not trust any man of them one inch!'

Parris smiled. 'My boatswain's mate Dacie is a good hand at that, Sir Richard.'

Figures flitted about the guns, and Bolitho heard some of the seamen whispering to one another as they rammed home the charges and shot. They were doing something they understood, which had been drummed into them every working day since they had walked or been dragged aboard a King's ship.

Jenour seemed to have a smattering of Swedish, and was speaking jerkily to the *Spica*'s mate. Eventually two large flags were produced, and quickly bent on to the halliards by Midshipman Hazlewood.

Bolitho moved across the deck, picking out faces, watching where each man had been stationed. Above, *Spica*'s wide topsail was now set and billowing out from its yard, and Bolitho could feel a rising excitement which even the nervous chant of the leadsman could not disperse. He could picture the schooner's slender hull as she plunged so confidently along the channel amongst the lurking sandbars, sometimes with only a few feet beneath her keel. If it was broad daylight they would be able to see *Spica*'s shadow keeping company with them on the bottom.

'All guns loaded, sir!'

'Very well.' He wondered how the abandoned Lieutenant Dalmaine was getting on with his two thirteen-inch mortars. If the attack failed, and *Thor* was unable to recover the men from the lighter, Dalmaine had orders to make his way ashore and surrender. Bolitho grimaced. He knew what he would do in those circumstances; what any sailor would attempt. Sailors mistrusted land. When others saw the sea as an enemy or a final barrier against escape, men like Dalmaine would take a chance, even in something as hopeless as a lighter.

Jenour joined them by the tiller and said, 'I was speaking with the Swedish mate, Sir Richard.'

Bolitho smiled. The lieutenant could barely suppress his eagerness.

'We are all ears.'

Jenour pointed into the darkness. 'He says we are past the battery. The biggest treasure-ship is anchored in line with the first fortress.' He added proudly. 'She is the *Ciudad de Sevilla*.'

Bolitho touched his arm. 'That was well done.' He pictured the marks on the chart. It was exactly as Price had described it, and the newly constructed fortress, which rose from the sea on a bed of rocks.

The leadsman called sharply, 'By th' mark two!'

Parris murmured, 'Christ Almighty.'

Bolitho said, 'Let her fall off a point.' He peered into the black cluster of shapes by the compass box. 'Who is that?'

'Laker, sir!'

Bolitho turned away. It would be. The seaman who was to have been flogged.

Laker called, 'Steady as she goes, sir! East-by-south!'

'By th' mark seven!'

Bolitho clenched his fists. In the time it had taken for the leadsman to recover and then cast his line from the chains, the *Spica* had ploughed out of the shallows and into deeper water. But if the chart with its sparse information was wrong . . .

'By th' mark fifteen!' Even the leadsman's voice sounded jubilant. It was not wrong. They were through.

He walked aft to the taffrail and peered at the boats astern, the gurgle of spray around each stem where lively phosphorescence painted the sea.

Allday said, 'Sun-up any minute, Sir Richard.' He sounded on edge. 'I'll be fair glad to see it go down again, an' that's no error.'

Bolitho loosened the hanger in its scabbard. It felt strange without the old sword. He pictured Adam wearing it as his own, Belinda's perfect face when she received the news that he had fallen.

He said harshly, 'Enough melancholy, old friend! We've faced worse odds!'

Allday watched him, his craggy face hidden in darkness.

'I knows it, Sir Richard. It's just that sometimes I get –'

His eyes shone suddenly and Bolitho grasped his thick forearm.

'The sun. Friend or foe, I wonder?'

'Stand by to come about!' Parris sounded untroubled. 'Two more hands on the forebrace, Keats.'

'Aye, aye, sir.'

Bolitho tried to recall the petty officer's face, but instead he saw other, older ones. *Hyperion*'s ghosts come back to watch him. They had waited over the years after their last battle. To claim him as their own, perhaps?

The thought made a chill run down his spine. He unclipped the scabbard and tossed it aside while he tested the hanger's balance in his hand.

More light, seeping and spreading across the water. There was the land to starboard, sprawling and shapeless. The flash of sunlight on a window somewhere, a ship's masthead pendant lifting to the first glow like the tip of a knight's lance.

The fortress was almost in line with the jib-boom, a stern, square contrast with the land beyond.

Bolitho let the hanger drop to his side and found that he had thrust his other hand inside his shirt. He could feel his heart pounding beneath the hot, damp skin, and yet his whole being felt cold; raw like steel.

'And there she lies!' He had seen the mastheads of the great ship below the fortress. She could be nothing else but Somervell's galleon. But instead of Somervell he saw Catherine's eyes watching him. Proud and captivating. Distant.

To tear himself from the mood he slowly raised his left arm, until the early sunlight spilled down the hanger as if he had dipped it into molten gold.

The sea noises intruded from every side. Wind and spray, the lively clatter of rigging and shrouds while the deck tilted to the change of tack.

Bolitho called, 'Look yonder, my lads! A reckoning indeed!'

But nobody spoke, for only *Hyperion*'s ghosts understood.

7

Perhaps The Greatest Victory

Bolitho held up the folded chart and strained his eyes in the faint sunlight. He would have wished to take more time to study it in the security of the schooner's tiny cabin, but every second was precious. It was all happening so swiftly, and when he glanced up again from the tilting compass-box he saw the grand roadstead opening up like some vast amphitheatre. More anchored shipping, the distance making them appear to be huddled together near the central fortress, then the coast itself, with white houses and the beginning of the twisting road which eventually led inland. Each mountain was brushed with sunshine, their blue-grey masses overlapping and reaching away, until they faded into mist and merged with the sky.

He stared for several seconds at the big Spanish ship. In size she matched *Hyperion*. It must have taken a month or more to load her with the gold and silver which had been brought overland on pack-mules and in wagons, guarded every mile of the way by soldiers.

At any minute now Lieutenant Dalmaine would open fire on the battery, before the sunlight reached out and betrayed *Thor* at her anchorage.

He tore his eyes away to look along the schooner's deck. Most of the *Spica*'s crew were sitting with their backs against the weather bulwark, their eyes fixed on the British seamen. No wonder they had offered no resistance. By contrast with the neat shirts of the Swedes, *Hyperion*'s men looked like pirates. He saw

Dacie the boatswain's mate, his head twisted at an angle so that he could watch his men and the *Spica*'s master at the same time. Dacie wore an eye patch to cover an empty socket; it gave him a villainous appearance. Parris had every right to have such confidence in him. Near the helm, Skilton, one of *Hyperion*'s master's mates, in his familiar coat with the white piping, was the only one who showed any sort of uniformity.

Even Jenour had followed his admiral's example and had discarded his hat and coat. He was carrying a sword which his parents had given him, with a fine blue blade of German steel.

Bolitho tried to relax as he studied the big Spanish ship. It was a far cry from that quiet room at the Admiralty when this plan had been discussed with all the delicacy of a conference at Lloyds.

He looked at Parris, his shirt open to the waist, his dark hair streaming above his eyes in the lively offshore breeze. Was Haven right to suspect him, he wondered? It certainly made sense that any woman might prefer him to his colourless captain.

A gull dived above the topsail yard, its mewing cry merging with the far-off blare of a trumpet. Ashore or at anchor, men were stirring, cooks groping for their pots and pans.

Parris stared at him across the deck and grinned. 'Rude awakening, Sir Richard!'

The crash when it came was still a surprise. It was like a double thunderclap which echoed across the water and then rolled back from the land like a returned salute.

Bolitho caught a sudden picture of Francis Inch when he had been given his first command of a bomb like Imrie's. He could almost hear his voice, as with his horse-face set in a frown of concentration he had walked past his mortars, gauging the bearing and each fall of shot.

'*Run the mortar up! Muzzle to the right! Prime! Fire!*'

As if responding to the memory both mortars fired again. But it was not Inch. He was gone, with so many others.

The double explosions sighed against the hull, and Bolitho tightened his grip on the hanger as flags broke from the big Spaniard's yards. They were awake now, right enough.

'Make the recognition signal, Mr Hazlewood!'

The two flags soared aloft and broke stiffly to the wind. All they needed now was for it to drop and leave them helpless and becalmed.

Parris yelled, 'Jump about, you laggards! Wave your arms and point astern, damn your eyes!' He laughed wildly as some of the seamen capered around the deck.

Bolitho waved. 'Good work! We are supposed to be running from the din of war, eh?'

He snatched up a glass and levelled it towards the anchored ship. Beyond her, about half a cable distant, was a second vessel. Smaller than the one named *Ciudad de Sevilla* but probably carrying enough booty to finance an army for months.

Parris called, 'She's got boarding nets rigged, Sir Richard!'

He nodded. 'Alter course to cross her bows!' It would appear that they were heading towards the nearest fortress for protection.

'Helm a-lee, sir!'

'Steady as she goes, Nor' east by east!'

Bolitho gripped a stay and watched the sails flapping and banging as the schooner lurched close to the wind; but she answered well. He winced as the mortars fired yet again, and still the shore battery remained silent. It seemed likely that the first shots had done their work, the massive balls falling to explode in a lethal flail of iron fragments and grape.

Astern there was a lot of smoke, haze too, so that the shallows where they had felt their way into the anchorage had completely vanished. It might delay *Thor*'s entrance, but at least she would be safe from the battery.

He said, 'Keep those other hands out of sight, Mr Parris!'

He saw Jenour watching him, remembering everything and perhaps feeling fear for the first time.

A man yelled, '*Guardboat*, starboard bow, sir!'

Bolitho trained his glass and watched the dark shape thrusting around the counter of an anchored merchantman.

Just minutes earlier each man would have been thinking of his bed. Then some wine perhaps in the sunshine before the heat drove them all to their siesta.

He saw the oars, painted bright red, pulling and backing to bring the long hull round in a tight turn.

And far beyond he could make out the shape of a Spanish frigate, her masts like bare poles while she completed a refit, or like the *Obdurate*, repairs after a violent Caribbean storm.

'Two points to starboard, Mr Parris!' Bolitho tried to steady the glass as the deck tilted yet again. He could hear more trumpet calls, most likely from the new fortress, and could imagine the startled artillerymen running to their stations, still unaware of what was happening.

Explosions maybe, but there was nothing untoward immediately obvious, except for the appearance of the Swedish schooner which was, reasonably, running for shelter. No enemy fleet, no cutting-out raid, and in any case the other fortresses would have taken care of such daring stupidity.

Bolitho watched the jib-boom swinging round until it seemed to impale the treasure-ship's forecastle, although she still stood a cable away. The guardboat was pulling towards them unhurriedly, an officer rising now to peer towards the smoke and haze.

Bolitho said, 'Pass the word. The guardboat will stand between us. Make it appear we are shortening sail.'

Jenour stared at him. '*Will* we, Sir Richard?'

Bolitho smiled. 'I think not.'

A sudden gust filled the topsail and a line parted high above the deck like a pistol shot.

Dacie, the formidable boatswain's mate, jabbed a seaman with his fist. 'Aloft with ye, boy! See to it!'

It took just a second and yet as Dacie peered aloft, the Swedish master sprang forward and seized a musket from one of the crouching sailors. He pointed it above the bulwark and fired towards the guardboat. Bolitho saw the musket smoke fan away even as the master hit the deck, felled by one of the boarding party.

The guardboat was frantically backing water, her blades churning the sea into a mass of foam. There was no time left.

Bolitho shouted, 'Run her down! *Lively!*' He forgot the shouts, even the crack of a solitary musket as the schooner tacked round and drove into the guardboat like a Trojan galley.

It felt like hitting a rock, and Bolitho saw oars and pieces of planking surging alongside, men floundering, their cries lost in the rising wind and the boom of canvas.

The treasure-ship seemed to tower above them, individual figures which moments earlier had been staring transfixed towards the explosions, running along the gangways, others pointing and gesticulating as the schooner charged towards them.

'*Stand by to board!*' Bolitho gripped the hanger and tightened the lanyard around his wrist. He had forgotten the danger, even the fear of his eye's treachery, as the last half-cable fell away.

'Down helm! Take in the tops'l!'

Shots whimpered overhead and one gouged a tall splinter from the deck like a clerk's quill.

'Hold your fire!' Parris strode forward, his eyes narrowed against the glare while he watched his men, as they hunched down close to the point of impact.

Bolitho saw the sagging boarding nets, faces peering through them at the schooner, one solitary figure reloading a musket, his leg wrapped around the foremast shrouds.

Halfway down the Spaniard's side a port-lid rose like an awakened man opening one eye.

Then he saw the gun muzzle lumber into view, and seconds later the livid orange tongue, followed by the savage bang of an explosion. It was a wild gesture and nothing more; the ball eventually hit open water like an enraged dolphin.

As the last of the sails were freed to the wind, the *Spica*'s jib-boom plunged through the Spaniard's larboard rigging and shivered to splinters. Broken cordage and blocks showered down on the forecastle before both ships jarred finally together with a terrible crash. *Spica*'s foretopmast fell like a severed branch, but men ran amongst torn canvas and snakes of useless rigging, oblivious to everything but the need to board the enemy.

'*Swivels!*' Bolitho dragged the midshipman aside as the nearest swivel jerked back on its mounting and blasted the packed canister across the other ship's beakhead. Men fell kicking into the sea, their screams lost as Parris signalled the six-pounders to add their weight to the attack.

Allday ran, panting at Bolitho's side as he leapt on to the bulwark, the hanger dangling from his wrist. To board her from aft would have been impossible; her high stern, a mass of gilded carving, rose above her reflection like an ornate cliff.

The forecastle was different. Men clambered across the beakhead, hacking aside resistance, while others slashed and cut their way through the nets.

A pike darted through a net like a serpent's tongue and one of Parris's men fell back, clutching his stomach, his eyes horrified as he dropped into the water below.

Another turned to stare after him then gurgled as a pike thrust into him, withdrew and struck again, the point taking him in the throat and reappearing through his neck.

But Dacie and some of the seamen were on deck, pausing to fire into the defenders before slashing aside the remaining nets. Bolitho felt someone seize his wrist and haul him through a hole in the netting. Another toppled against him, his eyes glazing as a ball smashed into his chest like the blow of a hammer.

'To me, Hyperions!' Parris waved his hanger and Bolitho saw it was running with blood. '*Starboard gangway!*'

Shots banged and whimpered over their heads, and two more men fell writhing and gasping, their agony marked by the stains across the planking.

Bolitho stared round wildly as some swivels blasted the Spaniard's high poop, cutting down a handful of men who had appeared there as if by magic. Mere seconds, and yet his mind recorded that they were only partly dressed or stark naked; probably some of the ship's officers roused from their sleep by the sudden attack.

Parris's men were on the starboard gangway, where another swivel was seized and depressed towards an open hatch as more faces peered up at them.

The remainder of Parris's boarders were already leaving the little schooner, and Bolitho heard the thud of axes as the Swedes took the opportunity to hack their vessel clear of the treasure-ship, complete with *Hyperion*'s longboats.

Dacie brandished his boarding axe. 'At 'em, you buggers!'

Every man Jack would know now that there was no retreat. It was victory or death. They would receive no quarter from the Spaniards after what they had done.

Bolitho paused on the gangway, his eyes watering from drifting smoke as the scrambling seamen spread out into purposeful patterns. Two to the big double-wheel below the poop, others already swarming aloft to loose the topsails while Dacie rushed forward to cut the huge anchor cable.

Shots cracked from hatchways to be answered instantly by reloaded swivels, the packed canister smashing into the men crammed on the companion ladders and turning them into flailing, bloody gruel. One Spaniard appeared from nowhere, his sword cutting down a seaman who crouched on all fours, already badly wounded from the first encounter.

Bolitho saw the little midshipman, Hazlewood, staring at the wild-eyed sailor, his dirk gripped in one hand while the Spaniard charged towards him.

Allday stepped between Bolitho and the enemy and shouted hoarsely, 'Over here, matey!' He could have been calling a pet dog. The Spaniard hesitated, his blade wavering, then saw his danger too late.

Allday's heavy cutlass struck him across the collar-bone with such force it seemed it might sever the head from his body. The man swung round, his sword clattering to the deck below as Allday struck him again.

Allday muttered, 'Get yerself a proper blade, *Mr* Hazlewood! That bodkin couldn't kill a rat!'

Bolitho hurried aft to the wheel, and watched as the bows appeared to swing towards the nearest fort with the cry, '*Cable's cut!*'.

'Loose tops'ls! Lively, you scum!' Dacie was peering aloft, his single eye gleaming like a bead in the sunlight.

Parris wiped his mouth with a tattered sleeve. 'We're under way! Put your helm down!'

There were unexplained splashes alongside, then Bolitho saw some Spanish seamen swimming away from the hull, or floundering in the current like exhausted fish. They must have clambered from the gun-ports to escape; anything rather than face the onslaught they had heard on deck.

Midshipman Hazlewood walked shakily beside Bolitho, his eyes downcast, fearful of what terrible scene he might witness next. Corpses sprawled in the scuppers who had been caught by the double-shotted six-pounders, and others who had been running to repel boarders when the swivels had scoured the decks with their murderous canister shot.

One jibsail cracked out to the wind and the great ship began to gather way. She appeared to be so loose in stays that she must be fully loaded with her precious cargo, Bolitho thought. What would the fort's battery commander do? Fire on her, or let her steal away under his eyes?

Bolitho saw the second treasure-ship as she appeared to glide towards them. Pin-pricks of light flashed from her tops, but at that range it would need a miracle to hit any of *Hyperion*'s topmen or those around the helm.

Bolitho snapped, 'Hand me the glass!' He saw Hazlewood fumbling with it, his mouth quivering from shock as he stared at the vivid splashes of blood across his breeches. He had been within a hair's breadth of death when Allday's cutlass had hacked the man down.

Bolitho took the glass and levelled it on the other ship. She lay between them and the fort. Once clear of her, every gun on the battery would be brought to bear.

If I were that commander I would shoot. To lose the ship was bad enough. To do nothing to prevent their escape would get little mercy from the Captain-General in Caracas.

There was a ragged cheer and Parris exclaimed, 'Here comes Imrie, by God!'

The *Thor* had spread every stitch of canvas so that her sails seemed to make one great golden pyramid in the early sunlight. All her snub-nosed carronades were run out like shortened teeth along her buff and black hull, and Bolitho saw the paintwork shine even more brightly as the helm went over and she tacked round towards the two treasure-ships. Compared with the *Ciudad de Sevilla*'s slow progress, *Thor* seemed to be moving like a frigate.

It must have taken everyone in the forts and ashore completely by surprise. First the Swedish schooner, and now a man-of-war, running it would appear from inshore, their own heavily-defended territory. Bolitho thought briefly of Captain Price. This would have been his moment.

'Signal *Thor* to attack the other treasure-ship.' They had discussed this possibility, even when it was originally intended to be a boat attack. Bolitho glanced at the bloodstained deck, the gaping corpses and moaning wounded. But for falling upon the schooner it now seemed unlikely they would have succeeded.

Bolitho trained the glass again and saw tiny figures stampeding along the other ship's gangways, sunlight flashing on pikes and bayonets. They expected *Thor* to attempt a second boarding, but this time they were ready. When they realised what Imrie intended it was already too late. A trumpet blared, and across the water Bolitho heard the shrill of whistles and saw the running figures colliding with each other, like a tide on the turn.

Almost delicately, considering her powerful timbers, *Thor* tacked around the other ship's stern, and then with a deafening, foreshortened roar so typical of the heavy 'smashers', the carronades fired a slow broadside, gun by gun as *Thor* crossed the Spaniard's unprotected stern.

The poop and counter seemed to shower gold as the bright carvings splashed into the sea or were hurled high into the air, and when a down-draft of wind carried the smoke clear, Bolitho saw that the whole stern had been blasted open into a gaping black cave.

The heavy grape would have cut through the decks from stern to bow in an iron avalanche, and anyone still below would have been swept away.

Thor was turning, and even as someone managed to cut the stricken ship's cable, she came about and fired another broadside from her opposite battery.

There was smoke everywhere, and the men trapped below Bolitho's feet must have been expecting to share the same fate. The other ship's mizzen and main had fallen in a tangle alongside, and the rigging trailed along the decks and in the water like obscene weed.

Bolitho cleared his throat. It was like a kiln.

'Get the forecourse on her, Mr Parris.' He gripped the midshipman's shoulder and felt him jump as if he had been shot. 'Signal *Thor* to close on me.' He retained his grip for a few seconds, adding, 'You did well.' He glanced at the staring eyes of the men at the wheel, their smoke-grimed faces and bare feet, the blood still drying on their naked cutlasses. 'You *all* did!'

The big foresail boomed out and filled to the wind, so that the deck tilted very slightly, and a corpse rolled over in the scuppers as if it had only feigned death.

He saw Jenour on the maindeck where two armed seamen were standing guard over an open hatch, although it was impossible to know how many of the enemy were still aboard. Jenour seemed to sense that he was looking at him, and raised his beautiful sword. It was like a salute. Like the thirteen year-old Hazlewood, it was probably his first blooding.

'*Thor* has acknowledged, sir!'

Bolitho made to sheathe his hanger and remembered he had dropped the scabbard before the fight. It was lying in the little schooner which even now was fading in sea-mist, like a memory.

'Steady as she goes, sir! Nor'-east by east!'

The open sea was there, milky-blue in the early light. Men were cheering, dazed, with joy or disbelief.

Bolitho saw Parris grinning broadly, gripping the master's mate's hand and wringing it so hard the man winced.

'She's *ours*, Mr Skilton! God damn it, we took her from under their noses!'

Skilton grimaced. 'We're not in port yet, sir!'

Bolitho raised the glass yet again; it felt like lead. And yet it had been less than an hour since they had driven into the anchored treasure-ship.

He saw a host of small boats moving out from the land, a brig making sail to join them as they all headed for the shattered treasure-ship. That last broadside must have opened her like a sieve, he thought grimly. Every boat and spare hand would be used to salvage what they could before she keeled over and sank. A worthwhile sacrifice. To try and take two such ships would have meant losing both. The master's mate was right about one thing. They still had a long way to go.

He dropped the hanger to the deck and looked at it. Unused. Like the midshipman's dirk; you never really knew what you could do until called to fight.

He examined his feelings and only glanced up as the main

topsail boomed out to the wind.

Death-wish? He had felt no fear. Not for himself. He looked at the sweating seamen as they slid down the backstays and rushed to the next task, where a hundred men should have been ready at halliards and braces.

They trusted him. That was perhaps the greatest victory.

Bolitho picked up a coffee cup and then pushed it away. Empty. Something Ozzard would never allow to happen in these circumstances. Wearily he rubbed his eyes and looked around the ornate cabin, palatial when compared with a man-of-war. He smiled wryly. Even for a vice-admiral.

It was mid-afternoon, and yet he knew that if he had the will to go on deck again and climb to the maintop he would still be able to see the coast of the Main. But in this case speed was as important as distance, and with the wind holding steady from the north-west he intended to use every stitch of canvas the ship would carry. He had had a brief and hostile interview with the ship's captain, an arrogant, bearded man with the face of some ancient *conquistador*. It was hard to determine which had angered the Spaniard more. To have his ship seized under the guns of the fortress, or to be interrogated by a man who proclaimed himself to be an English flag-officer, yet looked more like a vagrant in his tattered shirt and smoke-blackened breeches. He seemed to regard Bolitho's intention to sail the ship to more friendly waters as absurd. When the reckoning came, he had said in his strangely toneless English, the end would be without mercy. Bolitho had finished the interview right there by saying quietly, 'I would expect none, since you treat your own people like animals.'

Bolitho heard Parris shouting out to someone in the mizzen top. He seemed tireless, and was never too proud to throw his own weight on brace or halliard amongst his men. He had been a good choice.

Thor had placed herself between the ponderous treasure-ship and the shore, probably as astonished as the rest of them by their success. But great though that success had been it was not without cost, or the sadness which followed any fight.

Lieutenant Dalmaine had died even as his men had been hoisted into *Thor* from the waterlogged lighter. The two mortars had had to be abandoned, and their massive recoil had all but knocked out the lighter's keel. Dalmaine had seen his men to safety and had apparently run back to retrieve something. The lighter had suddenly flooded and taken Dalmaine and his beloved mortars to the bottom.

Four men had died in the attack, three more had been seriously wounded. One of the latter was the seaman named Laker, who had lost an arm and an eye when a musketoon had been discharged at point-blank range. Bolitho had seen Parris kneeling over him and had heard the man croak, 'Better'n bein' flogged, eh, sir?' He had tried to reach out for the lieutenant's hand. 'Never fancied a checkered shirt at th' gangway, 'specially for 'is sake!'

He must have meant Haven. If they met with *Hyperion* soon, the surgeon might be able to save him.

Bolitho thought of the holds far below his feet. Cases and chests of gold and silver plate. Jewel-encrusted crucifixes and ornaments – it had looked obscene in the light of a lantern held by Allday, who had never left his side.

So much luck, he thought wearily. The Spanish captain had let slip one piece of information. A company of soldiers were to have boarded the ship that morning to guard the treasure until they unloaded it in Spanish waters. A company of disciplined soldiers would have made a mockery of their attack.

He thought of the little schooner, *Spica*, and her master, who had tried to raise the alarm. Hate, anger at being boarded, fear of reprisal, it was probably a bit of each. But his ship was intact, although it was unlikely that the Spaniards would divert other vessels to convoy him to safer waters as intended. They might even blame him. One thing was certain; he would not want to trade with the enemy again, neutral or not.

Bolitho yawned hugely and massaged the scar beneath his hair. *Hyperion*'s imposing boatswain, Samuel Lintott, would have a few oaths to offer when he discovered the loss of the jolly boat and two cutters. Maybe the chance of prize-money would soften his anger. Bolitho tried to stop his head from lolling. He could not remember when he had last slept undisturbed.

This ship and her rich cargo would make a difference only in the City of London, and of course with His Britannic Majesty. Bolitho smiled to himself. The King who had not even remembered his name when he had lowered the sword to knight him. Perhaps it meant so little to those who had so much.

He knew it was sheer exhaustion which was making his mind wander.

There was more than one way of fighting a war than spilling blood in the cannon's mouth. But it did not feel right, and left him uneasy. Only pride sustained him. In his men, and those like Dalmaine who had put their sailors first. And the one called Laker, who had fought shoulder-to-shoulder with his friends, simply because it meant far more to him and to them than any flag or the cause.

He allowed his mind to touch on England, and wondered what Belinda was doing with her time in London.

But like a salt-blurred telescope her picture would not settle or form clearly, and he felt a pang of guilt.

He turned his thoughts to Viscount Somervell, although he knew it was a coward's way of opening the door to Catherine. Would they leave the Indies now that the treasure, or a large part of it, was taken?

His head touched his forearm and he jerked up, aware of two things at once. That he had fallen asleep across the table, and that a masthead lookout had pealed down to the deck.

He heard Parris call something and found himself on his feet, his eyes on the cabin skylight as the lookout shouted again.

'Deck there! Two sail to the nor'-west!'

Bolitho walked through the unfamiliar doors and stared at the deserted ranks of cabins. With the remaining crew members battened below where they could neither try to retake the ship nor damage her hull without risking their own lives, it was like a phantom vessel. All *Hyperion*'s hands were employed constantly on deck; or high above it amongst the maze of rigging, like insects trapped in a giant web. He noticed a portrait of a Spanish nobleman beside a case of books, and guessed it was the captain's father. Perhaps like the old grey house in Falmouth, he too had many pictures to retell the history of his family.

He found Parris with Jenour and Skilton, the master's mate, grouped by the larboard side, each with a levelled telescope.

Parris saw him and touched his forehead. 'Nothing yet, Sir Richard.'

Bolitho looked at the sky, then at the hard horizon line. Like the top of a dam, beyond which there was nothing.

It would not be dark for hours yet. Too long.

'*Hyperion*, maybe, Sir Richard?'

Their eyes met. Parris did not believe it either. Bolitho replied, 'I think not. With the wind in our favour we should have made contact by noon.' He ceased thinking out loud. 'Signal *Thor*. Imrie may not have sighted the ships as yet.' It gave him time to think. To move a few paces this way and that, his chin digging into his stained neckcloth.

The enemy then. He made himself accept it. The *Ciudad de Sevilla* was no man-of-war, nor did she have the artillery and skills of an Indiaman. The cannons with their ornate mountings and leering bronze faces were impressive, but useless against anything but pirates or some reckless privateer.

He glanced at some of the seamen nearby. The fight had been demanding enough. Friends killed or wounded, but survival and the usual dream of prize-money had left them in high spirits. Now it was changing again. It was a wonder they didn't rush the poop and take all the bullion for themselves. There was precious little Bolitho and his two lieutenants could do to prevent it.

The lookout yelled down, 'Two frigates, sir! Dons by the cut o' them!'

Bolitho controlled his breathing as some of the others looked at him. Somehow he had known Haven would not make the rendezvous. It was an additional mockery to recall he himself had given him the honourable way out.

Parris said flatly, 'Well, they say the sea is two miles deep under our keel. The Dons'll not get their paws on the gold again, unless they can swim that far down!' Nobody laughed.

Bolitho looked at Parris. *The decision is mine*. Signal *Thor* to take them and their Spanish prisoners on board? But with only half their boats available it would take time. Scuttle the great ship and all her wealth, and run, hoping *Thor* could outsail the frigates, at least until nightfall?

A victory gone sour.

Jenour moved closer. 'Laker just died, sir.'

Bolitho turned towards him, his eyes flashing. 'And for what – is that what you're asking? Must we all die now because of your vice-admiral's arrogance?'

Jenour, surprisingly, stood his ground. 'Then let's fight, Sir Richard.'

Bolitho let his arms fall to his sides. 'In God's name, Stephen, you mean it – don't you?' He smiled gravely, his anger spent. 'But I'll have no more dying.' He looked at the horizon. Is this how he would be remembered? He said, 'Signal *Thor* to heave-to. Then muster the prisoners on deck.'

The lookout yelled, 'Deck there! Two Spanish frigates an' another sail astern o' them!'

Parris muttered, 'Christ Almighty.' He attempted to smile. 'So, Mr Firebrand, will you still stand and fight the Dons?'

Jenour shrugged, then gripped his beautiful sword. It said more than any words.

Allday watched the officers and tried to fathom out what had gone wrong. It was not just failure which bothered Bolitho, that was as plain as a pikestaff. It was the old *Hyperion*. She had not come for him. Allday ground his teeth together. If ever he reached port again he would settle that bloody Haven once and for all, and swing for him to boot.

Bolitho must have felt it all the while in his blood. Why he had left the old sword behind. He *must* have known. Allday felt a chill run down his spine. *I should have guessed.* God alone knew it had happened to others.

They all stared up as the foremast lookout, forgotten until now, yelled down, 'Sail to the nor'-east, sir!'

Bolitho gripped his fingers together behind him. The newcomer must have run down on them while every eye was on the other strange sails.

He said, 'Get aloft, Stephen! Take a glass!'

Jenour paused just a few seconds as if to fix the importance and the urgency of the moment. Then he was gone, and was soon swarming hand over hand up the foremast shrouds to join the lookout on his precarious perch in the crosstrees.

It felt like an eternity. Other hands had climbed up to the tops or merely clung to the ratlines to stare at the eye-searing horizon. Bolitho felt a lump in his throat. It was not *Hyperion*. Her masts and yards would be clearly visible by now.

Jenour yelled down, his voice almost lost amongst the clatter of blocks and the slap of canvas.

'She's English, sir! Making her number!'

Parris climbed on to one of the poop ladders and levelled his own glass on the pursuers.

'They're fanning out, Sir Richard. They must have seen her too.' He added savagely, 'Not that it matters now, God damn them!'

Jenour called again, 'She's *Phaedra*, sloop-of-war!'

Bolitho felt Parris turning to watch him. Their missing sloop-of-war had caught up with them at last, only to be a spectator at the end.

Jenour shouted, faltered, then tried again, his voice barely audible. But this time it was not only because of the shipboard sounds.

'*Phaedra* has hoisted a signal, sir! *Enemy in sight!*'

Bolitho looked at the deck, at the blackened stain where a Spanish sailor had died.

The signal would be being read and repeated to all the other ships. He could picture his old *Hyperion*, her men running to quarters, clearing for action again to the beat of the drums.

Parris exclaimed with quiet disbelief, 'The Dons are standing away, Sir Richard.' He wiped his face, and perhaps his eyes. 'God damn it, old lady, don't cut it so fine next time!'

But as the Spanish topsails melted into the sea-mist, and the smart sloop-of-war bore down on the treasure-ship and her sole escort, it soon became obvious that she was quite alone.

The ill-assorted trio rolled in the swell, hove-to as *Phaedra*'s youthful commander was pulled across in his gig. He almost bounded up the high tumblehome, and doffed his hat to Bolitho, barely able to stop himself from grinning.

'There are no others?' Bolitho stared at the young man. 'What of the signal?'

The commander recovered his composure very slightly. 'My name is Dunstan, Sir Richard.'

Bolitho nodded. 'And how did you recognise *me*?'

The grin came back like a burst of sunlight.

'I had the honour to serve in *Euryalus* with you, Sir Richard.' He looked at the others with exclusive pride. 'As a midshipman. I recalled how you had used that deception yourself to confuse the enemy.' His voice trailed away. 'Although I was not sure it might work for *me*.'

Bolitho gripped his hand and held it for several seconds.

'Now I *know* we shall win.' He turned away and only Allday saw the emotion in his eyes.

Allday glanced across at the eighteen-gun *Phaedra*.

Perhaps after this Bolitho would accept what he had done for others. But he doubted it.

8

A Bitter Departure

The Right Honourable the Viscount Somervell looked up from the pile of ledgers and eyed Bolitho curiously.

'So you accepted Captain Haven's explanation, what?'

Bolitho stood beside a window, his shoulder resting against the cool wall. The air was heavy and humid although the wind which had stayed with them all the way to English Harbour remained quite firm. The small breakers near the harbour were no longer white, but in the sun's glare sighed over the sand like molten bronze.

He could see the great ship clearly from here. After the tumultuous welcome when they had sailed into harbour, the serious work of unloading her rich cargo had begun immediately. Lighters and boats plied back and forth, and Bolitho had never seen so many redcoats as the army guarded the booty every yard of the way, until, as Somervell had explained, it would be transferred and divided amongst several smaller vessels as an extra precaution.

Bolitho half-turned and glanced at him. Somervell had already forgotten his question about Haven. It was only yesterday morning that they had dropped anchor, and for the first time since he had met Somervell, Bolitho had noticed that he still wore the same clothes as when he had come out to the *Ciudad de Sevilla*. It was as if he could not bear leaving these detailed ledgers even to sleep.

They had met *Hyperion* and two of the brigs only a day out of

Antigua. Bolitho had decided to send for Haven rather than shift to his flagship, where there must have been speculation enough already.

Haven had been strangely confident as he had made his report. He had even presented it in writing to explain fully, if not excuse his action.

Hyperion and the little flotilla had closed with Puerto Cabello, and had even drawn the fire of a coastal battery when it had seemed they were about to force their way into harbour. Haven was certain that the captured frigate *Consort* was still there, and had sent the brig *Vesta* under the guns of a battery to investigate. The Spaniards had rigged a long boom from one of the fortresses and *Vesta* had run afoul of it. In minutes one of the batteries, using heated shot, had found *Vesta*'s range, and the helpless onlookers had seen her burst into flames before being engulfed in one devastating explosion.

Haven had said in his unemotional voice, 'Other enemy ships were heading towards us. I used my discretion,' his eyes had watched Bolitho without a flicker, 'as so ordered by you, Sir Richard, and withdrew. I considered that you would have succeeded or pulled back by that time, as I had offered the diversion required, with some risk to my command.'

After what they had done in taking the rich prize it was like a personal loss instead of a victory.

Haven could not be blamed. The presence of a boom might be expected or it might not. As he had said, he had used his discretion.

Tetrarch, another of the brigs, had risked sharing the same fate to sail amongst the smoke and falling shot to rescue some of her companion's people. One of the survivors had been her captain, Commander Murray. He was in an adjoining building with *Hyperion*'s wounded from the boarding party, and the remainder of the brig's company who had been plucked from the sea and the flames, a sailor's two worst enemies.

He said, 'For the moment, my lord.'

Somervell smiled as he turned over another leaf; he was gloating. 'Hell's teeth, even His Majesty will be satisfied with this!' He looked up, his eyes opaque. 'I know you grieve for the brig; so may the navy. But set against all this it will be seen as a noble sacrifice.'

Bolitho shrugged. 'By those who do not have to risk their precious skins. In truth I'd rather have cut out *Consort*, damn them!'

Somervell folded his arms reluctantly. 'You have been lucky. But unless you contain your anger or direct it elsewhere, I fear that same luck will desert you.' He put his head on one side. Like a sleek, fastidious bird. 'So make the most of it, eh?'

The door opened an inch and Bolitho saw Jenour peering in at him. Bolitho began, 'Excuse me, my lord. I left word with –' He turned away. Somervell had not heard; he was back again in the world of gold and silver.

Jenour whispered, 'I fear Commander Murray is going fast, Sir Richard.'

Bolitho fell into step beside him and they strode across the wide, flagged terrace to the archway which led to the temporary hospital. Bolitho had been grateful for that at least. Men who were suffering from their wounds should not share a place with garrison soldiers who died from yellow fever without ever hearing the sounds of war.

He glanced shortly at the sea before he entered the other building. Like the sky, it looked angry. A storm perhaps; he would have to consult with *Hyperion*'s sailing master.

Murray lay very still, his eyes closed as if already dead. Even though he had been on the West Indies station for two years, his features were like chalk.

Hyperion's surgeon, George Minchin, a man less callous than most of his trade, had remarked, 'A miracle he survived this far, Sir Richard. His right arm was gone when they pulled him from the sea, and I had to take off a leg. There is a chance, but –'

That had been yesterday. Bolitho had seen enough faces of death to know it was almost over.

Minchin rose from a chair near the bed and walked purposefully to a window. Jenour studied the sea through another window, thinking perhaps that Murray must have been staring at it too, like a handhold to life itself.

Bolitho sat beside the bed. 'I'm here –' He remembered the

young commander's name. 'Rest easy if you can, James.'

Murray opened his eyes with an effort. 'It was the boom, sir.' He closed his eyes again. 'Nearly tore the bottom out of the poor old girl.' He tried to smile but it made him look worse. 'They never took her though — never took her —'

Bolitho groped for his remaining hand and held it between his own.

'I shall see that your people are taken care of.' His words sounded so empty he wanted to cry out, to weep. 'Is there anyone?'

Murray tried again, but his eyes remained like feverish slits.

'I — I — ' his mind was clouding over. 'My mother — there's nobody else now —' His voice trailed away again.

Bolitho made himself watch. Like candles being snuffed out. He heard Allday outside the door, Jenour swallowing hard as if he needed to vomit.

In a remarkably clear voice Murray said, 'It's dark now, sir. I'll be able to sleep.' His hand bunched between Bolitho's. 'Thank you for —'

Bolitho stood up slowly. 'Yes, you sleep.' He pulled the sheet over the dead man's face and stared at the hard sunlight until he was blinded by it. *It's dark now.* For ever.

He crossed to the door by the terrace and knew Jenour was going to say something, to try and help when there was none to offer.

'Leave me.' He did not turn. '*Please.*'

Then he walked to the terrace wall and pressed both hands upon it. The stone was hot, like the sun on his face.

He raised his head and stared again at the glare. He could remember as a small boy seeing the family crest, carved in stone above the great fireplace at Falmouth. He had been tracing it with one finger when his father had entered and had picked him up in his arms.

The words below the crest stood out in his mind. *Pro Libertate Patria. For my country's freedom.*

What young men like Murray, Dunstan and Jenour all believed.

He clenched his fists until the pain steadied him.

They had not even begun to live yet.

He turned sharply as he heard footsteps to his left and seemingly below him. He had been staring so hard at the glare that he could see nothing but a vague shadow.

'Who is that? What do you want?' He twisted his head further, unaware of the edge to his voice or its helplessness.

She said, 'I came to find you.' She stood quite still at the top of some rough stone steps which led down to a small pathway. 'I heard what happened.' Another pause, which to Bolitho seemed endless, then she added quietly, 'Are you all right?'

He looked at the flagstones and saw the image of his shoes sharpen as the pain and mist in his eye slowly withdrew.

'Yes. One of my officers. I barely knew him –' He could not continue.

She remained at her distance as if afraid of him or what she might cause.

She said, 'I know. I am so sorry.'

Bolitho stared at the nearest door. 'How could you marry that man? I've met some callous bastards in my time, but –' He struggled to recover his composure. She had done it again. Like being stripped naked, with neither defence nor explanation.

She did not answer directly. 'Did he ask about the second treasure galleon?'

Bolitho felt the fight draining from him. He had almost expected Somervell to ask him just that. Both of them would have known where that might lead.

He said, 'I apologise. It was unforgivable of me. I had no right to question your motives, or his for that matter.'

She watched him gravely, one hand holding a lace mantilla in place over her dark hair as the hot wind whipped across the parapet. Then she stepped up on to the terrace and faced him. 'You look tired, Richard.'

He dared at last to look at her. She was wearing a sea-green gown, but his heart sank when he realised that her fine features and compelling eyes were still unclear. He must have been half-crazy with despair to stare at the sun. The surgeon in London had declared it to be his worst enemy.

He said, 'I hoped I would see you. I have thought of you a great

110

deal. More than I should; less than you deserve.'

She flicked open her fan and moved it in the wind like a bird's wing.

'I shall be leaving here quite soon. Perhaps we ought never to have met. We must both try —'

He reached out and took her wrist, not caring who might see, conscious only that he was about to lose even her, when he had lost everything else.

'I cannot try! It is hell to love another man's wife, but that is the truth, in God's name it is!'

She did not pull away, but her wrist was rigid in his grasp.

She answered without hesitation, 'Hell? You can never know what that is unless you are a woman in love with another woman's husband!' Her voice threw caution aside. 'I told you, I would have died for you once. Now, because you seem to think your chosen life is in ruins you can turn again to me! Don't you know what you're doing to me, damn you? Yes, I married Lacey because we needed one another, but not in a fashion you would ever understand! I cannot have a child, but then you probably know that too. Whereas *your wife* has given you a daughter I believe, so where's the rub, eh?' She tore her arm away, her dark eyes flashing as loose strands of hair broke from under the mantilla. 'I shall never forget you, Richard, God help me, but I pray that we never meet again, lest we destroy even that one moment of joy I held so dear!'

She turned and almost ran through the door.

Bolitho walked into the adjoining building and received his hat from a footman without even noticing. He saw Parris walking towards him and would have passed without a word had the lieutenant not touched his hat and said, 'I have been supervising the last of the treasure-chests, Sir Richard. I can still barely believe what we went through to get them!'

Bolitho looked at him vaguely. 'Yes. I shall note your excellent behaviour in my report to their lordships.' Even that sounded hollow. The aftermath. Letters to Murray's mother and Dalmaine's widow, arrangements for prize-money to be paid to the dependents of those others killed or discharged. His despatch would at least guarantee that.

Parris eyed him worriedly. 'I did not speak to you for praise, Sir Richard. Is something wrong?'

Bolitho shook his head, and felt the wind in his face, just as he could still sense her wrist under his fingers. In hell's name, what had he expected?

'No. Why should there be? It will be known as a noble sacrifice, I am given to understand, so be grateful that you serve and do not command!'

He walked away and Parris turned and saw Allday striding out into the angry sunlight.

'Sir Richard will require the barge, Cox'n.'

Allday shook his head. 'No, he'll walk a piece. When he's wore himself out, then he'll want the barge.'

Parris nodded, understanding perhaps for the first time. 'I envy the both of you.'

Allday walked slowly to the balustrade that overlooked the main anchorage. The sea was getting up right enough. He bit on an apple he had obtained from the commodore's cook. Bloody good job. Blow some of the bitterness clean out of sight.

He saw his barge standing off from the jetty to avoid scraping the paintwork as lively catspaws spattered the stone stairs with spray. Bolitho was all aback, just when he had believed things were getting better. Bloody women. He had said as much to Ozzard when they had returned in triumph with the treasure-ship. Ozzard had made one of his defensive remarks and Allday, too tired and angry to care, had exclaimed, 'What the hell do you know? You've never been married!' Strange how it had upset the little man. Allday had decided he would give him one of his precious bone carvings to make up for it. He tossed the apple core into the sun-dried grass and turned to leave. Then he saw her, standing on the terrace, watching him with those eyes of hers. That look could make a man turn to water.

She met his gaze and said, 'Do you remember me? You are Mr Allday.'

Allday replied carefully, 'Why, o' course I remember *you*, Ma'am. Nobody could forget what you done for the Captain, as he was then.'

She ignored the unspoken suggestion in his voice. 'I need your

112

help. Will you trust me?'

Allday felt his defences slipping. She was asking him to trust *her*. The wife of the high and mighty Inspector General, a man who needed watching if half what he had heard was true. But she had paid out her line first. She was the one who was taking all the risks.

He grinned slowly. *A sailor's woman.* 'I will.'

She moved towards him, and Allday saw the quick movement of her breasts beneath the fine gown. Not so cool and calm as she wanted to appear, he thought.

'Vice-Admiral Bolitho is not himself.' She hesitated; perhaps she had already gone too far. She had seen the grin fade, the instant hostility in the big man's eyes.

'I – I wish to help him, you see –' She dropped her gaze. 'In God's name, Mr Allday, must I beg of you?'

Allday said, 'I'm sorry, Ma'am. We've had a lot of enemies over the years, see.' He weighed it up. What was the worst thing that could happen? He said abruptly, 'He was nearly blinded.' He felt like ice despite the searing wind, but now he could not stop. 'He thinks he's losing the use of his left eye.'

She stared at him, the picture leaping into her mind like a stark dream. He had been staring at the sky or the sea when she had found him. Bolitho had looked so defeated, so lost that she had wanted to run to him and take him in her arms, forget security, life itself if only she could comfort and keep him a few moments more. She recalled his voice, the way he had looked at her without seeming to see her.

She heard herself whisper, 'Oh, dear God!'

Allday said, 'Remember, I've told you nothin', Ma'am. I'm often in hot water as it is without you adding more coals to it.' He hesitated, moved by her distress, her sudden loss of poise before him, a common seaman. 'But if you *can* help –' he broke off and touched his hat quickly. He whispered hoarsely, 'I sees yer husband hull-down on th' horizon, Ma'am. I'll be off now!'

She stared after him, a great, loping figure in flapping blue jacket and nankeen breeches, one scarred and hurt so badly she could see it on his homely features. But a man so gentle that she wanted to cry for him, for all of them.

But her husband did not come to her; she saw him walking along the terrace with the lieutenant called Parris.

When she looked down the sloping pathway which led to the harbour she saw Allday turn and lift his hat to her.

Just a small gesture, and yet she knew that he had accepted her as a friend.

The deckhead lanterns in *Hyperion*'s great cabin spiralled wildly, throwing insane shadows across the checkered deck covering and across the tightly lashed nine-pounders on either side.

Bolitho sipped a glass of hock, and watched while Yovell finished yet another letter and pushed it across the table for him to sign. Like actors on a stage, he thought, as Ozzard busied himself refilling glasses, and Allday entered and left the cabin like a player who had been given no lines to learn.

Captain Haven stood by the stern windows, now half-shuttered as the wind, made more fearsome by the darkness, broke the crests from the inshore waves, and flung spray over the anchored ships.

Bolitho felt the whole ship trembling as she tilted to her cable, and remembered the feeling of disbelief when Dacie had severed the Spaniard's mooring.

Haven concluded, 'That is everything I can determine, Sir Richard. The purser is satisfied with his storing, and all but one working party has been withdrawn from the shore.' He was speaking carefully, like a pupil repeating a hard-learned lesson to his teacher. 'I have been able to replace the three boats too, although they will need some work done on them.'

An observation, a reminder that it had been his admiral who had abandoned them. Haven was careful not to display his true feelings.

'Who is in charge of the last party?'

Haven looked at his list. 'The first lieutenant, Sir Richard.'

Always the title now, after their last clash. Bolitho swilled the hock around his glass. So be it then. Haven was a fool and must know that his admiral, any flag officer for that matter, could make or destroy his career. Or was it his way of exploiting Bolitho's sense of fairness?

Yovell looked over his steel-rimmed spectacles. 'I beg your pardon, Sir Richard, but did you intend this despatch to *Obdurate* to read in this fashion?'

Bolitho gave a wry smile. 'I did.' He did not need to be reminded.

You are directed and commanded to make ready for sea. Captain Robert Thynne of the other seventy-four could think what he liked. *Obdurate* was needed now more than ever. The vessels carrying the bulk of the treasure would have to be escorted clear of dangerous waters until they met with ships of Sir Peter Folliot's squadron, or until they could have the sea-room to manage for themselves. Bolitho would have preferred to bide his time until his own small squadron arrived, but the change of weather had altered all that.

He turned away from the others, glad of the lanterns' mellow light as he massaged his eye. It was still aching from his stupid contest with the sun. Or was it another snare of his imagination? He was glad to be aboard this old ship again. Somervell had guessed as much when he had said his farewell.

Somervell had explained that he and his lady were leaving after the main exodus, aboard a large Indiaman which was daily expected here. Personal comfort rated very high with Somervell.

Bolitho had seen the other side of the man when he had asked, 'I should like to take my leave of Lady Somervell.'

'Impossible.' Somervell had met his gaze insolently. Bolitho could well imagine those same cold eyes staring along the barrel of a duelling pistol in the dawn light, although it was known he favoured swords for such settlements.

He had added, 'She is not here.'

Antigua was a small island. If she had wanted to see him she could. Unless Somervell had grown tired of the game and had prevented it. Either way it did not matter now. It was over.

There was a tap at the door and Lieutenant Lovering, who was the officer-of-the-watch, took a pace into the cabin and reported, 'I beg your forgiveness for this intrusion, Sir Richard,' his eyes flickered between Bolitho and Haven, 'but a courier-brig has been reported running for harbour.'

Bolitho lowered his eyes. Maybe from England. Letters from

home. News of the war. Their lifeline. He thought of Adam, in command of his own brig, probably still carrying despatches for Nelson. Another world away from the heat and fever of the Indies.

Haven leaned forward. 'If there is any mail –' He recovered himself, and Bolitho recalled what Allday had said about his wife expecting a baby.

Bolitho signed more letters. Recommendations for promotion, for bravery, for transfers to other ships. Letters to the bereaved.

The lieutenant hesitated. 'Will you have any letters for the shore, Sir Richard?'

Bolitho looked at him. Lovering was the second lieutenant. Waiting for promotion, the chance to prove himself. If Parris fell . . . He shut the idea from his mind. 'I think not.' It came out easily. Was it that simple to end something which had been so dear?

Haven waited until the lieutenant had withdrawn. 'First light then, Sir Richard.'

'Yes. Call the hands as you will, and signal your intentions to *Obdurate* and the Commissioner of the Dockyard.'

When *Hyperion* returned to Antigua the Indiaman would have gone. Would they ever meet again, even by accident?

'It will take all day to work out of harbour and muster our charges into a semblance of order. This wind will decide then whether to be an ally or a foe.'

If the treasure-ships and their escort were contained in the shelter of English Harbour for much longer, the Spaniards and perhaps their French allies might even try to counter-attack before the new squadron arrived.

Left alone in the cabin Bolitho drank some more hock, but although his stomach was empty he was unable to face Ozzard's meal. With the old ship swaying and groaning around him, and the duty watch being mustered every few minutes, or so it appeared, to secure and lash down some loose gear, it was impossible to rest.

The hock was good, and Bolitho found time to wonder how Ozzard managed to keep it so cool even in the bilges.

He toyed with the idea of sending a note to Catherine and dismissed it immediately. In the wrong hands it could ruin her.

What it might do to his own career did not seem to matter any longer.

He heard the clank of pumps and remembered what he had been told about *Hyperion*'s age and service. It was like an additional taunt.

He lolled in his favourite chair but was awakened, it seemed within seconds, by Ozzard shaking his arm.

Bolitho stared at him. The ship was still in darkness, the din and movement as before.

'The first lieutenant wishes to see you, Sir Richard.'

Bolitho was wide awake. Why not the captain?

Parris entered, soaked with spray. He looked flushed despite his tan, but Bolitho knew he had not been drinking.

'What is it?'

Parris steadied himself against a chair as the deck swayed again. 'I thought you should know, Sir Richard. The guardboat reported earlier that a schooner left harbour. One of the commodore's own vessels, it seems.'

'Well?' Bolitho knew there was worse to come.

'Lady Somervell was on board.' He recoiled slightly under Bolitho's grey stare. 'I discovered that she intends to sail round to St John's.'

Bolitho stood up and listened to the wind. It was a gale now, and he heard the water surging against the hull like a flood tide.

'In *this*, man!' He groped round for his coat. 'Viscount Somervell must be informed.'

Parris watched dully. 'He knows. I told him myself.'

Haven appeared in the screen door, his sleeping attire covered by a boat-cloak. 'What's this I hear?' He glared at Parris. 'I shall speak to you later!'

Bolitho sat down. How could Somervell let her do it? He must have known when he had said it was impossible for her to make her farewell. A small schooner could founder if wrongly handled. He tried to remember who commanded Glassport's vessels.

Even in calm weather it was dangerous to make casual passages amongst the islands. Pirates were too commonplace to mention. For every one rotting in chains, or on the gallows, there were a hundred more in these waters.

He said, 'I can do nothing until daylight.'

Haven regarded him calmly. 'If you ask me –'

He fell silent then added, 'I must attend the watch on deck, Sir Richard.'

Bolitho sat down very slowly. *I did this to her.* He did not know if he had spoken aloud or not, but the words seemed to echo around the cabin like a shot.

He called to Ozzard, 'Rouse my flag lieutenant, if you please.'

He would send him ashore with a message for Somervell, in bed or not.

He stood up restlessly and walked to an unshuttered window. *If I go myself one of us will surely die.*

9

A Sloop Of War

Bolitho strode out on to the quarterdeck and felt the wind lift under his boat-cloak, and the spray which burst over the weather quarter like tropical rain.

He held on to the nettings and slitted his eyes against the gale. It was strong but clammy, so that it did nothing to refresh his tired limbs. Two days since they had clawed their way out of English Harbour to assemble their small but priceless convoy. In that time they had barely logged fifty miles.

By night they rode out the storm under a reefed maintopsail and little else, while the four transports and the smaller vessels lay hove-to as best they could under savage conditions.

Secrecy was now of secondary importance and *Hyperion* burned flares and her vice-admiral's top-lights to try and hold the ships together. Then as each dawn found them it had taken a full day to reassemble the badly scattered ships and to begin the formation all over again. Everything was wet, and as the men toiled aloft to fight the wind-crazed sails or stumbled to replace their companions on the bilge-pumps, many must have wondered what was keeping them afloat.

Bolitho stared abeam and saw the faint sheen of the sloop-of-war's topgallants. *Phaedra* was standing up to windward, heeling every so often as the waves lifted her slender hull like a toy. The brig *Upholder* was invisible, far ahead in the van, and the other brig *Tetrarch* was an equal distance astern.

Bolitho climbed up a few steps on a poop ladder and felt the cloak stream away from him, his shirt already soaked with spray and spindrift. There was *Obdurate*, half-a-mile astern, her black and buff bows shining like glass as the waves burst into her. It felt strange to have another third-rate in company again, although he doubted if Thynne was thanking him for it. After a long stay in harbour, repairing the last storm battering she had suffered, it was likely that *Obdurate*'s people were cursing their change of roles.

Bolitho climbed down to the deck again. There were four seamen at the big wheel, and nearby Penhaligon the master was in deep conversation with one of his mates.

The wind had backed decisively to the south-west and they had been blown many miles off their original course. But if the sailing master was troubled he did not show it.

All around, above and along the maindeck, men were working to repair any storm damage. Lines to be replaced or spliced, sails to be sent down, to be patched or discarded.

Bolitho glanced at the nearest gangway where a boatswain's mate was supervising the unrigging of a grating.

Another flogging. It had been worse than usual, even after Ozzard had closed the cabin skylight. The wild chorus of the wind through stays and shrouds, the occasional boom of reefed topsails, and all the while the rattle of drums and the sickening crack of the lash across a man's naked back.

He saw blood on the gangway, already fading and paling in the flung spray. Three dozen lashes. A man driven too far in the middle of the storm, an officer unable to deal with it on the spot.

Haven was in his quarters writing his log, or re-reading the letters which had been brought in the courier bag.

Bolitho was glad he was not here. Only his influence remained. The men who hurried about the decks looked strained, resentful. Even Jenour, who had not served very much at sea, had remarked on it.

Bolitho beckoned to the signals midshipman. 'The glass, if you please, Mr Furnival.' He noticed the youth's hands, raw from working all night aloft, and then trying to assume the dress and bearing of a King's officer by day.

Bolitho raised the glass and saw the sloop-of-war swim sharply into focus, the creaming wash of sea as she tilted her gunports into a deep swell. He wondered what her commander, Dunstan, was thinking as he rode out the wind and waves to hold station on his admiral. It was a far cry from *Euryalus*'s midshipman's berth.

He moved the glass still further and saw a green brush-stroke of land far away on the larboard bow. Another island, Barbuda. They should have left it to starboard on the first day. He thought of the schooner, of Catherine who had asked the master to take her around Antigua to St John's instead of using the road.

A small vessel like that would stand no chance against such a gale. Her master could either run with the wind, or try to find shelter. Better ships would have suffered in the storm; some might have perished. He clenched his fingers around the telescope until they ached. Why did she do it? She could be lying fathoms deep, or clinging to some wreckage. She might even have seen *Hyperion*'s toplights, have known it was his ship.

He heard the master call to the officer-of-the-watch, 'I would approve if you could get the t'gallants on her, Mr Mansforth.'

The lieutenant nodded, his face brick-red from the salt spray. 'I – I shall inform the Captain.' He was very aware of the figure by the weather side, with the boat-cloak swirling around him. Hatless, his black hair plastered to his forehead, he looked more like a highwayman than a vice-admiral.

Jenour emerged from the poop and touched his hat. 'Any orders, Sir Richard?'

Bolitho returned the glass to the midshipman. 'The wind has eased. Please make a signal to the transports to keep closed up. We are not out of trouble yet.'

The four ships which were sharing most of the treasure were keeping downwind of the two seventy-fours. With a brig scouting well ahead, and the other trailing astern like a guard-dog, they should be warned in time should a suspicious sail show itself. Then *Hyperion* and *Obdurate* could gauge their moment before running down on the convoy, or beating up to windward to join *Phaedra*.

Flags soared up to the yards and stiffened to the wind like painted metal.

'Acknowledged, Sir Richard.' Then in a hushed voice Jenour added, 'The Captain is coming.'

Bolitho felt the bitterness rising within him. They were more like conspirators than of one company.

Haven walked slowly across the streaming planking, his eyes on the gun-breechings, flaked lines, coiled braces, everything.

He was apparently satisfied that he had nothing to fear from what he saw, and crossed the deck to Bolitho.

He touched his hat, his face expressionless while his eyes explored Bolitho's wet shirt and spray-dappled breeches.

'I intend to make more sail, Sir Richard. We should carry it well enough.'

Bolitho nodded. 'Signal *Obdurate* so that they conform. I don't want us to become separated.' Captain Thynne had lost two men overboard the previous day and had backed his mizzen topsail while he had attempted to send away the quarter boat. Neither of the luckless men was recovered. They had either fallen too far from aloft and been knocked senseless when they hit the sea, or like most sailors, were unable to swim. Bolitho had not intended to mention it.

But Haven snorted, 'I will make the signal *at once*, Sir Richard. Thynne wants to drill his people the better, and not dawdle about when some fool goes outboard through his own carelessness!'

He gestured to the lieutenant of the watch.

'Hands aloft and loose t'gan'sls, Mr Mansforth!' He looked at the midshipman. 'General signal. *Make more sail.*' His arm shot out across the quarterdeck rail. '*That man!* Just what the bloody hell is he about?'

The seaman in question had been wringing out his checkered shirt in an effort to dry it.

He stood stockstill, his eyes on the quarterdeck, while others moved aside in case they too might draw Haven's wrath.

A boatswain's mate yelled, ''Tis all right, sir! I told him to do it!'

Haven turned away, suddenly furious.

But Bolitho had seen the gratitude in the seaman's eyes and knew that the boatswain's mate had told him nothing of the kind. Were they all so sick of Haven that even the afterguard were against him?

'Captain Haven!' Bolitho saw him turn, the anger gone. It was unnerving how he could work up a sudden rage and disperse it to order. 'A word, if you please.'

The midshipman called, 'All acknowledged, sir.'

Bolitho said, 'This ship has never been in action under your command or beneath my flag. I'll trouble you to remember it when next you berate a man who has been running hither and thither for two days and nights.' He was finding it hard to keep his voice level and under control. 'When the time comes to beat to quarters in earnest, you will expect, nay, demand instant loyalty.'

Haven stammered, 'I know some of these troublemakers –'

'Well, hear me, Captain Haven. All these men, good and bad, saints and *troublemakers*, will be called on to fight, do I make myself clear? Loyalty has to be earned, and a captain of your experience should not need to be told! Just as you should not require me to remind you that I will not tolerate senseless brutality from anyone!'

Haven stared back at him, his eyes sparking with indignation.

'I am not supported, Sir Richard! Some of my wardroom are as green as grass, and my senior, Mr Parris, is more concerned with gaining favour for himself! By God, I could tell you things about that one!'

Bolitho snapped, 'That is enough. You are my flag captain, and you have my support.' He let the words sink in. 'I know not what ails you, but if you abuse my trust once again, I shall put you in the next ship for England!'

Parris had appeared on deck and as the calls trilled to muster the topmen once again for making more sail, he glanced at Bolitho, then at his captain.

Haven tugged his hat more firmly over his ginger hair and said, 'Carry on, Mr Parris.'

Bolitho knew Parris was surprised. There was no additional threat or warning.

As the seamen poured up the ratlines like monkeys, and the masthead pendant whipped sharply for the first time to prove that the wind was indeed easing, Haven said stiffly, 'I have standards too, Sir Richard.'

Bolitho dismissed him and turned again towards the far-off

island. Allday stood a few paces away. He never seemed to trust him alone any more, Bolitho thought.

Allday said, 'Them island schooners is hardy craft, Sir Richard.'

Bolitho did not turn but touched his arm. 'Thank you, old friend. You always know what I'm thinking.' He watched two gulls rising above the wave crests, their wings spread and catching a brighter sunlight as it broke through the clouds. Like Catherine's fan.

He said desperately, 'I feel so helpless.' He looked at Allday's strong profile. 'Forgive me. I should not pass my burden to you.'

Allday's eyes narrowed as he stared at the leaping waves, their long crests curling over to the wind's thrust.

It was like gauging the fall of shot. Up one. Down one. The next would hit home.

He said, 'Matter of fact, she spoke to me afore we left harbour.'

Bolitho stared. 'To *you*?'

Allday sounded ruffled. 'Well, some women feels free to speak with the likes o' me.'

Bolitho touched his arm again. 'Please, no games, old friend.'

Allday said, 'Told me she was fair bothered about you. Wanted you to know it, like.'

Bolitho banged his fist on the weathered rail. 'I didn't even try to understand. Now I've lost her.' It was spilling out of him, and he knew that only Allday would understand, even if he did not always agree.

Allday's eyes were faraway. 'Knew a lass once in a village where I was livin'. She was fair taken with the squire's son, a real young blade 'e was. She was made for him, an' he never even knew she was alive, the bastard, beggin' your pardon, Sir Richard.'

Bolitho watched him, wondering if Allday had wanted that girl.

Allday said simply, 'One day she threw herself down in front of the squire's coach. She couldn't take no more, I 'spect, and wanted to *show him*.' He looked at his scarred hands. 'She was killed.'

124

Bolitho wiped the spray from his face. To *show him*. Was that what Catherine had done because of him?

Why had he not seen it, accepted that love could never be won the easy way? He thought of Valentine Keen, and his girl with the moonlit eyes. He had risked so much, and won everything because of it.

He heard Allday move away, probably going below for a *wet* with his friends, or with Ozzard in his pantry.

He walked towards the poop and saw Mr Penhaligon watching the set of each sail, his beefy hands on his hips. Haven pouting as he peered at the compass, Parris watching him, waiting to dismiss the watch below.

Bolitho listened to the regular clank of pumps; the old *Hyperion* carried all of them. She had seen hundred of hopes dashed, bodies broken on these same decks.

Bolitho's ears seemed to fasten on to a new intrusion.

He exclaimed, '*Gunfire!*'

Several men jumped at the sharpness in his voice; Allday, who was still on the ladder, turned and looked towards him.

Then the signals midshipman said excitedly, 'Aye, I hear it, sir!'

Haven strode to the quarterdeck rail, his head moving from side to side, still unable to hear the sound.

Jenour came running from the poop. 'Where away?' He saw Bolitho and flushed. 'I beg your pardon, Sir Richard!'

Bolitho shaded his eyes as the midshipman yelled, 'From *Phaedra*, sir! *Sail to the nor'-west!*'

Bolitho saw men climbing into the shrouds, their discomfort forgotten. For the moment.

Jenour asked anxiously, 'What does it mean, Sir Richard?'

Bolitho said, 'Signal *Phaedra* to investigate.' Minutes later when the midshipman's signalling party had run the flags up to the yard Bolitho replied, 'Small cannon, Stephen. Swivels or the like.'

Why had he heard, when so many others around him had not?

He said, 'Signal *Tetrarch* to close on the flag.'

Allday said admiringly, 'God, look at 'er go!' He was watching the sloop-of-war turning away, showing her copper in the misty sunlight, as she spread more canvas and rounded fiercely until she was close-hauled on the larboard tack.

Allday added, 'Like your *Sparrow*, eh, Cap'n?' He grinned awkwardly. 'I *mean* Sir Richard!'

Bolitho took a telescope from the rack. 'I remember. I hope young Dunstan appreciates the greatest gift as I once did.'

None of the others understood and once again Allday was moved by the privilege.

Bolitho lowered the glass. Too much spray and haze, whirling in the wind like smoke.

A privateer perhaps? Crossing swords with a Barbuda trader. Or one of the local patrols braving the wind and sea to chase an enemy corvette? *Phaedra* would soon know. It might also be a decoy to draw their flimsy defences away from the gold and silver.

He smiled bitterly. How would Haven react to that, he wondered?

'Nor'-west-by-north, sir!' The helmsman had to yell to make himself heard above the roar of wind through the canvas and rigging, pushing the sloop-of-war hard over until it was impossible to stand upright.

Commander Alfred Dunstan gripped the quarterdeck rail and tugged his cocked hat more firmly over his wild auburn hair. He had been *Phaedra*'s captain for eighteen months, his first command, and with luck still on his side might soon be transferring his single epaulette to his right shoulder, the first definite step to post-rank.

He shouted, 'Bring her up two points to wind'rd, Mr Meheux! God damn it, we'll not let it escape, whatever it is!'

He saw the first lieutenant exchange a quick glance with the sailing master. *Phaedra* seemed to be sailing as close to the wind as she dared, so that her braced yards and bulging sails appeared to be almost fore-and-aft, thrusting her over, the sea boiling around her gunports and deluging the bare-backed seamen until their tanned bodies shone like crude statuary.

Dunstan strained his eyes aloft to watch every sail, and his topmen straddled out along the yards, some doutbless remembering *Obdurate*'s hands who had been lost overboard in the storm.

'Full-an'-bye, sir! Nor'-west-by-west!'

The deck and rigging protested violently, the shrouds making a vibrant thrumming sound as the ship heeled over still further.

The first lieutenant, who was twenty-three, a year younger than his captain, shouted, 'She'll not take much more, sir!'

Dunstan grinned excitedly. He had a sensitive, pointed face and humorous mouth, and some people had told him he looked like Nelson. Dunstan liked the compliment, but had discovered the resemblance himself long ago, even as a midshipman in Bolitho's big first-rate *Euryalus*.

'A plague on your worries! What are you, an old woman?'

They laughed like schoolboys, for Meheux was the captain's cousin, and each knew almost what the other was thinking.

Dunstan tightened his lips as a line parted on the foretopsail yard with the echo of a pistol shot. But two men were already working out to repair it, and he replied, 'We must beat up to wind'rd in case the buggers show us a clean pair of heels an' we lose them!'

Meheux did not argue; he knew him too well. The sea boiled over the gangway and flung two men, cursing and floundering, into the scuppers. One came up against a tethered cannon and did not move. He had been knocked senseless, or had broken a rib or two. He was dragged to a hatchway, the others crouching like athletes as they gauged the moment to avoid the next incoming torrent of water.

Meheux enjoyed the excitement, just as Dunstan was never happier than when he was free of the fleet's apron strings or an admiral's authority. They did not even know the meaning or source of the gunfire; they might discover that it was another British man-of-war engaged in taking an enemy blockade-runner. If so, there was no chance of sharing the prize-money this time. The other captain would see to that.

Dunstan climbed up the ratlines of the lee shrouds, the waves seeming to swoop at his legs as he hung out to train his telescope while he waited for the next cry from the masthead.

The lookout yelled, 'Fine on the starboard bow, sir!' He broke off as the ship lifted then plunged deeply into a long trough, hard down until her gilded figurehead was awash, as if *Phaedra* was on her way to the bottom. The crash must have all but shaken the lookout from his precarious perch.

Then he called, 'Two ships, sir! One dismasted!'

Dunstan climbed back again and grinned as he poured water from his hat. 'Fine lookout, Mr Meheux! Give him a guinea!'

The first lieutenant smiled. 'He's one of *my* men, sir.'

Dunstan was wiping his telescope. 'Oh, good. Then you give the feller a guinea!'

There was more sporadic firing, but because of the lively sea and the drifting curtains of spray it was impossible to determine the other vessels, except from the masthead.

Phaedra heeled upright, and the main topsail boomed and thundered violently as the wind went out of it.

'Man the braces there! Let her fall off three points!' Dunstan released his grip on the rail. The wind was dropping significantly so that the hull had to be brought under command to take advantage of it.

'Nor'-nor'-west, sir! Steady as she goes!'

Meheux gasped, 'By God, there they are.'

Dunstan raised his glass again. 'Hell's teeth! It's that damn schooner we were looking for!'

Meheux studied his profile, the wild hair flapping beneath the battered hat which Dunstan always wore at sea. Once, in his cups, Dunstan had confided, 'I'll get meself a new hat when I'm posted, not before!'

Meheux said, 'The one with the Inspector General's lady aboard?'

Dunstan grinned broadly. Meheux was a reliable and promising officer. He was a child where women were concerned.

'I can see why our vice-admiral was so concerned!'

A man yelled, 'They're casting adrift, sir! They've seen us, by God!'

Dunstan's smile faded. 'Stand by on deck! Starboard battery load, but don't run out!' He gripped the lieutenant's arm. 'A bloody pirate if I'm any judge, Josh!'

The first lieutenant's name was Joshua. Dunstan only used it when he was really excited.

Dunstan said urgently, 'We'll take him first. Put some good marksmen in the tops. She's a fancy little brigantine, worth a guinea or two, wouldn't you say?' He saw Meheux hurry away, the glint of steel as a boarding party was mustered clear of the gun crews and their rammers.

The schooner was dismasted although someone had tried to put up a jury rig. In that gale it must have been a nightmare.

Meheux came back, strapping on his favourite hanger.

'What about the others, sir?'

Dunstan trained the glass, then swore as a puff of smoke followed by a sharp bang showed that the pirate had fired on his ship.

'God blast their bloody eyes!' Dunstan raised his arms as he had seen Bolitho do when they had prepared for battle, so that his coxswain could clip on his sword. 'Open the ports! *Run out!*'

He recalled what Meheux had just asked him. 'If they're alive we'll take them next, if not –' He shrugged. 'One thing is certain, they're not going anywhere!'

He glanced around and winced as the pirate fired again and a ball slapped down alongside. The stage was set.

Dunstan drew his sword and held it over his head. He felt the chill run down his arm, as if the blade was made of ice. He remembered crouching with another midshipman on *Euryalus*'s quarterdeck, sick with terror, yet unable to tear his eyes away as the enemy's great mountain of sails had towered above the gangway. And Bolitho standing out on the exposed deck, his sword in the air, each gun-captain watching, sweating out the agonising seconds whch had been like hours. Eternity.

Dunstan grinned and brought his arm down with a flourish. '*Fire!*'

The small brigantine came up floundering into the wind, her foremast gone, her decks covered with torn canvas and piles of rigging. That well-aimed broadside had also shot away the helm, or killed the men around it. The vessel was out of control, and one man who ran on to the poop with a raised musket was shot down instantly by *Phaedra*'s marksmen.

'*Hands aloft! Shorten sail!* Take in the main-course!' Dunstan sheathed his sword and watched the other vessel reeling under *Phaedra*'s lee. The fight was already over. 'Stand by to board!' Some of the seamen were clambering into the shrouds, their muskets cocked and ready, while others waited like eager hounds to get to grips. It was rare to catch a pirate. Dunstan watched his first lieutenant bracing his legs to jump as the sloop-of-war sidled heavily alongside. He knew it would be a madman who put up a defence. This was what his sailors did best. They would offer no quarter if one of their own was cut down.

There was a ragged cheer as the red ensign was hoisted up the brigantine's mainmast.

Dunstan glanced at the low-lying shape of the schooner. She must be badly holed, and looked ready to capsize.

It would mean risking a boat despite the lively waves.

He called, 'Mr Grant! Jolly boat, lively with you! Stand clear if the buggers fire on you!'

The boat lifted and dipped away from the side, the other lieutenant trying to stay upright as he looked towards the schooner. Once he stared astern, then gestured wildly towards *Phaedra*.

Dunstan stared up and then laughed aloud, feeling some of the tension draining out of him.

Bolitho would have had something to say about that. He shouted, 'Run up the Colours!' He saw Meheux clambering inboard again. 'We fought under no flag, dammit!'

He saw his cousin's face and asked, 'How was it, Josh?'

The lieutenant sheathed his hanger and let out a long sigh.

'One of the bastards had a go at us, slashed poor Tom Makin across the chest, but he'll live.'

They both watched as a corpse splashed down between the two hulls.

'He'll not try that again!'

Leaving the prize crew on board, *Phaedra* cast off, and under reduced canvas, edged towards the listing schooner.

Dunstan watched as the boarding party climbed across her sloping deck. Two men, obviously pirates who had been left stranded by the brigantine, charged to the attack. Lieutenant Grant shot one with his pistol; the other ducked and retreated towards the companionway. A seaman balanced his cutlass and then flung it like a spear. In the telescope's lens everything was silent, but Dunstan swore he could hear the scream as the man tumbled headlong, the blade embedded in his back.

'I'll not go alongside. Stand by to come about! Ready on deck!'

Dunstan lowered the glass, as if what he saw was too private. The woman, her gown almost torn off her back, yet strangely proud as she allowed the sailors to guide her towards the jolly boat. Dunstan saw her pause just once as she passed the dead pirate, shot down by Lieutenant Grant. He saw her spit on him and kick the cutlass from his hand. Hate, contempt and anger; but no sort of fear.

Dunstan looked as the first lieutenant. 'Man the side, Josh. This is something we shall all remember.'

Then later, when *Phaedra* with her prize making a painful progress astern, sighted the flagship, Dunstan discovered another moment which he would never forget.

She had been standing beside him, wrapped in a tarpaulin coat which one of the sailors had offered her, her chin uplifted and her eyes wide while she had watched *Hyperion*'s yards swinging, her sails refilling on to the tack which would bring them together.

Dunstan had said, 'I'll make a signal now, my lady. May I order my midshipman to spell out your name?'

She had shaken her head slowly, her eyes on the old two-decker, her reply almost lost in the crack of sails and rigging.

'No, Captain, but thank you.' Quieter still, 'He will see me. I know it.'

Only once had Dunstan seen her defences weaken. The master's mate had shouted, 'There, lads! The old girl's goin'!'

The schooner had lifted her stern and was turning in a circle of foam and bubbles, like a pale hand revolving in a chandler's butt of grain. The hull was surrounded by bobbing flotsam and a few corpses when suddenly it dived, as if eager to be gone from those who had wronged her.

Dunstan had glanced at her and had seen her clutching a fan to her breast. He could not be certain but he thought he saw her

131

speak two words. *Thank you.*

Afterwards Dunstan had said, 'Make it *two* guineas, Josh. It was more important than either of us realised.'

10

Harbour

Two weeks after *Phaedra*'s capture of the pirate brigantine and the release of the captives, *Hyperion* and *Obdurate* returned to Antigua.

The island was sighted at dawn, but as if to taunt their efforts, the wind all but died completely and it was nearly dusk before they edged their way into English Harbour and dropped anchor.

Bolitho had been on the quarterdeck for most of the afternoon, idly watching the hands trimming the sails while the island seemed to stand away at the same distance.

Any other time it would have been a proud moment. They had met with ships of Sir Peter Folliot's squadron, which even now would be escorting the treasure convoy all the remainder of the way to England.

The lookouts had eventually reported that there were three ships-of-the-line in harbour and Bolitho guessed they were the other vessels of his squadron, with each captain doubtless wondering about his immediate future under Bolitho's flag.

That too should have been like a tonic, after the strain of escorting the treasure and fighting a daily battle with the weather. Now, Bolitho was somehow grateful that it would not be until the next day that he could meet his new captains and while they studied him, he would measure the men who would be serving him.

When both the two-deckers finally dropped their anchors Bolitho had gone aft to his quarters where the great cabin was already transformed by several cheerful lanterns.

He walked to the stern windows and leaned out over the darkening water to watch a full-blooded sunset, but his mind was still hanging on to that moment when Catherine had been hoisted up the ship's side in the rough tarpaulin coat.

It did not seem possible that she had been here in this same cabin, alone with him.

Alone with him and yet still at a measured distance. He walked around the cabin and looked at his sleeping quarters, which he had given her during her brief stay on board. There should still be some sign of her presence. A breath of her perfume, a garment forgotten perhaps when she had been carried over to Admiral Folliot's flagship when the two formations of ships had found each other.

Bolitho crossed to the fine mahogany wine cabinet and ran his fingers along it. Made by one of the best craftsmen, it had been her gift to him after he had left her in London, where he had last seen her until Antigua. He smiled sadly as he remembered his old friend Thomas Herrick's disapproval when the cabinet had been brought aboard his *Lysander*, after he had been appointed Bolitho's flag captain.

Herrick had always been a loyal friend, but had mistrusted anything and anyone he thought might damage Bolitho's name and career. Even young Adam had been involved because of the so-called liaison between them for that short, precious time. He had fought a duel with another hot-headed lieutenant at Gibraltar in defence of his uncle's reputation. It seemed as if everyone Bolitho cared for was hurt or damaged by the contact.

He turned and looked along the cabin, and saw the marine sentry's shadow through the screen door. She had stood here, quite still, only her breathing rapid and uncontrolled as she had stared around, the coat bunched to her throat as if she was cold.

Then she had noticed the cabinet, and for just a moment he had seen her mouth quiver.

He had said quietly, 'It goes everywhere with me.'

Then she had walked right up to him and had laid her hand on his face. When he had made to put his arms round her she had shaken her head with something like desperation.

'*No!* It is hard enough to be here like this. Do not make it worse. I just want to look at you. To tell you how much it means to be alive because of you. God, Fate, I know not which, once brought us together. And now I fear what it might do to us.'

He had seen the great rent in her gown and had asked, 'Can I not have it mended? Your maid, where is she?'

She had walked away but had kept her eyes on him. 'Maria is dead. They tried to rape her. When she fought them with her bare hands they killed her, cut her down like some helpless animal.' She added slowly, 'Your little ship came just in time. For me, that is. But I made sure that some of those filthy pigs never breathe the same air again.' She had looked at her hands, at the soiled fan which she still grasped in one of them. 'I wish to God I could be there when they make those vermin dance on their ropes!'

The screen door opened slightly and Jenour looked in at him. 'The Commodore's boat has been sighted, Sir Richard.' His eyes moved around the cabin. Maybe he could see her too.

'Very well.' Bolitho sat down and looked at the deck between his feet. Glassport was the last man he wanted to see just now.

He thought of that final moment when he had accompanied her across to Sir Peter Folliot's big three-decker.

The admiral was a slight, sickly man, but there was nothing wrong with his quick mind. Despite the poor communications he seemed to know all about the preparations for the raid on La Guaira, and the actual amount of booty down to the nearest gold coin.

'Quite an escapade, eh?' He had greeted Catherine with lavish courtesy, and had announced that he would place her in the care of one of his best frigate captains, who would make all speed to return her to her husband in Antigua.

Maybe he knew something about that as well, Bolitho thought.

He had watched the powerful forty-four gun frigate making sail to take her away from him for the last time, and had stayed on deck until only the topgallant sails showed above the evening horizon like pink shells.

The big Indiaman had gone from the harbour, and he had pictured Catherine with her husband drawing further and further away with each turn of the glass.

The door opened again and Captain Haven took a few paces into the cabin.

'I am about to greet the Commodore, Sir Richard. May I signal your captains to repair on board tomorrow forenoon?'

'Yes.' It was all so empty, so coldly formal. Like a great wall between them.

Bolitho tried again. 'I did hear your wife was expecting a child, Captain Haven.' He recalled how tense Haven had been since he had received his letters from the courier brig. Like a man in a trance; he had even allowed Parris to manage the ship's affairs for him.

Haven's eyes narrowed. 'From whom, Sir Richard, may I ask?'

Bolitho sighed. 'Does it matter?'

Haven looked away. 'A baby boy.'

Bolitho saw his fingers clench around his cocked hat. Haven was driving himself mad.

'I congratulate you. It must have been on your mind a great deal.'

Haven swallowed hard. 'Yes, er, thank you, Sir Richard –'

Mercifully, shouted orders floated from the quarterdeck and Haven almost fled from the cabin to meet Commodore Glassport as he came aboard.

Bolitho stood up as Ozzard entered with his dress coat. Was it really Parris's child, he wondered? How would they settle it?

He looked down at Ozzard. 'Did I thank you for taking good care of our guest while she was amongst us?'

Ozzard brushed a speck of dust from the coat. He had mended Catherine's torn gown. There seemed no end to his skills.

The little man gave a shy smile. 'You did, Sir Richard. It was a pleasure.' He reached into a drawer and pulled out the fan she had brought with her from the sinking schooner.

'She left this.' He flinched under Bolitho's stare. 'I – I cleaned it up. There was some blood on it, y'see.'

'*Left it?*' Bolitho turned the fan over in his hands, remembering it, seeing her expression above it. He turned aside from a lantern as his eye misted over very slightly. He repeated, 'Left it?'

Ozzard watched him anxiously. 'All the rush. I expect she forgot.'

Bolitho gripped the fan tightly. No, she had not forgotten it.

Feet tramped towards the door and then Commodore Glassport, followed by the flag captain and Jenour, entered the cabin. Glassport's features were bright scarlet, as if he had been running uphill.

Bolitho said, 'Be seated. Some claret perhaps?'

Glassport seemed to revive at the word. 'I'd relish a glass, Sir Richard. Dammee, so much excitement, I think I should have retired long since!'

Ozzard filled their glasses and Bolitho said, 'To victory.'

Glassport stuck out his thick legs and licked his lips.

'A very fair claret, Sir Richard.'

Haven remarked, 'There are some letters, Sir Richard; they came in the last packet ship.' He watched as Jenour brought a small bundle and laid it on the table by Bolitho's elbow.

Bolitho said, 'See to the glasses, Ozzard.' Then, 'If you will excuse me, gentlemen.'

He slit open one letter. He recognised Belinda's handwriting immediately.

His glance moved rapidly across the letter, so that he had to stop and begin again.

My dear husband. It was as if the letter was for someone else. Belinda wrote briefly of her latest visit to London, and that she was now staying in a house which she had leased to await his approval. Elizabeth had had a cold, but was now well and had taken to the nurse whom Belinda had hired. The rest of the letter seemed to be about Nelson, and how the whole country was depending on him as he stood between the French and England.

Jenour asked quietly, 'Not bad news, Sir Richard?'

Bolitho tucked the letter into his coat. 'Really, Stephen, I wouldn't know.'

There had been nothing about Falmouth and people there he had known all his life. No concern, not even anger or remorse at the way they had parted.

Glassport said heavily, 'It is a mite quieter here now that the King's Inspector General is departed.' He gave a deep chuckle. 'I would not wish to get on the wrong side of that one.'

Haven said primly, 'His is another world. It is certainly not mine.'

Bolitho said, 'I shall see my captains tomorrow —' He looked at Glassport. 'By how much was the Indiaman delayed?'

Glassport peered at him, his mind already blurred by several large glasses of claret.

'When the gale eased, Sir Richard.'

Bolitho stood up without realising it. He must have misheard. 'Without waiting for Lady Somervell? By what vessel did she take passage after she arrived in the frigate?' Surely even Somervell, so eager to present the treasure to His Majesty in person, would have waited to be assured of Catherine's safety?

Glassport sensed his sudden anxiety and said, 'She did not leave, Sir Richard. I am still awaiting her instructions.' He seemed confused. 'Lady Somervell is at the house.'

Bolitho sat down again, then glanced across at the fan which lay on the wine cabinet.

He said, 'Once again, please excuse me, gentlemen. I will speak with you tomorrow.'

Later, as he listened to the trill of calls and the thud of Glassport's launch alongside, he walked to the stern windows and stared at the land. Pinpricks of light from the harbour and the houses behind it. A slow, glassy swell which tilted *Hyperion*'s heavy bulk just enough to make the rigging and blocks stir uneasily. A few pale stars. Bolitho took time to count them, to contain the sudden realisation which moments earlier had been disbelief.

Would you risk everything? The voice seemed to speak out loud.

Jenour re-entered silently and Bolitho saw his reflection in the thick glass beside him.

Bolitho said, 'Fetch Allday, if you would, Stephen, and call away my barge. I am going ashore directly.'

Jenour hesitated, unwilling to pit his beliefs against Bolitho's sudden determination.

Jenour had watched him when Glassport had blurted out about the woman *Phaedra* had snatched from the sea and the nearness of brutal rape and death. It had been like seeing a light rekindled. A cloud passing away.

He said, 'May I speak, Sir Richard?'

'Have I ever prevented you from doing so, Stephen?' He half turned, feeling the young lieutenant's uncertainty and discomfort. 'Is it about my leaving the ship?'

Jenour replied huskily, 'There is not a man under the flag who would not die for you, Sir Richard.'

Bolitho said, 'I doubt that.' He immediately sensed Jenour's dismay and added, 'Please continue.'

Jenour said, 'You intend to visit the lady, Sir Richard.' He fell silent, expecting an instant rebuff. When Bolitho said nothing he continued, 'By tomorrow the whole squadron will know. This time next month, all England will hear of it.' He looked down and said, 'I – I am sorry to speak out in this fashion. I have no right. It is just that I care very much.'

Bolitho took his arm and shook it gently. 'It took courage to speak as you did. An old enemy, John Paul Jones, was quoted as saying that "he who will not risk cannot win". Whatever his other faults may have been, a lack of courage was not one of them.' He smiled gravely. 'I *know* the risk, Stephen. Now fetch Allday.'

On the other side of the pantry door Ozzard withdrew his ear from the shutter and nodded very slowly.

He was suddenly grateful he had discovered the fan.

Bolitho barely noticed anything as he strode through the shadows to leave the harbour behind him. Only once he paused to regain his breath, and to try and test his feelings and the depth of his actions. He watched the anchored ships, their open gunports glittering across the even swell, the heavier, darker shape of the captured *Ciudad de Sevilla*. What would become of her? Would she be commandeered or sold to some wealthy merchant company, or even offered in trade to the Spaniards in an attempt to recover *Consort*? The latter was unlikely. The Dons would be humiliated enough at losing the treasure-ship and having another destroyed under their own fortress without adding to it.

When he arrived at the white walls of the house he paused again, conscious of his heart against his ribs, of the realisation that he had no plan in mind. Perhaps she would not even see him?

He walked up the carriage-drive and entered the main door, which was open to tempt any sea-breeze into the house. A sleeping servant, curled in a tall wicker chair by the entrance, did not even stir as Bolitho passed.

He stood in the pillared hall, staring at the shadows, some heavy tapestry glowing in the light from two candelabra. It was very still, and there seemed to be no air at all.

Bolitho saw a handbell on a carved chest by another door and played with the idea of ringing it. In that last fight aboard the treasure-ship, death had been a close companion, but it was no stranger to him. He had felt no fear at all, not even afterwards. He gripped his sword tightly. Where was that courage now that he really needed it?

Maybe Glassport had been mistaken and she had gone from here, overland this time to St John's. She had friends there. He recalled Jenour's anxiety, Allday's watchful silence as the barge had carried him to the jetty. Some Royal Marines on picket duty had scrambled into a semblance of attention as they realised that the vice-admiral had come ashore without a word of warning.

Allday had said, 'I shall wait, Sir Richard.'

'No. I can call for a boat when I need one.'

Allday had watched him leave. Bolitho wondered what he thought about it. Probably much the same as Jenour.

'Who is that?'

Bolitho turned and saw her on the curved stairway, framed against another dark tapestry. She wore a loose, pale gown, and was standing very still, a hand on the rail, the other concealed in the gown.

Then she exclaimed, 'You! I – I did not know –'

She made no move to come down and Bolitho walked slowly up the stairway towards her.

He said, 'I have just heard. I believed you gone.' He paused with one foot on the next step, afraid she would turn away. 'The Indiaman sailed without you.' He was careful not to mention Somervell by name. 'I could not bear to think of you here. Alone.'

She turned and he realised that she was holding a pistol.

He said, 'Give it to me.' He moved closer and held out his hand. 'Please, Kate.'

He took it from her fingers and realised it was cocked, ready to fire. He said quietly, 'You are safe now.'

She said, 'Come to the drawing room.' She might have shivered. 'There is more light.'

Bolitho followed her and waited for her to close the door behind them. It was a pleasant enough room, although nothing looked personal; it was occupied too often by visitors, strangers.

Bolitho laid the pistol on a table and watched her draw shutters across the window, where some moths were tapping against the glass, seeking the light.

She did not look at him. 'Sit there, Richard.' She shook her head vaguely. 'I was resting. I must do something to my hair.' Then she did turn to study him, a lingering, searching glance, as if she was seeking an answer to some unspoken question.

She said, 'I knew he would not wait. He took his mission very seriously. Put it above all else. It was my fault. I knew the matter was so dear to him, so urgent once you had made the plan into reality. I should not have gone in the schooner.' She repeated slowly, 'I knew he would not wait.'

'Why did you do it?'

She looked away and he saw her hand touch the handle on the other door, which was in deep shadow, away from the lights.

She replied, 'I felt like it.'

'You might have been killed, and then –'

She swung round, only her eyes flashing in the shadows. 'And *then*?'

She tossed her head with something like anger. 'Did you ask yourself that question too when you went after the *Ciudad de Sevilla*?' The ship's name seemed to intrude like a person. It had rolled so easily off her tongue, a cruel reminder that she had been married to a Spaniard. She continued, 'Someone of *your* value and rank, you of all people must have realised that you were taking a terrible risk? You knew that, I can see it on your face – must have known that any junior captain could have been sent, just as you once seized the ship I was aboard, when I first laid eyes on you!'

Bolitho was on his feet and for several seconds they stared at each other, both hurt and vulnerable because of it.

She said abruptly, 'Do not leave.' Then she vanished through the other door although Bolitho did not even see it open and close.

What had he expected? He was a fool, and looking a worse one. He had harmed her enough, too much.

Her voice came from beyond. 'I have put down my hair.' She waited until he faced the door. 'It is not quite right yet. Yesterday and today I walked along the foreshore. The salt air is cruel to vain women.'

Bolitho watched the long, pale gown. In the deep shadows she appeared to be floating like a ghost.

She said, 'You once gave me a ribbon for it, remember? I have tied it around my hair.' She shook her head so that one shoulder vanished in shadow, which Bolitho knew was her long dark hair.

'Do you see it, or had you forgotten that?'

He replied quietly. 'Never. You liked green so much. I had to get it for you —' He broke off as she put out her arms and ran towards him. It seemed to happen in a second. One moment she was there, pale against the other door, and the next she was pressed against him, her voice muffled while she clutched his shoulders as if to control her sudden despair.

She exclaimed, 'Look at me! In God's name, Richard, I *lied* to you, don't you see?'

Bolitho took her in his arms and pressed his cheek into her hair. It was not the ribbon he had bought in London from the old lady selling lace. This one was bright blue.

She ran her hand up to his neck and then laid it against his face. When she raised her eyes he saw that they were filled with emotion, pity.

She whispered, 'I did not *know*, Richard. Then, before you sailed with the convoy, I — I heard something about it — how you —' She held his face between her hands now. 'Oh, dearest of men, I had to be sure, to know!'

Bolitho pulled her closer so that he could hide his face above her shoulder. It must have been Allday. Only he would take the risk.

He heard her whisper, 'How bad is it?'

He said, 'I have grown used to it. Just sometimes it fails me.

142

Like the moment you stood there in the shadows.' He tried to smile. 'I was never able to outwit you.'

She leaned back in his arms and studied him. 'And the time you came to the reception here, when you almost fell on the stair. I should have known, ought to have understood!'

He watched the emotions crossing her face. She was tall and he was very aware of her nearness, of the trick which had misfired.

He said, 'I will leave if you wish.'

She slipped her hand through his arm. She was thinking aloud as they walked around the room, like lovers in a quiet park.

'There are people who must be able to help.'

He pressed her wrist to his side. 'They say not.'

She turned him towards her. 'We will *go on trying*. There is always hope.'

Bolitho said, 'To know that you care so much means everything.' He half-expected her to stop him but she remained quite still, her hands in his, so that their linked shadows appeared to be dancing across the walls.

'Now that we are together I never want to lose you. It must sound like madness, the babbling of some besotted youth.' The words were flooding out of him and she seemed to know how he needed to speak. 'I thought my life was in ruins, and knew that I had done a terrible harm to yours.' Then she made to speak but he shook her hands in his. 'No, it is all true. I was in love with a ghost. The realisation ripped me apart. Someone suggested I had a death-wish.'

She nodded slowly. 'I can guess who that was.' She met his gaze steadily, without fear. 'Do you really understand what you are saying, Richard? How high the stakes may be?'

He nodded. 'Even greater for you, Kate. I remember what you said about Nelson's infatuation.'

She smiled for the first time. 'To be called a whore is one thing; to be one is something very different.'

He gripped her hands even tighter. 'There are so many things –'

She twisted from his grip. 'They must wait.' Her eyes were very bright. 'We cannot.'

He said quietly, 'Call me what you did just now.'

'Dearest of men?' She pulled the ribbon from her hair and shook it loose across her shoulder. 'Whatever I have been or done, Richard, you have always been that to me.' She looked at him searchingly. 'Do you want me?'

He reached for her but she stepped away. 'You have answered me.' She gestured towards the other door. 'I need just a moment, *alone.*'

Without her the room seemed alien and hostile. Bolitho removed his coat and sword, and as an afterthought slid the latch on the door. His glance fell on the pistol and he uncocked it, seeing her face when she had discovered him. Knowing that she would have fired at the first hint of danger.

Then he walked to the door and opened it, the shadows and the fears forgotten as he saw her sitting on the bed, her hair shining in the candlelight.

She smiled at him, her knees drawn up to her chin like a child.

'So the proud vice-admiral has gone, and my daring captain has come in his place.'

Bolitho sat beside her, and then eased her shoulders down onto the bed.

She wore a long robe of ivory silk, tied beneath her throat by a thin ribbon. She watched him, his eyes as they explored her body, remembering perhaps how it had once been.

Then she took his hand and pulled it to her breast, tightening his fingers until he thought he must hurt her.

She whispered, 'Take me, Richard.' Then she shook her head very slowly. 'I know what you fear now, but I tell you, it is not out of pity, it is from the love I have never given to another man.'

She thrust her hands out on either side like one crucified and watched as he untied the ribbon and began to remove the robe.

Bolitho could feel the blood rushing through his brain; while he too felt momentarily like an onlooker as he bared her breasts and her arms until she was naked to the waist.

He gasped, 'Who did this to you?'

Her right shoulder was cruelly discoloured, one of the worst bruises he had ever seen.

But she reached up with one hand and dragged his mouth down to hers, her breathing as wild as his own.

She whispered, 'A Brown Bess has a fearsome kick, like a mule!'

She must have been firing a musket when the pirates had attacked the schooner. Like the pistol.

The kiss was endless. It was like sharing everything in a moment. Clinging to it, never wanting it to finish, but unable to hold on for a minute longer.

He heard her cry out as he threw the robe on the floor, saw her fists clench as he touched her, then covered her in his hand as if to prolong the need they had for each other.

She watched him tear off his clothes and touched the scar on his shoulder, remembering that too, and the fever she had held at bay.

She said huskily, 'I don't care about *afterward*, Richard.'

He saw her looking at him as his shadow covered her like a cloak. She said something like 'It's been so long —' Then she arched her body and gave a sharp cry as he entered her, her fingers pulling at him, dragging him closer and deeper until they were one.

Later, as they lay spent in each other's arms and watched the smoke standing up from the guttering candles, she said softly, 'You needed love. *My* love.' He held her against him as she added, 'Who cares about the tomorrows.'

He spoke into her hair. 'We shall make them ours too.'

Down on the jetty Allday seated himself comfortably on a stone bollard and began to fill his new pipe with tobacco. He had sent the barge back to the ship.

Bolitho would not be needing it for a bit yet, he thought. The tobacco was rich, well dampened with rum for good measure. Allday had dismissed the barge but found that he wanted to remain ashore himself. *Just in case.*

He put down a stone bottle of rum on the jetty and puffed contentedly on his new clay.

Perhaps there was a God in Heaven after all. He glanced towards the darkened house with the white walls.

Only God knew how this little lot might end, but for the present, and that was all any poor Jack could hope for, things were looking better for Our Dick. He grinned and reached down for the bottle. *An' that's no error.*

Gibraltar
1805

11

The Letter

His Britannic Majesty's Ship *Hyperion* heeled only very slightly as she changed tack yet again, her tapering jib-boom pointing almost due east.

Bolitho stood by the quarterdeck nettings and watched the great looming slab of Gibraltar rise above the larboard bow, misty-blue in the afternoon glare. It was mid-April.

Men moved purposefully about the decks, the lieutenants checking the set of each sail, conscious perhaps of this spectacular landfall. They had not touched land for six weeks, not since the squadron had quit English Harbour for the last time.

Bolitho took a telescope from the rack and trained it on the Rock. If the Spaniards ever succeeded in retaking this natural fortress, they could close the Mediterranean with the ease of slamming a giant door.

He focused the glass on the litter of shipping which seemed to rest at the foot of the Rock itself. More like a cluster of fallen moths than ships-of-war. It was only then that a newcomer could realise the size of it, the distance it still stood away from the slow-moving squadron.

He looked abeam. They were sailing as close as was prudently safe to the coast of Spain. Sunlight made diamond-bright reflections through the haze. He could imagine just how many telescopes were causing them as unseen eyes watched the small procession of ships. *Where bound? For what purpose?* Riders would be carrying intelligence to senior officers and lookout stations. The Dons could study the comings and goings with ease here at the narrowest part of the Strait of Gibraltar.

As if to give weight to his thoughts he heard Parris say to one of the midshipmen on the quarterdeck, 'Take a good look, Mr Blessed. Yonder lies the enemy.'

Bolitho tucked his hands behind him and thought over the past four months, since his new squadron had finally assembled at Antigua. Since Catherine had taken passage for England. The parting had been harder than he had expected, and still hurt like a raw wound.

She had sent one letter in that time. A warm, passionate letter, part of herself. *He was not to worry. They would meet again soon. There must be no scandal.* She was, as usual, thinking of him.

Bolitho had written back, and had also sent a letter to Belinda. The secret would soon be out, if not already; it was right if not honourable that she should hear it from him.

He moved across the quarterdeck and saw the helmsmen drop their eyes as his glance passed over them. He climbed a poop ladder and raised the glass again to study the ships which followed astern. It had kept his mind busy enough while the squadron had worked up together, had got used to one another's ways and peculiarities. There were four ships-of-the-line, all third-rates which to an ignorant landsman would look exactly like *Hyperion* in the van. Apart from *Obdurate*, the others had been new to Bolitho's standards, but watching them now he could feel pride instead of impatience.

Holding up to windward in the gentle north-westerly breeze he saw the little sloop-of-war *Phaedra*, sailing as near as she dared to the Spanish coast, Dunstan hoping possibly for a careless enemy trader to run under his guns.

Perhaps the most welcome addition was the thirty-six gun frigate *Tybalt*, which had arrived from England only just in time to join the squadron. She was commanded by a fiery Scot named Andrew McKee, who was more used to working independently. Bolitho understood the feeling even if he could not condone it. The life of any frigate captain was perhaps the most remote and monastic of all. In a crowded ship he remained alone beyond his cabin bulkhead, dining only occasionally with his officers, completely cut off from other ships and even the men he commanded. Bolitho smiled. Until now.

They had achieved little more in the Caribbean. A few indecisive attacks on enemy shipping and harbours, but after the reckless cutting-out of the treasure-ship from La Guaira all else seemed an anti-climax. As Glassport had said when the squadron had set sail for Gibraltar. *After that, life would never be the same.*

In more ways than one, Bolitho thought grimly.

It had been a strange feeling to quit Antigua. He had the lurking belief that he would never see the islands again. The Islands of Death, as the luckless army garrisons called them. Even *Hyperion* had not been immune from fever. Three seamen employed ashore had been taken ill, and had died with the disbelief of animals at slaughter.

He stepped from the ladder as Haven crossed the deck to speak with Penhaligon the master.

The latter remarked confidently, 'The wind stands fair, sir. We shall anchor at eight bells.'

Haven kept very much to himself, and apart from a few fits of almost insane anger, seemed content to leave matters to Parris. It was a tense and wary relationship, which must affect the whole wardroom. And yet the orders when they came by courier brig had been welcome. The storm was still brewing over Europe, with the antagonists watching and waiting for a campaign, even a single battle which might tip the balance.

The captured frigate *Consort*, renamed *Intrépido*, had slipped out of port unseen and unchecked. It was said that she too had left for Spain, to add her weight to His Catholic Majesty's considerable navy. She would be a boost to public morale as well. A prize snatched from the English, who were as ever desperate for more frigates.

Bolitho stared at the towering Rock. *Gibraltar for orders.* How many times had he read those words? He looked along the busy maindeck, the hands trimming the yards, or squinting up at the restless sails. It had been in Gibraltar that he had first met with *Hyperion*, when this endless war had barely begun. Did ships wonder about their fates? He saw Allday lounging by the

151

boat tier, his hat tilted down to shade his eyes from the hard glare. He would be remembering too. Bolitho saw the coxswain put one hand to his chest and grimace, then glance suspiciously around to make sure nobody had noticed. He was always in pain, but would never rest. Thinking about his son, of the girl at the Falmouth inn; of the last battle, or the next one.

Allday turned and looked up at the quarterdeck. Just a brief glance of recognition, as if he knew what Bolitho was thinking.

Like that dawn when he had gone to the jetty after leaving Catherine.

Allday had been there, had put his fingers to his mouth to give his piercing whistle which dismissed any boatswain's call to shame, to summon a boat.

When he had last seen Catherine he had argued with her, tried to persuade her to move away from London until they could face the storm together. She had been adamant. She intended to see Somervell, to tell him the truth. *Our love must triumph*.

When Bolitho had voiced his fears for her safety she had given the bubbling, uninhibited laugh he remembered so well. 'There has been no love between us, Richard. Not as you thought it was. I wanted a marriage for security, Lacey needed my strength, my backing.'

It still hurt to hear her use his name.

He could see her now, on that last evening before she had sailed. Those compelling eyes and high cheekbones, her incredible confidence.

He heard Jenour's footsteps on the worn planking. Ready to convey his orders to the other captains.

Bolitho saw a brig riding untidily on the blue water, her yards alive with flags as she conveyed news of the squadron to the Rock fortress. There might even be word from Catherine. He had reread her only letter until he knew each line perfectly.

Such a striking, vibrant woman. Somervell must be mad not to fight for her love.

One night when they had been lying together, watching the moonlight through the shutters, she had told him something of her past. He already knew about her first marriage to an English soldier-of-fortune who had died in a brawl in Spain before the

Franco-Spanish Alliance. She had been just a young girl at the time, who had been raised in London, *a part you would not dare to believe, dear Richard!* She had laughed, and nuzzled his shoulder, but he had heard the sadness too. Before that she had been on the stage. When she was fourteen. A long hard journey to become the wife of the Inspector General. Then there had been Luis Pareja, who had been killed after Bolitho had taken their ship as a prize, then defended it against Barbary pirates.

Pareja had been twice her age, but she had cared for him deeply; for his gentle kindness above all, something which until then had been denied her.

Pareja had provided for her well, although she had had no idea that she owned anything but some jewellery she had been wearing aboard that ship when Bolitho had burst into her life.

Their first confrontation had been one of fire. She had spat out her bitter despair and hate. It was still hard to fathom when all that had changed to an equally fiery love.

He took the telescope again and trained it on the brig.

Catherine had missed the sight she had sworn to witness. Almost the last thing Bolitho had seen when *Hyperion* left English Harbour had been a line of grisly gibbets, their sun-blackened remains left as a reminder and a warning to other would-be pirates.

He saw Parris standing forward along the starboard gangway, to make sure that when they anchored nobody ashore would find even the smallest fault in the manoeuvre.

Parris had taken a working party ashore at Antigua to move Catherine's trunks aboard the packet-ship.

Catherine had slipped her hand through Bolitho's arm while they had watched the sailors carrying the boxes towards the jetty.

She had said, 'I don't like that man.'

Bolitho had been surprised. 'He's a good officer, brave too. What don't you like about him?'

She had shrugged, eager to change the subject. 'He gives me the shivers.'

Bolitho glanced again at the first lieutenant. How simply he could raise a grin from a seaman, or the obvious awe of a midshipman. Maybe he reminded her of someone in her past? It would be easy to picture Parris as a soldier-of-fortune.

Jenour remarked, 'My first time here, Sir Richard.'

Bolitho nodded. 'I've been glad enough to see the Rock once or twice after a rough passage.'

Captain Haven called, 'Stand by to alter course two points to larboard!'

Bolitho watched his shoulders and wondered. Or had Catherine recognised in Parris what Haven obviously believed?

Bolitho took out his watch as the seamen hurried to the braces and halliards.

'General signal. *Tack in succession.*'

The waiting midshipmen bustled amongst a mass of bunting, while their men bent on each flag with the speed of light.

'All acknowledged, sir!'

Haven glowered. 'About time, dammit!'

Jenour said carefully, 'I was wondering about our orders, Sir Richard?'

Bolitho smiled. 'You are not alone. North to Biscay and the damned blockade of Brest and Lorient. Or join Lord Nelson? The dice can fall either way.'

Bolitho shaded his eyes to watch the other ships shortening sail in preparation for the last leg to the anchorage.

Astern of *Obdurate* was another veteran, *Crusader*. Twenty-five years old, and like most third-rates she had tasted the fire of battle many times. Bolitho had seen her at Toulon and in the West Indies, seeking French landings in Ireland, or standing in the blazing line at the Nile. *Redoubtable* and *Capricious* completed the squadron, the latter being commanded by Captain William Merrye, whose grandfather had once been an infamous smuggler; or so the story had it. Seventy-fours were the backbone of the fleet, any fleet. Bolitho glanced up at his flag at the fore. It looked right and proper there.

Then the drawn-out ceremony of gun-salutes to the Rock, repeated and acknowledged until the anchorage was partly hidden by smoke, the echoes sighing across to Algeciras like an added insult.

Bolitho saw the guardboat with its huge flag and motionless

oars. Marking where they should drop anchor. He thought suddenly of the Spanish boat at La Guaira, smashed apart under the schooner's stem.

'*Anchor!*'

They must make a fine, if familiar, sight to the people on the shore, Bolitho thought.

Leviathans turning into the gentle wind, with all canvas clewed up but for topsails and jibs.

'Tops'l clew lines! *Start that man!* Lively there!'

'Helm a-lee!'

Bolitho clenched his fists as Parris's arm fell. '*Let go!*'

The great anchor threw up a pale waterspout, while high overhead the topsails vanished against their yards as if to a single hand.

Bolitho looked quickly at the other ships, swinging now to their cables, each captain determined to hold a perfect bearing on his vice-admiral.

Boats were already being swayed out, the excitement of seeing the great harbour after weeks at sea contained and suppressed by leather-lunged boatswain's mates and petty officers.

'Gig approaching, sir!'

Bolitho saw the small boat rising and dipping smartly across the slight swell. Their first encounter.

'I shall go aft, Mr Jenour.' He spoke formally in front of Haven. 'As soon as –'

He turned as the quartermaster yelled the age-old challenge.

'Boat ahoy?'

The answer came back from the gig. '*Firefly!*'

Jenour said, 'Someone's captain coming to see us already, Sir Richard.' Then he saw Bolitho's eyes, his look of relief and something more.

Bolitho said, 'I shall greet *Firefly*'s captain myself.'

The young commander almost bounded up *Hyperion*'s tumblehome. Those who did not know stared with astonishment as their admiral threw his arms about the youthful officer who at first glance could have been his brother.

Bolitho held him and shook his shoulders gently. 'Adam. Of all people.'

Commander Adam Bolitho of the brig *Firefly* grinned with delight, his teeth very white in his sunburned face.

All he could say was, 'Well, Uncle!'

Bolitho stood in the centre of his cabin, while Yovell and Jenour sorted through a bag of despatches and letters which Adam had brought from the shore.

Adam said, 'It was amazing bad luck, Uncle. The Frogs put to sea under Admiral Villeneuve, and Our Nel went looking for them. But while the little admiral was searching around Malta and Alexandria, Villeneuve slipped through the Strait and into the Atlantic. In God's name, Uncle, had your orders been sent earlier you might have met up with 'em! Thank the high heavens you did not!'

Bolitho smiled quietly. Adam spoke with the ease and confidence of a seasoned old campaigner, and he was twenty-four years old; twenty-five in two months' time.

Adam said, 'This old ship, Uncle. Look at us now, eh?'

Bolitho nodded as Yovell placed an official Admiralty envelope before him. Adam had joined *Hyperion* as his first ship, a thin, pale youth, but with all the determination and wildness of a young colt.

Indeed, he thought. Look at us now.

So the French had put to sea at last. Past Gibraltar and across the Atlantic with Nelson eventually in hot pursuit. Villeneuve had apparently sailed westward, though for what purpose nobody seemed quite sure. Bolitho read swiftly, aware of Adam watching him. Wanting to talk with him more than anything, but needing to know what was happening; it might affect them all.

Bolitho handed the letter to Yovell and said, 'So the French are on the move. Is it a trick or are they out to divide our forces?'

Adam was right. Had he been ordered to leave Antigua earlier they might well have met up with the enemy. Five third-rates against one of the finest fleets in the world. The outcome would have been in no doubt. But at least they might have delayed Villeneuve until Nelson caught up with them. He smiled. *Our Nel* indeed.

Bolitho took the next letter, already opened by Jenour, who

had barely taken his eyes off the young commander since he had stepped aboard. A part of the Bolitho story he did not yet share.

Bolitho said softly, 'Hell's teeth. I am to relieve Thomas Herrick at Malta.' He examined his feelings. He should be happy to see the man who was his best friend. After the court of enquiry into Valentine Keen's behaviour, when only Bolitho's word had prevented a court-martial, he was not so certain. Deep in his heart Bolitho knew Herrick had been in the right. *Would I have twisted the rules in his place?* The question had never been answered.

Adam eyed him gravely. 'But first you sail for England, Uncle.' He forced a grin. 'With me.'

Bolitho took the envelope from him and slit it open. It was strange that of all his people who were dear to him, only Adam had ever met the famous Nelson, had carried more despatches from him in his brig *Firefly* than anybody.

The new squadron would rest and take on victuals at Gibraltar. Nelson had written in his strange sloping hand, 'Doubtless the care and attention of English Harbour will have left much to complain on!' Was there anything he did not know about?

Bolitho was to be released from his command for a brief visit to their Lordships of Admiralty. The letter ended with the barb Nelson so enjoyed. 'There you may discover how well they fight their wars with words and paper instead of ordnance and good steel. . . .'

It was true that the squadron could do with fresh victualling and some spare spars. The blockade was likely to be a lengthy one. The French must return to port, if only to await reinforcements from their Spanish ally. One of which would likely be the *Intrépido*.

Bolitho glanced at the pile of charts on a nearby table. The vastness of a great ocean which could hide or swallow a fleet with ease. Thank God Catherine had written her letter from England, otherwise he would have been fretting that she had been taken by the enemy.

He looked at Adam and saw the sudden apprehension in his eyes.

Bolitho said to the others, 'Please leave us a while.' He touched

157

Jenour's arm. 'Delve through the rest of the pile, Stephen. I am afraid I have come to rely too much on you.'

The door closed behind them and Adam said quietly, 'That was kindly done, Uncle. The flag lieutenant is another one caught in your spell.'

Bolitho asked, 'What is wrong?'

Adam stood up and crossed to the stern windows. How like his father, Bolitho thought. Hugh would have been proud of him this day, to see him in command of his own ship.

'I know you hate deceit, Uncle.'

'So?'

'I once fought a stupid duel over yonder.'

'I've not forgotten, Adam.'

He shifted his feet on the checkered canvas deck. 'Is it true what they're saying?'

'I expect so. Some of it anyway.'

Adam turned, his hair shining in the sunlight. 'Is it what you want?'

Bolitho nodded. 'I will see that no harm is done to you, Adam. You have been hurt enough, if not by your family then because of it.'

Adam's chin lifted. 'I shall be all right, Uncle. Lord Nelson said to me that England needs all her sons now –'

Bolitho stared. His father had said those same words when he had given him the old sword, which should have been Hugh's but for his disgrace. It was uncanny.

Adam continued, 'If one man can love another, then you have mine, Uncle. You know that already, but you may wish to remember it when others turn against you, which they will. I do not know the lady, but then I do not really know the Lady Belinda.' He looked down, embarrassed. 'In God's name, I am out of my depth!'

Bolitho walked to the windows and stared hard at the nearest ship's motionless reflection.

'She has my heart, Adam. With her I am a man again. Without her I am like a ship denied sails.'

Adam faced him. 'I believe this call to London is for you to settle matters. To clear the air.'

'By denying the truth?'

'It is what I think, Uncle.'

He smiled sadly. 'So wise a head on so young a pair of shoulders.'

Adam shrugged, and appeared suddenly vulnerable. Like the fourteen-year old midshipman who had once walked all the way from his home in Penzance to join Bolitho's *Hyperion* after the death of his mother. A whore she might have been, but she had tried to care for the boy. And Hugh had known nothing about it, not until it was all too late.

Adam said, 'At least we will keep one another company. I have more despatches from Lord Nelson.' He eyed him steadily. 'I am to carry you back to the squadron when your affairs in London are settled.'

Who had decided that, Bolitho wondered? Nelson himself, getting his own back on those who despised his infatuation with Emma Hamilton, and showing them he had a kindred spirit? Or someone more highly placed, who would use family unity to make him change his mind? He could still not accept that he was going to see Catherine again so soon. Even the news of a temporary French breakout seemed unimportant by comparison.

He recalled the others to the cabin and said, 'I shall require you to remain here in my absence, Stephen.' He shook his head to cool down the protests and added, 'I need you in *Hyperion*; do you know what I am saying?'

He saw understanding clearing the disappointment from the lieutenant's eyes.

Bolitho said, 'An ally, if you like, someone who will send me word if anything untoward happens.'

He looked at Yovell. 'Help the flag lieutenant all you can.' He forced a smile. 'A rock in stormy seas, eh?'

Yovell did not smile. 'I'm worried about *you*, Sir Richard.'

Bolitho looked at them. 'Good friends, all of you. But just now and then I have to act alone.'

He thought suddenly of the livid scar on Somervell's neck. Was that what was intended to settle the matter? A duel?

He dismissed the idea immediately. Somervell was too anxious to please the King. No, it was to be a skirmish of a different kind.

He said, 'I shall take Allday with me.'

Adam clapped one hand over his hair and exclaimed, 'I am an idiot! I completely forgot it!' He pointed vaguely through the windows. 'I have taken young Bankart as my own coxswain! He marched aboard *Firefly* at Plymouth when I called there for orders.'

'That was good of you, Adam.'

He grinned but it did not reach his eyes. 'Only right that one bastard should help another!'

The little brig *Firefly* weighed and put to sea the following day. It was a rush from the moment Bolitho had read the despatches, and he barely had time to summon his captains and to tell them to use the next weeks to supply and refurbish their ships.

Haven had listened to the instructions without any show of surprise or excitement. Bolitho had impressed on him more than any other, that as flag captain it was his obliged duty to watch over the squadron, and not merely the affairs of his own command. He had also made it very clear that no matter what impressive plan Captain McKee of the frigate *Tybalt* should put forward as an excuse to steal away and regain his independence, it was to be denied. *I need that frigate as much, if not more than I need him.*

After *Hyperion*'s cabin, the brig's quarters seemed like a cupboard. Only beneath the skylight could Bolitho stand upright, and he knew that the ship's company had to exist in some parts where the deckhead was only four feet six inches high.

But the vessel seemed as lively inboard as out, and Bolitho quickly noticed that there was a very relaxed feeling between afterguard and forecastle, and was secretly proud of what his nephew had done.

He was disturbed by the fact there had been no more news from Catherine and had told himself she was trying to keep up normal appearances until the gossip died, or was transferred to another. But it worried him nevertheless, especially after reading the one letter which had been sent by Belinda.

It was a cool, and what his mother would have called a *sensible* letter. She referred only briefly to the infatuation with *this woman*, something which could be forgiven if not understood. Nothing would be allowed to stand between them. *I shall not tolerate it.* Had she written in anger he might have felt less troubled. Perhaps she had already met Catherine at one of the receptions which attracted Belinda so much. But that also seemed unlikely.

Once into the Western Ocean *Firefly* began to live up to her name. Adam kept her standing well out and away from land as day by day they beat their way around the southern shores of Portugal, then north towards the Bay of Biscay. When he asked Adam why he was standing so far out from land he explained with an awkward grin that it was to avoid the weatherbeaten ships of the blockading squadrons. 'If any captain sees *Firefly* he'll make a signal for me to heave-to so that he can pass over mail for England! This time, I do not have an hour to waste!'

Bolitho found time to pity the men of the blockading squadrons. Week in and week out they tacked up and down in all weathers, while the enemy rested safely in harbour and watched their every move. It was the most hated duty of all, as *Hyperion*'s newer hands would soon appreciate.

The passage of twelve hundred miles from Gibraltar to Portsmouth was one of the liveliest Bolitho could recall. He spent much of the time on deck with Adam, shouting to each other above the roar of spray and wind as the brig spread her canvas to such a degree that Bolitho wondered why the sticks were not torn out of her.

It was exhilarating to be with him again, to see how he had changed from the eager lieutenant to a man in command. Who knew the strain of every piece of cordage and canvas, and could give confidence to those who did not. Sometimes he liked to quote Nelson, the hero he so obviously admired. His first lieutenant, quite new to Bolitho, had asked him nervously about reefing when the Biscay gales had sprung up suddenly like some fierce tribe.

Adam had called above the din, 'It is time to reef when you *feel* like it!'

Another time he had quoted his uncle when a master's mate had asked about getting the men fed, before or after changing tack?

Adam had glanced across at Bolitho and smiled. 'The people come first this time.'

Then into the Western Approaches and up the Channel, exchanging signals with watchful patrols, and then on a glorious spring morning they sighted the Isle of Wight. Five and a half days from Gibraltar. They had flown right enough.

Bolitho and Adam went to a smaller inn, and not the George, to await the *Portsmouth Flier* to London. Perhaps they had both spoken so much about the last time they had left Portsmouth together. Too many memories, maybe? Like being cleansed of something bad.

It had been like a tonic to see Allday with his son throughout the lively passage. Now they too were saying their farewells, while young Bankart remained with his ship and Allday boarded the coach. Bolitho protested that Allday had to be an outsider, because the coach was filled to capacity.

Allday merely grinned and looked scornfully at the plump merchants who were the other passengers.

'I want to see the land, Sir Richard, not listen to th' bleatings o' th' likes o' them! I'll be fine on the upper deck!'

Bolitho settled in a corner, his eyes closed as a defence against conversation. Several people had noticed his rank, and were probably waiting to ask him about *the war*. At least the merchants appeared to be doing well out of it, he thought.

Adam sat opposite him, his eyes distant as he watched the rolling Hampshire countryside, his reflection in the coach window like the portraits at Falmouth.

On and on, stops for fresh horses, tankards of ale from saucy wenches at the various coaching inns. Heavy meals when they halted so that the passengers could ease their aching muscles and test their appetites on anything from rabbit pie to the best beef. The further you went from the sea, the less sign of war you found, Bolitho decided.

The coach ground to a halt at the final inn at Ripley in the county of Surrey.

Bolitho walked along the narrow street, his cloak worn to conceal his uniform although the air was warm and filled with the scent of flowers.

England. *My England.*

He watched the steaming horses being led to their stables and sighed. Tomorrow they would alight at the George in Southwark. *London.*

Then she would give him back his confidence. Standing there, without a uniform in sight, and the sound of laughter from the inn he found he was able to say it out loud.

'Kate. I love thee.'

12

The One-Legged Man

Admiral Sir Owen Godschale watched while his servant carried a decanter of claret to a small table and then withdrew. Outside the tall windows the sun was shining, the air hot and dusty, remote like the muffled sounds of countless carriage wheels.

Bolitho took time to sip the claret, surprised that the Admiralty could still make him ill-at-ease and on the defensive. Everything had changed for him; it should be obvious, he thought. He and Adam had been ushered into a small, comfortably furnished library, something quite different from the large reception room he had seen earlier. It had been crowded with sea-officers, mostly captains, or so it had appeared. Restlessly waiting to meet a senior officer or his lackey, to ask favours, to plead for commands, new ships, almost anything. *As I once was*, he had thought. He still could not get used to the immediate respect, the servility of the Admiralty's servants and guardians.

The admiral was a handsome, powerfully built man who had distinguished himself in the American Revolution. A contemporary of Bolitho's, they had in fact been posted on the same day. There was little to show of that youthful and daring frigate captain now, Bolitho thought. Godschale looked comfortably sleek, his hands and features pale as if he had not been at sea for years.

He had not held this high appointment for very long. It seemed likely he would discourage anything controversial which might delay or damage his plans to enter the House of Lords.

Godschale was saying, 'It warms the heart to read of your exploits, Sir Richard. We in Admiralty too often feel cut adrift from the actual deeds which we can only plan, and which with God's guidance, can be brought to a victorious fruition.'

Bolitho relaxed slightly. He thought of Nelson's wry comment on wars fought with words and paper. Across the room, his eyes alert, Adam sat with an untouched glass by his side. Was it a courtesy, or part of a plot to include him in this meeting?

Godschale warmed to his theme. 'The treasure-ship was one such reward, *although*. . . .' his voice dragged over the word. 'There are some who might suggest you took too much upon yourself. Your task is to lead and to offer the encouragement of your experience, but that is in the past. We have to think of the future.'

Bolitho asked, 'Why was I brought here, Sir Owen?'

The admiral smiled and toyed with his empty glass. 'To put you in the position of knowing what is happening in Europe, and to reward you for your gallant action. I believe it is His Majesty's pleasure to offer you the honorary rank of Lieutenant Colonel in the Royal Marines.'

Bolitho looked at his hands. When was Godschale getting to the point? An honorary appointment to the Royal Marines was only useful if you were faced by a confrontation between Army and Navy in some difficult campaign. It was an honour, of course, but it hardly warranted bringing him away from his squadron.

Godschale said, 'We believe that the French are gathering their fleet in several different areas. Your transfer to the flag at Malta will enable you to disperse your squadron to best advantage.'

'The French are said to be at Martinique, Sir Owen. Nelson declares –'

The admiral showed his teeth like a gentle fox. 'Nelson is not above being wrong, Sir Richard. He may be the country's darling; he is not immune to false judgement.'

The admiral included Adam for the first time. 'I am able to tell your nephew, and it is my honour so to do, that he is appointed captain from the first of June.' He smiled, pleased with himself. 'The *Glorious* First of June, eh, Commander?'

165

Adam stared at him, then at Bolitho. 'Why, I thank you, Sir Owen!'

The admiral wagged his finger. 'You have more than earned your promotion. If you continue as you have I see no reason for your advancement to falter, eh?'

Bolitho saw the mixed emotions on Adam's sunburned features. Promotion. Every young officer's hope and dream. Three years more and he could be a post-captain. But was it a just reward, or a bribe? With the rank would come a different command, maybe even a frigate, what he had always talked about; as his uncle had once been, his father too, except that Hugh had fought on the wrong side.

Godschale turned to Bolitho. 'It is *good* to be here with you today, Sir Richard. A long, long climb since the Saintes in eighty-two. I wonder if many people realise how hard it is, how easy to fall from grace, sometimes through no fault of ours, eh?'

He must have seen the coldness in Bolitho's eyes and hurried on, 'Before you quit London and return to Gibraltar, you must dine with me.' He glanced only briefly at Adam. 'You too, of course. Wives, a few friends, that kind of affair. It does no harm at all.'

It was not really a request, Bolitho thought. It was an order.

'I am not certain that Lady Belinda is still in London. I have not had the time yet to –'

Godschale looked meaningly at a gilded clock. 'Quite so. You are a busy man. But never fear, my wife saw her just a day back. They are good company for one another while you and I deal with the dirtier matters of war!' He chuckled. 'Settled then.'

Bolitho stood up. He would have to see her anyway, but why no word from or about Catherine? He had gone alone to her house against Adam's wishes, but had got no further than the entrance. An imposing footman had assured him that his visit would be noted, but Viscount Somervell had left the country again on the King's service, and her ladyship was most likely with him.

He knew a lot more than he was saying. And so did Godschale. Even the cheap comment to Adam had an edge to it. The promotion was his right; he had won it without favour and against all prejudice.

Outside the Admiralty building the air seemed cleaner, and Bolitho said, 'What did you make of that?'

Adam shrugged. 'I am not that much of a fool that I could not recognise a threat, Uncle.' His chin lifted again. 'What do you want me to do?'

'You may become involved, Adam.'

He grinned, the strain dropping away like an unwanted mask. 'I *am* involved, sir!'

'Very well. I shall go to the house I mentioned.' He smiled at a memory. 'Browne, once my flag lieutenant, placed it at my disposal whenever I needed it.' *Browne with an 'e'*. Since the death of his father, he had succeeded to the title and had taken his place well ahead of Godschale in the House of Lords.

Adam nodded. 'I will put the word about.' He glanced at the imposing buildings and richly dressed passers-by. 'Though this is not some seaport. A man could be lost forever here.'

He glanced at him thoughtfully, 'Are you quite sure, Uncle? Maybe she *has* gone, thinking it best for you,' he faltered, 'as it might well be. She sounds like a most honourable lady.'

'I am sure, Adam, and thank you for that. I know not where Valentine Keen is at present, and there is no time to reach him by letter. I have days, not weeks.'

He must have displayed his anxiety, and Adam said, 'Rest easy, Uncle. You have many friends.'

They fell into step and walked into the sunshine. There were some people watching the passing carriages and one turned as the two officers appeared.

He called, 'Look, lads, 'tis 'im!' He waved a battered hat. 'God bless you, Dick! Give the Frogs another drubbin'!'

Someone gave a cheer and shouted, 'Don't you listen to them other buggers!'

Bolitho smiled, although his heart felt like breaking.

Then he said quietly, 'Yes, I do have friends after all.'

True to the promise of his one-time flag lieutenant, Bolitho was warmly received at the house in Arlington Street. The master was away in the North of England, the housekeeper explained, but she had her instructions, and conducted them to a suite of pleasant rooms on the first floor. Adam left almost at once to see friends who might be able to shed some light on Catherine's disappearance; for Bolitho was now convinced that she had vanished. He dreaded that Adam might be right, that she had gone away with Somervell for appearance's sake, to save their reputations.

On the first morning Bolitho left the house. He had an immediate clash with Allday, who protested at being left behind.

Bolitho had insisted. 'This is not the quarterdeck with some Frenchie about to board us, old friend!'

Allday had glared out at the busy street. 'The more I'm in London, the less I trust th' place!'

Bolitho had said, 'I need you here. In case someone comes. The housekeeper might turn him away otherwise.'

Or her, Allday thought darkly.

It was not a long walk to the quiet square of which Belinda had written in her letter.

He paused to look at some children who were playing in the grassy centre of the square, their nursemaids standing nearby, gossiping about their respective families, he thought.

One of the little girls might be Elizabeth. It brought him all aback to realise that she must have changed a lot since he had last seen her. She would be three soon. He saw two of the nursemaids curtsy to him, and touched his hat in reply.

Another sailor home from the sea. It seemed ironic now. How would he conduct the next moments in his life?

The house was tall and elegant, like many which had been built in His Majesty's reign. Wide steps flanked by ornate iron railings, with three stories above to match the houses on either side. A servant opened the door and stared at him for several seconds. Then she bobbed in a deep curtsy, and, stammering apologies, took his hat and showed him into a pillared hall with a blue and gilt-leafed ceiling.

'This way, sir!'

She opened a pair of doors, and stood aside while he walked into an equally fine drawing-room. The furniture looked foreign to him, and the curtains and matching carpets were, he guessed, newly made. He thought of the rambling grey house in Falmouth. Compared with this it was like a farm.

He caught sight of himself in a tall, gilded mirror, and automatically straightened his shoulders. His face looked deeply tanned above his spotless waistcoat and breeches, but the uniform made him look like someone he did not know.

Bolitho tried to relax, to pitch his ear to the muted sounds above him in the house. Another world.

The doors opened suddenly and she walked quickly into the room. She was dressed in dark blue which almost matched his own coat, and her hair was piled high to show her small ears and the jewellery around her neck. She looked very composed, defiant.

He said, 'I sent a note. I hope this is convenient?'

She did not take her eyes from him; she was examining him as if to seek some injury or disfigurement, or that he had changed in another way.

'I think it absurd that you should be staying in somebody else's house.'

Bolitho shrugged. 'It seemed best until —'

'Until you saw how I would behave to you, is that it?'

They faced each other, more like strangers than husband and wife.

He replied, 'I tried to explain in my letter —'

She waved him down. 'My cousin is here. He begged me to forgive your foolishness, for all our sakes. I have been much embarrassed by your reckless affair. You are a senior officer of repute, yet you behave like some foul-mouthed seaman with his doxy on the waterfront!'

Bolitho looked around the room; his heart, like his voice, was heavy.

'Some of those foul-mouthed sailors are dying at this very moment to protect houses like this.'

She smiled briefly, as if she had discovered what she had been seeking. 'Tut, Richard! Your share of prize money from the Spanish galleon will more than cover it, so do not lose the issue in hypocrisy!'

Bolitho said flatly, 'It is not an affair.'

'I see.' She moved to a window and touched a long curtain. 'Then where is this woman you seem to have lost your mind to?' She swung round, her eyes angry. 'I shall tell you! She is with her husband Viscount Somervell, who is apparently more willing to forgive and forget than I!'

'You saw him?'

She tossed her head, her fingers stroking the curtain more quickly to reveal her agitation.

'Of course. We were both very concerned. It was humiliating and degrading.'

'I regret that.'

'But not what you did?'

'That is unfair.' He watched her, amazed that his voice was calm when his whole being was in turmoil. 'But not unexpected.'

She looked past him at the room. 'This belonged to the Duke of Richmond. It is a fine house. Suitable for us. For you.'

Bolitho heard a sound and saw a small child being led past the doors. He knew it was Elizabeth despite her disguise of frothy lace and pale blue silk.

She turned just once, hanging to the hand of her nursemaid. She stared at him without recognition and then walked on.

Bolitho said, 'She knew me not.'

'What did you expect?' Then her voice softened. 'It can and must change. Given time –'

He looked at her, hiding his despair. 'Live here? Give up the sea when our very country is in peril? What is this madness, when people cannot see the danger?'

'You can still serve, Richard. Sir Owen Godschale commands the greatest respect both at Court and in Parliament.'

Bolitho rested his hands on the cool marble mantel. 'I cannot do it.'

She watched him in the mirror. 'Then at least escort me to Sir Owen's reception and dinner. I understand we shall receive notice of it this day.' She hesitated for the first time. 'So that people can see the emptiness of the gossip. She has gone, Richard. Have no doubt of that. Maybe it was an honest reaction, or perhaps she saw where her best fortune lies.' She smiled as he turned hotly towards her. 'Believe what you will. I am thinking of you now. After all, I do have the *right*!'

Bolitho said quietly, 'I shall stay at the other house until tomorrow. I have to think.'

She nodded, her eyes very clear. 'I understand. I know your moods. Tomorrow we shall begin again. I shall forgive, while you must try to forget. Do not damage your family name because of a momentary infatuation. We parted badly, so I must carry some of the blame.'

She walked beside him to the entrance hall. At no time had they touched, let alone embraced.

She asked, 'Is everything well with you? I did hear that you had been ill.'

He took his hat from the gaping servant. 'I am well enough, thank you.'

Then he turned and walked out into the square as the door closed behind him.

How could he go to the reception and act as if nothing had happened? If he never saw Catherine again, he would never forget her and what she had done for him.

Almost out loud he said, 'I cannot believe she would run away!' The words were torn from him, and he did not even notice two people turn to stare after him.

Allday greeted him warily. 'No news, Sir Richard.'

Bolitho threw himself into a chair. 'Fetch me a glass of something, will you?'

'Some nice cool hock?'

Allday watched worriedly as Bolitho replied, 'No. Brandy this time.'

He drank two glasses before its warmth steadied his mind.

'In God's name, I am in hell.'

Allday refilled the glass. It was likely the best thing to make him forget.

He stared round the room. Get back to the sea. *That* he could understand.

Bolitho's head lolled and the empty glass fell unheeded on the carpet.

The dream was sudden and violent. Catherine pulling at him, her breasts bared as she was dragged away from him, her screams probing at his brain like hot irons.

He awoke with a start and saw Allday release his arm, his face full of concern.

Bolitho gasped, 'I – I'm sorry! It was a nightmare –' He stared round; the room was darker. 'How long have I been here?'

Allday watched him grimly. 'That don't matter now, beggin' yer pardon.' He jabbed his thumb at the door. 'There's someone here to see you. Wouldn't talk to no one else.'

Bolitho's aching mind cleared. 'What about?' He shook his head. 'No matter, fetch him in.'

He got to his feet and stared at his reflection in the window. *I am losing my sanity.*

Allday pouted. 'Might be a beggar.'

'Fetch him.'

He heard Allday's familiar tread, and a strange clumping step which reminded him of an old friend he had lost contact with. But the man who was ushered in by Allday was nobody he recognised, nor was his rough uniform familiar.

The visitor removed his outdated tricorn hat to reveal untidy greying hair. He was badly stooped, and Bolitho guessed it was because of his crude wooden leg.

He asked, 'Can I help you? I am –'

The man peered at him and nodded firmly. 'I knows 'oo you are, zur.'

He had a faint West Country accent, and the fashion in which he touched his forehead marked him as an old sailor.

But the uniform with its plain brass buttons was like nothing Bolitho had ever seen.

He said, 'Will you be seated?' He gestured to Allday. 'A glass for – what may I call you?'

The man balanced awkwardly on a chair and nodded again very slowly. 'You won't recall, zur. But me name's Vanzell –'

Allday exclaimed, 'Bless you, so it is!' He stared at the one-legged man and added, 'Gun-captain in th' *Phalarope.*'

Bolitho gripped the back of a chair to contain his racing thoughts. All those years, and yet he could not understand why he had not recognised the man called Vanzell. A Devonian like Yovell. It was over twenty years back, when he had been a *boy-captain* like Adam would soon be.

The Saintes Godschale had dismissed as a sentimental memory. It was not like that to Bolitho. The shattered line of

172

battle, the roar of cannon fire while men fell and died, including his first coxswain, Stockdale, who had fallen protecting him. He glanced at Allday, seeing the same memory on his rugged features. He had been there too, as a pressed man, but one who was still with him as a faithful friend.

Vanzell watched their recognition with satisfaction. Then he said, 'I never forget, y'see. 'Ow you helped me an' th' wife when I was cast ashore after losin' me pin to a Froggie ball. You saved us, an' that's a fact, zur.' He put down the glass and stared at him with sudden determination.

'I 'eard you was in London, zur. So I come meself. To try an' repay what you did for me an' th' wife, God rest her soul. There's only me now, but I'll not forget what 'appened after them bastards raked our decks that day.'

Bolitho sat down and faced him. 'What are you doing now?' He tried to conceal the anxiety and urgency in his bearing. This man, this tattered memory from the past, was frightened. For some reason it had cost a lot for him to come.

Vanzell said, 'It will lose me me job, zur.' He was thinking aloud. 'They all knows I once served under you. They'll not forgive me, not never.'

He made up his mind and studied Bolitho searchingly. 'I'm a watchman, zur, it was all I could get. They've no time for half-timbered Jacks no more.' His hand shook as he took another glass from Allday. Then he added huskily. 'I'm at th' Waites, zur.'

'What is that?'

Allday said sharply, 'It's a prison.'

Vanzell downed the glass in one gulp. 'They got 'er there. I know, 'cause I saw 'er, an' I 'eard what the others was sayin' about you both.'

Bolitho could feel the blood rushing through his brain.

In a prison. It was impossible. But he knew it was true.

The man was saying to Allday, 'It's a filthy place full o' scum. Debtors an' lunatics, a bedlam you'd not believe.'

Allday glanced tightly at Bolitho. 'Oh, yes I would, matey.'

Bolitho said, 'Tell the housekeeper I shall need a carriage at once. Do you know where this place is?' Allday shook his head.

Vanzell said, 'I – I'll show 'ee, zur.'

'Good.' Bolitho's mind was suddenly clear, as if it had been doused in icy water.

He asked, 'Would you care to work for *me* at Falmouth? There'll be a cottage.' He looked away, unable to watch the gratitude. 'There are one or two old *Phalaropes* working there. You'll feel at home.'

Allday came back and handed him his cloak. Bolitho saw that he had donned his best blue coat with the gilt buttons, and he carried a brace of pistols in his other hand.

Allday watched him while he clipped on his sword. 'It might still be a mistake, Sir Richard.'

'Not this time, old friend.' He looked at him for a few seconds. 'Ready?'

Allday waited for the other man to lead the way to a smart carriage standing outside the door.

The words kept repeating themselves over and over again.

She did not run away. She had not left him.

The Waites prison was just to the north of London and it was almost dark by the time they got there.

It was a grim, high-walled place, and would look ten times worse in daylight.

Bolitho climbed down from the coach and said to Vanzell, 'Wait here. You have done your part.' To Allday he added shortly, 'So let's be about it.'

He hammered on a heavy door and after a long pause it was opened just a few inches. An unshaven man, wearing the same uniform as Vanzell, peered out at them.

'Yeh? 'Oo calls at this late hour?' He held up a lantern, and at that moment Bolitho let his cloak fall from his shoulders so that the light glittered on his epaulettes.

'Tell the governor, or whoever is in charge, that Sir Richard Bolitho wishes to see him.' He stared at the man's confusion and added harshly, '*Now!*'

They followed the watchman up a long, untidy pathway to the main building and Bolitho noticed that he was limping. They evidently found it cheaper to employ unwanted ex-servicemen, he thought bitterly. Another door, and a whispered conversation while Bolitho stood in a dank room, his hand on his sword, aware of Allday's painful breathing close behind him.

Allday gasped as a piercing scream, followed by shouts and thuds, echoed through the building. Other voices joined in, until the place seemed to cringe in torment. More angry yells, and someone banging on a door with something heavy; and then eventual silence again.

The door opened and the watchman waited to allow Bolitho to enter. The contrast was startling. Good furniture, a great desk littered with ledgers and papers, and a carpet which was as much out of place here as the man who rose to greet him.

Short, and jolly-looking, with a curly wig to cover his baldness, he had all the appearances of a country parson.

'Sir Richard Bolitho, this is indeed an honour.' He glanced at a clock and smiled, like a saucy child. 'And a *surprise* at this late hour.'

Bolitho ignored his out-thrust hand. 'I have come for Lady Somervell. I'll brook no argument. Where is she?'

The man stared at him. 'Indeed, Sir Richard, I would do anything rather than offend such a gallant gentleman, but I fear that someone has played a cruel game with you.'

Bolitho recalled the terrible scream. 'Who do you hold here?'

The little man relaxed slightly. 'Lunatics, and those who plead insanity to avoid their debts to society –'

Bolitho walked around the desk and said softly, 'She is here and you know it. How could you hold a lady in this foul place and not know? I do not care what name she is given, or under what charge. If you do not release her into my care I will see that you are arrested and tried for conspiracy to conceal a crime, and for falsifying the deeds of your office!' He touched the hilt of his sword. 'I am in no mood for more lies!'

The man pleaded, 'Tomorrow perhaps I can discover –'

Bolitho felt a strange calm moving over him. *She is here.* For just a moment the man's confidence had made him doubt.

He shook his head. 'Now.' By tomorrow she would have been taken elsewhere. Anything could have happened to her.

He said curtly, 'Take us to her room.'

The little man pulled open a drawer and squeaked with fright as Allday responded instantly by drawing and cocking a pistol in

175

one movement. He raised a key in his shaking hands.

'Please, *be careful*!' He was almost in tears.

Bolitho caught his breath as they walked into a dimly lit corridor. There was straw scattered on the flagstones, and one of the walls was dripping wet. The stench was foul. Dirt, poverty and despair. They stopped outside the last door and the little governor said in a whisper, 'In God's name I had naught to do with it! She was given in my charge until a debt was paid. But if you are certain that —'

Bolitho did not hear him. He stared in through a small window which was heavily barred, each one worn smooth by a thousand desperate fingers.

A lantern shone through a thick glass port, like those used in a ship's hanging magazine. It was a scene from hell.

An old woman was leaning against one wall, rocking from side to side, a tendril of spittle hanging from her mouth as she crooned some forgotten tune to herself. She was filthy, and her ragged clothes were deeply soiled.

On the opposite side Catherine sat on a small wooden bench, her legs apart, her hands clasped between her knees. Her gown was torn, like the day she had come aboard *Hyperion*, and he saw that her feet were shoeless. Her long hair, uncombed, hung across her partly bared shoulders, hiding her face completely.

She did not move or look up as the key grated in the lock and Bolitho thrust open the door.

Then she whispered very quietly, 'If you come near me, I shall kill you.'

He held out his arms and said, 'Kate. Don't be frightened. Come to me.'

She raised her head and brushed the hair from her eyes with the back of her hand.

Still she did not move or appear to recognise him, and for a moment Bolitho imagined that she had been driven mad by these terrible circumstances.

Then she stood up and stepped a few paces unsteadily towards him.

'Is it you? Really you?' Then she shook her head and exclaimed, 'Don't touch me! I am unclean —'

Bolitho gripped her shoulders and pulled her against him, feeling her protest give way to sobs which were torn from each awful memory. He felt her skin through the back of the gown; she wore nothing else beneath it. Her body was like ice despite the foul, unmoving air. He covered her with his cloak, so that only her face and her bare feet showed in the flickering lanterns.

She saw the governor in the doorway and Bolitho felt her whole body stiffen away from him.

Bolitho said, 'Remove your hat in the presence of my lady, *sir*!' He found no pleasure in the man's fear. 'Or by God I'll call you out here and now!'

The man shrank away, his hat almost brushing the filthy floor.

Bolitho guided her along the corridor, while some of the inmates watched through their cell doors, their hands gripping the bars like claws. But nobody cried out this time.

'Your shoes, Kate?'

She pressed herself against his side as if the cloak would protect her from everything.

'I sold all I had for food.' She raised her head and studied him. 'I have walked barefoot before.' Her sudden courage made her look fragile. 'Are we really leaving now?'

They reached the heavy gate and she saw the carriage, with the two stamping horses.

She said, 'I will be strong. For you, dear Richard, I –' She saw the shadowy figure inside the coach and asked quickly, 'Who is that?'

Bolitho held her until she was calm again.

He said, 'Just a friend who knew when he was needed.'

13

Conspiracy

Belinda dragged the doors of the drawing room shut behind her and pressed her shoulders against them.

'Lower your voice, Richard!' She watched his shadow striding back and forth across the elegant room, her breasts moving quickly to betray something like fear. 'The servants will hear you!'

Bolitho swung round. 'God damn them, and you too for what you did!'

'What is the matter, Richard? Are you sick or drunk?'

'It is fortunate for both of us that it is not the latter! Otherwise I fear what I might do!'

He stared at her and saw her pale. Then he said in a more controlled voice, 'You knew all the time. You connived with Somervell to have her thrown into a place which is not even fit for pigs!' Once again the pictures flashed across his mind. Catherine sitting in the filthy cell, and later when he had taken her to Browne's house in Arlington Street, when she had tried to prevent him from leaving her.

'Don't go, Richard! It's not worth it! We're together, that's all that matters!'

He had turned by the waiting carriage and had replied, 'But those liars intended otherwise!'

He continued, 'She is no more a debtor than you, and you knew it when you spoke with Somervell. I pray to God that he is as ready with a blade as he is with a pistol, for when I meet with him —'

She exclaimed, 'I have never seen you like this!'

'Nor will you again!'

She said, 'I did it for *us*, for what we were and could be again.'

Bolitho stared at her, his heart pounding, knowing how close he had come to striking her. Catherine had told him in jerky sentences as the coach had rolled towards the other house, an unexpected rain pattering across the windows.

She had loaned Somervell most of her own money when they had married. Somervell was in fear of his life because of his many gambling debts. But he had friends at Court, even the King, and a government appointment had saved him.

He had deliberately invested some of her money in her name, then left her to face the consequences when he had caused those same investments to fail. All this Somervell had explained to Belinda. It made Bolitho's head swim to realise just how close to success the plan had been. If he had moved into this house, and then been seen at Admiral Godschale's reception, Catherine would have been told that they were reconciled. A final and brutal rejection.

Somervell had left the country; that was the only known truth. When he returned he might have expected Catherine half-mad or even dead. Like a seabird, Catherine could never be caged.

He said, 'You have killed that too. Remember what you threw in my face on more than one occasion after we were married? That because you *looked* like Cheney, it did not mean that you had anything in common. By God, that was the truest thing you ever said.' He stared round the room and realised for the first time that his uniform was soaked with rain.

'Keep this house, by all means, Belinda, but spare a thought sometimes for those who fight and die so that you may enjoy what they can never know.'

She moved away, her eyes on him as he wrenched open the doors. He thought he saw a shadow slip back from the stairway, something for the servants to chew on.

'You will be ruined!' She gasped as he stepped towards her as if she expected a blow.

'That is my risk.' He picked up his hat. 'Some day I shall speak with my daughter.' He looked at her for several seconds. 'Send for all you need from Falmouth. You rejected even that. So enjoy your new life with your proud friends.' He opened the front door. 'And God help you!'

He walked through the dark street, heedless of the rain which soothed his face like a familiar friend. He needed to walk, to marshal his thoughts into order, like forming a line of battle. He would make enemies, but that was nothing new. There had been those who had tried to discredit him because of Hugh, had even tried to hurt him through Adam.

He thought of Catherine, where she should stay. Not at Falmouth, not until he could take her himself. If she would come. Would she see double-meanings in his words because of what had happened? Expect another betrayal?

He dismissed the thought immediately. She was like the blade at his hip, almost unbreakable. Almost.

One thing was certain. Godschale would soon hear what had happened, although no one would speak openly about it without appearing like a conspirator.

He gave a bleak smile. It would be Gibraltar for orders very soon.

His busy mind recorded a shadow and the click of metal. The old sword was in his hand in a second and he called, '*Stand!*'

Adam sounded relieved. 'I came looking, Uncle.' He watched as Bolitho sheathed his blade.

'It's done then?'

'Aye. 'Tis done.'

Adam fell into step and removed his hat to stare up into the rain. 'I heard most of it from Allday. It seems I cannot leave you alone for a moment.'

Bolitho said, 'I can still scarce believe it.'

'People change, Uncle.'

'I think not.' Bolitho glanced at two army lieutenants walking unsteadily towards St James's. 'Circumstances may, but not people.'

Adam tactfully changed the subject. 'I have discovered Captain Keen's whereabouts. He is in Cornwall. They had gone there to settle some matters relating to Miss Carwithen's late father.'

Bolitho nodded. He had been afraid that Keen would be married without his being there to witness it. How strange that such a simple thing could still be so important after all which had happened.

'I sent word by courier, Uncle. He *should* know.'

They fell silent and listened to their shoes on the pavement.

He probably did already. The whole fleet would by now. Offensive to many, but a welcome scandal as far as the overcrowded messdecks were concerned.

They reached the house, where they found Allday sharing a jug of ale with Mrs Robbins, the housekeeper. She was a Londoner born and bred in Bow and despite her genteel surroundings had a voice which sounded like a street trader's. Mrs Robbins got straight down to business.

'She's in bed now, Sir Richard.' She eyed him calmly. 'I give 'er a small guest room.'

Bolitho nodded. He had taken her point. There would be no scandal in this house, no matter how it might appear.

She continued, 'I stripped 'er naked as a brat and bathed 'er proper. Poor luv, she could do wiv it an' all. I burned 'er clothes. They was alive.' She opened her red fist. 'I found these sewn in the 'em.'

They were the earrings he had given her. The only other time they had been in London together.

Bolitho felt a lump in his throat. 'Thank you, Mrs Robbins.'

Surprisingly, her severe features softened.

'It's nuffink, Sir Richard. Young Lord Oliver 'as told me a few yarns about when you saved 'is rump for 'im!' She went off chuckling to herself.

Allday and Adam entered and Bolitho said, 'You heard all that?'

Allday nodded. 'Best to leave her. Old Ma Robbins'll call all hands if anything happens in the night.'

Bolitho sat down and stretched his legs. He had not eaten a crumb since breakfast but he could not face it now.

It had been a close thing, he thought. But perhaps the battle had not even begun.

*   *   *

Catherine stood by a tall window and looked down at the street. The sun was shining brightly, although this side of the street was still in shadow. A few people strolled up and down, and very faintly could be heard the voice of a flower-girl calling her wares.

She said quietly, 'This cannot last.'

Bolitho sat in a chair, his legs crossed, and watched her, still scarcely able to believe it had ever happened, that she was the same woman he had snatched from squalor and humiliation. Or that he was the man who had risked everything, including a court-martial, by threatening the governor of the Waites jail.

He replied, 'We can't stay here. I want to be alone with you. To hold you again, to tell you things.'

She turned her head so that her face too was in shadow. 'You are still worried, Richard. You have no need to be, where my love for you is concerned. It never left me, so how can we lose it now?' She walked slowly around his chair and put her hands on his shoulders. She was dressed in a plain green robe, which the redoubtable Mrs Robbins had bought for her the previous day.

Bolitho said, 'You are protected now. Anything you need, all that I can give, it is yours.' He hurried on as her fingers tightened their grip on his shoulders, glad that she could not see his face. 'It may take months longer even to retrieve what he has stolen from you. You gave him everything, and saved him.'

She said, 'In return he offered me security, a place in society where I could live as I pleased. Foolish? Perhaps I was. But it was a bargain between us. There was no love.' She laid her head against his and added quietly, 'I have done things I am too often ashamed of. But I have never sold my body to another.'

He reached up and gripped her hand. 'That, I know.'

A carriage clattered past, the wheels loud on the cobbles. At night, this household, like others nearby, had servants to spread straw on the road to deaden the sound. London never seemed to sleep. In the past few days Bolitho had lain awake, thinking of Catherine, the code of the house which kept them apart like shy suitors.

She said, 'I want to be somewhere I can hear about you, what you are doing. There will be more danger. In my own way I shall share it with you.'

182

Bolitho stood up and faced her. 'I will likely receive orders to return to the squadron very soon. Now that I have declared myself, they will probably want rid of me from London as soon as possible.' He smiled and put his hands on her waist, feeling her supple body beneath the robe, their need for each other. There was colour in her cheeks now, and her hair, hanging loose down her back, had recovered its shine.

She saw his eyes and said, 'Mrs Robbins has taken good care of me.'

Bolitho said, 'There is my house in Falmouth.' Instantly he saw the reluctance, the unspoken protest, and added, 'I *know*, my lovely Catherine. You will wait until –'

She nodded. 'Until you carry me there as your kept woman!' She tried to laugh but added huskily, 'For that is what they will say.'

They stood holding hands and facing each other for a full minute.

Then she said, 'And I'm not lovely. Only in your eyes, dearest of men.'

He said, 'I want you.' They walked to the window and Bolitho realised that he had not left the house since that night. 'If I cannot marry you –'

She put her fingers on his mouth. 'Enough of that. Do you think I care? I will be what you wish me to be. But I shall always love you, be your tiger if others try to harm you.'

A servant tapped on the door and entered with a small silver salver. On it was a sealed envelope with the familiar Admiralty crest. Bolitho took it, felt her eyes on him as he slit it open.

'I have to see Sir Owen Godschale tomorrow.'

She nodded. 'Orders then.'

'I expect so.' He caught her in his arms. 'It is inevitable.'

'I know it. The thought of losing you –'

Bolitho considered her being alone. He must do something.

She said, 'I keep thinking, we have another day, one more night.' She ran her hands up to his shoulders and to his face. 'It is all I care for.'

He said, 'Before I leave –'

She touched his mouth again. 'I know what you are trying to say. And yes, dearest Richard, I want you to love me like you did in Antigua, and all that time ago here in London. I told you once that you needed to be loved. I am the one to give it to you.'

Mrs Robbins looked in at them. 'Beg pardon, Sir Richard.' Her eyes seemed to measure the distance between them. 'But yer nephew is 'ere.' She relented slightly. 'You're lookin' fair an' bright, m'lady!'

Catherine smiled gravely. 'Please, Mrs Robbins. Do not use that title.' She looked steadily at Bolitho. 'I have no use for it now.'

Mrs Robbins, or 'Ma' as Allday called her, wandered slowly down the stairway and saw Adam tidying his unruly black hair in front of a looking-glass.

It was a rum do, she thought. God, everyone in the kitchen was talking about it. It had been bad enough for Elsie, the upstairs maid, when her precious drummer-boy had gone off with a blackie in the West Indies. Not what you expected from the quality; although old Lord Browne had been one for the ladies before he passed on. Then she thought of Bolitho's expression when she had given him the earrings she had rescued from the filthy gown. There was a whole lot more to this than people realised.

She nodded to Adam. ' 'E'll be down in a moment, sir.'

Adam smiled. It was strange, he thought. He had always loved his uncle more than any man. But until now he had never envied him.

Admiral Sir Owen Godschale received Bolitho immediately upon his arrival. Bolitho had the impression that he had cut short another interview, perhaps to get this meeting over and done with without further delay.

'I have received intelligence that the French fleet outran Lord Nelson's ships. Whether he can still call them to battle is doubtful. It seems unlikely that Villeneuve will be willing to fight until he has combined forces with the Spaniards.'

Bolitho stared at the admiral's huge map. So the French were still at sea but could not remain so for long. Nelson must have believed the enemy's intention was to attack British possessions and bases in the Caribbean. Or was it merely one great exercise in strength? The French had fine ships, but they had been sealed up in harbour by an effective blockade. Villeneuve was too experienced to make an attack up the English Channel, to pave the way for Napoleon's armies, with ships and men whose skills and strength had been sapped by inactivity.

Godschale said bluntly, 'So I want you to hoist your flag again and join forces with the Maltese squadron.'

'But I understood that Rear-Admiral Herrick was to be relieved?'

Godschale looked at his map. 'We need every ship where she can do the most good. I have sent orders today by courier-brig to Herrick's command.' He eyed him impassively. 'You know him, of course.'

'Very well.'

'So it would appear that the reception I had planned must now be postponed, Sir Richard. Until quieter times, eh?'

Their eyes met. 'Would I have been invited to attend *alone*, Sir Owen?' He spoke calmly but the edge was clear in his voice.

'Under the circumstances I think that would have been preferred, yes.'

Bolitho smiled. 'Then under those same circumstances I am glad it is postponed.'

'I resent your damned attitude, sir!'

Bolitho faced his bluff. 'One day, Sir Owen, you may have cause to remember this disgraceful conspiracy. The last time we met you told me that Nelson was not above being wrong. And neither, sir, are you! And should you too fall from grace you will most certainly discover who your true friends are!' He strode from the room, and heard the admiral slam a door behind him like a thunderclap.

Bolitho was still angry when he reached the house. Until he saw Catherine speaking with Adam, and heard a familiar voice from the adjoining study.

Then Allday stepped out of the passageway which led from the kitchen, his jaw still working on some food. They were all staring at him.

Bolitho said, 'I am to return to the squadron as soon as is convenient.'

185

A shadow fell across the passage, and Captain Valentine Keen stepped into the light.

Bolitho clasped his hands. 'Val! This is a miracle!'

Beyond his friend he saw the girl Zenoria, exactly as he had remembered her. Both of them were travel-stained, and Keen explained, 'We have been on the road for two days. We were already on our way back from Cornwall and by a stroke of fate we met with the courier at a small inn where he was changing his mount.'

Fate. That word. Bolitho said, 'I don't understand.' He saw the girl's face as she walked up to him and held him, while he kissed her on the cheek. Something more had happened.

Keen said, 'I am to be your flag captain, Sir Richard.' He gave Zenoria a despairing glance. 'I was asked. It seemed right.' He handed Bolitho a letter. 'Captain Haven is under arrest. The day after you left in *Firefly* he attacked another officer and attempted to kill him.' He watched Bolitho's face. 'The commodore at Gibraltar awaits your orders.'

Bolitho sat down while Catherine stood beside him, her hand on his shoulder.

Bolitho looked up at her. *My tiger.* That poor, wretched man had broken under the strain. There was nothing much in the letter, but Bolitho knew the other officer must be Parris. He at least was alive.

Keen looked from one to the other. 'I was about to suggest that your lady might care to share my home with Zenoria and my sister until we return.'

Bolitho clasped Catherine's hand; he could tell from the way the dark-haired girl from Cornwall was looking at her that it was a perfect arrangement. God alone knew they both had plenty in common.

Keen had rescued Zenoria from the transport ship *Orontes* after she had been wrongly charged and convicted of attempted murder. She had been trying to defend herself from being raped. Transportation to the penal colony in New South Wales; and she had been innocent. Keen had boarded the transport and cut her down when she was about to be flogged at the ship's master's command. She had taken one blow across her naked back before

Keen had stopped the torment. Bolitho knew she would carry the scar all her life. It made him go cold to realise that the same fate could have been thrown at Catherine, but for different reasons. Jealousy and greed were pitiless enemies.

He said, 'What say you, Kate?' The others seemed to fade away as if his damaged eye would only focus on her. 'Will you do it?'

She said nothing but nodded very slowly. Only a blind man would have failed to see the light, the communion, between them.

'It's settled then.' Bolitho looked at their faces. 'Together again.'

It seemed to include them all.

Lieutenant Vicary Parris sat in his cabin only half paying attention to the ship noises above and around him. Compared with the upper deck the cabin with its open gunport seemed almost cool.

The fifth lieutenant, *Hyperion*'s youngest, stood beside the small table and stared at the open punishment book.

Parris asked again, 'Well, do you think it fair, Mr Priddie?'

It was chilling, Parris thought. The vice-admiral had barely quit the Rock in *Firefly* when Haven had gone on the rampage. At sea, fighting the elements and working the ship, men were often too busy or desperate to question the demands of discipline. But *Hyperion* was in harbour, and in the hot sunshine, work about the ship and taking on fresh stores made its own slower and more comfortable routine, when men had the time to watch and to nurse resentment.

'I – I am not certain.'

Parris swore under his breath. 'You wanted to pass for lieutenant, but now that you share the wardroom you seem prepared to accept any excuse for a flogging without care or favour?'

Priddie hung his head. 'The Captain insisted –'

'Yes, he would.' Parris leaned back and counted seconds to restore his temper. At any other time he would have requested, even demanded a transfer to another ship, and to hell with the consequences. But he had lost his last command; he wanted, no, he *needed* any recommendation which might offer the opening to another promotion.

He had served under several captains. Some brave, some too cautious. Others ran their ships like the King's Regulations and would never take a risk which might raise an admiral's eyebrow. He had even served under the worst kind of all, a sadist who punished men for the sake of it, who had watched every breath-stopping stroke of the cat until the victim's back had been like seared meat.

There was no defence against Haven. He simply hated him. He used the weapon of his complete authority to punish seamen without proper consideration as if to force his first lieutenant to challenge it.

He touched the book. 'Look at this, man. Two dozen lashes for fighting. They were skylarking in the dog watches, nothing more; you must have seen that?'

Priddie flushed. 'The Captain said that discipline on deck was lax. That eyes ashore would be watching. He would tolerate no more slackness.'

Parris bit off a harsh retort. Priddie had not yet forgotten what it was like to be a midshipman. As first lieutenant he should do something. He could appeal to no one; the other captains would see his behaviour as betrayal, something which might rebound on their own authority if encouraged. Right or wrong, the captain was like a god. Only one man cared enough to stop it, and he was on passage for England with trouble enough of his own if he did not bow down to threats. It seemed unlikely that Bolitho would bend a knee to anyone if he believed what he was doing was right.

Parris considered the ship's surgeon, George Minchin. But he had tried before to no avail. Minchin was a drunkard like so many ships' surgeons. Butchers, at whose hands more men died than ever did because of their original injury or wound.

Hyperion was supposed to be getting a senior surgeon, one of several being sent into the various squadrons to observe and report on what they discovered. But that was later. It was now he was needed.

Parris said, 'Leave it to me.' He saw the lieutenant's eyes light up, thankful that he was no longer involved.

Parris added angrily, 'You'll never hold a command, Mr Priddie, unless you face up to the rank you carry.'

He climbed to the quarterdeck and watched the seamen sway-ing up new rigging to the mizzen top. There was a strong smell of fresh tar for blacking-down, the sounds of hammers and an adze as Horrocks the carpenter and his mates completed work on a new cutter, built from materials to hand. They worked well, he thought, would even be happy, but for the cloud which always hung over the poop.

With a sigh he made his way aft and waited for the Royal Marine sentry to announce him.

Captain Haven was sitting at his desk, papers arranged within easy reach, his coat hanging from the chairback as he fanned his face with his handkerchief.

'Well, Mr Parris? I have much to do.'

Parris made himself ignore the obvious dismissal. He noticed that the pens on the desk were all clean and dry. Haven had written nothing. It was as if he had prepared for this, had been expecting his visit despite the hint of rejection.

Parris began carefully, 'The two men for punishment, sir.'

'Oh, which two? I was beginning to believe that the people did much as they pleased.'

'Trotter and Dixon, sir. They have not been in any trouble before. Had the fifth lieutenant come to me –' He got no further.

Haven snapped, 'But you were not aboard, sir. No, you were elsewhere, I believe?'

'Under your orders, sir.'

'Don't be impertinent!' Haven shifted on his chair. It reminded Parris of a fisherman he had watched when he had felt something take the hook.

Haven said, 'They were behaving in a disgusting and disorderly fashion! I saw them. As usual I had to stop the rot!'

'But two dozen lashes, sir. I could give them a week's extra work. Discipline would be upheld, and I think Mr Priddie would learn from it.'

'I see, you are blaming the junior lieutenant now.' He smiled. Parris could feel the strain clutching at him like claws. 'Men will be flogged, and Mr Priddie will take the blame for it. God damn your eyes, sir! Do you think I give a sniff for what they think? I

command here, they will do my bidding, *do I make myself clear?*'
He was shouting.

Parris said, 'You do, sir.'

'I am glad to hear it.' Haven watched him, his eyes slitted in the
filtered sunlight. 'Your part in the cutting-out will be known at
the Admiralty, I have no doubt. But you can crawl after our
admiral's coat-tails as long as you like. I shall see that your
disloyalty and damned arrogance are noted fully when your case
for promotion is considered again!'

Parris felt the cabin sway. 'Did you call me disloyal, sir?'

Haven almost screamed at him. 'Yes, you lecherous swine, I
bloody well did!'

Parris stared at him. It was worse than anything which had
happened before. He saw the sunlight at the bottom of the
captain's door blackened in places by feet. There were men out
there listening. God, he thought, despairingly, what chance do
we have if we stand into battle?

He said, 'I think we may both have spoken out of turn, sir.'

'Don't you ever dare to reprimand me, blast you! I suppose
that when you lie in your cot you think of me down aft, sneer
because of the foul deed you committed – well, answer me, you
bloody hound!'

Parris knew he should summon another officer, just as he knew
he would strike Haven down in the next few seconds. Something,
like a warning in his sleep, seemed to stay his anger and
resentment. *He wants you to strike him. He wants you as his next
victim.*

Haven slumped back in his chair, as if the strength and fury
had left him. But when he looked up again Parris saw it was still
there in his eyes, like fires of hate.

In an almost conversational voice Haven said, 'You really
thought I would not find you out? Could you be *that* stupid?'

Parris held his breath, his heart pounding; he had believed that
nothing more could unseat him.

Haven continued, 'I know your ways and manners, the love
you bear for yourself. Oh yes, I am not without some wit and
understanding.' He pointed at the portrait of his wife but kept his
eyes on Parris.

He said in a hoarse whisper, 'The guilt is as plain as day on your face!'

Parris thought he had misheard. 'I met the lady once, but –'

'Don't you dare to speak of her in my presence!' Haven lurched to his feet. 'You with your soft tongue and manners to match, just the sort she'd listen to!'

'*Sir*. Please say nothing more. We may both regret it.'

Haven did not appear to be listening. 'You took her when I was occupied in this ship! I worked myself sick pulling this damned rabble into one company. Then they hoisted the flag of a man much like you, I suspect, who thinks he can have any woman he chooses!'

'I can't listen, sir. It is not true anyway. I saw –' He hesitated and finished, 'I did not touch her, I swear to God!'

Haven said in a small voice, 'After all that I gave her.'

'You are wrong, sir.' Parris looked at the door. Someone must come surely? The whole poop must hear Haven's rantings.

Haven shouted suddenly, 'It's *your child*, you bloody animal!'

Parris clenched his fists. So that was it. He said, 'I am leaving now, sir. I will not listen to your insults or your insinuations. And as far as your wife is concerned, all I can say is that I am sorry for her.' He turned to go as Haven screamed, 'You'll go nowhere, God damn you!'

The roar of the pistol in the confined space was deafening. It was like being struck by an iron bar. Then Parris felt the pain, the hot wetness of blood even as he hit the deck.

He saw the darkness closing in. It was like smoke or fog, with just one clear space in it where the captain was trying to ram another charge into his pistol.

Before the pain bore him into oblivion Parris's agonised mind was able to record that Haven was laughing. Laughing as if he could not stop.

14

For Or Against

It was early morning on a fine June day when Bolitho rehoisted his flag above *Hyperion*, and prepared his squadron to leave the Rock.

During *Firefly*'s speedy passage to Gibraltar, Bolitho and Keen had had much to discuss. If Keen had been unsettled at being made flag captain of a squadron he knew nothing about he barely showed it, while for Bolitho it was the return of a friend; like being made whole again.

At the commodore's request he had visited Haven at the place where he was being confined ashore. He had expected him to be in a state of shock, or at least ready to offer something in the way of a defence for shooting Parris down in cold blood.

A garrison doctor had told Bolitho that Haven either did not remember, or did not care about what had happened.

He had risen as Bolitho had entered his small room and had said, 'The ship is ready, Sir Richard. I took steps to ensure that old or not, *Hyperion* will match her artillery against any Frenchman when called to!'

Bolitho had said, 'You are relieved. I am sending you to England.'

Haven had stared at him. 'Relieved? Has my promotion been announced?'

Upon returning to the ship Bolitho had been handed a letter addressed to Haven, which had just been brought by a mail schooner from Spithead. Under the circumstances Bolitho decided to open it; he might at least be able to spare someone in England the bitter truth about Haven, until the facts were released at his inevitable court-martial.

Afterwards, Bolitho was not certain he should have read it. The letter was from Haven's wife. It stated in an almost matter-of-fact fashion that she had left him to live with a wealthy mill-owner who was making uniforms for the military, where she and her child would be well cared for.

It seemed that the mill-owner was the father of the child, so it was certainly not Parris's. When Haven eventually came to his senses, if he ever did, that would be the hardest cross to bear.

The first lieutenant must be born lucky, Bolitho thought. The pistol ball had lifted too much in the short range of the cabin, and had embedded itself in his shoulder and chipped the bone. He must have suffered terrible agony as Minchin had sought to probe it out. But the shot had been intended for his heart.

Keen had asked Bolitho, 'Do you wish to keep him aboard? The wound will take weeks to heal, and I fear it was roughly treated.' He had probably been remembering how a great splinter had speared into his groin; rather than allow him to face the torture of a drunken surgeon, it had been Allday who had cut the jagged wood away.

'He is an experienced officer. I have hopes for his promotion. God knows we can use some skilled juniors for command.'

Keen had agreed. 'It will certainly put the other lieutenants on their mettle!'

And so with mixed feelings the squadron sailed and headed east into the Mediterranean, the sea which had seen so many battles, and where Bolitho had almost died.

With *Hyperion* in the van, Bolitho's flag at the fore, and the other third-rates following astern, heeling steeply to a lively north-westerly, their departure probably roused as much speculation as their arrival. Bolitho watched the Rock's famous silhouette until it was lost in haze. The strange cloud of steam rising against an otherwise clear sky was a permanent feature when the wind cooled the overheated stones, so that from a distance it appeared like a smouldering volcano.

Most of *Hyperion*'s company had grown used to one another

since the ship had commissioned, and Keen was almost the only stranger amongst them.

As day followed day, and each ship exercised her people at sail or gun drill, Bolitho was thankful for the fates which had brought Keen back to him.

Unlike Haven, he did know Bolitho's ways and standards, had served him both as a midshipman and lieutenant before eventually becoming his flag captain. The ship's company seemed to sense the bond between their captain and admiral, and the older hands would note and appreciate that if Keen did not know something about his ship he was not too proud to ask. It never occurred to Bolitho that Keen had perhaps learned it from him.

It had been sad to part with *Firefly*, but she had bustled on to deliver more despatches to admirals and captains who were eagerly awaiting the latest news of the French. Amongst *Firefly*'s mountain of despatches there would doubtless be a few like the one which Haven had still not read. War was as cruel in the home as it was on the high seas, he thought.

When he met with Adam again his promotion would have been confirmed. It seemed strange to consider it. He could imagine what they would think and say at Falmouth when the latest Captain Bolitho came home. Unless Adam eventually met and married the girl of his choice, he would be the last captain to arrive at the house in Cornwall.

He often thought of Catherine and their farewell. They had shared their passion and love equally, and she had insisted that she accompany him all the way to Portsmouth to board the little *Firefly*. Keen had said his own goodbyes earlier when he had gone to Portsmouth with Adam in another carriage.

With the horses stamping and steaming in the sunshine Catherine had clung to him, searching his face, touching it with tenderness and then dismay when Allday had told them the boat was waiting at the sally port.

He had asked her to wait by the carriage but she had followed him to the wooden stairs where so many sea-officers had left the land. There had been a small crowd watching the ships and the officers being pulled out to them.

Bolitho had noticed that there were very few of the age for

service. It would be a fool who risked the press gang's net if he had no stomach for the fight.

The people had raised a cheer, and some of them recognised Bolitho, as well they might.

One had shouted, 'Good luck, Equality Dick, an' to yer lady as well!'

He had faced her and he had seen tears for the first time.

She had whispered, 'They included *me!*'

As the boat had pulled clear of the stairs Bolitho had looked back, but she had vanished. And yet as they had bumped over a choppy Solent where *Firefly* tugged at her cable, he had sensed that she was still there. Watching him to the last second. He had written to ask her just that, and to tell her what her love meant to him.

He remembered what Belinda had said about their *infatuation.* Allday had described Catherine as *a sailor's woman, an' that's no error.* When he said it, it sounded the greatest compliment of all.

While the frigate *Tybalt* and the sloop-of-war *Phaedra* chased and questioned any coaster or trader foolish enough to be caught under their guns, Bolitho and Keen studied the scanty reports, as day by day they sailed deeper into the Mediterranean.

It was said that Nelson was still in the Atlantic and had joined up with his friend and second-in-command Vice-Admiral Collingwood. Nelson had probably decided that the enemy were trying to divide the British squadrons by ruses and quick dashes from safe harbours. Only when that was achieved would Napoleon launch his invasion across the Channel.

As Yovell had mildly suggested, 'If that is so, Sir Richard, then you are the senior officer in the Mediterranean.'

Bolitho had barely considered it. But if true, it meant one thing to him. When the enemy came his way he would need to ask no one what he must do. It made the weight of command seem more appealing.

One forenoon as he took his walk on the quarterdeck he saw Lieutenant Parris moving along a gangway, his arm strapped to his side, his steps unsteady while he gauged the rise and fall of the hull. He appeared to have withdrawn more into himself since Haven's attack with intent to murder him. Keen had said that he was well content to have him as his senior, but had not known him before so could not make a comparison.

Parris moved slowly to the lee side of the quarterdeck and clung to a stay to watch some seabirds swooping and diving alongside.

Bolitho walked across from the weather side. 'How do you feel?'

Parris tried to straighten his back but winced and apologised. 'It is slow progress, Sir Richard.' He stared up at the bulging sails, the tiny figures working amongst and high above them. 'I'll feel a mite better when I know I can climb up there again.'

Bolitho studied his strong, gipsy profile. A ladies' man? An enigma?

Parris saw his scrutiny and said awkwardly, 'May I thank you for allowing me to remain aboard, Sir Richard. I am less than useless at the moment.'

'Captain Keen made the final decision.'

Parris nodded, his eyes lost in memory. 'He makes this old ship come alive.' He hesitated, as if measuring the confidence. 'I was sorry to hear of your trouble in London, Sir Richard.'

Bolitho looked at the blue water and tensed as his damaged eye misted slightly in the moist air.

'Nelson has a saying, I believe.' It was like quoting one of Adam's favourites. 'The boldest measures are usually the safest.'

Parris stood back as Keen appeared below the poop-deck, but added, 'I wish you much joy, Sir Richard. Both of you.'

Keen joined him by the nettings. 'We shall sight Malta tomorrow in the forenoon watch.' He glanced over at the master's powerful figure. 'Mr Penhaligon *assures* me.'

Bolitho smiled. 'I was speaking with the first lieutenant. A strange fellow.'

Keen laughed. 'It is wrong, I know, to jest on it, but I have met captains I would have dearly liked to shoot. But never the other way about!'

Down by the boat-tier Allday turned as he heard their laughter. Keen's old coxswain had been killed aboard their last ship, *Argonaute*. Allday had selected a new man for him, but secretly wished it was his son.

Keen's coxswain was named Tojohns, and he had been captain of the foretop. He glanced aft with him and said, 'A new ship since he stepped aboard.' He studied Allday curiously. 'You've known him a long while then?'

Allday smiled. 'A year or two. He'll do me, an' he's good for Sir Richard, that's the thing.'

Allday thought about their parting at Portsmouth Point. The people cheering and waving their hats, the women smiling fit to burst. It *had* to work this time. He frowned as the other coxswain broke into his thoughts.

Tojohns asked, 'Why did you pick me?'

Allday gave a lazy grin. Tojohns was a fine seaman and knew how to put himself about in a fight. He was not in the least like old Hogg, Keen's original coxswain. Chalk and cheese. *What they said about me and Stockdale.*

Allday said, ' 'Cause you talk too much!'

Tojohns laughed but fell silent as a passing midshipman glanced sharply at him. It was hard to accept his new role. He would no longer have to be up there at the shrill of every call, fighting wild canvas with his foretopmen. Like Allday he was apart from all that. Somebody, for the first time.

'Mind you.' Allday watched him gravely. 'Whatever you sees down aft, you keep it to yerself, right, matey?'

Tojohns nodded. *Down aft.* Yes, he was somebody.

Six bells chimed out from *Hyperion*'s forecastle and Captain Valentine Keen touched his hat to Bolitho, barely able to suppress a smile.

'The master was right about our arrival here, Sir Richard.'

Bolitho raised his telescope to scan the familiar walls and batteries of Valletta. 'Only just.'

It had been a lengthy passage from Gibraltar, over eight days to log the weary twelve hundred miles. It had given Keen time to impress his methods on the whole ship, but had filled Bolitho with misgivings at the forthcoming meeting with Herrick.

He said slowly, 'Only three ships-of-the-line, Val.' He had recognised Herrick's flagship *Benbow* almost as soon as the masthead lookouts. Once his own flagship, and like *Hyperion*,

197

full of memories. Keen would be remembering her for very different reasons. Here he had faced a court of enquiry presided over by Herrick. It could have ruined him, but for Bolitho's intervention. Past history? It seemed unlikely he would ever forget.

Bolitho said, 'I can make out the frigate yonder, anchored beyond *Benbow*.' He had been afraid that she would have been sent elsewhere. She was named *La Mouette*, a French prize taken off Toulon while Bolitho had been at Antigua. She was a small vessel of only twenty-six guns, but beggars could not be choosers. Any frigate was welcome at this stage of the war against the new cat-and-mouse methods used by the French.

Keen said, 'But it raises our line of battle to eight.' He smiled. 'We have managed with far less in the past.'

Jenour stood slightly apart, supervising the signals midshipmen with their bright flags strewn about in apparent disorder.

Bolitho crossed to the opposite side to watch as the next astern, Thynne's *Obdurate*, took in more sail and tacked slowly after her admiral.

He pictured Herrick in *Benbow*, watching perhaps as the five major ships of Bolitho's squadron moved ponderously on a converging tack in readiness to anchor. It was very hot, and Bolitho had seen the sunlight flash on many telescopes amongst the anchored ships. Would Herrick be regretting this meeting, he wondered? Or thinking how their friendship had been born out of battle and a near mutiny in that other war against the American rebels?

He said, 'Very well, Mr Jenour, you may signal now.'

He glanced at Keen's profile. 'We shall just beat eight bells, Val, and so save Mr Penhaligon's reputation!'

'All acknowledged, sir!'

As the signal was briskly hauled to the deck, the ships faced up to the feeble breeze and dropped anchor.

Bolitho said, 'I have to go aft. I shall require my barge directly.'

Keen faced him. 'You'll not wait for the rear-admiral to come aboard, Sir Richard?'

Keen must have guessed that he was going to visit *Benbow* mainly to avoid having to greet Herrick with all the usual forma-

198

lities. Their last meeting had been across the court's table. When next they met it would have to be as man-to-man. For both their sakes.

'Old friends do not need to rest on tradition, Val.' Bolitho hoped it sounded more convincing than it felt.

He tried to push it from his mind. Herrick had been here a long time; he might well have news of the enemy. Intelligence was everything. Without the little scraps of information gathered by the patrols and casual encounters they were helpless.

He heard Allday calling hoarsely to his barge crew, the creak of tackles as the boat, soon followed by others, was swayed up and over the gangway.

A few local craft were already approaching the ships, their hulls crammed with cheap wares to tempt the sailors to part with their money. Like Portsmouth and any other seaport, there would be women too for the land-starved men if the captains turned a blind eye. It must be hard for any man to accept, Bolitho thought. The officers came and went as duty permitted, but only trusted hands and those of the press-gangs were ever allowed to set foot ashore. Month in and year out, it was a marvel there had not been more outbreaks of rebellion in the fleet.

He thought of Catherine as he had left her. Keen would be thinking the same about Zenoria. It would be ten thousand times worse if they could not meet until the war had ended, or they had been thrown on the beach as rejected cripples, like the one-legged man.

He went to his cabin and collected some letters which had been brought on board *Firefly* at the last moment. For Herrick. He gave a grim smile. Like bearing gifts.

Ozzard pattered round him, his eyes everywhere, to make sure that Bolitho had forgotten nothing.

It made Bolitho think of Catherine's face when he had presented her with the fan Ozzard had cleaned.

She had said, 'Keep it. It is all I have to give you. Have it by you. Then I shall be near when you need me.'

He sighed and walked out past the sentry and Keen's open cabin door, where fresh white paint disguised where Haven's pistol had been fired. Haven was lucky that Parris was still alive.

Or was he? His career was wrecked, and there would be nothing waiting for him when he eventually reached his home.

He walked into the bright sunlight and saw the Royal Marines assembled at the entry port, boatswain's mates with their silver calls, Keen and Jenour ready to pay their respects.

Major Adams of the Royal Marines raised his sword and barked:

'Guard ready, *sir*!'

Keen looked at Bolitho. 'Barge alongside, Sir Richard.'

Bolitho raised his hat to the quarterdeck and saw bare-backed seamen working aloft on the mizzen yard peering down at him, their feet dangling in space.

One ship. One company.

Bolitho hurried down to the barge. The memories would have to wait.

Rear-Admiral Thomas Herrick stood with his hands grasped behind his back and watched the other ships anchoring, while the wind fell away to leave their sails almost empty. Gunsmoke from exchanged salutes drifted towards the shore, and Herrick tensed as he saw the green barge being lowered alongside *Hyperion* almost as soon as the Jack was hoisted forward.

Captain Hector Gossage remarked, 'It seems that the vice-admiral is coming to us immediately, sir.'

Herrick grunted. There were so many new faces in his command, and his flag captain had only been with him for a few months. His predecessor, Dewar, had gone home in ill health and Herrick still missed him.

Herrick said, 'Prepare to receive him. Full guard. You know what to do.'

He wanted to be left alone, to think. When he had received his new orders from Sir Owen Godschale at the Admiralty, Herrick had thought of little else. The last time he had met Bolitho had been here in the Mediterranean when *Benbow* had been under heavy attack from Jobert's squadron. Re-united in battle, friends meeting against the heartless terms of war. But afterwards, when Bolitho had sailed for England, Herrick had thought a great deal about the court of enquiry, how Bolitho had cursed them after he had heard of Inch's death. Herrick still believed that Bolitho's hurt and anger had been directed at him, not the anonymous court.

He thought of Godschale's personal letter, which had accompanied the changed orders. Herrick had already learned of the liaison between Bolitho and the woman he had known as Catherine Pareja. He had always felt ill-at-ease with her, out of his depth. A proud, uninhibited woman. In his eyes she lacked modesty, humility. He thought of his dear, loving Dulcie at their new house in Kent. Not a bit like her at all.

How brave Dulcie had been when she had been told finally that she could not bear him any children. She had said softly, 'If only we had met earlier, Thomas. Maybe we would have had a fine son to follow you into the navy.'

He thought of Bolitho's life in Falmouth, the same old grey house where he had been entertained when Bolitho had commanded *Phalarope*, and he had risen to become his first lieutenant. It seemed like a century ago.

Herrick had always been stocky, but he had filled out comfortably since he had married Dulcie, and had risen to the unbelievable height of rear-admiral as well. He had been out here so long that his round, honest face was almost the colour of mahogany, which made his bright blue eyes and the streaks of grey in his hair seem all the more noticeable.

What could Richard Bolitho be thinking of? He had a lovely wife and daughter he could be proud of. Any serving officer could envy his record, fights won at cost to himself, but never failing to hold his men's values close to his heart. His sailors had called him Equality Dick, a nickname taken up by the popular newsheets ashore. But some of those were telling a very different story now. Of the vice-admiral who cared more for a lady than his own reputation.

Godschale had skirted round it very well in his letter.

'I know you are both old friends, but you may find it difficult now to serve under him when you were expecting quite rightly to be relieved.'

By saying nothing, Godschale had said everything. A warning or a threat? You could take it either way.

He heard the marines falling in at the entry port, their officer snapping out commands as he inspected the guard.

Captain Gossage rejoined him and watched the array of anchored ships.

He said, 'They look fine enough, sir.'

Herrick nodded. His own ships needed to be relieved, if only for a quick overhaul and complete restoring. He had only been able to release one vessel at a time for watering or to gather new victuals, and the sudden change of orders to place him under Bolitho's flag had left everyone surprised or resentful.

Gossage was saying, 'I served with Edmund Haven a few years ago, sir.'

'Haven?' Herrick pulled his mind back. 'Bolitho's flag captain.'

Gossage nodded. 'A dull fellow, I thought. Only got *Hyperion* because she was little more than a hulk.'

Herrick dug his chin into his neckcloth. 'I'd not let Sir Richard hear you say that. It is not a view he would share.'

The officer-of-the-watch called, 'The barge is casting off, sir!'

'Very well. Man the side.'

In her last letter Dulcie had said little about Belinda. They had been in touch, but it seemed likely that any confidences would be kept secret. He smiled sadly. Even from him.

Herrick thought too of the girl Bolitho had once loved and married – Cheney Seton. Herrick had been at the marriage. It had been his terrible mission to carry the news of her tragic death to Bolitho at sea. He had known that Belinda was not another like her. But Bolitho had seemed settled, especially after he had been presented with a daughter. Herrick tried to keep things straight. It had nothing to do with the cruel fact that Dulcie was beyond the age to give him children. Even as he arranged his thoughts he recognised the lie. Could almost hear the comparison. *Why them and not us?*

And now there was Catherine. Rumours were always blown up out of all proportion. Like Nelson's much-vaunted affair. Later, Nelson would regret it. When he laid down his sword for the last time, there would be many old enemies eager to forget his triumphs and his worth. Herrick came of a poor family and knew how hard it was to rise above any superior's dislike, let alone outright hostility. Bolitho had saved him from it, had given him the chance he would otherwise never have had. There was no denying that. And yet –

Gossage straightened his hat. 'Barge approaching, sir!'

A voice yelled, 'Clear the upper deck!'

It would not look right to have the gundeck and forecastle crowded with idlers when Bolitho came aboard. But they were there all the same, despite some tempting smells from the galley funnel.

Herrick gripped his sword and pressed it to his side. Old friends. None closer. How could it happen like this?

The calls shrilled and the Royal Marine fifers struck into *Heart of Oak*, while the guard slapped their muskets to the present in a small cloud of pipeclay.

Bolitho stood framed against the sea's silky blue and doffed his hat.

He had not changed, Herrick thought. And as far as he could see, he had no grey hairs, although he was a year older than Herrick himself.

Bolitho nodded to the Royal Marines and said, 'Smart guard, Major.' Then he strode across to Herrick and thrust out his hand.

Herrick seized it, knowing how important this moment was, perhaps to Bolitho as well.

'Welcome, Sir Richard!'

Bolitho smiled, his teeth white against his sunburned skin.

'It is good to see you, Thomas. Though I fear you must hate this change of plans.'

Together they walked aft to the great cabin while the guard was dismissed, and Allday cast off the barge to idle comfortably within *Benbow*'s fat shadow.

In the cabin it seemed cool after the quarterdeck, and Herrick watched as Bolitho seated himself by the stern windows, saw his eyes moving around while he recalled it as it had once been. His own flagship. There had been other changes too. That last battle had made certain of that.

The servant brought some wine and Bolitho said, 'It seems that Our Nel is still in the Atlantic.'

Herrick swallowed his wine without noticing it. 'So they say. I have heard that he may return to England and haul down his flag, as it looks unlikely that the French will venture out in strength. Not this year anyway.'

'Is that what you think?' Bolitho examined the glass. Herrick was on edge. More than he had expected. 'It is possible, of course, that the enemy may slip through the Strait again and run for Toulon.'

Herrick frowned. 'If so, we shall *have 'em*. Caught between us and the main fleet.'

'But suppose Villeneuve intends to break out from another direction? By the time their lordships got word to us, he would be beating up the Channel, while we remain kicking our heels in ignorance.'

Herrick stirred uneasily. 'I am keeping up my patrols –'

'I knew you would. I see you are short of a ship?'

Herrick was startled. '*Absolute*, yes. I sent her to Gibraltar. She's so rotten, I wonder she remains afloat.' He seemed to stiffen. 'It was my responsibility. I did not know then that you were assuming total command.'

Bolitho smiled. 'Easy, Thomas. It was not meant as a criticism. I might have done the same.'

Herrick looked at the deck. *Might*. He said, 'I shall be pleased to hear of your intentions.'

'Presently, Thomas. Perhaps we might sup together?'

Herrick looked up and saw the grey eyes watching him. Pleading with him?

He replied, 'I'd relish that.' He faltered. 'You could bring Captain Haven if you wish, although I understand –'

Bolitho stared at him. Of course. He would not have heard yet.

'Haven is under arrest, Thomas. In due course I expect he will stand trial for attempting to murder his first lieutenant.' He almost smiled at Herrick's astonishment. It probably sounded completely insane. He added, 'Haven imagined that the lieutenant was having an affair with his wife. There was a child. He was wrong, as it turned out. But the damage was done.'

Herrick refilled his glass and spilled some wine on the table without heeding it.

'I have to speak out, Sir Richard.'

Bolitho watched him gravely. 'No rank or title 'twixt us, Thomas – unless you need a barricade for your purpose?'

Herrick exclaimed, 'This woman. What can she mean to you except –'

Bolitho said quietly, 'You and I are friends, Thomas. Let us remain as such.' He looked past him and pictured Catherine in the shadows. He said, 'I am in love with her. Is that so hard to understand?' He tried to keep the bitterness from his tone. 'How would you feel, Thomas, if some stranger referred to your Dulcie as *this woman*, eh?'

Herrick gripped the arms of his chair. 'God damn it, Richard, why do you twist the truth? You know, you *must* know what everyone is saying, that you are besotted by her, have thrown your wife and child to the winds so that you can lose yourself, and to hell with all who care for you!'

Bolitho thought briefly of the grand house in London. 'I've thrown nobody to the winds. I *have* found someone I can love. Reason does not come into it.' He stood up and crossed to the windows. 'You must know I do not act lightly in such matters.' He swung round. 'Are you judging me too? Who are you – Christ?'

They faced each other like enemies. Then Bolitho said, 'I need her, and I pray that she may always need me. Now let that be an end to it, man!'

Herrick took several deep breaths and refilled both glasses.

'I shall never agree.' He fixed Bolitho with the bright blue eyes he had always remembered. 'But I'll not let it put my duty at risk.'

Bolitho sat down again. 'Duty, Thomas? Don't speak to me of that. I've had a bellyful of late.' He made up his mind. 'This combined squadron is our responsibility. I am not usurping your leadership and that you must know. I don't share their lordships' attitude on the French, that is if they indeed have one. Pierre Villeneuve is a man of great intelligence; he is not one to go by the book of fighting instructions. He needs to be cautious on the one hand, for if he fails in his ultimate mission to clear the Channel for invasion, then he must die at the guillotine.'

Herrick muttered, '*Barbarians!*'

Bolitho smiled. 'We must explore every possibility and keep

our ships together except for the patrols. When the time comes, it will be a hard sail to find and support Nelson and brave Collingwood.' He put down his glass very slowly. 'You see, I do not believe that the French will wait until next year. They have run the course.' He looked through the sun's glare towards the anchored ships. 'So have we.'

Herrick felt safer on familiar ground. 'Who do you have as flag captain?'

Bolitho watched him and said dryly, 'Captain Keen. There is none better. Now that you are promoted beyond my reach, Thomas.'

Herrick did not hide his dismay. 'So we are all drawn together?'

Bolitho nodded. 'Remember Lieutenant Browne — how he called us *We Happy Few*?'

Herrick frowned. 'I don't need reminding.'

'Well, think on it, Thomas, my friend, there are even fewer of us now!'

Bolitho stood up and reached for his hat. 'I must return to *Hyperion*. Perhaps later –' He left it unsaid. Then he placed the packet of letters for Herrick on the table.

'From England, Thomas. There will be more *news*, I expect.' Their eyes met and Bolitho ended quietly, 'I wanted you to hear it from me, as a friend, rather than assault your ears with more gossip from the sewers.'

Herrick protested, 'I did not mean to hurt you. It is for you that I care.'

Bolitho shrugged. 'We will fight the war together, Thomas. It seems that will have to suffice.'

They stood side-by-side at the entry port while Allday manoeuvred the barge alongside once again. Allday had never been caught out before and would be fuming about it.

Like everyone else he must have expected him to remain longer with his oldest friend.

Bolitho walked towards the entry port as the marine guard presented their muskets to the salute, the bayonets shining like ice in the glare.

He caught his shoe in a ring-bolt, and would have fallen but for a lieutenant who thrust out his arm to save him.

'Thank you, sir!'

He saw Herrick standing at him with sudden anxiety, the major of marines swaying beside the guard with his sword still rigid in his gloved hand.

Herrick exclaimed, 'Are you well, Sir Richard?'

Bolitho looked at the nearest ship and gritted his teeth as the mist partly covered his eye. A close thing. He had been so gripped with emotion and disappointment at this visit that he had allowed his guard to fall. As in a sword-fight, it only took a second.

He replied, 'Well enough, thank you.'

They looked at one another. 'It shall not happen again.'

Some seamen had climbed into the shrouds and began to cheer as the barge pulled strongly from the shadow and into the sunlight. Allday swung the tiller bar and glanced quickly at Bolitho's squared shoulders, the familiar ribbon which drew his hair back above the collar. Allday could remember it no other way.

He listened to the cheers, carried on by another of the seventy-fours close by.

Fools, he thought savagely. What the hell did they know? They had seen nothing, knew even less.

But he had watched, and had felt it even from the barge. Two friends with nothing to say, nothing to span the gap which had yawned between them like a moat around a fortress.

He saw the stroke oarsman watching Bolitho instead of his loom and glared at him until he paled under his stare.

Allday swore that he would never take anyone at face value again. *For or against me, that'll be my measure of a man.*

Bolitho twisted round suddenly and shaded his eyes to look at him.

'It's *all right*, Allday.' He saw his words sink in. 'So be easy.'

Allday forgot his watching bargemen and grinned awkwardly. Bolitho had read his thoughts even with his back turned.

Allday said, 'I was rememberin', Sir Richard.'

'I know that. But at the moment I am too full to speak on it.'

The barge glided to the main chains and Bolitho glanced up at the waiting side-party.

207

He hesitated. 'I sometimes think we may hope for too much, old friend.'

Then he was gone, and the shrill of calls announced his arrival on deck.

Allday shook his head and muttered, 'I never seen him like this afore.'

'What's that, Cox'n?'

Allday swung round, his eyes blazing. 'And *you*! Watch your stroke in future, or I'll have the hide off ye!'

He forgot the bargemen and stared hard at the towering tumblehome of the ship's side. Close to, you could see the gouged scars of battle beneath the smart buff and black paintwork.

Like us, he thought, suddenly troubled. Waiting for the last fight. When it came, you would need all the friends you could find.

15

A Time For Action

Bolitho leaned on one elbow and put his signature on yet another despatch for the Admiralty. In the great cabin the air was heavy and humid, and even with gunports and skylight open, he felt the sweat running down his spine. He had discarded his coat, and his shirt was open almost to his waist, but it made little difference.

He stared at the date on the next despatch which Yovell pushed discreetly before him. September; over three months since he had said his farewell to Catherine and returned to Gibraltar. He looked towards the open stern windows. *To this.* Hardly a ripple today, and the sea shone like glass, almost too painful to watch.

It seemed far longer. The endless days of beating up and down in the teeth of a raw Levantine, or lying becalmed without even a whisper of a breeze to fill the sails.

It could not go on. It was like sitting on a powder-keg and worse. Or was it all in his mind, a tension born of his own uncertainties? Fresh water was getting low again, and that might soon provoke trouble on the crowded messdecks.

Of the enemy there was no sign. *Hyperion* and her consorts lay to the west of Sardinia, while Herrick and his depleted squadron maintained their endless patrol from the Strait of Sicily to as far north as Naples Bay.

The other occupant of the cabin gave a polite cough. Bolitho glanced up and smiled. 'Routine, Sir Piers, but it will not take much longer.'

Sir Piers Blachford settled down in his chair and stretched out his long legs. To the officers in the squadron his arrival in the last courier-brig had been seen as another responsibility, a civilian sent to probe and investigate, a resented intruder.

It had not taken long for this strange man to alter all that. If they were honest, most of those who had taken offence at his arrival would be sorry to see him leave.

Blachford was a senior member of the College of Surgeons, one of the few who had volunteered to visit the navy's squadrons, no matter at what discomfort to themselves, to examine injuries and their treatment in the spartan and often horrific conditions of a man-of-war. He was a man of boundless energy and never seemed to tire as he was ferried from one ship to the other, to meet and reason with their surgeons, to instruct each captain on the better use of their meagre facilities for caring for the sick.

And yet he was some twenty years older than Bolitho, as thin as a ramrod, with the longest and most pointed nose Bolitho had ever seen. It was more like an instrument for his trade than part of his face. Also, he was very tall, and creeping about the different decks and peering into storerooms and sickbays must have taxed his strength and his patience, but he never complained. Bolitho would miss him. It was a rare treat to share a conversation at the end of a day with a man whose world was healing, rather than running an elusive enemy to ground.

Bolitho had received two letters from Catherine, both in the same parcel from a naval schooner.

She was safe and well in the Hampshire house which was owned by Keen's father. He was a powerful man in the City of London, and kept the country house as a retreat. He had welcomed Catherine there, just as he had Zenoria. The favour went two ways, because one of Keen's sisters was there also, her husband, a lieutenant with the Channel Fleet, having been lost at sea. A comfort, and a warning too.

He nodded to Yovell, who gathered up the papers and withdrew.

Bolitho said, 'I expect that your ship will meet with us soon. I hope we have helped in your research?'

Blachford eyed him thoughtfully. 'I am always amazed that

casualties are not greater when I see the hell-holes in which they endure their suffering. It will take time to compare our findings at the College of Surgeons. It will be well spent. The recognition of wounds, the responses of the victims, a division of causes, be they gunshot or caused by thrusting or slashing blades. Immediate recognition can save time, and eventually lives. Mortification, gangrene and the terror it brings with it, each must be treated differently.'

Bolitho tried to imagine this same, reedy man with the wispy white hair in the midst of a battle. Surprisingly, it was not difficult.

He said, 'It is something we all dread.'

Blachford smiled faintly. 'That is very honest. I am afraid one tends to think of senior officers as glory-seeking men without heart.'

Bolitho smiled back. 'Both our worlds appear different from the outside. When I joined my first ship I was a boy. I had to learn that the packed, frightening world between decks was not just a mass, a mindless body. It took me a long time.' He stared at the glittering reflections that moved across one of the guns which shared the cabin, as *Hyperion* responded to a breath of wind. 'I am still learning.'

Through the open skylight he heard the shrill of a call, the slap of bare feet as the watch on deck responded to the order to man the braces yet again, and retrim the great yards to hold this cupful of wind. He heard Parris, too, and was reminded of a strange incident when one of the infrequent Levantine gales had swept down on them from the east, throwing the ship into confusion.

A man had gone overboard, probably like Keen's sister's husband, and while the ship forged away with the gale, the sailor had floundered astern, waiting to perish. For no ship could be brought about in such a blow without the real risk of dismasting her. Some captains would not even have considered it.

Keen had been on deck and had yelled for the quarter-boat to be cast adrift. The man overboard could obviously swim; there was a chance he might be able to reach the boat. There were also some captains who would have denied even that, saying that any boat was worth far more than a common seaman who might die anyway.

But Parris had shinned down to the boat with a handful of volunteers. The next morning the wind had backed and dropped, its amusement at their efforts postponed. They had recovered the boat, and the half-drowned seaman.

Parris had been sick with pain from his wounded shoulder, and Blachford had examined it afresh, and had done all he could. Bolitho had seen respect on Keen's face, just as he had recorded Parris's fanatical determination to prove himself. Because of him, there was one family in Portsmouth who would not grieve just yet. Blachford must also have been thinking of it, as well as all the other small incidents which when moulded into one hull made a fighting ship.

He remarked, 'That was a brave thing your lieutenant did. Not many would even attempt it. It can be no help to see your own ship being carried further and further away until you are quite alone.'

Bolitho called for Ozzard. 'Some wine?' He smiled. 'You are only unpopular aboard this ship if you ask for water!'

The joke hid the truth. They had to divide the squadron soon. If they did not water the ships. . . . He shut it from his mind as Ozzard entered the cabin.

And all the time he felt Blachford watching him. He had only once touched on the subject of his eye, but had dropped the matter when Bolitho had made light of it.

Blachford said abruptly, 'You must do something about your eye. I have a fine colleague who will be pleased to examine it if I ask him.'

Bolitho watched Ozzard as he poured the wine. There was nothing on the little man's face to show he was listening to every word.

Bolitho spread his hands. 'What can I do? Leave the squadron when at any moment the enemy may break out?'

Blachford was unmoved. 'You have a second-in-command. Are you afraid to delegate? I did hear that you took the treasure galleon because you would not risk another in your place.'

Bolitho smiled. 'Perhaps I did not care about the risk.'

Blachford sipped his wine but his eyes remained on Bolitho. Bolitho was reminded of a watchful heron in the reeds at Falmouth. Waiting to strike.

'But that has changed?' The heron blinked at him.

'You are playing games with me.'

'Not really. To cure the sick is one thing. To understand the leaders who decide if a man shall live or die is another essential part of my studies.'

Bolitho stood up and moved restlessly about the cabin. 'I am the cat on the wrong side of every door. When I am at home I fret about my ships and my sailors. Once here and I yearn for just a sight of England, the feel of grass underfoot, the smell of the land.'

Blachford said quietly, 'Think about it. A raging gale like the one I shared with you, the sting of salt spray and the constant demands of duty are no place for what you need.' He made up his mind. 'I tell you this. If you do not heed my warning you will lose all sight in that eye.'

Bolitho looked down at him and smiled sadly. 'And if I hand over my flag? Can you be sure the eye will be saved?'

Blachford shrugged. 'I am certain of nothing, but –'

Bolitho touched his shoulder. 'Aye, the *but*; it is always there. No, I cannot leave. Call me what you will, but I am *needed* here.' He waved his hand towards the water. 'Hundreds of men are depending on me, just as their sons will probably depend on your eventual findings, eh?'

Blachford sighed. 'I call you stubborn.'

Bolitho said. 'I am not ready for the surgeon's wings-and-limbs tub just yet, and I do not yearn for glory as some will proclaim.'

'At least think about it.' Blachford waited and added gently, 'You have another to consider now.'

Bolitho looked up as a far-off voice cried out, 'Deck there! Sail on the lee bow!'

Bolitho laughed. 'With luck that will be your passage to England. I fear I am no match for your devious ways.'

Blachford stood up and ducked his head between the massive beams. 'I never thought it, but I'll be sorry to go.' He looked at Bolitho curiously. 'How can you know that from a masthead's call?'

Bolitho grinned. 'No other ship would dare come near us!'

Later, as the newcomer drew closer, the officer-of-the-watch reported to Keen that she was the brig *Firefly*. The vessel which, like the old *Superb* in Nelson's famous squadron, sailed when others slept.

Bolitho watched as Blachford's much-used chests and folios were carried on deck and said, 'You will meet my nephew. He is good company.'

But *Firefly* was no longer captained by Adam Bolitho; it was another young commander who hurried aboard the flagship to make his report.

Bolitho met him aft and asked, 'What of my nephew?'

The commander, who looked like a midshipman aping his betters, explained that Adam had received his promotion. It was all he knew, and was almost tongue-tied at meeting a vice-admiral face to face. Especially one who was now well known for reasons other than the sea, Bolitho thought bleakly.

He was glad for Adam. But he would have liked more than anything to see him.

Keen stood beside him as *Firefly* spread more sails, and tacked around in an effort to catch the feeble wind.

Keen said, 'It seems wrong without him in command.'

Bolitho looked up at *Hyperion*'s braced yards, the masthead pendant lifting and curling in the glare.

'Aye, Val, I wish him all the luck –' he faltered and remembered Herrick's Lady Luck. 'With men like Sir Piers Blachford taking an interest at long last, maybe Adam's navy will be a safer one for those who serve the fleet.'

He watched the brig until she was stern-on and spreading more canvas, and her upper yards were touched with gold. In two weeks' time *Firefly* would be in England.

Keen moved away as Bolitho began to pace up and down the weather side of the quarterdeck.

In his loose, white shirt, his lock of hair blowing in the breeze, he did not look much like an admiral.

Keen smiled. *He was a man.*

A week later the schooner *Lady Jane*, sailing under Admiralty warrant, was sighted by the frigate *Tybalt*, whose captain immediately signalled his flagship.

The wind was fair but had veered considerably, so that the smart schooner had to beat back and forth for several hours before more signals could be exchanged.

On *Hyperion*'s quarterdeck, Bolitho stood with Keen and watched the schooner's white sails fill to the opposite tack, while Jenour's signals party ran up another acknowledgement.

Jenour said excitedly, 'She is from Gibraltar with despatches, Sir Richard.'

Keen remarked, 'They must be urgent. The schooner is making heavy weather of it.' He gestured to Parris. 'Prepare to heave-to, if you please.'

Calls trilled between decks and men swarmed through hatchways and along the upperdeck to be mustered by their petty officers.

Bolitho touched his eyelid and pressed it gently. It had barely troubled him since Sir Piers Blachford had left the ship. Was it possible that it might improve, despite what he had said?

'*Lady Jane*'s hove-to, Sir Richard. She's putting down a boat.'

Someone chuckled, 'Gawd, her captain looks about twelve years old!'

Bolitho watched the small boat rising and dipping over the smooth-sided swell.

He had been in his cabin when the hail had come from the masthead about *Tybalt*'s signal. He had been composing fresh orders for Herrick and his captains. *Divide the squadron. Delay no longer.*

Bolitho glanced at the nearest gangway, the bare-backed seamen clinging to the nettings to watch as the boat pulled nearer. Was it wrong to curse boredom when the alternative could be sudden death?

'Heave-to, if you please!'

Parris raised his speaking trumpet. 'Main tops'l braces!' Even he seemed to have forgotten his wound.

Hyperion came slowly into the wind, while Bolitho kept his gaze on the approaching boat.

Suppose it was just one more despatch, which in the end meant nothing? He swung away to hide the anger he felt for himself. In God's name, he should be used to that by now.

215

Lady Jane's captain, a pink-cheeked lieutenant named Edwardes, clambered through the entry port and stared around like someone trapped.

Keen stepped forward. 'Come aft, sir. My admiral will speak with you.'

But Bolitho stared at the second figure who was being hauled unceremoniously on deck, accompanied by grins and nudges from the seamen.

Bolitho exclaimed, 'So you could not stay away!'

Sir Piers Blachford waved a warning hand as a sailor made to drop his case of instruments on the deck. Then he said simply, 'I had reached Gibraltar. There I was told that the French are massed at Cadiz with their Spanish allies. I could not see my way to joining the fleet, so I decided to return here in the schooner.' He smiled gently. 'I have the blessing of authority behind me, Sir Richard.'

Keen smiled wryly. 'You are more likely to get sunburn or dry rot if you stay with *us*, Sir Piers!' But his eyes were on Bolitho, seeing the change in him. It never failed to move him, just to watch his expression, the sudden glint in his dark grey eyes.

In the cabin Bolitho slit open the weighted canvas envelope himself. The shipboard sounds seemed to be muffled, as if *Hyperion* too was holding her breath.

The others stood around like unrehearsed players. Keen, feet astride, his fair hair and handsome features picked out in a bar of sunlight. Yovell by the table, a pen still gripped in his hand. Sir Piers Blachford, sitting down because of his height, but unusually subdued, as if he knew this was a moment he must share and remember. Jenour by the table, close enough for Bolitho to hear his rapid breathing. And Lieutenant Edwardes who had carried the despatches under all sail from the Rock, gulping gratefully from a tankard which Ozzard had put into his hand.

And of course, Allday. Was it by chance, or had he taken his stance by the rack with its two swords to mark the moment?

Bolitho said quietly, 'Last month Lord Nelson hauled down his flag and returned home after failing to bring the French to battle.' He glanced at Blachford. 'The French fleet is at Cadiz, so too the Spanish squadrons. Vice-Admiral Collingwood is blockading the enemy in Cadiz.'

Jenour whispered, 'And Lord Nelson?'

Bolitho looked at him. 'Nelson has rejoined *Victory*, and is now doubtless with the fleet.'

For a long moment nobody spoke. Then Keen asked, 'They will break out? They must.'

Bolitho gripped his hands behind him. 'I agree. Villeneuve is ready. He has no choice. Which way will he head? North to Biscay, or back here, Toulon perhaps?' He studied their intent faces. 'We shall be ready. We are ordered to prepare to join Lord Nelson, to blockade or to fight; only Villeneuve knows which.'

He felt every muscle relax, as if a weight had been lifted from his shoulders.

He looked at the pink-cheeked lieutenant. 'So you are on your way?'

'Aye, Sir Richard.' He waved vaguely. 'First to Malta, and then. . . .'

Bolitho watched the sparkle in his eyes; he was planning how he would relate to his friends, how he had carried the word to the rest of the fleet.

'I wish you Godspeed.'

Keen left to see the young man over the side and Bolitho said, 'Make a signal to *Tybalt*, repeated to *Phaedra*. Captain to close the Flag and repair on board without delay.'

Jenour wrote in his book and said, 'Immediately, Sir Richard.' He almost ran from the cabin.

Bolitho looked at Blachford. 'I shall send *Phaedra* to recall the rest of the squadron. When Herrick joins me, I intend to move to the west. If there is to be a fight, then we shall share it.' He smiled and added, 'You will be more than welcome here if that happens.'

Keen came back and asked, 'Will you send *Phaedra*, Sir Richard?'

'Yes.'

Bolitho thought, Val's mind matches my own. He is thinking it a pity it could not be Adam going to tell Herrick the news.

Blachford remarked, 'But it may end in another blockade?'

Keen shook his head. 'I think not, Sir Piers. There is too much at stake here.'

217

Bolitho nodded. 'Not least, Villeneuve's honour.'

He walked to the stern windows and wondered how long it would take Dunstan to work his sloop-of-war back to the squadron.

So Nelson had quit the land to rejoin his *Victory*? He must feel it too. Bolitho ran his palms over the worn sill of the stern windows and watched the sea rise and fall beneath the counter. Two old ships. He thought of the sally port where he had released his hold on Catherine that last time. Nelson would have used those same stairs. One day they would meet. It was inevitable. Dear Inch had met him, and Adam was on speaking terms. He smiled to himself. *Our Nel.*

There were whispers at the screen door, then Keen said, '*Phaedra* is in sight, Sir Richard.'

'Good. We'll send her on her way before dusk with any luck.'

Bolitho threw off his gold-laced coat and sat at the table. 'I shall write my orders, Mr Yovell. Tell your clerk to prepare copies for every captain.'

He stared at the sun glinting across the fresh ink.

Upon receipt of these orders you are to proceed with all despatch – Right or wrong, it was a time for action.

Herrick sat squarely in *Hyperion*'s stern cabin and grasped a tankard of ginger-beer with both hands.

'It feels strange.' He dropped his eyes. 'Why should that be?'

Bolitho walked about the cabin, remembering his own feelings when the lookouts had sighted *Benbow* and her two consorts in the dawn light.

He could understand Herrick's feelings. Two men drawn together like passing ships on an ocean. Now he was here, and not even the coolness Bolitho had seen between him and Keen as the latter had greeted his arrival on board could dispel a sense of relief.

Bolitho said, 'I have decided to head west now that we are joined, Thomas.'

Herrick looked up, but his eyes seemed drawn to the elegant wine cabinet in the corner of the cabin. He probably saw Catherine's hand here too.

'I am not certain it is wise.' He pouted, and then shrugged. 'But if we are called to support Nelson, then the closer we are to the Strait the better, I suppose.' He did not sound very certain. 'At least we can face the enemy if he comes our way in the narrows.'

Bolitho listened to the tramp of feet as the afterguard manned the mizzen braces for changing tack again. Eight ships-of-the-line, a frigate and a small sloop-of-war. It was no fleet, but he was as proud of them as a man could be.

Only one was missing, the little prize frigate *La Mouette* which Herrick had sent further north to scout for any coastal shipping from which she might glean some information.

Herrick said, 'If the Frogs decide not to venture out, we shall remain in ignorance of their next plan of attack. What then?' He waved Ozzard aside as he made to bring the tray and some claret. 'No, I would relish some more ginger-beer.'

Bolitho turned away. Was it really that, or had Herrick become so rigid in his bias against Catherine that he would take nothing from her cabinet? He tried to dismiss the thought as unworthy, petty, but it still persisted.

He said, 'We'll move in separate formations, Thomas. If the weather remains our ally, we shall stand two miles or more apart. It will give our mastheads a better scan of the horizons. If the enemy is chased our way, we should have good warning of it, eh?' He made to smile. 'It is never wise to stand in the path of a charging bull!'

Herrick said abruptly, 'When we return home, what will you do?' He moved his shoes on the deck. 'Share your life with another?'

Bolitho braced his legs as the ship heeled slightly to an extra thrust in her canvas.

He replied, 'I share nothing. Catherine *is* my life.'

'Dulcie said –' The blue eyes lifted and watched him stubbornly. 'She believes you will regret it.'

Bolitho glanced at the wine cabinet, the folded fan lying on top of it.

'You can go with the stream, Thomas, or fight against it.'

'Our friendship means a lot to me.' Herrick frowned as Ozzard padded in with a fresh tankard. 'But it gives me the right to speak my mind. I can never accept this –' he licked his lips, 'this lady.'

Bolitho faced him sadly. 'Then you have made your decision, Thomas.' He sat down and waited for Ozzard to refill his glass. 'Or have you had it made by others?' He watched Herrick's angry reaction and added, 'Perhaps the enemy will decide our future.' He raised the glass. 'I give you a sentiment, Thomas. May the best man win!'

Herrick stood up. 'How can you jest about it!'

The door opened and Keen peered in. 'The rear-admiral's barge is standing by, Sir Richard.' He did not glance at Herrick. 'The sea is getting up, and I thought –'

Herrick looked round for his hat. Then he waited for Keen to withdraw and said flatly, 'When we meet again –'

Bolitho held out his hand. 'For friendship?'

Herrick grasped it, his palm as hard as it had ever been.

He said, 'Aye. Nothing can break that.'

Bolitho listened to the calls as Herrick was piped over the side for the lively pull to his flagship.

Allday lingered in the other doorway, his rag moving up and down on the old sword.

Bolitho said wearily, 'They say love is blind, old friend. It seems to me that only those who have never known it are blind.'

Allday smiled and replaced the sword on its rack.

If it took war and the risk of a bloody fight to make Bolitho's eyes shine again, then so be it.

He said, 'I knew a lass once –'

Bolitho smiled, and recalled his thoughts when he had written his orders.

A time for action. It was like an epitaph.

16

Articles Of War

The twenty-six gun frigate *La Mouette* was completely shrouded in a heavy sea-mist. The lookouts could barely see more than a few yards on either beam, and from the deck the upper shrouds and limp sails were invisible.

There was a slow, moist breeze, but the mist kept pace with the ship to add a sense of being motionless.

Occasionally the disembodied voice of a leadsman floated aft, but the water was deep enough, although if the mist suddenly lifted the ship might be close inshore, or completely alone on an empty sea.

Aft by the quarterdeck rail the first lieutenant, John Wright, stared at the dripping maincourse until his eyes smarted. It was eerie, like thrusting into something solid. He could picture the jib-boom feeling the way like a blind man's stick. There was nothing beyond the pale patch of the figurehead, a fierce-looking seagull with its beak wide in anger.

Around and behind him the other watchkeepers stood about like statues. The helmsman, the sailing master close by. The midshipman of the watch, a boatswain's mate, their faces shining with moisture, as if they had been standing in a rainfall.

Nobody spoke. But that was nothing new, Wright thought. He longed for the chance of a command for himself. Anything. It had meant the next step on the ladder just being first lieutenant. He had not bargained for a captain like Bruce Sinclair. The captain was young, probably twenty-seven or so, Wright decided. A man with fine cheekbones, his chin always high, like a haughty pose, someone who was always quick to seek out slackness and inefficiency in his command.

A visiting admiral had once praised Sinclair for the smartness of his ship. Nobody ever walked on the upper deck, orders were carried out at the double, and any midshipman or petty officer who failed to report a man for not doing so would also face punishment.

They had been in several single-ship actions with privateers and blockade runners, and Sinclair's unyielding discipline had, on the face of it, worked well enough to satisfy any admiral.

The master joined him at the rail and said in a low voice, 'This mist can't last much more, Mr Wright.' He sounded anxious. 'We could be miles off course by now. I'm not happy about it.'

They both looked at the gundeck as a low groan made the men on watch glance uneasily at each other.

Like all the other ships in the squadron *La Mouette* was short of fresh water. Captain Sinclair had ordered it to be severely rationed for all ranks, and two days ago had cut the ration still further. Wright had suggested they might call at some island provided there was no sign of an enemy, if only to replenish a portion of the water supply. Sinclair had studied him coldly. 'I am ordered to seek information about the French, Mr Wright. I cannot spare any time for spoonfeeding the people merely because their lot is not to their taste!'

Wright stared at the man by the larboard gangway. He was quite naked, his legs braced apart by irons, his arms tied back to a gun so that he looked as if he had been crucified. The man occasionally rolled his head from side to side, but his tongue was too swollen in his blistered mouth to make sense of his pleas.

Aboard any King's ship a thief was despised. The justice meted out by the lower deck against such an offender was often far harsher than that of a proper authority.

The seaman McNamara had stolen a gallon of fresh water one night, when a Royal Marine sentry had been called away by the officer-of-the-watch.

He had been caught by a boatswain's mate, drinking the rancid water in secret while his messmates had slept in their hammocks.

Everyone had expected his punishment to be severe, especially as McNamara was a regular defaulter, but Sinclair's reaction had taken even the most hardened sailor aback. For five days he had been in irons on the upper deck, in blazing sunlight, and in the chill of the night. Naked, and in his own filth, he had been doused with salt water by other hands under punishment, to clean up the deck rather than afford him any relief from his torment.

Sinclair had turned up the hands to read the relevant sections of the Articles of War, and had ended by saying that McNamara would be awarded three dozen lashes when the example of his theft was completed.

Wright shivered. It seemed unlikely that McNamara would live long enough to face the flogging.

The master hissed, 'Cap'n's comin' up, Mr Wright.'

It was like that. Whispers. Fear. Smouldering hatred for the man who ruled their daily lives.

Sinclair, neatly dressed, his hand resting on his sword hilt, strode first to the compass, then to the quarterdeck rail to study the set of any visible sails.

'Nor'-west-by-west, sir!'

Sinclair waited as Wright made his report, then said, 'Direct a boy to fetch your hat, Mr Wright.' He smiled faintly. 'This is a King's ship, not a Bombay trader!'

Wright flushed. 'I'm sorry, sir. This heat –'

'Quite.' Sinclair waited until a ship's boy had been sent below for the hat and remarked, 'Deuced if I know how much longer I can waste time like this.'

The wretched man on the gundeck gave another groan. It sounded as if he was choking on his tongue.

Sinclair snapped, 'Keep that man silent! God damn his eyes, I'll have him seized up and put to the lash here and now if I hear another squeak from him!' He looked aft. 'Bosun's mate! See to it! I'll have no bleatings from that bloody thief!'

Wright wiped his lips with his wrist. They felt dry and raw.

'It *is* five days, sir.'

'I too keep a log, Mr Wright.' He moved to the opposite side and peered down at the water as it glided past. 'It may help others to think twice before they follow his miserable example!'

Sinclair added suddenly, 'My orders are to rendezvous with the squadron.' He shrugged, the dying seaman apparently forgotten. 'The meeting is overdue, thanks to this damnable weather. Doubtless Rear-Admiral Herrick will send someone to seek us out.'

Wright saw the boatswain's mate merge with the swirling mist as he hurried towards the naked man. It made him feel sick just to imagine what it must be like. Sinclair was wrong about one thing. The anger of the ship's company had already swung to sympathy. The torture was bad enough. But Sinclair had stripped McNamara of any small dignity he might have held. Had left him in his own excrement like a chained animal, humiliated before his own messmates.

The captain was saying, 'I'm not at all sure that our gallant admiral knows what he is about.' He moved restlessly along the rail. 'Too damn cautious by half, if you ask me.'

'Sir Richard Bolitho will have his own ideas, sir.'

'I wonder.' Sinclair sounded faraway. 'He will combine the squadrons, that is my opinion, and then –' He looked up, frowning at the interruption as a voice called, 'Mist's clearin', sir!'

'God damn it, make a proper report!' Sinclair turned to his first lieutenant. 'If the wind gets up, I want every stitch of canvas on her. So call all hands. Those idlers need work to keep their fingers busy!'

Sinclair could not restrain his impatience and strode along the starboard gangway, which ran above a battery of cannon and joined quarterdeck to forecastle. He paused amidships and looked across at the naked man. McNamara's head was hanging down. He could be dead.

Sinclair called, 'Rouse that scum! *You*, use your starter, man!'

The boatswain's mate stared up at him, shocked at the captain's brutality.

Sinclair put his hands on his hips and eyed him with contempt.

'Do it, or by God you'll change places with him!'

Wright was thankful as the hands came running to halliards and braces. The muffled stamp of bare feet at least covered the sound of the rattan across McNamara's shoulders.

The second lieutenant came hurrying aft and said to the

master, 'Lively, into the chartroom. We shall be expected to fix our position as soon as we sight land!'

Wright pursed his lips as the master's mate of the watch reported the hands ready to make more sail.

If there was no land in sight, God help them all, he thought despairingly.

He watched some weak sunshine probing through the mist and reaching along the topsail yards, then down into the milky water alongside.

The leadsman cried out again, 'No bottom, sir!'

Wright found that he was clenching his fingers so tightly that he had cramp in both hands. He watched the captain at the forward end of the gangway, one hand resting on the packed hammock nettings. A man without a care in the world, anyone might think.

'Deck there! Sail on the weather bow!'

Sinclair strode aft again, his mouth in a thin line.

Wright ran his finger round his neckcloth. 'We'll soon know, sir.' Of course, the lookout would be able to see the other ship now, if only her topgallant yards above the creeping mist.

The lookout shouted again, 'She's English, sir! Man-o'-war!'

'Who is that fool up there?' Sinclair glared into the swirling mist.

Wright answered, 'Tully, sir. A reliable seaman.'

'Hmph. He had better be.'

More sunlight exposed the two batteries of guns, the neatly flaked lines, the pikes in their rack around the mainmast, perfectly matched like soldiers on parade. No wonder the admiral had been impressed, Wright thought.

Sinclair said sharply, 'Make sure our number is bent on and ready to hoist, Mr Wright. I'll have no snooty post-captain finding fault with my signals.'

But the signals midshipman, an anxious-looking youth, was already there with his men. You never fell below the captain's standards more than once.

The foretopsail bellied out from its yard and the master exclaimed, 'Here it comes at last!'

'Man the braces there!' Sinclair pointed over the rail. 'Take that man's name, Mr Cox! God damn it, they are like cripples today!'

The wind tilted the hull, and Wright saw spray lift above the beakhead. Already the mist was floating ahead, shredding through the shrouds and stays, laying bare the water on either beam.

The naked seaman threw back his head and stared, half-blinded, at the sails above, his wrists and ankles rubbed raw by the irons.

'Stand by on the quarterdeck!' Sinclair glared. 'Ready with our number. I don't want to be mistaken for a Frenchie!'

Wright had to admit it was a wise precaution. Another ship new to the station might easily recognise *La Mouette* as French-built. Act first, think later, was the rule in sea warfare.

The lookout called, 'She's a frigate, sir! Runnin' with the wind!'

Sinclair grunted, 'Converging tack.' He peered up to seek out the masthead pendant, but it was still hidden above a last banner of mist. Then like a curtain rising the sea became bright and clear, and Sinclair gestured as the other ship seemed to rise from the water itself.

She was a big frigate, and Sinclair glanced above at the gaff to make certain his own ensign was clearly displayed.

'She's hoisting a signal, sir!'

Sinclair watched as *La Mouette*'s number broke from the yard.

'You see, Mr Wright, if you train the people to respond as they should –'

His words were lost as somebody yelled, 'Christ! *She's runnin' out!*'

All down the other frigate's side the gunports had opened as one, and now, shining in the bright sunshine, her whole larboard battery trundled into view.

Wright ran to the rail and shouted, '*Belay that! Beat to quarters!*'

Then the world exploded into a shrieking din of flame and whirling splinters. Men and pieces of men painted the deck in vivid scarlet patterns. But Wright was on his knees, and some of the screams he knew were his own.

His reeling mind held on to the horrific picture for only seconds. The naked man tied to the gun, but no longer complaining. He had no head. The foremast going over the side, the signals midshipman rolling and whimpering like a sick dog.

The picture froze and faded. He was dead.

Commander Alfred Dunstan sat cross-legged at the table in *Phaedra*'s cramped cabin and studied the chart in silence.

Opposite him, his first lieutenant Joshua Meheux waited for a decision, his ear pitched to the creak and clatter of rigging. Astern through the open windows he could see the thick mist following the sloop-of-war, heard the second lieutenant calling another change of masthead lookouts. In any fog or mist even the best lookout was subject to false sightings. After an hour or so he would see only what he expected to see. A darker patch of fog would become a lee shore, or the topsail of another vessel about to collide. He watched his cousin. It was incredible how Dunstan was able to make his ship's company understand exactly what he needed from them.

He glanced round the small cabin, where they had had so many discussions, made plans, celebrated battles and birthdays with equal enthusiasm. He looked at the great tubs of oranges and lemons which filled most of the available space. *Phaedra* had run down on a Genoese trader just before the sea-mist had enveloped them.

They were short of water, desperately so, but the mass of fresh fruit which Dunstan had *commandeered*, as he had put it, had tilted the balance for the moment.

Dunstan glanced up from the chart and smiled. 'Smells like Bridport on market day, don't it?'

His shirt was crumpled and stained, but better that than have the ship's company believe that water rationing did not apply to the officers as well.

Dunstan tapped the chart with his dividers. 'Another day, and I shall have to come about. We are sorely needed with the squadron. Besides, Captain Sinclair will have an alternative rendezvous. But for this mist, I'd wager we would have sighted his ship days ago.'

Meheux asked, 'Do you know him?'

Dunstan lowered his head to peer more closely at his calculations. 'I know *of* him.'

The lieutenant smiled to himself. Dunstan was in command. He would go no further in discussing another captain. Even with his cousin.

Dunstan leaned back and ruffled his wild auburn hair. 'God, I itch like a poxed-up whore!' He grinned. 'I think Sir Richard intends to join the fleet under Nelson. Though he will take all the blame if the French outpace him and slip back into port in these waters.'

He reached under the table and then produced a decanter of claret. 'Better than water anyway.' He poured two large glasses. 'I'll bet that our vice-admiral will be in enough hot water as it is! God damn it, any man who can accept the wrath of Admiralty and that of the dandified Inspector General must be made of stern stuff.'

'What was he like as a captain?'

Dunstan looked at him, his eyes distant. 'Brave, courteous. No conceit.'

'You liked him?'

Dunstan swallowed the claret; the casual question had slipped through his guard.

'I worshipped the deck he walked on. All of us in the gunroom did, I believe.' He shook his head. 'I'd stand beside him any day.'

There was a tap at the door and a midshipman, dressed in an even grubbier shirt than his captain's, peered in at them.

'The second lieutenant's respects, sir, and he thinks the mist may be clearing.'

They looked up as the deck quivered very slightly, and the hull murmured a gentle protest at being disturbed again.

'By God, the wind *is* returning.' Dunstan's eyes gleamed. 'My compliments to the second lieutenant, Mr Valliant. I shall come up presently.' As the boy left he winked at Meheux. 'With a name like his he should go far in the navy!'

Dunstan held up the decanter and grimaced. It was almost empty.

He remarked, 'It will be a drier ship than usual, I fear.' Then he

228

became serious again. 'Now this is what I intend –'

Meheux stared at the decanter as the glass stopper rattled for several seconds.

Their eyes met. Meheux said, 'Thunder?'

Dunstan was groping for his shabby hat. 'Not this time, by God. That came from iron guns, my friend!'

He slipped his arms into his coat and climbed up the companion ladder to the deck.

He glanced through the drifting mist, seeing his seamen standing and listening. Such a small vessel, yet so many men, he thought vaguely. He tensed as the booming roar sighed through the mist and imagined he could feel the sullen vibration against the hull. Faces had turned aft towards him. Instantly he remembered Bolitho, when they had all stared at him as if expecting salvation and understanding, because he had been their captain.

Dunstan tucked one hand into his old seagoing coat with the tarnished buttons. *I am ready. Now they look to me.*

Meheux was the first to speak.

'Shall we stand away until we are sure what is happening, sir?'

He did not reply directly. 'Call all hands. Have the people lay aft.'

They came running to the pipe, and when they were all packed from side to side, with some clinging to the mizzen shrouds and on the upturned cutter, Meheux touched his hat, his eyes curious.

'Lower deck cleared, sir.'

Dunstan said, 'In a moment we shall clear for action. No fuss, no beat of a drum. Not this time. You will go to quarters in the manner you have learned so well.' He looked at those nearest him, youngsters like their officers, grizzled old hands such as the boatswain and the carpenter. Faces he had taught himself to know and recognise, so that he could call any one of them by name even in pitch darkness. At any other time the thought would have made him smile. For it was often said that his hero Nelson had the same knack of knowing his people, even now that he had reached flag rank.

But he did not smile. 'Listen!' The booming roar echoed through the mist. Each man would hear it differently. Ships at war, or the sound of enraged surf on a reef. Thunder across the hills in a home land which had produced most of these men.

'I intend to continue on this tack.' His eyes moved over them. 'One of those ships must be a friend. We shall carry word of our finding to Sir Richard Bolitho and the squadron.'

A solitary voice raised a cheer and Dunstan gave a broad grin. 'So stand-to, my lads, and God be with you all!'

He stood back to watch as they scattered to their various stations, while the boatswain and his own party broke out the chain slings and nets for the yards to offer some protection to the gun crews should the worst happen.

Dunstan said quietly, 'I think we may have found *La Mouette*.' He kept the other thought to himself. That he hoped Sinclair was as ready for a fight as he was with the lash.

The thuds of screens being taken down, stores and personal belongings being lowered to the orlop deck, helped to muffle the occasional sound of distant thunder.

Lieutenant Meheux touched his hat and reported, 'Cleared for action, sir.'

Dunstan nodded and again recalled Bolitho. 'Ten minutes this time. They take fairly to their work.' But the mood eluded him and he smiled. 'Well done, Josh!'

The sails billowed out loudly, like giants puffing their chests. The deck canted over and Dunstan said, 'Bring her up a point! Steer nor'-nor'-west!'

He saw Meheux clipping on his hanger and said, 'The people are feeling this.' He looked at the crouching gun crews, the ship's boys with their buckets of sand, the others at the braces or with their fingers gripping the ratlines, ready to dash aloft when the order was piped to make more sail.

Dunstan made up his mind. 'Load if you please, I –'

There was a great chorus of shouts and Dunstan stared as the mist lifted and swirled to one violent explosion.

He said sharply, '*Load*, Mr Meheux! Keep their minds in your grasp!'

Each gun captain faced aft and raised his fist.

'All loaded, sir!'

They looked aloft as the mist faded more swiftly and laid bare the rippling ensign above the gaff.

Dunstan plucked his chin. 'We are ready this time anyway.'

All eyes turned forward as the mist lost its greyness. Something like a fireball exploded through it, the sound going on and on until eventually lost in the beat of canvas, the sluice of water alongside.

'Ship on the starboard bow, sir!'

Dunstan snatched a glass. 'Get aloft, Josh. I need your eyes up there today.'

As the first lieutenant swarmed up the mainmast shrouds a warning cry came from the forecastle.

'Wreckage ahead!'

The master's mate of the watch threw his weight onto the wheel with that of the two helmsmen but Dunstan yelled, 'Belay that! Steady as you go!' He made himself walk to the side as what appeared to be a giant tusk loomed off the bow. It was always best to meet it head on, he thought grimly. *Phaedra* did not have the timbers of a liner, nor even a frigate. That great pitching spar might have crashed right through the lower hull like a ram.

He watched the severed mast pass down the side, torn shrouds and blackened canvas trailing behind it like foul weed. There were corpses too. Men trapped by the rigging, their faces staring through the lapping water, or their blood surrounding them like pink mist.

Dunstan heard a boatswain's mate bite back a sob as he stared at one of the bobbing corpses. It wore the same blue jacket with white piping as himself.

There was no more doubt as to who had lost the fight.

Some of the small waves crumpled over as the rising wind felt its way across the surface.

Dunstan watched the mist drawing clear, further and further. leaving the sea empty once again. He stiffened as more shouts came from forward.

Something long and dark which barely rose above the uneasy water. There was much weed on it. One of the vessels which should have been released for a much needed overhaul. Surrounded by giant bubbles and a great litter of flotsam and charred remains, it was a ship's keel.

231

Dunstan said, 'Up another point. Hands aloft, Mr Faulkner! As fast as you like!'

High above it all, Lieutenant Meheux clung to the main crosstrees beside the lookout and watched the mist rolling away before him. He saw the other ship's topgallant masts and braced yards, and then as the mist continued to outpace the thrust of the sails, the forepart of the hull and her gilded figurehead.

He slid down a backstay and reached Dunstan in seconds.

Dunstan nodded very slowly. 'We both remember *that* ship, Josh. She's *Consort* – in hell's name I'd know her anywhere!'

He raised his telescope and studied the other vessel as more sails broke to the wind, and her shining hull seemed to shorten while she leaned over on a fresh tack. Towards *Phaedra*.

The midshipman was pointing wildly. 'Sir! There are men in the water!' He was almost weeping. 'Our people!'

Dunstan moved the glass until he saw the thrashing figures, some clinging to pieces of timber, others trying to hold their comrades afloat.

Dunstan climbed into the shrouds and twisted his leg around the tarred cordage to hold himself steady.

The masthead lookout yelled, 'Ships to the nor'-east!'

But Dunstan had already seen them. With the mist gone, the horizon was sharp and bright; it reminded him of a naked sword.

Someone was shouting, 'It'll be th' squadron! Come on, lads! Kill them buggers!'

Others started to cheer, their voices broken as they watched the survivors from *La Mouette*. Men like themselves. The same dialects, the same uniforms.

Dunstan watched the ships on the horizon until his eye ached. He had seen the red and yellow barricades around their fighting-tops in the powerful lens, something the lookout had not yet recognised.

He lowered the glass and looked sadly at the midshipman. 'We must leave those poor devils to die, Mr Valliant.' He ignored the boy's horrified face. 'Josh, we will come about and make all haste to find Sir Richard.'

Meheux waited, dazed by the swiftness of disaster.

His captain gestured towards the horizon. 'The Dons are

coming. A whole bloody squadron of them.'

The air cringed as a shot echoed across the sea. The frigate had fired a ranging ball from one of her bow chasers. The next one —

Dunstan cupped his hands. 'Hands aloft! Man the braces! Stand by to come about!' He bit his lip as another ball slammed down and threw up a waterspout as high as the topsail yard. Men ran to obey, and as the yards swung round *Phaedra*'s lee bulwark appeared to dip beneath the water.

Another shot pursued her as the frigate made more sail, her yards alive with men.

Meheux was waving to his topmen with the speaking trumpet. He shouted breathlessly, 'If they reach our squadron before we can warn them —'

Dunstan folded his arms and waited for the next fall of shot. Any one of those nine pounders could cripple his command, slow her down until she reeled beneath a full broadside as Sinclair had done.

'I think it will be more than a squadron at stake, Josh.'

A ball crashed through the taffrail and seared across the deck like a furnace bar. Two men fell dead, without even uttering a cry. Dunstan watched as two others took their place.

'Run, my beauty, *run!*' He looked up at the hardening sails, the masts curving like coachmen's whips.

'Just this once, you are the most important ship in the fleet!'

17

Prepare For Battle!

Captain Valentine Keen walked up the slanting deck and hunched his shoulders against the wind. How quickly the Mediterranean could change her face at this time of year, he thought. The sky was hidden by deep-bellied clouds, and the sea was no longer like blue silk.

He stared at the murky horizon, at the endless serried ranks of short, steep white horses. It looked hostile and without warmth. There had been some heavy rain in the night and every available man had been roused on deck to gather it in canvas scoops, even in humble buckets. A full glass, washed down with a tot of rum for all hands, seemed to have raised their spirits.

The deck heaved over again, for *Hyperion* was butting as close to the wind as she dared, her reefed topsails glinting with spray as she held station on the other ships astern.

For as Isaac Penhaligon, the master, had commented, with the wind veered again to the nor'-east, it was hard enough to dawdle until Herrick's ships joined them, without the additional problem of clawing into the wind, watch in and watch out. For if they were driven too far to the west, they would find it almost impossible to steer for Toulon should the enemy try to re-enter that harbour.

Keen pictured the chart in his mind. They were already at that point right now, another cross, a new set of bearings and the noon sights. With such poor visibility they could be miles off their estimated course.

Keen walked to the quarterdeck rail and stared along the maindeck. As usual it was busy despite the weather. Trigge the sailmaker with his assistants, squatting on the deck, their needles and palms moving intricately like parts of a mill as they repaired heavy-weather canvas brought up from below.

Trigge was experienced enough to know that if they entered the Atlantic in search of the enemy, every spare sail would be needed.

Sheargold the purser, his unsmiling features set in a permanently suspicious frown, was watching as some casks of salt-beef were hoisted through another hatch. Keen did not envy anyone in that trade. Sheargold had to plan for every league sailed, each delay or sudden change of orders which might send the ship in an opposite direction without time to restock his provisions.

Hardly anybody ever felt grateful to Sheargold. It was generally believed between decks that most pursers retired rich, having won their fortunes by scrimping on the sailors' meagre rations.

Major Adams was up forward, standing at an angle on the tilting deck while he studied a squad of marines being put through their paces. How bright the the scarlet coats and white cross belts looked in the dull light, Keen thought.

He heard the boatswain, Sam Lintott, discussing the new cutter with one of his mates. The latter was the villainous-looking one named Dacie. Keen had been told of his part in the cutting-out of the Spanish treasure-ship. He could believe all that he had heard. With his eye patch, and crooked shoulder, Dacie would frighten anybody.

Lieutenant Parris approached the rail and touched his hat.

'Permission to exercise the quarterdeck guns this afternoon, sir?'

Keen nodded. 'They will not thank you, Mr Parris, but I think it a good idea.'

Parris looked out to sea. 'Shall we meet the French, sir?'

Keen glanced at him. Outwardly easy and forthcoming with the sailors, there was something else within the man, something he was grappling with, even in casual conversation. Getting his command? Keen did not know why he had lost it in the first place. He had heard about Haven's animosity towards him. Maybe there had been another superior officer with whom he had crossed swords.

He replied, 'Sir Richard is torn between the need to watch the approaches to Toulon, and the strong possibility we will be called to support the fleet.' He thought of Bolitho in the cabin, dictating letters to Yovell or his clerk, telling young Jenour what might be expected of him if they met with the enemy. Keen had already discussed the possibility with Bolitho.

Bolitho had seemed preoccupied. 'I do not have the time to call all my captains aboard. I must pray that they know me well enough to respond when I so order.'

I do not have the time. It was uncanny. Bolitho seemed to accept it, as if a battle was inevitable.

Parris said, 'I wonder if we shall see Viscount Somervell again.'

Keen stared at him. 'Why should that concern you?' He softened his tone and added, 'I would think he is better off away from us.'

Parris nodded. 'Yes, I – I'm sorry I mentioned it, sir.' He saw the doubt in Keen's eyes. 'It is nothing to do with Sir Richard's involvement.'

Keen looked away. 'I should hope not.' He was angry at Parris's interest. More so with himself for his instant rush of protectiveness. *Involvement*. What everybody was probably calling it.

Keen walked to the weather side and tried to empty his mind. He took a telescope from the midshipman-of-the-watch and steadied it on the ships astern.

The three seventy-fours were somehow managing to hold their positions. The fourth, Merrye's *Capricious*, was almost invisible in spray and blown spume. She was far astern of the others, while work was continued to replace the main topgallant mast which had carried away in a sudden squall before they could shorten sail.

He smiled. A captain's responsibility never ceased. The man who was seen by others as a kind of god, would nevertheless pace his cabin and fret about everything.

A lookout yelled, 'Deck there! *Tybalt* is signallin'!'

Keen looked at the midshipman. 'Up you go, Mr Furnival. *Tybalt* must have news for us.'

Later, Keen went down to the cabin and reported to Bolitho.

'*Tybalt* has the rest of the squadron in sight to the east'rd, Sir Richard.'

Bolitho glanced across his scattered papers and smiled. He looked and sounded tired.

'That is something, Val.' He gestured to a chair. 'I would ask you to join us, but you will need to be on deck until the ships are closer.'

As he left, Sir Piers Blachford said, 'A good man. I like him.' He was half-lying in one of Bolitho's chair. *The heron at rest.*

Yovell gathered up his letters and the notes he would add to his various copies.

Ozzard entered to collect the empty coffee cups, while Allday, standing just inside the adjoining door, was slowly polishing the magnificent presentation sword. Bolitho's gift from the people of Falmouth for his achievements in this same sea and the events which had led up to the Battle of the Nile.

Bolitho glanced up. 'Thank you, Ozzard.'

Blachford slapped one bony fist into his palm.

'Of course. I remember now. Ozzard is an unusual name, is it not?'

Allday's polishing cloth had stilled on the blade.

Blachford nodded, remembering. 'Your secretary and all the letters he has to copy must have brought it back to me. My people once used the services of a scrivener down by the London docks. Unusual.'

Bolitho looked at the letter which he might complete when the others had left him. He would share his feelings with Catherine. Tell her of his uncertainty about what lay ahead. It was like speaking with her. Like the moments when they had lain together, and she had encouraged him to talk, had shared those parts of his life which were still a mystery to her.

He replied, 'I've never asked him about it.'

But Blachford had not heard. 'I don't know how I could have forgotten it. I was directly involved. There was the most dastardly murder done, almost opposite the scrivener's shop. How could one forget that?'

There was a crash of breaking crockery from the pantry and Bolitho half-rose from his chair.

But Allday said quickly, 'I'll go. He must have fallen over.'

Blachford picked up a book he had been reading and remarked, 'Not surprised in this sickening motion.'

Bolitho watched him, but there was nothing on his pointed face to suggest anything other than passing interest.

Bolitho had seen Allday's expression, had almost heard his unspoken warning.

Coincidence? There had been too many of those. Bolitho examined his feelings. *Do I want to know more?*

He stood up. 'I am going to take my walk.'

He could feel Blachford's eyes following him as he left the cabin.

It was not until the next day that Herrick's three ships were close enough to exchange signals.

Bolitho watched the flags soaring aloft, Jenour's unusual sharpness with the signals midshipmen, as if he understood the mood which was gripping his vice-admiral.

Bolitho held on to a stay and studied the new arrivals, the way they and his own seventy-fours lay about haphazardly under reduced canvas, as if they and not their captains were awaiting instructions.

The weather had not improved, and overnight had built the sea into a parade of steep swells. Bolitho covered his damaged eye with one hand. His skin was wet and hot, indeed like the fever which had brought him and Catherine together.

Keen crossed the slippery planking and stood beside him, his telescope tilted beneath his arm to keep the lens free of salt spray.

'The wind holds steady from the nor'-east, Sir Richard.'

'I know.' Bolitho tried not to listen to the clank of pumps. The old ship was working badly, and the pumps had continued all through the night watches. Thank God Keen knew his profession and the extent of his complete authority. Haven would have been flogging his luckless sailors by now, he thought bitterly. Hardly an hour had passed without the hands being piped aloft to make or shorten sail. Manning the pumps, lashing loose gear in the uncomfortable motion – it took patience as well as discipline to keep men from flying at each other's throats. The officers were not immune to it. Tempers flared out of all proportion if a lieutenant was just minutes late relieving his opposite number; he had heard Keen telling one of them to try and act up to the coat he wore. It was not easy for any of them.

Bolitho said, 'If it gets any worse we'll not be able to put down any boats.' He studied his scattered ships. *Waiting for his lead.* He saw *Benbow* swaying steeply as she hove-to, her sails billowing and cracking, shining in the filtered glare like buckled breastplates.

Herrick was coming to see him. Face-to-face. It was typical of him.

Herrick's barge had to make three attempts before the bowman could hook on to the main chains.

In the cabin the sounds faded, and only the sloping horizon, blurred by the thick glass of the stern windows, appeared to be swaying, as if to tip the weatherbeaten ships into a void.

Herrick got straight to the point.

'I wish to know what you intend.' He shook his head as Ozzard hovered nearby with a tray in his hand. 'No, but thank you.' To Bolitho he added, 'I'd not want to be marooned here, away from my flagship.' He glanced at the spray running down the glass. 'I don't like this at all.'

Bolitho said, 'No sign of *La Mouette*, Thomas?' He saw Herrick shake his head. 'I sent *Phaedra* to hunt for her.'

Herrick leaned forward in his chair. 'Captain Sinclair knows what he is about. He will find the squadron.'

Bolitho said, 'I will use every vessel which can scout for us. It was not a criticism.'

Herrick settled back again. 'I think we should stand towards Toulon. Then we shall know, one way or the other.'

Bolitho rested his hands on the table. He could feel the whole ship shivering through it, the rudder jerking against helm and wind.

'If the enemy intend to re-enter the Mediterranean, Thomas,

239

we could lose them just as easily as Nelson lost contact when they ran to the west.' He made up his mind. 'I intend to head for Gibraltar. If we still have no news we shall proceed through the Strait and join the fleet. I see no other choice.'

Herrick eyed him stubbornly. 'Or we can stay here and wait. No one can blame us. We shall certainly be damned if we miss the enemy when they break through to Toulon.'

'I would blame *myself*, Thomas. My head tells me one thing, instinct directs me otherwise.'

Herrick cocked his head to listen to the pumps. 'Is it that bad?'

'She will stand more of it.'

'I sent *Absolute* into harbour because she was too rotten.'

Bolitho retorted, 'I could use her too, rotten or not.'

Herrick stood up and walked to the stern windows. 'I should leave. I mean no disrespect, but my barge will have a hard pull as it is.'

Bolitho faced him. '*Listen to me*, Thomas. I don't care what you think about my private life, for private it is not apparently. I need your support, for fight we shall.' He clapped his hand to his heart. 'I know it.'

Herrick watched him as if seeking a trap. 'As your second-in-command I will be ready *if* we are called to battle. But I still believe you are misguided.'

Bolitho said despairingly, 'You are not listening, man! I am not commanding you, I am asking for your help!' He saw Herrick's astonishment as he exclaimed, 'In God's name, Thomas, must I plead? *I am going blind*, or did that piece of gossip rouse no interest amongst you?'

Herrick gasped, 'I had no idea —'

Bolitho looked away and shrugged. 'I will trouble you to keep it to yourself.' He swung round, his voice harsh. 'But if I fall, you must lead these men, you will make them perform miracles if need be — are you listening now?'

There was a tap at the door, and Bolitho shouted, '*Yes?*' His anguish tore the word from his throat.

Keen entered and glanced between them. 'Signal from *Phaedra*, sir, repeated by *Tybalt*.'

Herrick asked quickly, 'What of *La Mouette*?'

Keen was looking only at Bolitho. He guessed what had happened, and wanted to share it with him.

He answered abruptly, 'She is down.'

Bolitho met his gaze, grateful for the interruption. He had almost broken that time.

'News, Val?'

'There is an enemy squadron on the move, Sir Richard. Heading west.'

Herrick asked, 'How many?'

Still Keen avoided his eyes. 'Phaedra has not yet reported. She is damaged after a stern-chase.' He took a step towards him, then let his arms fall to his sides. 'They are Spanish, Sir Richard. Sail of the line, that we do know.'

Bolitho ran his fingers through his hair and asked, 'How many ships does Nelson have?'

Keen looked at him, and then his eyes cleared with understanding.

'It was last reported as two dozen of the line, Sir Richard. The French and their Spanish ally are said to have over thirty, which will include some of the largest first-rates afloat.'

Bolitho listened to the moan of the wind. *Divide and conquer.* How well Villeneuve had planned it. And now with this new formation of ships, discovered only accidentally by *Phaedra*, Nelson's fleet would be overwhelmed and hopelessly outnumbered.

He said simply, 'If they slip through the Strait we may never catch them in time.' He looked at Keen. 'Signal *Phaedra* to close on the Flag.' He caught his arm as he made to leave. 'When that brave little ship draws close enough, spell out *well done*.'

When Keen left Herrick said with sudden determination, 'I am ready. Tell me what to do.'

Bolitho stared through the stained windows. 'Minimum signals, Thomas. As we discussed.'

'But your eyesight?' Herrick sounded wretched.

'Oh no, *not any more*, Thomas. Little *Phaedra* has lifted my blindness. But hear me. If my flag comes down, *Benbow* will take the van.'

Herrick nodded. 'Understood.'

241

Bolitho said, 'So hold back your conscience, my friend, and together we may yet win the day!'

He turned to look at the breaking wave-crests, and did not move until he heard the door shut.

Bolitho put his signature to his final letter and stared at it for several minutes.

The swell was as steep as before, but the wind had lessened, so that the hull seemed to rise and fall with a kind of ponderous majesty. He glanced at the quarter windows as a pale shaft of sunlight penetrated the sea-mist and showed up the salt stains on the glass like ice-rime. He hoped the sun would break through completely before the day ended. The air was heavy with damp; hammocks, clothing, everything.

He reread the last of the letter which *Phaedra* would carry to the fleet. He tried to picture Nelson eventually reading it, understanding as a sailor, better than any other, what Bolitho's ships and men were trying to do.

He had finished with, '*And I thank you, my lord, for offering my nephew, who is most dear to me, the same inspiration you have given to the whole fleet.*'

He pushed it aside for Yovell to seal and turned the other letter over in his fingers, while he imagined Catherine's dark eyes as she read the words, his declaration of love *which now can never die*. There would be many letters going in *Phaedra*. What would Herrick say to his Dulcie, he wondered? Their parting yesterday had left a bad taste. Once, such a thing would have seemed impossible. Maybe people did change, and he was the one who was mistaken.

Keen would have written to his Zenoria. It was a great comfort that she would be with Catherine. He stood up, suddenly chilled to the marrow despite the damp, humid air. *Nothing must happen to Val.* Not after what they had shared. The pain and the joy, the fulfilment of a dream which had been snatched from Keen and had left him like half a man. Until Zenoria. The girl with the moonlit eyes; another whose love had been forged from suffering.

Keen looked in. '*Phaedra*'s captain is come aboard, Sir Richard.'

Bolitho faced the door as Dunstan almost bounded into the cabin.

A young man of tireless energy, and certainly one of the scruffiest captains Bolitho had ever laid eyes on.

'It was good of you to come.' Bolitho held out his hand. 'I believe it was intended we should pass the despatches over by line and tackle.'

Dunstan beamed and looked around the cabin. 'I thought, damn the sea, Sir Richard. I'll go myself.'

Bolitho gestured to the letters. 'I place these in your hands. There is one for Lord Nelson. When you have run him to ground I would wish you to present it to him personally.' He gave a quick smile. 'It seems I am fated not to meet him in person!'

Dunstan took the letter and stared at it as if he expected it to look different from all the others.

Bolitho said, 'I am told that you had some casualties.'

'Aye, Sir Richard. Two killed, another pair cut down by splinters.'

For just a moment Bolitho saw the young man behind the guise of captain. The memory and the risks, the moment of truth when death sings in the air.

Dunstan added, 'I am only sorry I could not linger to estimate the full array of Spanish vessels.' He shrugged. 'But that damn frigate was at my coat-tails, and the mist hid many of the enemy.'

Bolitho did not press him. Keen would have laid all of his findings and calculations alongside his own on *Hyperion*'s charts.

Dunstan said, 'It struck me that war is an odd game, Sir Richard. It was just a small fight by today's standard, but how strange the contestants.'

Bolitho smiled. 'I know. A captured British frigate fighting under Spanish colours against a French prize beneath our own flag!'

Dunstan looked at him squarely. 'I would ask that you send another to seek out Lord Nelson. My place is here with you.'

Bolitho took his arm. 'I need the fleet to know what is happening, and my intention to prevent these ships of yours from joining with Villeneuve. It is vital. In any case I can spare nobody else.'

He shook his arms gently. '*Phaedra* has done enough. For me, and for us all. Remember that well and tell your people.'

Dunstan nodded, his eyes searching Bolitho's face as if he wanted to remember the moment.

He said, 'Then I shall leave, Sir Richard.' Impetuously he thrust out his hand. 'God be with you.'

For a long while afterwards Bolitho stood alone in the cabin, watching the sloop-of-war as she went about, her gunports awash as she took the wind into her courses and topsails.

He heard distant cheers, from *Phaedra* or the other ships he could not tell.

He sat down and massaged his eye, hating its deception.

Allday clumped into the cabin and regarded him dubiously.

'She's gone then, Sir Richard?'

'Aye.' Bolitho knew he must go on deck. The squadron was waiting. They must assume their proper formation long before dusk. He thought of his captains. How would they react? Perhaps they doubted his ability, or shared Herrick's opposition to his intentions.

Allday asked, 'So, it's important?'

'It could well be, old friend.' Bolitho looked at him fondly. 'If we head them off, they *must fight*. If they have already outrun us then we shall give chase.'

Allday nodded, his eyes faraway. 'Nothin' new then.'

Bolitho grinned, the tension slipping away like soft sand in a glass.

'No, nothing new! My God, Allday, they could do with you in Parliament!'

By the next morning the weather had changed yet again. The wind had veered and stood directly from the east. That at least put paid to any hope of beating back to Toulon.

The squadron, lying comfortably on the starboard tack, headed north-west with the Balearic Islands lying somewhere beyond the starboard bow.

Sixth in the line leading his own ships, Rear-Admiral Herrick had been up since dawn, unable to sleep, and unwilling to share his doubts with Captain Gossage.

He stood in one corner of *Benbow*'s broad quarterdeck and watched the ships ahead. They made a fine sight beneath an almost clear sky, broken only by fleecy patches of cloud. His face softened as he remembered his mother, in the little house where he had been born in Kent.

Watch the big sheep, Tommy! She had always said that.

Herrick looked around at the busy seamen, the first lieutenant in a close conversation with several warrant officers about today's work.

What would that dear, tired old lady think of her Tommy now?

Captain Gossage crossed the deck, his hat tilted at the jaunty angle which he seemed to favour.

Herrick did not wish to pass the time in idle conversation. Each turn of the log was taking his ships further westward. He felt uneasy, as if he had suddenly been stripped of his authority. He shaded his eyes to peer across the starboard nettings. Their one remaining frigate was far away from the squadron. *Tybalt* would be the first to sight any enemy shipping. He bit his lip until it hurt. If the enemy had not already slipped past them. Slamming a door after the horse had bolted.

Gossage remarked, 'I suppose that *Phaedra*'s captain was not mistaken, sir?'

Herrick glared. 'Well, somebody sunk *La Mouette*, he did not imagine that!'

Gossage grunted. 'Had we been relieved from the Maltese station we would have been at Gibraltar anyway, sir. Then our ships would have had the honour –'

Herrick snapped, 'Honour be damned! Sir Richard Bolitho is not the kind of man to seize glory for himself!'

Gossage raised his eyebrows, 'Oh, I see, sir.'

Herrick turned away, quietly fuming. *No, you don't.* Try as he might he could not tear his thoughts from the twenty-odd years that he had known Bolitho.

All the battles, some hard-won, others surprisingly kind to them. Bad wounds, old friends lost or maimed, sea-passages and landfalls when at times they had wondered if they might ever walk ashore again. Now it had gone rotten, thrown away because of –

Gossage tried again. 'My wife wrote to me and says that there is talk of Sir Richard being relieved.'

Herrick stared at him. Dulcie had said nothing of the kind. 'When?'

Gossage smiled. He had caught his admiral's attention at last. 'Next year, sir. The fleet will be reformed, the squadrons allocated differently. In this article she read —'

Herrick gave a cold grin. 'Bloody rubbish, man! Sir Richard and I have been hearing the bleats of shorebound experts all our lives. God damn it, the day we —'

The masthead yelled, 'Deck there! Signal from *Flag*!'

A dozen telescopes rose as one and the signals midshipman called, '*General*, sir! Have *Tybalt* in sight to the north!'

Gossage hissed to the officer-of-the-watch, 'Why in hell's name did they sight her first?'

Herrick smiled wryly. 'Acknowledge it.' To the first lieutenant he called, 'Send a good master's mate aloft, Mr O'Shea!'

The lieutenant turned as if to confirm the order with Gossage but Herrick snapped, 'Just do it!'

He moved away, his hands grasped behind his back. He had never got used to flag rank, nor had he expected it, no matter what flattering things Dulcie had said about the matter.

He knew he was being petty but he felt better for it. At heart he would always remain a captain and not leave it to others to carry out his plans.

All down the line of eight ships, the air would be buzzing with speculation. Herrick thought of the missing third-rate *Absolute*. He had done the right thing. One great gale like the last one, and that poor, rotten ship would surely have foundered.

Bolitho's refusal to accept his action still rankled deeply. He took his own telescope, the latest and most expensive one which Dulcie could find, and trained it on the ships astern. In perfect formation, their masthead pendants licking out like serpents' tongues, the sunlight glistening on the checkered patterns of gunports.

The new voice hailed from the masthead. '*Tybalt* in sight, sir!'

Herrick climbed up the starboard poop ladder and levelled his beautiful telescope. He could just make out the frigate's topgallant sails, like the fleecy clouds, pink-edged and delicate against the hard horizon. The edge of the sea, he thought. Deep, dark blue. Still no sign of rain. Perhaps Bolitho would decide after all to send some of the ships to seek fresh water.

He saw the tiny pin-pricks of colour rise against the frigate's pyramid of sails. Herrick blinked his eyes. His vision was not as good as it had been, although he would never admit it. He thought of Bolitho's expression, the anguish when he had revealed to him about his damaged eyesight.

It troubled Herrick for several reasons, not the least being that he had failed Bolitho when he had most needed him.

Herrick's flag lieutenant, a willowy young man called De Broux, called, 'From *Tybalt*, sir!'

Herrick waited impatiently. He had never really liked his flag lieutenant. He was soft. Even had a Frenchie-sounding name.

Unaware of Herrick's distaste De Broux said, '*Strange sail bearing north-east!*'

Several of the officers nearby chuckled amongst themselves and Herrick felt his face smart with anger, and embarrassment too for Bolitho.

Gossage said cheerfully, 'A strange sail, eh? Damn my eyes if I don't think that our eight *liners* can't take care of it, what?' He turned to his officers. 'We can leave *Tybalt* outside to act as umpire!'

Herrick said harshly, 'Hold your damn noise!' He spoke to the lieutenants. It was meant for Gossage.

'From *Flag*, sir. *General. Make more sail.*'

Herrick watched the acknowledgement dashing aloft.

Gossage, sulking slightly, called, 'Hands aloft, Mr O'Shea! Shake out all reefs!' His tone suggested it was merely to cover Bolitho's confusion.

Herrick raised the telescope and climbed up two more steps.

She had been so proud when she had bought it for him, from one of the best instrument makers in London's Strand. His heart sank. She had gone there with Belinda.

De Broux shouted suddenly, '*Tybalt* to *Flag*, sir!' For once he seemed unsure of himself. Then he stammered, '*Estimate twelve sail-of-the-line!*'

247

Herrick climbed down to the quarterdeck again. He was uncertain how he felt. Resigned, or stunned by the last signal.

Gossage was staring at him, and made to speak as De Broux called desperately, '*General signal*, sir. *Prepare for battle!*'

Herrick met Gossage's disbelief with something close to complete calm. To feel that way under such circumstances was almost unnerving.

Herrick asked coolly, 'Well, Captain Gossage, how do the odds appeal to you now?'

18

In Danger's Hour

Bolitho held out his arms and tried to contain his impatience as Ozzard nimbly buttoned his white waistcoat. After all the shortages it felt strange to be dressed from head to toe in clean clothing. Over Ozzard's shoulder he watched Keen, who was standing just inside the cabin so that he could still hear the shouted commands and replies from the quarterdeck.

Hyperion had not yet cleared for action; he would leave it to Herrick and the individual captains to do it when they were ready, and in their own time.

Hyperion's company were snatching a last hasty meal, although how the average sailor managed to eat anything before a fight was beyond Bolitho.

Keen said, 'If the Dons continue that approach, Sir Richard, neither of us will hold the wind-gage. It would seem that the enemy is on a converging tack.' His eyes were clouded with concentration as he tried to picture the distant ships. A day later and the enemy would have slipped past them to close with the coast of Spain before a final dash through the Strait.

Bolitho said, 'I must take the wind-gage from them. Otherwise, ship-to-ship they will swamp us.' He could feel Keen watching him as the plan formed itself so that they could both see it. As if it was here and now. 'We shall hold our forces together until the last moment. I intend to alter course to starboard and form two columns. Herrick knows what to do. His will be the shorter line, but no matter. Once battle is joined we may throw the Dons into confusion.' He allowed Ozzard to offer him his coat and hat.

Keen said, 'I must protest, Sir Richard.' He looked at the gold lace, the Nile medal which Bolitho would hang about his neck. 'I know your custom. I have shared this suspense too many times to forget.'

Allday entered by the other door and reached up for the old sword. Over his shoulder he remarked, 'You're wastin' your time, with all respect, Cap'n Keen.'

Keen and Allday looked at one another. Allday recalled better than any how he had seen Bolitho on board the embattled *Phalarope* at the Saintes. In his best uniform, a ripe target for any sharp-eyed marksman, *so that the people should see him.* Oh yes, Allday knew it was impossible to talk him out of it.

Bolitho slipped his arms into the coat and waited for Ozzard to stand on tip-toe to adjust the bright epaulettes with the twin silver stars.

'This will not be a battle to test each other's mettle, Val. We must not even consider losing it. It is vital; you accept that now.'

Keen smiled sadly. 'I know it.'

There was a muffled hail from the masthead, and a lieutenant came running from the quarterdeck.

He stared at Bolitho and then said, 'The first lieutenant's respects, sir.' He tore his eyes from his vice-admiral and faced Keen. 'The mainmast lookout has just reported the enemy in sight. Steering south-west.'

Keen glanced at Bolitho, who nodded, then said, 'General signal. Enemy in sight.'

As the lieutenant hurried away Keen said, 'Brief and to the point. As you like it, Sir Richard.'

Bolitho smiled, and beckoned to Ozzard. 'You may clear the cabin. The bosun's party is waiting to carry the bits and pieces to the hold.' He rested his hand on Ozzard's bony shoulder. 'Go with them. No heroics today.' He saw his wistful gaze and added, 'I know not what ails you, but I will deal with it. Remember that, eh?'

As Ozzard made to pick up some small items Bolitho called, 'No! Not that!' He took the fan from Ozzard's hand and looked at it. Remembering.

Keen watched as Bolitho slipped the fan into his coat-pocket.

Bolitho reached for his hat. 'A small thing, I know, Val. But it is all I have of hers.'

Allday followed them from the cabin, then he paused, the old sword over one arm as he stared back at the place he knew so well. Why should this time be any different? The odds were bad, but that was nothing new, and the enemy were Dons. Allday felt he wanted to spit. Even the Frogs were better fighters than them. He took a last glance round, then touched his chest where the Spanish blade had thrust into him.

The cabin was deserted. He turned away, angry with the thought. For it looked as if it would remain empty forever.

On deck Bolitho walked to the centre of the quarterdeck rail and took a telescope from the senior midshipman. He looked at him more closely, then at the other officers and master's mates near the wheel. Everyone appeared to be dressed in his best clothing.

Bolitho smiled at the midshipman. 'That was nicely done, Mr Furnival.'

He raised the glass and found *Tybalt*'s sails almost immediately. He moved it still further and saw the dark flaws on the horizon, like the rippling edge of some distant tidal wave.

Bolitho returned the glass and looked up at the sky. The pendant was still pointing towards the larboard bow. The wind held steady, but not too strong. He recalled something his father had said. *A good wind for a fight.* But out here that could easily change, if the mood took it.

Keen stood watching him, his fair hair ruffling beneath the brim of his hat, even though it had been cut in the modern fashion. Bolitho gripped the rail with both hands. *Like Adam's.*

He felt the old wood, hot in the sunshine. So dented and pitted with the years, yet worn smooth by all the hands which had rested here.

He watched Major Adams with his lieutenant, Veales, standing below the quarterdeck. The major was frowning with concentration as he pulled on a fresh pair of white gloves.

Bolitho said, 'It is time.' He saw Keen nod, the lieutenants glance at one another, probably wondering who might still be here when the smoke cleared.

Keen said, 'The wind is firm, Sir Richard. They'll be up to us before noon.'

Penhaligon remarked indifferently, 'Fine day for it anyway.'

Bolitho drew Keen to one side. 'I have to say something, Val. We must clear for action directly; after that we shall be divided by our duties. You have come to mean a great deal to me, and I think you must know it.'

Keen answered quietly, 'I understand what you are trying to say, Sir Richard. But it will not happen.'

Bolitho gripped his arm tightly. 'Val, Val, how can we know? It will be a hard fight, maybe the worst we have endured.' He gestured towards the ships astern. '*All these men* following like helpless animals, trusting the Flag to carry them through, no matter what hell awaits them.'

Keen replied earnestly, 'They will be looking to you.'

Bolitho gave a quick smile. 'It makes it less easy to bear. And you, Val, what must you be thinking as the Dons draw to an embrace? That but for me you would be at home with your lovely Zenoria.'

Keen waited while Allday stepped up with the sword.

Then he said simply, 'If I never lived beyond this day I have still known true happiness. Nothing can take that away.'

Allday clipped on the old sword and loosened it in its scabbard.

He said gruffly, 'Amen to that, I says, Cap'n.'

Bolitho looked at both of them. 'Very well. Have the marines beat to quarters.' He touched his pocket and felt the fan inside. Her presence. 'You may clear for action, Captain Keen!'

They faced each other, and Keen formally touched his hat.

He smiled, but it did not reach his eyes. 'So be it.'

The stark rattle of drums, the rush of feet from every hatch and along both gangways made further speech impossible. Bolitho watched the gun crews throwing themselves around their charges, topmen swarming aloft to rig the slings and nets, ready to whip or splice their repairs even in the carnage of a broadside.

Jenour appeared on deck, his hat tugged well down on his forehead, the beautiful sword slapping against his hip. He looked stern, and somehow older.

As the ship fell silent once more, Parris strode aft and faced up to the captain. He wore a pair of fine hessian boots.

'Cleared for action, sir. Galley fire doused. Pumps manned.'

Keen did not take out his watch but said, 'Nine minutes, Mr Parris. The best yet.'

Bolitho smiled. Whether it was true or not, those who had heard Keen's praise would pass it on to each deck. It was little enough. But it all helped.

Keen came aft. 'Ready, Sir Richard.'

Bolitho saw him hesitate and asked, 'What is it, Val?'

'I was wondering, Sir Richard. Could we have the fifers strike up? Like we did in *Tempest*?'

Bolitho looked at the sea, the memory linking them once again. 'Aye, make it so.'

And as the old *Hyperion* leaned over to the same starboard tack, and while the edge of the horizon broke into more silhouettes and mastheads, the Royal Marine fifers struck up a lively march. Accompanied by the drums from the poop, and the seamen's bare feet stamping on the sanded planking, they strode up and down as if they were on parade at their barracks.

Bolitho met Keen's glance and nodded. *Portsmouth Lass*. It was even the same tune.

Bolitho raised his telescope and slowly examined the Spanish line from end to end. The two rearmost ships were well out of formation, and Bolitho suspected that the very end vessel was standing away so that the other one could complete some repairs as *Olympus* had done.

He shifted his gaze to the solitary frigate. It was easy to see why *La Mouette*'s captain had been deceived. It took much more than a foreign ensign to disguise an English-built frigate.

He knew that *Consort* had been launched on the Medway, near Herrick's home. Would he be thinking of that now, he wondered?

Twelve sail-of-the-line. The flagship in the van had already been identified by Parris, who had met with her before. She was the ninety-gun *San Mateo*, flagship of Almirante Don Alberto Casares, who had commanded the Spanish squadrons at Havana.

Casares would know all about *Hyperion*'s part in the attack on Puerto Cabello. Some of these very ships had probably been intended to escort the treasure galleons to Spain.

Bolitho watched the *Intrépido*. At least the two squadrons had something in common, two frigates between them.

He heard Parris saying to the signals midshipmen, 'It will be a while yet.'

Bolitho glanced at the two youths, who could barely drag their eyes from the enemy. How much worse for anyone who had never faced a line of battle, he thought. It could take hours to draw together. At the Saintes it had taken all day. First the few mastheads topping the horizon, then they had risen and grown until the sea's face had seemed to be covered.

A lieutenant who had written home after the Saintes had described the French fleet as 'rising above the horizon, like the armoured knights at Agincourt'. It had been a fair description.

Bolitho walked forward to the rail and looked along the maindeck. The men were ready; the gun captains had selected the best-fashioned balls and grape for the first, double-shotted broadside. This time they would need to fight both sides of the ship at once, so there would be no extra hands to spare. They had to break through the line – after that, it was every ship for herself.

The Royal Marines were in the fighting tops, the best marksmen Major Adams could find, with some others to man the vicious swivels. The bulk of the marines lined the poop, not yet standing to the packed hammock nettings to mark down their targets, but waiting in gently swaying ranks, Sergeant Embree and his corporals talking to each other without appearing to move their mouths.

Penhaligon and his master's mates were near the wheel, with two extra hands at the helm in case of casualties.

Apart from the sea noises and the occasional slap of the great driver sail above the poop, it seemed quiet after the fifers had stopped playing. Bolitho raised his glass yet again and saw a seaman turn from a maindeck eighteen-pounder to watch him.

The enemy flagship was much nearer. He could see the glint of sunlight on swords and fixed bayonets, men swarming up the ratlines of her foremast, others rising from their guns to watch the approaching squadron.

The Spanish admiral might expect his opposite number to fight ship-to-ship. His ninety guns against this old third-rate. Bolitho smiled grimly. It would even be unwise to cross *San Mateo*'s ornate stern in the first stage of the engagement. To be crippled breaking the line would throw the following ships into disorder, and Herrick would be left to attack on his own with just three ships.

Bolitho said, 'Signal *Tybalt* to take station astern of *Olympus*. It might add some weight to Herrick's line.' He heard the flags rushing aloft but continued to watch the big Spanish flagship.

Keen must have read his thoughts. 'May I suggest we break the line astern of the third or fourth ship, as it may present itself?'

Bolitho smiled. 'The further away from that beauty the better. Until we have lessened the odds anyway.'

Jenour was standing near the signals party and heard Bolitho's casual comment. Was it all a bluff, or did he really believe he could win against so many? Jenour tried to concentrate on his parents, how he would word his next letter. His mind reeled when he realised that the concept eluded him. Perhaps there would *be* no more letters. He felt a sudden terror and stared up at the wispy clouds directly above Bolitho's flag at the foremast truck. *He was going to be killed.*

Midshipman Springett, who was the youngest in the ship, appeared on deck. His station was on the lower gundeck, to relay messages back and forth to the poop. In the bright sunlight he had to blink several times after the gloom of the sealed gundeck.

Bolitho saw the boy turn, watched his expression as he gazed at the enemy ships, seeing them probably for the first time.

For those few moments his uniform and the proud, glinting dirk at his belt meant nothing. He drove his knuckles into his mouth as if to hold back a cry of fear. He was a child again.

Jenour must have seen him, and strode across. 'Mr Springett, isn't it? I could do with you assisting me today.' He gestured to the two signals midshipmen, Furnival, the senior, and Mirrielees, who had red hair and a face covered with freckles. 'These *old men* are getting past it, I fear!' The two in question grinned and nudged one another as if it were all a huge joke.

The boy stared at them. Mesmerised. He whispered, 'Thank you, sir.' He held out a paper. 'Mr Mansforth's respects, sir.' He turned and trotted back to the ladder without once looking at the imposing ranks of sails.

Keen said quietly, 'Your flag lieutenant just about saved that lad from bursting into tears.'

Bolitho watched more flags rising and dipping above the *San Mateo*. To himself he said, 'And it saved Stephen Jenour, I suspect.'

Even across the expanse of glistening swell you could hear the slow rumble of gun trucks, while something like a sigh came from the waiting sailors as shadows painted the *San Mateo*'s tall side. All her larboard battery had been run out. It was like looking into the mouth of every one of them.

Bolitho heard the blare of a trumpet, and pictured the enemy gun crews at their quarters. Eyes peering over the muzzles, the next shots and charges already to hand.

'Hoist *Benbow*'s number.' Bolitho took Keen aside as the flags were swiftly bent on to the halliards. 'I dare not wait too much longer, Val.' They both stared at the converging lines of ships, like one great arrowhead which must soon meet at some invisible westerly point.

There was a dull bang and Bolitho saw a puff of smoke drifting away from *San Mateo*'s side. The ball hit the sea, rebounded and smacked down, flinging a ragged waterspout half a cable clear. A ranging shot? Or was it merely to raise the spirits of the Spanish seamen who had been sharing the same agony of suspense as *Hyperion*'s?

'*Benbow*'s acknowledged, sir!'

Make the signals as few as possible. Bolitho had always believed it a good idea in principle. It was not difficult for an enemy to guess or determine the next move from another's signals. It was likely too that the prize, *Intrépido*, had been captured with some secret signals still intact.

When poor Captain Price had run his ship aground he could never have visualised any of this.

Bolitho looked at Keen and his first lieutenant. 'We will alter course in succession. *Hyperion* and *Benbow* will lead the two divisions.' He saw them nod; Parris was watching his lips as if to read what he had not said.

'It will be as close to the wind as she can lie, so it will reduce our progress.' He saw their understanding. It might also mean that it would give the enemy more time to traverse his guns. Bolitho walked to the starboard side and stood on the truck of a quarterdeck nine-pounder, his hand gripping the bare shoulder of one of its crew.

He could see *Benbow*'s masts beyond the others astern, Herrick's flag rippling out from the mizzen. *Benbow* was still flying her acknowledgement, just as *Hyperion* had kept her number hoisted close-up. Like a trumpet signalling a cavalry charge into the jaws of hell. A charge which cannot be halted once it has been urged to attack. Bolitho felt the man's shoulder tense as he turned to stare up at him. Bolitho looked at him. About eighteen. The sort of face you saw around the farms and lanes of Cornwall. But not in times of war.

He said, 'Naylor, am I right?'

The youth grinned while his mates winked at each other. 'Aye, Sir Richard!'

Bolitho kept his eyes on him, thinking of the terrified midshipman, and Jenour, who was more frightened of showing fear than of fear itself.

'Well, Naylor, there is our enemy. What say you?'

Naylor stared at the nearest ships with their trailing banners and curling pendants, some of which almost touched the water. 'I reckon we can take 'em.' He nodded, satisfied. 'We can clear the way for t'others, Sir Richard!'

Some of the gun crews cheered and Bolitho climbed down, afraid that his eye might choose this moment to betray him.

Just an ordinary sailor, who if he survived today, would likely end in another battle before he was a year older.

He thought suddenly of the grand London house, and Belinda's scathing words to him.

He nodded to the bare-backed seaman called Naylor. 'So we shall!' He turned quickly. 'Captain Keen!' Again, time seemed to stop for both of them. Then Bolitho said in a more level tone,

'Alter course three points to starboard, steer nor'-by-west!' He waved to Jenour. '*Now! Execute!*'

Every man in Herrick's flagship must have been poised for the moment. For as the flags were hauled down *Benbow* appeared to swing immediately out of the line, as if she, and she alone, was mounting a solitary attack on the enemy.

Keen watched closely, as pursued by Parris's speaking trumpet the scrambling seamen hauled on the braces, while others freed the big maincourse even as the yards creaked round.

Penhaligon spread his legs while the deck leaned to larboard, as the wind explored the braced sails and thrust the ship over.

Then Keen was at the compass, although Bolitho had not seen him move.

'*Meet her!* Steady as you go!'

The sails boomed and thundered in protest, and the driver rippled from peak to foot as if it was about to tear apart. She could stand no closer to the wind, and from the Spanish line it must appear as if all her sails were overlapping fore-and-aft.

Bolitho clutched the rail and stared at the enemy. Someone was firing, but the nets rigged above the maindeck gunners, and the huge billowing maincourse hid the flashes.

Bolitho saw *Benbow* drawing level abeam, barely three cables away. The others astern of her were already following round, with *Tybalt* tacking wildly to take station as the last of the line.

Keen exclaimed, 'The Dons are taken aback, by God!'

Bolitho looked at the Spanish flagship. Now she seemed to be heading away from *Hyperion*'s larboard bow, two others still following her as before.

Bolitho shouted, 'Load and run out, Captain Keen!'

The order was repeated to the deck below, and it seemed barely a minute had passed before each gun captain was faced aft, his fist above his head.

'All loaded, sir!'

'Open the ports! Run out!'

Squeaking noisily, the guns were hauled up to their ports. On the lee side the sea appeared to be curling up to the black muzzles as if to drive them inboard again.

Hyperion's deck shivered violently as the nearest enemy ships opened fire. But the two small divisions had taken the Spanish admiral by surprise, and most of his guns could not be brought to bear. Several tall waterspouts shot above the gangways, and Bolitho felt the tell-tale crash of a ball hitting *Hyperion*'s lower hull.

'Brail up the courses!'

Shots whimpered overhead, and the gun crews crouched even lower, their faces running with sweat as each group peered through their open port, waiting for a target.

As the forecourse was brailed up the scene opened on either bow as if a giant curtain had been raised.

Bolitho heard one of the midshipmen gasp with alarm as the stern of the nearest Spaniard appeared from nowhere, or from the depths – her high, ornate gallery, stabbing musket fire from above, and her name, *Castor*, reflecting the spray beneath her counter.

'Stand by to larboard!' Lovering, the second lieutenant, was striding inboard from the first division of guns. 'As you bear!'

Keen raised his sword, then sliced it down. '*Fire!*'

The larboard carronade on the forecastle hurled its huge ball into *Castor*'s stern with terrible effect. Bolitho heard the roar of its explosion within the other ship's hull, could imagine the scything horror of the packed grape as it swept through the ship. Cleared for action, any man-of-war was most vulnerable when an enemy was able to cross her stern.

The ship on the other side was looming through the smoke, her guns shooting out vivid orange tongues.

'*Fire!*'

Bolitho was deafened by the roar of guns as both sides vanished in swirling smoke and charred fragments from the charges. The ship to starboard was already being engaged by *Obdurate*, and Bolitho could see just her mastheads rising above the dense smoke like lances. He felt the deck jar again and again, Parris yelling, 'On the uproll, lads!' Then the next division fired as one, and Bolitho saw the *Castor*'s mizzen mast topple, suspended momentarily in the rigging and stays before going over the side with a sound like thunder.

'*Fire!*'

Keen strode across the quarterdeck, his eyes streaming, as the upper battery recoiled singly and in pairs on their tackles, the crews leaping forward with sponges and rammers, ready to tamp home the next ball. To do what they had been taught, to keep on firing no matter what was happening about them.

Jenour coughed in the smoke, then shouted, '*Obdurate* is in collision with a Spaniard, Sir Richard!' He winced as a musket ball slammed into the deck nearby and added, 'She requests assistance!'

Bolitho shook his head.

Keen said tersely, '*Inability!*'

The flags bearing Keen's curt signal lifted and vanished into a great pall of smoke which came surging inboard as the lower battery roared out to starboard.

Parris shouted, 'We're through, we're through!' He waved his hat wildly. 'Huzza, lads! *We've broken the line!*'

More sails loomed like giant ghosts astern. *Crusader*, and *Redoubtable*, the latter almost colliding with another Spaniard which had either lost her steering or had her helmsmen shot down.

'Stand by to alter course to larboard!' Bolitho tossed his telescope to one of the midshipmen. 'I don't need this now!' He could feel his lips set in a grin.

'Deck there!' Someone up there above the smoke and shrieking iron was keeping his head. '*Benbow*'s through the line!'

There were more wild cheers and coughs as the larboard battery fired a full broadside through the smoke, some into the *Castor*'s side, while the rest fell on and around the second ship in the enemy column.

'Lay her on the larboard tack, Mr Penhaligon! Afterguard, man the mizzen braces there!' Selected marines put down their muskets and ran to help, while some of their comrades squinted above the hammocks, their weapons cradled to their cheeks, seeking a target.

Bolitho looked up and saw lengths of severed cordage dangling on the protective nets, while above it all there was still the same peaceful sky.

A ball slammed into the larboard side, and crashed amongst

the men by one of the forward eighteen-pounders. Bolitho gritted his teeth as two were smashed to bloody ribbons, and another rolled across the deck, his leg held on by a thread of skin.

He tried to concentrate. All his ships must be engaged now. The roar of battle seemed to roll all around, as if vessels were on every hand, masked from each other by their own smoke. Sharper gunfire, like the staccato beat of drums, echoed over the water, as if it were another part of destiny.

Bolitho shouted, 'General signal. Close on the Flag. Reform line of battle!'

How they could work with their flags was a miracle, Bolitho thought.

'All acknowledged, Sir Richard!' Jenour tried to grin. 'I think!'

'No matter!' Bolitho strode to the rail as he saw a Spanish two-decker standing out from the others as she made more sail. Her captain either wished to rejoin his own flagship, or he had increased sail to avoid hitting the crippled Castor.

Bolitho pointed, 'There, Val! Engage her!'

Keen yelled, 'Stand by to starboard!'

The newcomer seemed to gather speed as the distance fell away, but Bolitho knew it was the illusion made by smoke. He watched the Spaniard changing tack so that she would cross Hyperion's bowsprit; he could see the scarlet and gold banner of Spain, the huge cross on her forecourse.

Keen's sword rose in the air. 'As you bear!'

The other ship fired almost at the same time. Iron and wooden splinters flew across the maindeck, while overhead the sails flailed and kicked, shot through so many times that some could not hold a cupful of wind. Bolitho wiped his face and saw the other ship's foremast going down in the smoke, rigging and pieces of canvas vanishing into bursting spray alongside.

But he could ignore even that. Hyperion had been badly wounded. He had felt part of the enemy's broadside crash into the lower hull with the weight of a falling cliff.

He made to cross the deck but something held his shoe. He looked down and saw it was the young seaman, Naylor. He was lying against his upended gun, and was trying to speak, his face creased with pain, and the effort to find words.

Keen called, 'Over here, Sir Richard! I think we may –' He stopped, his feet slipping on blood as he saw Bolitho drop to his knee beside the dying seaman.

Bolitho took the youth's hand. The Spaniards must have used extra grape in their broadside. Naylor had lost half of his leg, and there was a hole in his side big enough for a fist.

'Easy, Naylor.' Bolitho held his hand tightly as the deck seemed to leap beneath him. He was needed, probably urgently. Around them the battle raged without let-up. Obeying his instruction. *No matter what.*

The seaman gasped, 'I – I think I'm dyin', sir!' There were tears in his eyes. He seemed oblivious to his blood, which poured unchecked into the scuppers. It was as if he was puzzled by what was happening. He almost prized his broken body away from the gun, and Bolitho felt a sudden strength in his grip.

The youth asked, 'Why me, sir?' He fell back, blood making a thin line from a corner of his mouth. '*Why me?*'

Keen waited while Bolitho released his hand and let it fall to the deck.

Keen said, '*Capricious* is in support, Sir Richard! But there is another Don breaking through yonder!' He stared at his own raised arm. There was a strip torn from his sleeve. Yet he had not even felt the ball hiss past.

Bolitho hurried to the side and saw the second ship already overhauling the one which had fired the last broadside.

Bolitho nodded. 'Trying to join her admiral.'

Keen waved his hand. 'Mr Quayle! Pass word to the lower battery! We will engage this one immediately!'

The fourth lieutenant was no longer pouting disdainfully. He was almost beside himself with terror.

Keen turned. 'Mr Furnival!' But the midshipman had fallen too, while his companion stood rigidly beside Jenour, his eyes on the flags where his dead friend lay as if resting from the heat of battle.

Bolitho snapped, 'Get below, Mr Quayle! That is an order!'

Keen dashed the hair from his forehead and realised that his hat had been plucked away.

'God damn,' he said.

'*Ready*, sir!'

Keen sliced down with his sword. '*Fire!*'

Gun by gun the broadside painted the heaving water between the ships in the colours of the rainbow. It was possible to hear *Hyperion*'s weight of iron as it crashed into the other ship's side, smashing down men and guns in a merciless bombardment.

The smoke swirled away in a rising breeze and Keen exclaimed, 'She'll be into us! Her rudder's shot away!'

Bolitho heard a splash and when he turned his head he saw some of the boatswain's party hurrying from the upended gun. Naylor's corpse had gone over the side. There was only blood left to mark where he had fought and died.

Bolitho could still hear his voice. *Why me?* There were many more who would ask that question.

He saw Allday with a bared cutlass in his fist, watching the oncoming Spaniard with a cold stare.

Parris yelled, 'Stand by to repel boarders!'

Major Adams went bustling forward, as the other ship's tapering jib-boom rose through the smoke and locked into *Hyperion*'s bowsprit with a shudder which made even the gun crews pause at their work.

Keen shouted, '*Continue firing!*'

Hyperion's lower battery of thirty-two pounders fired relentlessly across the littered triangle of smoky water. Again, and yet once more, before the enemy's jib-boom shattered to fragments and with a great lurch she began to sidle alongside, until the gun muzzles of both friend and enemy clashed together.

Muskets cracked from the tops and a dozen different directions. Men dropped at their guns, or collapsed as they ran to hack away fallen rigging and blocks.

The swivels barked out from *Hyperion*'s maintop, and Bolitho saw a crowd of Spanish sailors blasted away even as they swung precariously across the boarding nets.

Keen shouted, 'We've lost steerage way, Sir Richard! We'll have to fight free of this one, and I think the other two-decker is snared into *her!*'

'Clear the lower battery, Val. Seal the ports! I want every spare hand up here!'

They dared not fire into the ship alongside now. They were locked together. It only needed one flaming wad from a gun to turn both ships into an inferno.

The seamen from the lower battery, their half-naked bodies blackened by the trapped smoke, surged up to join Major Adams's men as they charged to meet the attack.

Keen tossed his scabbard aside and tested the balance of his sword in his hand. He stared around in the drifting smoke, picking out his lieutenants amongst the darting figures. 'Where's my bloody coxswain?' Then he gave a quick grin as Tojohns ran to join him, his cutlass held high to avoid the other hurrying seamen.

'Here, sir!' He glanced at Allday. 'Ready when you are, sir!'

Keen's eyes settled on Parris by the rail. 'Stay here. Hold the quarterdeck.' Just the flicker of a glance towards Bolitho. It was as if they had clasped hands.

Then he too was up and running along the starboard gangway, as the enemy clambered aboard, or fired down from their own ship. Lieutenant Lovering pointed with his hanger and yelled, 'To the fo'c'stle, lads!' Then he fell, the hanger dangling from his wrist as an unseen marksman found his victim.

Dacie the one-eyed boatswain's mate was already there on the beakhead, swinging a boarding axe with terrible effect, cutting down three of the enemy before some of Adams's marines jumped down to join him, their bayonets licking through the nets, hurling aside the men caught there like flies in a web.

The swivels in the maintop banged out again, and some of Spanish sailors about to join the first boarders were scattered in a deadly hail of canister. Those already aboard *Hyperion* fell back, one throwing away his cutlass as the marines cornered him on the forecastle, but it was already too late for quarter. Gunsmoke drifted over the deck and when it cleared, there were only corpses as the jubilant marines fought their way across to the other ship's deck.

Jenour stood close beside Bolitho, his sword drawn, his face like one already dead. He shouted, 'Two of the Dons have struck, Sir Richard!'

Despite the clash of steel and the sporadic bang of muskets, there were faint cheers from another ship, and Bolitho imagined he could hear drums and fifes.

He climbed up the poop ladder and rubbed his eyes before peering through the enveloping smoke. He could just make out *Obdurate*, now completely dismasted and lashed alongside the Spanish two-decker she had collided with. A British ensign flew above the other vessel's deck, and Bolitho guessed it was Captain Thynne's men who were cheering.

Then he saw *Benbow*, pushing past another crippled Spaniard, pouring a slow broadside into her as she moved by. Masts toppled like felled trees, and Bolitho saw Herrick's flag curling above the smoke, so bright in the mocking sunlight.

He thought wildly, *Hyperion* had cleared the way, just as Naylor had promised she would.

Allday shouted, 'Here, watch out!'

Bolitho turned and saw a group of Spanish seamen clamber up over the starboard gangway, slashing aside the nets before anyone had noticed them. They must have climbed from the main chains; they could have been creatures from the sea itself.

Bolitho drew his sword, and saw some of Adams's red-coated marines already hacking their way aft on the other ship. These boarders had no chance at all. Their own vessel would have to strike unless the other two-decker could come to her aid. But another broadside hurled smoke and debris high in the air and even on to *Hyperion*'s maindeck, as one of Bolitho's squadron, probably *Crusader*, raked her from stern to bow.

There was a lieutenant leading the small group, and as he saw Bolitho he brandished his sword and charged to the attack.

Jenour stood his ground, but the Spaniard was a fine swordsman. He parried the blue blade aside as if it was a reed, twisted it with his hilt and sent it flying. He drew back to balance himself for a last thrust, then stared with horror at the boarding pike which lunged up through the quarterdeck ladder. The seaman gave an insane yell, tugged the pike free and drove it into the lieutenant's stomach.

Bolitho faced another Spaniard who was armed only with a heavy cutlass.

Bolitho yelled, 'Surrender, *damn you!*'

But whether he understood or not the seaman showed no sign of giving in. The wide blade swung in a bright arc and Bolitho stepped aside easily, then almost fell as a shaft of sunlight probed through the smoke haze and touched his injured eye. It was like that other time. Like being struck blind.

He felt himself swaying, the old sword held straight out, pointing uselessly at nothing.

Parris yelled, 'Stop that man!' Bolitho could only guess what was happening, and waited for the searing agony of the cutlass he could not see. Someone was screaming, and occasional yells told Bolitho that more of Keen's men were running to vanquish the last of the attackers.

Allday sliced his blade at an angle, his mind numb as he saw the other man lunging towards Bolitho, who was apparently unable to move. The blade took the man on one side of his head, a glancing blow, but it had Allday's strength and memory behind it. As he pivoted round, squinting into the sudden glare, he saw Allday looming towards him.

Jenour heard the next blow even as he scrabbled in the blood-stained scuppers to retrieve his sword. Parris, who was sobbing with pain from a slash across his wounded shoulder, saw the cutlass hit the Spaniard on the forearm; could only stare as the arm, complete with cutlass, clattered across the deck.

Allday spat, 'An' this is for me, matey!' He silenced the man's scream with one final blow across the neck.

He grasped Bolitho's arm. 'You all right, Sir Richard?'

Bolitho took several deep breaths. His lungs felt as if they were filled with fire; he could barely breathe.

'Yes. Yes, old friend. The sun. . . .'

He looked for Jenour. 'You have true courage, Stephen!'

Then he saw Jenour's features change yet again and thought for an instant he had already been wounded. There were wild cheers from the ship snared alongside by a tangle of fallen rigging, but as a freak gust of wind drove the smoke away Bolitho knew the reason for Jenour's stunned look of dismay.

He turned, covering his left eye with his hand, and felt his body cringe.

The Spanish admiral's flagship San Mateo had stayed clear of the close-action, or maybe it had taken her this long to put about. She seemed to shine above her own tall reflection; there was not a scar or a stain on her hull or a shot hole in her elegant sails. She was moving very slowly, and Bolitho's mind recorded that there were many men aloft on her yards. She was preparing to change tack again. Away from the battle.

Bolitho could feel his limbs quivering, as if they would never stop. He heard Parris shout, 'In Christ's name! She's going to fire!'

San Mateo had run out every gun, and at the range of some fifty yards could not miss with any of them, even though two of her own consorts lay directly in the path of her broadside.

Bolitho's mind refused to clear. It was *Hyperion* they wanted. The defiant ship with his flag still at the fore which had somehow broken their line, and inspired the others to follow. He looked at Allday but he was staring at the enemy flagship, his cutlass hanging loosely from his fist.

Together. Even now.

Then the flagship fired. The sound was deafening, and as the weight of the broadside smashed into the drifting *Hyperion*, Bolitho felt the deck rear up as if the ship was sharing their agony.

He was thrown to the side of the quarterdeck, his ears deaf to the thundering roar of falling spars, of men crying and screaming before the torn rigging dragged them over the side like corpses in a huge net.

Bolitho crawled to Midshipman Mirrielees and dragged at his shoulder to turn him on to his back. His eyes were shut tight, and there was moisture like tears beneath the lids. He was dead. He saw Allday crouching on his knees, his mouth wide as he sucked in the air. Their eyes met and Allday tried to grin.

Bolitho felt someone pulling him to his feet, his eyes blinded again by the sunlight as it laid bare the destruction.

Then the smoke drifted lower and hid *San Mateo* from view.

19

The Last Farewell

Sir Piers Blachford steadied himself against the makeshift table while the guns thundered out yet again and shook the whole ship. He wiped his streaming face and said, 'Take this man away. He's dead.'

The surgeon's assistants seized the naked corpse and dragged it away into the shadows of the orlop deck.

Blachford reached up and felt the massive beam by his head. If there was really a hell, he thought, it must surely look like this.

The swinging lanterns which dangled above the table made it worse, if that were possible, casting shadows up the curved sides of the hull one moment, and laying bare the huddled or inert shapes of the wounded who were being brought down to the orlop with hardly a let-up.

He looked at his companion, George Minchin, *Hyperion*'s own surgeon, a coarse-faced man with sprouting grey hair. His eyes were red-rimmed, and not only from fatigue. There was a huge jug of rum beside the table, to help ease the agony or the passing moments of the pitiful wounded who were brought to the table, stripped, then held like victims under torture until the work was done. Minchin seemed to drink more than his share.

Blachford had seen the most terrible wounds. Men without limbs, with their faces and bodies burned, or clawed by flaying splinters. The whole place, which was normally the midshipmen's berth, where they slept, ate and studied their manuals by the dim light of their glims, was filled with suffering. It stank of blood, vomit and pain. Each thundering roar of a broadside, or the sickening crash of enemy balls hitting the ship around them, brought cries and groans from the figures who waited to be attended.

Blachford could only guess what was happening up there, where it was broad daylight. Here on the orlop, no outside light ever penetrated. Below the waterline it was the safest place for this grisly work, but it revolted him none the less.

He gestured to the obscene tubs below the table, partly filled with amputated limbs, a stark warning to those who would be the next to be carried to endure what must be an extension of their agony. Only death seemed like a blessed relief here. 'Take them out!'

He listened to the beat of hammers in the narrow carpenter's walks, which ran around the ship below the waterline. Like tiny corridors between the inner compartments and the outer hull, where the carpenter and his mates repaired shot holes or leaks as the iron smashed again and again into the side.

There was a long drawn out rumbling directly overhead, and Blachford stared at the red-painted timbers as if he expected them to cave in.

A frightened voice called from the shadows. 'What's that, Toby?'

Someone replied, 'They're runnin' in the lower battery, that's what!'

Blachford asked quickly, 'Why would they do that?'

Minchin took a cupful of rum and wiped his mouth with a blood-stained fist.

'Clearing it. We're alongside one o' the buggers. They'll need every spare Jack to fight 'em off!'

He shouted hoarsely, 'Next one, Donovan!'

Then he eyed Blachford with something like contempt. 'Not quite what you're used to, I expect? No fancy operating rooms, with lines of ignorant students hanging on your every word.' He blinked his red-rimmed eyes as smoke eddied through the deck. 'I hope you learn something useful today, *Sir Piers*. Now you know what we have to suffer in the name of medicine.'

A loblolly boy said, 'This one's an officer, sir.'

Blachford leaned over the table as the lieutenant was stripped of his torn shirt and pressed flat on the table.

It was the second lieutenant, Lovering, who had been shot down by a Spanish marksman.

Blachford studied the terrible wound in his arm. The blood looked black in the swinging lanterns, the skin ragged where the ball had split apart upon hitting the bone.

Lovering stared at him, his eyes glazed with pain. 'Oh God, is it bad?'

Minchin touched his bare shoulder. It felt cold and clammy. 'Sorry, Ralph.' He glanced at Blachford. 'It's got to come off.'

Lovering closed his eyes. 'Please God, not my arm!'

Blachford waited for an assistant to bring his instruments. He had had to order them to to be cleaned again and again. No wonder men died of gangrene. He said gently, 'He's right. For your own sake.'

The lieutenant rolled his head away from the nearest lantern. He was about twenty-two, Blachford thought.

Lovering said in a whisper, 'Why not kill me? I'm done for.'

More crashes shook the hull and several instruments fell to the deck. Blachford stooped to retrieve one of them and stared, sickened, as a rat scurried away into the shadows.

Minchin saw his disgust and set his teeth. Coming here with all his high-and-mighty talk. What did he know about war?

From one corner of his eye he saw the lamplight glint on Blachford's knife.

'Here, Ralph.' He placed a wedge of leather between his jaws before he could protest. 'I'll give you some proper brandy after this.'

A voice yelled through the misty smoke. 'Another officer, sir!'

An assistant held up his lantern and Blachford saw Lieutenant Quayle slipping down against one of the massive timbers, trying to cover his face with his coat.

A seaman protested angrily, ' 'E's not even marked!'

Lieutenant Lovering struggled on the table, and but for the assistant holding his uninjured arm, and Minchin's hands on his shoulders, would have fought his way to his feet.

'You bloody bastard! You cowardly –' His voice trailed away

as he fell back in a faint on the table.

Blachford glanced again at Quayle; he was gripping his fingers and whimpering like a child.

'Call him what you will, but he's as much a casualty as any of them!'

Minchin replaced the leather wedge between Lovering's jaws. Brutal, callous; they were the marks of his trade. He held Lovering's shoulders and waited for him to feel the first incision of the knife. With luck he might lose consciousness completely before the saw made its first stroke.

Minchin could dismiss what Blachford and others like him thought about the navy's surgeons. He could even ignore Lovering's agony, although he had always liked the young lieutenant.

Instead he concentrated on his daughter in Dover, whom he had not seen for two years.

'Next.' Lovering was carried away; the amputated limb fell into the tub. The *wings and limbs* tub as most of them called it. Until it was their turn.

Blachford waited for a seaman whose foot had been crushed beneath a careering gun-truck to be laid before him. Around him the loblolly boys and their helpers held the flickering lanterns closer. Blachford looked at his own arms, red to the elbows, like Minchin's and the rest. *No wonder they call us butchers.*

The man began to scream and plead but sucked greedily on a mug of rum which Minchin finished before laying bare the shattered foot. The hull quivered again, but it felt as if the battle had drawn away. There seemed to be cannon fire from all directions, occasional yells which were like lost spirits as they filtered through the other decks.

Hyperion might have been boarded, Blachford thought, or the enemy could have drawn away to reform. He knew little about sea-warfare other than what he had been told or had read about in the *Gazette*. Only since his travels around the fleet had he thought about the men who made victories and defeats real, into flesh and blood like his own.

'*Next!*' It never stopped.

This time a marine ran down a ladder and called, 'We've taken the Don alongside, lads!' He vanished again, and Blachford was

271

amazed that some of the wounded could actually raise a weak cheer. No wonder Bolitho loved these sailors.

He looked down at the young midshipman. A child.

Minchin probed open part of his side where the ribs showed white through the blood.

Blachford said quietly, 'God, he looks so young.'

Minchin stared at him, wanting to hurt him, to make him suffer.

'Well, Mr Springett won't be getting any older, Sir Piers. He's got a fistful of Spanish iron inside him!' He gestured angrily. 'Take him away.'

'How old was he?'

Minchin knew the boy was thirteen, but something else caught his attention. It was the sudden stillness, which even the far-off gunfire could not break. The deck was swaying more slowly, as if the ship was heavier in the water. But the pumps were still going. God, he thought, in this old ship they never seemed to stop.

Blachford saw his intent expression. 'What is it?'

Minchin shook his head. 'Don't know.' He glanced at the dark shapes of the wounded along the side of the orlop. Some already dead, with no one to notice or care. Others waiting, still waiting. But this time. . . . He said harshly, 'They're all sailors. They *know* something is wrong.'

Blachford stared at the smoke-filled ladder which mounted to the lower gundeck. It was as if they were the only ones left aboard. He took out his watch and peered at it. Minchin reached down and refilled his cup with rum, right to the brim.

He had seen the fine gold timepiece with the crest engraved on its guard. God rot him!

The roar of the broadside when it came was like nothing Minchin had ever experienced. There must have been many guns, and yet they were linked into one gigantic clap of thunder which exploded against the ship as if the sound, and not the massive weight of metal, was striking into the timbers.

The deck canted right over, shivered violently as it reared against the ship alongside, but the din did not stop. There was an outstanding, splitting crack which seemed to come right through the deck; it was followed immediately by a roar of crashing spars

272

and rigging, and heavy thuds which he guessed were guns being hurled back from their ports.

The wounded were shouting and pleading, some dragging themselves to the ladder, their blood marking the futility of their efforts. Blachford heard the broken spars thudding against the hull, then sudden screams from the carpenter's walk, men clawing their way in darkness as the lanterns were blown apart.

Minchin picked himself up from the deck, his ears still ringing from the explosion. He saw some rats scurrying past the bodies of those who were beyond pain, and shook his head to clear it.

As he brushed past, Blachford called, 'Where are you going?'

'My sickbay. All I own in this bloody world is in there.'

'In Heaven's name, *tell me*, man!'

Minchin steadied himself as the deck gave another great shudder. The pumps had finally stopped. He said savagely, 'We're going down. But I'm not staying to watch it!'

Blachford stared round. *If I survive this.* . . . Then he took a grip on his racing thoughts.

'Get these men ready to move on deck.' The assistants nodded, but their eyes were on the ladder. *Going down.* Their life. Their home, whether from choice or impressment; it could not happen. Shoes clattered on the ladder, and Dacie, the one-eyed boatswain's mate, peered down at them.

'Will you come up, Sir Piers? It's a bloody shambles on deck.'

'What about these wounded?'

Dacie gripped the handrail and wiped his remaining eye. He wanted to run, run, keep on running. But all his life he had been trained to stand fast, to obey.

'I'll pass the word, Sir Piers.' Then he was gone.

Blachford picked up his bag and hurried to the ladder. As he climbed the first steps he felt they were different. At an angle. He sensed the chill of fear for the first time.

He thought of Minchin's anger.

Going down.

Lieutenant Stephen Jenour retained his grip on Bolitho's arm even after he had pulled him from the deck. He was almost incoherent in his relief and horror. 'Thank God, oh thank God!'

Bolitho said, 'Take hold, Stephen.' His eyes moved across the quarterdeck and down to the awful spread of destruction. No wonder Jenour was close to a complete breakdown. He had probably imagined himself to be the only one left alive up here.

It was as if the whole ship had been stripped and laid bare, so that no part of her wounds should be hidden. The mizzen mast had gone completely, and the whole of the foretopmast had been severed as if by some gigantic axe, and was pitching alongside with all the other wreckage. Spars, ropes, and men. The latter either floated in the weed of rigging, or floundered about like dying fish.

Jenour gasped, 'The first lieutenant, Sir Richard!' He tried to point, but his body was shaking so violently he almost fell.

Bolitho forgot his own despair as he hurried down a splintered ladder to the maindeck. Guns lay up-ended and abandoned, their crews strewn around them, or crawling blindly for the nearest hatch to hide. Parris was pinned beneath an overturned eighteen-pounder, his eyes staring at the sky until he saw Bolitho.

Bolitho dropped beside him. To Jenour he said, 'Send some one for the surgeon.' He held his coat. 'And Stephen, remember to *walk*, will you? Those who have survived will need all their confidence in us.'

Parris reached up to touch his arm. Through gritted teeth he gasped, 'God, that was bad!' He tried to move his shoulders. 'The *San Mateo*, what of her?'

Bolitho shook his head. 'She has gone. There was no point in continuing the fight after this.'

Parris released a great sigh. 'A victory.' Then he looked at Bolitho, his eyes pleading. 'My face – is it all right, sir?'

Bolitho nodded. 'Not a mark on it.'

Parris seemed satisfied. 'But I can't feel my legs.'

Bolitho stared at the overturned gun. The barrel was still hot from being fired, yet Parris could feel nothing. He could see his hessian boots protruding from the other side of the truck. Both legs must have been crushed.

'I'll wait here until help comes.' He looked along the shattered deck. Only the foremast still stood as before, with his flag rippling from the truck above the shredded sails.

He felt the deck quiver. The pumps had stopped, probably choked or smashed apart. He made himself face the truth. *Hyperion* was dying, even while he waited. He glanced across at the dead midshipman Mirrielees, whose body had been hurled down from the quarterdeck where he had been killed. He was sixteen. *I was just his age when Hyperion's keel tasted salt water for the first time.*

He heard voices and hurrying feet and saw seamen and marines returning from the Spanish two-decker alongside. It was strange, but Bolitho had not even glanced at their battered prize.

He saw Keen, an arm wrapped around Tojohns' shoulders, a bloody bandage tied about one leg, limping anxiously towards him.

'I died a dozen times back there, Sir Richard. I – I thought you must have fallen in that broadside.' He saw Parris and said, 'We should move him.'

Bolitho took his arm. 'You *know*, don't you, Val?'

Their eyes met. Keen replied, 'Yes. She's sinking. There's little we can do.' He stared at the abandoned cannon, unable to watch Bolitho's pain. 'Even if we could cast these guns overboard. But time is against us.'

Parris gave a groan and Bolitho asked, 'Is the prize safe, Val?'

'Aye. She's *Asturias* of eighty guns. She took much punishment too from that battering, as did her neighbour. But she is useful for repeating signals.'

Bolitho tried to clear his throbbing mind; his ears were still aching from that terrible broadside.

'Signal *Benbow* to secure the prizes and then give chase with whatever forces we have still seaworthy. The Dons will doubtless be running for the nearest Spanish port.' He stared at the bloody decks. 'Leaving their friends as well as their enemies to manage for themselves!'

Keen tightened his hold on his coxswain. 'Come, Tojohns! We must muster the hands!'

Bolitho said to Jenour, 'Go below and take charge of the boatswain's party. Can you do that?'

Jenour stared at Parris. 'What about him, Sir Richard?'

'I'll wait for the surgeon.' Bolitho lowered his voice. 'He will want to amputate both legs, I fear.'

Parris said vaguely, 'I am sorry about this, Sir Richard.' He gasped as a great pain went through him. 'I – I could have helped. Should have come to you earlier when I learned about your troubles in London.'

He was rambling. Bolitho leaned over him and grasped his hand. *Or was he?*

Parris continued in the same matter-of-fact tone, 'I *should* have known. I wanted a new command so much, just as I hated to lose the other. I suppose I didn't want it quite enough.'

Figures were clambering over from the other ship, voices of command emerged from chaos, and he saw Penhaligon, the master, with one of his mates coming from the wrecked poop, carrying the ship's chronometer, the same one she had carried in all her years of service. He half-listened to Parris's vague sentences but he was thinking of this ship he had known better than any other. *Hyperion* had carried three admirals, served fifteen captains, and countless thousands of sailors. There had been no campaign of note she had missed except for her time as a hulk.

Parris said, 'Somervell became very dear to me. I fought against it, but it was no use.'

Bolitho stared at him, for a moment not understanding what he was saying.

'You and Somervell – is *that* how it was?' It came at him like a blow, and he was stunned at his own blindness. Catherine's dislike for Parris, not because he was a womaniser as Haven had believed, but because of his liaison with her husband. *There was no love between us.* He could almost hear her words, her voice. It must have been why Parris had lost his only command, the matter dropped by some authority which required the scandal to be buried.

Parris gazed at him sadly. 'How it was. I wanted to tell you – you of all people. After what you did for me and this ship what you had to endure because of my folly.'

Bolitho heard Blachford hurrying along the deck. He should have felt anger or revulsion, but he had been in the navy since he had been twelve years old; what he had not seen in that time he had soon learned about.

He said quietly, 'Well, you've told me now.' He touched his shoulder. 'I shall speak with the surgeon.'

The deck gave a shudder, and broken blocks and discarded weapons clattered from a gangway like so much rubbish.

Blachford looked as white as a sheet, and Bolitho could guess what it had been like for him in the cockpit.

'Can you do it here on deck?'

Blachford nodded. 'After this I can do anything.'

Keen came limping down from the quarterdeck and called, 'Benbow has acknowledged, Sir Richard. Rear-Admiral Herrick wishes you well, and offers you all assistance!'

Bolitho smiled sadly, 'Tell him no, but thank him.' Dear Thomas was alive, unharmed. Thank God for that.

Keen watched Blachford stooping to open his bag. His eyes said, it could have been either of us, or both. He said, 'Six of the Dons have struck, Sir Richard, including Intrépido which was the last to haul down her colours to Tybalt.'

There was the crack of a line parting and Keen added, 'She drags heavily on Asturias, Sir Richard.'

'I know.' He stared round. 'Where's Allday?'

A passing seaman called, 'Gone below, Sir Richard!'

Bolitho nodded. 'I can guess why.'

Blachford said, 'I'm ready.'

There was another loud crack but this time it was a pistol shot. Bolitho and the others stared at Parris as his arm fell to the deck, the pistol he always carried still smoking in his fingers.

Blachford closed his bag, and said quietly, 'Perhaps his was the best way, better than mine. For such a courageous young man, I think living as a cripple would have proved unbearable.'

Bolitho removed his hat and walked to the quarterdeck ladder. 'Leave him there. He will be in good company.'

Afterwards he thought it sounded like an epitaph.

Scarlet coats moved into the ship, and Major Adams, hatless but apparently unmarked, was bellowing orders.

Bolitho said, 'The wounded first, Major. Over to the Spaniard. After that —' He did not finish.

Instead he turned to watch as Benbow, accompanied by Capricious, passed down the opposite side. There were no cheers this time, and Bolitho could envision how *Hyperion* must look. Was it imagination, or were the figurehead's muscled shoulders already closer to the sea? He stared until his damaged eye throbbed.

He could think of nothing else. *Hyperion* was settling down. They could not even anchor, for here the sea had no bottom, so her exact position could never be marked.

Men moved briskly around him, but like the moment he had hoisted his flag aboard, the faces he saw were different ones.

He touched the fan in his pocket. *Sharing it with her.*

He saw Rimer, the wizened master's mate who had accompanied him on the cutting-out of the treasure galleon. He was sitting against a bollard, his eyes fixed and unmoving, caught at the moment the shot had cut him down. Loggie the ship's corporal, sprawled headlong across another marine he had been trying to haul to safety when a marksman had found him too.

The first of the wounded were being swayed up through one of the hatchways. A few cried out as their wounds touched the coaming or the tackles, but most of them just stared like the dead Rimer; they had never expected to see daylight again.

Allday reappeared by his side; he had brought Ozzard with him.

He said, 'He was still in the hold, Sir Richard.' He forced a grin. 'Didn't know the fight was over, bless 'im!' He did not say that he had found Ozzard sitting on the hold's ladder, Bolitho's fine presentation sword clutched against his chest, staring at the last lantern's reflections on the black water which was creeping slowly towards him. He had not intended to leave.

Bolitho touched the little man's shoulder. 'I am very glad to see you.'

Ozzard said, 'But all that furniture, the wine cabinet from her ladyship –' He sighed. 'All gone.'

Keen limped over and said, 'I hate to trouble you, Sir Richard, but –'

Bolitho faced him. 'I know, Val. You continue your work. I shall attend the ship.' He saw the protest die on Keen's lips as he added, 'I know her somewhat better than you.'

Keen stood back. 'Aye, aye, Sir Richard.' He glanced at the

tautening hawsers to the ship alongside. 'There may not be long.'

'I know. Single-up your lines.' Then almost to himself he added, 'I have never lost a ship before.'

He saw Minchin coming on deck with one of his assistants, their clothing dark with blood, each carrying a bag.

Minchin approached Bolitho and said, 'Permission to leave with the wounded, Sir Richard?'

'Yes, and thank you.'

Minchin forced a grin to his ruined face. 'Even the rats have gone.'

Bolitho said to Ozzard, 'Leave with the others.'

Ozzard clutched the bright sword. 'No, Sir Richard, I'm staying –'

Bolitho nodded. 'Then remain here, on deck.'

He looked at Allday. 'Are you coming with me?'

Allday watched him despairingly. *Must you go down there?* Aloud he said, 'Have I ever left you?'

They walked beneath the poop and down the first companionway to the lower gundeck. The ports were still sealed, but most of those on the larboard side had been blasted open, their guns hurled from their breechings. There were few dead here. Mercifully Keen had cleared the deck to storm the Spaniard alongside. But there were some. Lolling figures, eyes slitted as if because of the smoky sunlight, watching as they passed. Half a man, chopped neatly in two by a single ball even as he had run with his sponge to the nearest gun. Blood everywhere; no wonder the sides were painted red, but it still showed itself. Lieutenant Priddie, second-in-command of the lower gundeck, lay face down, his back pierced with long splinters which had been blasted from the planking. He was still holding his sword.

Down another ladder, to the orlop, where Bolitho had to duck beneath each low beam. There were still one or two lanterns alight here. The dead lay in neat rows covered by sail-cloth. Others remained around the bloodied table, where they had died while they waited. Above their heads a heavy object fell to the deck, and then after a few seconds began to rumble along the scarred planking, like something alive.

Allday whispered, 'In the name of Christ!'

Bolitho looked at him. It must be a thirty-two pounder ball which had broken free of its garland and was now rolling purposefully down towards the bows.

They paused by the last hatchway and Allday dragged back the cover. It was one of the holds, where Ozzard always kept his vigil when the ship was in action.

Bolitho dropped to his knees and peered down while Allday lowered a lantern beside him.

He had expected to see water amongst the casks and crates, the chests and the furniture, but it was already awash from side to side. Barrels floated on the dark water, and lapped around a marine who had been clinging to a ladder when he had died. A sentry put to guard against terrified men running below in battle. He might have been killed by one of them, or like Ozzard had been trying to find refuge from the hell on deck.

The deck quivered again, and he heard heavy fragments booming against the carpenter's walk where more of his men had been trapped and drowned.

The orlop, and the holds and magazines beneath it, places which had remained in total darkness for all of Hyperion's thirty-three years. When they had returned the old ship to service after a hasty refit, it was more than likely the dockyard had missed something. Probably down there, where the first heavy broadside had smashed into the hull, there had still been some rot, unseen and undiscovered. Gnawing at the timbers and frames as far down as the keelson. San Mateo's last bombardment had dealt the mortal blow.

Bolitho watched Allday shut the hatch and made his way back to the ladder.

So many memories would go with this ship. Adam as a midshipman; Cheney whom he had loved in this same hull. So many names and faces. Some would be out there now in the battered squadron where they waited to secure the prizes after their victory. Bolitho thought of them watching Hyperion, remembering her perhaps as she had once been, while the younger ones like Midshipman Springett. . . . He cursed and held his hand to his eyes. No, he was gone too, with so many others he could nót even remember.

Allday murmured, 'I think we'd better get a move on, sir.'

The hull shook once more, and Bolitho thought he saw the gleam of water in the reflected light, creeping through the deck seams; soon it would cover the blood around Minchin's table.

They climbed to the next deck, then threw themselves to one side as a great thirty-two pounder gun came to life and squealed down the deck, as if propelled by invisible hands. *Load! Run out! Fire!* Bolitho could almost hear the orders being screamed above the roar of battle.

On the quarterdeck once more Bolitho found Keen and Jenour waiting for him.

Keen said quietly, 'The ship is cleared, Sir Richard.' His eyes moved up to the flag, so clean in the afternoon sunlight.

'Shall I have it hauled down?'

Bolitho walked to the quarterdeck rail and grasped it as he had so many times as captain and now as her admiral.

'No, if you please, Val. She fought under my flag. She will always wear it.'

He looked at the Spanish *Asturias*. He could see much more of her damage, her side pitted by *Hyperion*'s own broadsides. She appeared much higher in the water now.

Bolitho looked at the sprawled figures, Parris's outflung arm with the pistol he had chosen as his final escape.

They had succeeded in driving off and scattering the enemy. Looking at the drifting ships and abandoned corpses, it seemed like a hollow victory.

Bolitho said, '*You are my ship.*'

The others stood near him but he seemed quite alone as he spoke.

'No more as a hulk. This time with honour!' He swung away from the rail. 'I am ready.'

It took another hour for *Hyperion* to disappear. She dipped slowly by the bows, and standing on the Spaniard's poop Bolitho heard the sea rushing through the ports, sweeping away wreckage, eager for the kill.

Even the Spanish prisoners who gathered along the bulwarks to watch were strangely silent.

Hammocks floated free of the nettings, and a corpse by the

wheel rolled over as if it had been only feigning death.

Bolitho found that he was gripping his sword, pressing it against the fan in his pocket with all his strength.

They were all going with her. He held his breath as the sea rolled relentlessly aft towards the quarterdeck until only the poop, and the opposite end of the ship, his flag above the sinking masthead, marked her presence.

He remembered the words of the dying sailor.

Hyperion cleared the way, as she always had.

He said aloud, 'There'll be none better than you, old lady!'

When he looked again she had gone, and only bubbles and the scum of flotsam remained as she made her last voyage to the seabed.

Keen glanced at the stricken survivors around him and was inclined to agree.

Epilogue

Bolitho paused near the edge of the cliff and stared hard across Falmouth Bay. There was no snow on the ground, but the wind which swept the cliffs and hurled spume high above the rocks below was bitterly cold, and the low dark-bellied clouds hinted at sleet before dusk.

Bolitho felt his hair whipping in the wind, drenched with salt and rain. He had been watching a small brig beating up from the Helford River, but had lost sight of her in the wintry spray which blew from the sea like smoke.

It was hard to believe that tomorrow was the first day in another year, that even after returning here he was still gripped by a sense of disbelief and loss.

When *Hyperion* had gone down he had tried to console himself that she had not made a vain sacrifice, nor had the men who had died that day in the Mediterranean sunshine.

Had the Spanish squadron been able to join with the Combined Fleet at Cadiz, Nelson might well have been beaten into submission.

Bolitho had transferred to the frigate *Tybalt* for passage to Gibraltar and had left Herrick in command of the squadron, although most of the ships would need dockyard care without delay.

At the Rock he had been stunned by the news. The Combined Fleet had broken out without waiting for more support, but outnumbered or not, Nelson had won a resounding victory; in a single battle had smashed the enemy, had destroyed or captured two-thirds of their fleet, and by so doing had laid low any hope Napoleon still held of invading England.

But the battle, fought in unruly seas off Cape Trafalgar, had cost Nelson his life. Grief transmitted itself through the whole fleet, and aboard *Tybalt* where none of the men had ever set eyes on him, they were shocked beyond belief, as if they had known him as a friend. The battle itself was completely overshadowed by Nelson's death, and when to Bolitho eventually reached Plymouth he discovered it was the same wherever he went.

Bolitho watched the sea boil over the rocks, then tugged his cloak closer about his body.

He thought of Nelson, the man he had so wanted to meet, to walk and talk with him as sailor to sailor. How close their lives had been. Like parallel lines on a chart. He recalled seeing Nelson just once during the ill-fated attack on Toulon. It was curious to recall that he had seen Nelson only at a distance aboard the flagship; he had waved to Bolitho, a rather shabby young captain who was to change their world. Stranger still, the flagship Nelson had been visiting for orders was that same *Victory*. He thought also of the few letters he had received from him, and all in the last months aboard *Hyperion*. Written in his odd, sloping hand, self-taught after losing his right arm, *There you may discover how well they fight their wars with words and paper instead of ordnance and good steel.* He had never spared words for pompous authority.

And the words which had meant so much to Bolitho when he had asked for, and had been reluctantly given, *Hyperion* as his flagship. *Give Bolitho any ship he wants. He is a sailor, not a landsman.* Bolitho was glad that Adam had met him, and been known by him.

He glanced back along the winding cliff path towards Pendennis Castle. The battlements were partly hidden by mist, like low cloud; everything was grey and threatening. He could not remember how long he had been walking or why he had come. Nor did he remember when he had ever felt so alone.

Upon returning to England he had paid a brief visit to the Admiralty with his report. No senior had been available to see him. They were all engaged in preparing for Nelson's funeral, apparently. Bolitho had ignored the obvious snub, and had been glad to leave London for Falmouth. There were no letters for him from Catherine. It was like losing her again. But Keen would see her when he joined Zenoria in Hampshire.

Then I shall write to her. It was surprising how nervous it made him feel. Unsure of himself, like the first time. How would she see him after their separation?

He walked on into the wind, his boots squeaking in the sodden grass. Nelson would be buried at St Paul's, with all the pomp and ceremony which could be arranged.

It made him bitter to think that those who would be singing hymns of praise the loudest, would be the very same who had envied and disdained him the most.

He thought of the house now hidden by the brow of the hill. He had been glad that Christmas had been over when he reached home. His moods of loneliness and loss would have cast a wet blanket over all festivities. He had seen no one, and he imagined Allday back at the house, yarning with Ferguson about the battle, adding bits here and there as he always did.

Bolitho had thought often of the battle. At least there had been no mourning in Falmouth. Only three of *Hyperion*'s company had come from the port, and all had survived.

There had been a letter from Adam waiting for him. The one shining light to mark his return.

Adam was at Chatham. He had been appointed captain, in command of a new fifth-rate now completing in the Royal Dockyard there. He had got his wish. He had earned it.

He stopped again, suddenly tired, and realising he had eaten nothing since breakfast. Now it was afternoon, and darkness would soon arrive to make this path a dangerous place to walk. He turned, his cloak swirling about him like a sail.

How well his men had fought that day. *The Gazette* had summed it up in a few lines, overshadowed by a nation's sense of mourning. *On 15th October last, some hundred miles to the East of Cartagena ships of the Mediterranean squadron under the flag of Vice-Admiral Sir Richard Bolitho KB encountered a superior Spanish force of twelve sail-of-the-line. After a fierce engagement the enemy withdrew, leaving six prizes in British hands. God Save The King.* Hyperion was not mentioned, nor the men who now lay with her in peace. Bolitho quickened his pace and almost stumbled, not from any blindness, but because of the emotion which blurred his eyes.

God damn them all, he thought. Those same hypocrites would praise the little admiral now that they no longer had to fear his honesty. But the true people would remember his name, and so would ensure that it lived forever. For Adam's new navy, and the ones which would follow.

A figure was approaching by way of the path which ran closest to the edge. He peered through the mist and rain and saw the person wore a blue cloak like his own.

In an hour, maybe less, it would be dangerous here. A stranger perhaps?

. . . She came towards him very slowly, her hair, as dark as his own, streaming untied in the bitter wind off the sea.

Allday must have told her. He was the only one in the house who knew about this walk. This *particular* walk they had both taken after his fever, a thousand years ago.

He hurried towards her, held her at arms' length and watched her laughing and crying all in one. She was dressed in the old boat-cloak he kept at the house for touring the grounds in cold weather. A button missing, a rent near the hem. When it lifted to the wind he saw she was wearing a plain dark red gown beneath. So far a cry from the fine carriage and the life she had once shared.

Then Bolitho clutched her against his body, feeling her wet hair on his face, the touch of her hands. They were like ice, but neither of them noticed.

'I was going to write —' He could not go on.

She studied him closely, then gently stroked his brow near his injured eye.

'Val told me everything.' She pressed her face against his, while the wind flung their cloaks about them. 'My dearest of men, how terrible it must have been. For you and your old ship.'

Bolitho turned her and put his arm over her shoulders. As they mounted the path over the hill he saw the old grey house, light already gleaming in some of the windows.

She said, 'They say I am a sailor's woman. How could I stay away?'

Bolitho squeezed her shoulder, his heart too full to speak.

Then he said, 'Come, I'll take you home.'

He paused at the bottom to help her over the familiar old stile-gate where he had played as a child with his brother and sisters.

She looked down at him from the stile, her hands on his shoulders. 'I love thee, Richard.'

He made the moment last, sensing that peace like a reward had come to them in the guise of fate.

He said simply, 'Now it's your home, too.'

The one-legged ex-sailor named Vanzell touched his hat as they passed; but they did not see him.

Fate.

Form Line of Battle

Alexander Kent

June 1793, Gibraltar

The gathering might of revolutionary France prepares to engulf Europe in another bloody war. As in the past, Britain will stand or fall by the fighting power of her fleet.

For Richard Bolitho, the renewal of hostilities means a fresh command and the chance of action after long months of inactivity. However, his mission to support Lord Hood in the monarchist-inspired occupation of Toulon has gone awry. Bolitho and the crew of the *Hyperion* are trapped by the French near a dry Mediterranean island. The great ship-of-the-line's battered hull begins to groan as her sails snap in the hot wind.

'One of our foremost writers of naval fiction'
Sunday Times

arrow books

Man of War

Alexander Kent

Antigua, 1817, and every harbour and estuary is filled with ghostly ships, the famous and the legendary now redundant in the aftermath of war. In this uneasy peace, Adam Bolitho is fortunate to be offered the seventy-four gun *Athena*, and as flag captain to Vice-Admiral Sir Graham Bethune once more follows his destiny to the Caribbean.

But in these haunted waters where Richard Bolitho and his 'band of brothers' once fought a familiar enemy, the quarry is now a renegade foe who flies no colours· and offers no quarter, and whose traffic in human life is sanctioned by flawed treaties and men of influence. And here, when *Athena*'s guns speak, a day of terrible retribution will dawn for the innocent and the damned.

'One of our foremost writers of naval fiction'
Sunday Times

arrow books

Relentless Pursuit

Alexander Kent

It is December 1815 and Adam Bolitho's orders are unequivocal. As captain of His Majesty's Frigate *Unrivalled* of forty-six guns, he is required to *'repair in the first instance to Freetown Sierra Leone, and reasonably assist the senior officer of the patrolling squadron'*. But all efforts of the British anti-slavery patrols to curb a flourishing trade in human life are hampered by unsuitable ships, by the indifference of a government more concerned with old enemies made distrustful allies, and by the continuing belligerence of the Dey of Algiers, which threatens to ignite a full-scale war.

For Adam, also, there is no peace. Lost in grief and loneliness, his uncle's death still avenged, he is uncertain of all but his identity as a man of war. The sea is his element, the ship his only home, and a reckless, perhaps doomed attack on an impregnable stronghold his only hope of settling the bitterest of debts.

'As ever, Kent evokes the blood and smoke of battle in crimson-vivid prose'
Mail on Sunday

'A splendid yarn'
The Times

arrow books

Success to the Brave

Alexander Kent

Spring, 1802

Richard Bolitho is summoned to the Admiralty to receive his orders for a diffcult and thankless mission . . .

The recent Peace of Amiens is already showing signs of strain as old enemies wrangle over colonies won and lost during the war. In the little 64-gun *Achates*, Bolitho sails west for the Caribbean, to hand over the island of San Felipe to the French.

But diplomacy is not enough . . .

'One of our foremost writers of naval fiction . . .'
Sunday Times

arrow books

Colours Aloft!

Alexander Kent

SEPTEMBER 1803

Vice-Admiral Sir Richard Bolitho finds himself the new master of the *Argonaute*, a French flagship taken in battle. With the Peace of Armiens in ruins, he must leave the safety of Falmouth.

What lies ahead is the grim reality of war at close quarters - where Bolitho who will be called upon to anticipate the overall intention of the French fleet. But the battle has also become a personal vendetta between himself and the French admiral who formerly sailed the *Argonaute*.

Bolitho and his men are driven to a final rendezvous where no quarter is asked or given.

arrow books

Sloop of War

Alexander Kent

SPRING 1778

The year marks a complete transformation for Richard Bolitho and his future in the Royal Navy. It is the year that the American War of Independence changes to an all-out struggle against British rule – and the year when he takes command of Sparrow, a fast, well-armed sloop of war.

As the pace of the war increases, the Sparrow is called from one crisis to another; and when the great fleets of Britain and France converge on the Chesapeake, Bolitho must be ready to come of age in a sea battle that will decide the fate of a whole continent.

'A splendid yarn'
The Times

arrow books

ALSO AVAILABLE IN ARROW

The Only Victor

Alexander Kent

FEBRUARY 1806

The frigate carrying Vice-Admiral Sir Richard Bolitho drops anchor off the shores of southern Africa. It is only four months since the resounding victory over the combined Franco-Spanish fleet at Trafalgar, and the death of England's greatest naval hero.

Bolitho's instructions are to assist in hastening the campaign in Africa, where an expeditionary force is attempting to recapture Cape Town from the Dutch. Outside Europe few have yet heard of the battle of Trafalgar, and Bolitho's news is met with both optimism and disappointment as he reminds the senior officers that, despite the victory, Napolean's defeat is by no means assured. The men who follow Bolitho's flag into battle are to discover, not for the first time, that death is the only victor.

arrow books

TO FIND OUT MORE ABOUT

Alexander Kent

Visit www.bolithomaritimeproductions.com
or you may wish to subscribe to
The Bolitho Newsletter.

To join our mailing list to receive *The Bolitho Newsletter*,
send your name and address to:

The Bolitho Newsletter
William Heinemann Marketing Department
20 Vauxhall Bridge Road
London
SW1V 2SA

If at any stage you wish to be deleted from *The Bolitho Newsletter*
mailing list, please notify us in writing at the address above.

*Your details will be held on our database in order for us to send
you *The Bolitho Newsletter* and information on Alexander Kent,
Douglas Reeman and any of our other authors you may find
interesting. Your personal details will not be passed to any third
parties. If you do not wish to receive information on any other
author please clearly state so when subscribing to the newsletter.

arrow books

To Glory We Steer

Alexander Kent

JANUARY 1782

Captain Richard Bolitho is ordered to take the frigate *Phalarope* to the Caribbean, where the hard pressed royal squadrons are fighting for their lives against the combined fleets of France and Spain and American privateers.

It should have been a proud commission for Bolitho, but *Phalarope* has been driven to near mutiny by her previous commander. Bolitho sets about restoring the ship's pride. Caught between inner conflict and the broadsides of the enemy, the great battle of the Saintes provides captain and crew with the ultimate chance of redemption.

'As ever, Kent evokes the blood and smoke of battle in crimson-vivid prose'
Mail on Sunday